PRAISE FOR
HOLLYWOOD NORTH

"Libling's assured, quietly menacing debut, based on his World Fantasy Award-nominated novella of the same title [*Hollywood North*], is steeped in bittersweet childhood nostalgia and coming-of-age foibles. . . . The leisurely telling belies the hint of evil simmering just below the town's almost aggressively mundane surface, and there are a few surprises in store. Fans of *Stand by Me* and the like will find much to enjoy."

—*Publishers Weekly*

"A beautifully deceptive mystery and fantasy noir novel. The book is filled with humor and heartbreak and great homages to classic films. While immersed in this Hollywood North, I felt like I was watching a mesmerizing movie unfold."

—Sheila Williams, Editor, *Asimov's Science Fiction Magazine*

"I don't use the word 'brilliant' promiscuously, never have, never will, but with Michael Libling's wonderful first novel I use it very comfortably. For another reader, *Hollywood North* might be simply 'ingenious' or 'charming' or 'outrageously engaging', but I believe it's more than that—a novel that film buffs will love, along with anyone living in a society with the hand of popular culture upon them as baptism or drowning (or both). Yes, it's charming and human and light-hearted in its seriousness, and clever and rich with a film-lover's allusions, nods and hats-off; but that's another matter. One of the best first novels I've read in a decade."

—Bruce McAllister, author of *Dream Baby*
and *The Village Sang to the Sea: A Memoir of Magic*

"*Hollywood North*, perhaps the cleverest use of the so-called unreliable narrator that I have ever seen outside of Nabokov or perhaps Evan S. Connell Jr., is also so devastating as to go far beyond the clever. Michael Libling's first novel is the work of a prodigy with no reference to age and it explores the darkness of human complexity with bravura."

—Barry Malzberg, author of *The Bend at the End of The Road*,
Breakfast in the Ruins, and many others

"A simultaneously heartwarming and heartbreaking coming-of-age story set in the small town of Trenton, Ontario, against the backdrop of a little known chapter of Canada's cinematic past. Michael Libling is to be celebrated for this gem of a book."

—Maude Barlow, activist/author of *Blue Gold*,
Boiling Point, and many others

Michael Libling

HOLLYWOOD NORTH

a novel in six reels

Distributed in Canada by
Fitzhenry & Whiteside Limited
195 Allstate Parkway
Markham, Ontario L3R 4T8
Phone: (905) 477-9700
e-mail: bookinfo@fitzhenry.ca

Distributed in the U.S. by
Consortium Book Sales & Distribution
34 Thirteenth Avenue, NE, Suite 101
Minneapolis, MN 55413
Phone: (612) 746-2600
e-mail: sales.orders@cbsd.com

Library and Archives Canada Cataloguing in Publication

Title: Hollywood North : a novel in six reels / Michael Libling.
Names: Libling, Michael, 1949- author.
Description: First edition.
Identifiers: Canadiana (print) 20190107782 | Canadiana (ebook) 20190107790 | ISBN 9781771485234
   (hardcover) | ISBN 9781771484909 (softcover) | ISBN 9781771484916 (PDF)
Classification: LCC PS8623.I35 H65 2019 | DDC C813/.6—dc23

CHIZINE PUBLICATIONS
Peterborough, Canada
www.chizinepub.com
info@chizinepub.com

Edited by: Brett Savory
Copyedited and proofread by Alan Smithee

Canada Council   Conseil des arts
for the Arts   du Canada

We acknowledge the support of the Canada Council for the Arts which last year invested $20.1 million in writing and publishing throughout Canada.

ONTARIO ARTS COUNCIL
CONSEIL DES ARTS DE L'ONTARIO
an Ontario government agency
un organisme du gouvernement de l'Ontario

Published with the generous assistance of the Ontario Arts Council.

Printed in Canada

HOLLYWOOD NORTH

a novel in six reels

Dedications

To Pat,
the first girl I ever met
who read the same books I did.
Later, she read my stories, too,
and somehow still married me.
She is, by far, the best part of my story.

In memory of my parents,
the original Bert and Mollie,
who in the unlikeliest of plot twists
made Trenton their home
and the Theatre Bar their business.
I hope they know how much they gave me.

———

Based on true events
(as They say)

Nigh upon the Quinte, abreast the River Trent,
Abides my dear sweet Trenton, where my youth was spent.
Perfidious rabble a-hounding, ere my forefathers fled,
Royalists and Loyalists, to the British Crown they pledged.

**—Agnes Meyers Johns, from *Nigh Upon the Quinte*,
Lost Poems of the Dominion (1921)**

Cafés and shops and industries.
Airbase, schools and charities.
Fires and floods and jeopardies.
Together we rise from tragedies.
Front Street, King Street, Dundas, too,
Stroll around, check out what's new!
Sail the Quinte, hike Hanna woods,
Cannon on Pelion, where Champlain stood.
That's my Trenton, my neighbourhood.

**—Darrell Minden, Jr., from *Together We Rise*,
Honourable Mention, Trenton Office of Tourism Song Competition
(1982)**

PRODUCTION _____

DIRECTOR _____

CAMERA _____

DATE _____ SCENE _____ TAKE _____

First Reel

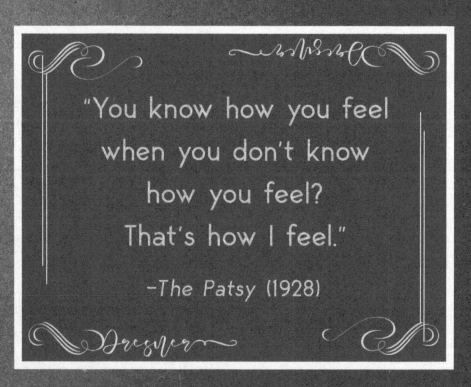

"You know how you feel
when you don't know
how you feel?
That's how I feel."

–*The Patsy* (1928)

# ONE

1988 and I was on the 3:10 to Yuma
with Jack, a girl, and Frankie Laine

The lawyer didn't need to ask me twice. Any reason to get out of Winnipeg in January was reason enough. Even if it sent me home. "It'll be worth your while," he said. By then, I guess, curiosity outweighed the fear, and my death instinct had kicked in.

The train was rolling as I clambered into the car, my bag thrust out front as I cast about for a window seat. Last to board, my odds were slim. It wasn't the view so much as the comfort I was after. I had two days of sitting-up ahead of me. A window would be an extra place to rest my head.

I was halfway down the aisle before Jack tripped me up, pulled what I'd come to call his Orson Welles entrance. Like Harry Lime in *The Third Man*. A stray cat at his wingtips, a slash of light to reveal the mischief in his eyes. Unexpected, only if you've never seen a Welles picture. Or don't know jack about Jack.

My old pal got right to it, picked up as if nothing had changed between us. "Best kid-without-a-dad movie—*The Day the Earth Stood Still* or *The Seven Faces of Dr. Lao*?"

Jack could find me anywhere.

"Hottest TV mom, then? Donna Reed or June Lockhart?"

He was good at that. Finding, I mean.

You know how it is. Everyone has people inside their heads, drop-ins, slugs, and residents. Thoughts of home brought Jack to mine. Even when he wasn't with me he was with me. I wager he'd have said the same of me.

But this was my end of the story. His entrance was premature. I swung my bag right through him and forged on to the rear of the car, the four seats facing.

A woman had beaten me to it, her space staked out. Her knee-high leather boots were stowed by the heater. Her stockinged feet were folded under her, taking advantage of the seat adjacent. I apologized for my invasion. "Uh-huh," she said, dragged her briefcase from my newly claimed territory, the bench opposite, and returned to the paperback tucked close to her chin. *Women Who Love Too Much* by Robin Norwood.

She was younger than me, though not by much. Thirty-three, thirty-four. A toss-and-tease blonde. Business professional sporty. Petite. Ex-figure skater relegated to coaching—a fantasy I could run with. And I did.

My thing for women on trains goes back to Frankie Laine and *3:10 to Yuma*. Not the theme he sang for the movie, but the radio version, where Frankie falls hard for this girl with "golden hair," and then moans the whole song through because he lets her exit the train without a peep between them, even as her eyes bid him "a sad goodbye." Great singer, that Frankie, and thick as a rump roast.

Jack persisted. "What about Gene Tierney in *Leave Her to Heaven*? Now there was a woman on a train, hoo-boy!"

I could have punched him in the face. He knew it, too.

The train was stopped. I wasn't sure where we were or how long I'd been dozing. Nothing but moonlit snow on either side of Canada's acclaimed middle of nowhere. My travelling companion glanced up from her book, sympathized with my confusion. "They're clearing drifts from the tracks again," she said. "Last I heard, we'll be a half-day late into Toronto."

I checked my watch, feigned like-minded annoyance. She had places to be and zero time to waste and I had rarely seen a woman like her with patience for the train, least of all the entire stretch in coach. I could have sworn she'd read my mind: "I was on Air Canada Flight 797," she said, assessing my degree of cluelessness before expanding. "The plane that caught fire a few years back? June 2, 1983? Dallas . . . Montreal?"

"Oh, yeah. Of course." In truth, I did and mostly didn't. How many accidents and disasters is a person obligated to remember, anyhow? I was full up, thank you very much.

"We made an emergency landing in Cincinnati. Eighteen of us got out. But twenty-three . . . it was horrific . . . awful . . . you can't imagine . . . the poor man sitting next to me . . . turned out I'd gone to high school with his daughter. . . ." Tears loomed. She lowered her head, hugged herself till the impulse passed. "I can't believe it's coming up on five years. I haven't flown since. But the way this trip is going . . . could this be any more exhausting?"

"I hate to fly, too," I said, as trite as anything I'd ever come out with. I should've been a walking-talking phrase book of commiseration by then, catastrophe and me, our long and special relationship. Mercifully, she let me off the hook.

"So, what's waiting for you in Toronto?" she asked.

"A rental car and another hundred miles."

"Me, it's our annual sales meeting. I rep for Pfizer in Vancouver."

I wanted to ask if she'd been a figure skater, but did not. I was as much of a rump roast as Frankie Laine, for Christ's sake.

"And you, if not Toronto?" she said.

"Trenton."

"Where the Air Force base is?"

"One claim to fame."

"You live there?"

"Used to."

"But you still have family in the town? Friends?"

"Tons," I said.

"I love going home. The reminiscing and all . . ."

I nodded as if I knew where she was coming from, then shook my head, strummed a heartstring. "This trip, sad to say, it's for the reading of a will." The chitchat never lags when you've got puppies, babies, or death to turn to.

"Oh, my. I am so sorry. Someone close?"

"No. Not really."

"Hmm . . ." She dog-eared a page, set her book aside. "You make it sound intriguing."

"Do I?" *Did I? I did.*

"Like in the movies—and you're heir to an unforeseen fortune. A castle in Scotland or something."

Her eyes were girlfriend blue, ready to love me as soon as despise me. "It's a long story," I told her.

"Isn't it always?" she laughed, as if she'd heard it all and expected to hear more, and Jack, I guess, had heard enough. He tossed up a card from our collection.

Good choice, I thought, and fired back.

"I understand," Jack said. "Beauty, charm, and plane crash survivor. A woman after your own heart. Too bad she's not in the script this time out."

"You don't know that. She could be the one."

"There's only ever been one, you know that."

"What about 'a sad goodbye'?"

"There are better Frankie Laine songs."

"C'mon, Jack. That's not fair."

"Let her go, Gus. Let her remember you as you are—the distracted loony who blanked mid-conversation and started yammering aloud to himself. She'll tell the story to friends, embellish it in parts, describe you as off your meds and supremely disturbed—but not as disturbed as you really are—and promptly forget she ever had the misfortune to cross your path. I'm doing you a favour, man."

"What if there's a bridge out up ahead and the train plunges into a ravine and I never get another chance to—"

"You wish you could be that lucky," Jack said.

"Excuse me? Are you speaking to me?" She was nervous, nursey, like she might whip out a thermometer, a cold compress. "Are you all right? Is something wrong?"

The train lurched. Couplings grumbled down the line.

Jack and me, we came up with the TV Guide blurb together.

1:00 5 HOLLYWOOD NORTH—Movie
After many years away, a man returns to his boyhood home to claim a mysterious inheritance.

I was thirty-seven years old, January of 1988, my future behind me, my past dead ahead.

# TWO

Jack was the boy who found things

Jack Levin was the boy who found things. When he was eight, a meteorite. When he was nine, a message in a bottle. When he was ten, a gold ring. Jack made the front page of the *Trent Record* every time.

LOCAL BOY FINDS METEORITE IN GARDEN
LOCAL BOY FINDS TRAGIC MESSAGE IN BOTTLE
LOCAL BOY FINDS LONG-LOST WEDDING BAND

On school days, boiled eggs, toast soldiers, and the paper were my breakfast, and my mother kept watch to ensure I digested all. "Don't forget, this is the same breakfast Alexander Graham Bell's mother gave him," she'd say, Mr. Bell in regular rotation with Edison, Einstein, and Walt Disney. On weekends, it would be Rice Krispies or Sugar Pops and the paper, which happened to be the same breakfast Winston Churchill's mother gave him. Either way, Mom promised, "You'll look back on this some day and thank me."

I have never stopped looking back. It's the thank-you that's been tough.

My mother was like most mothers. She believed me to be a better person than I would ever know myself to be.

The news was local. Fires. Fender benders. Drownings. Thefts. Fires. Drownings. Public intoxication. Fires. Death notices. Drownings. Pee Wee hockey. Fires. I skimmed the pages, bluffed interest with an intensity that swelled Mom's heart. Oh, I was good, all right. She'd get downright soppy as she gushed to friends about her wonderful son and his passion for the world about him. "So much like his dad, you have no idea."

Had she quizzed me, she'd have seen I retained no specifics, save for the life and times of *Superman, Beetle Bailey, Mandrake the Magician,* and Jack Levin.

We were spiritual bookends, Jack and me. That's how I saw it, anyhow. He found things. I wanted things. The front page was of no value to me unless he was on it.

"Quite the adventurer, isn't he?" Mom observed from her post behind my right shoulder. It was Jack's debut. The meteorite story. June 1958. "You can tell even now he's going to grow up to be a somebody. Just like you." My mother's endorsement of Jack should have had me running the other way. Her previous candidates for playmates had ranged from co-workers' nephews to the sundry spawn of checkout line acquaintances. The ensuing playtimes were footnotes from *The Book of the Damned.* I'd learned to dismiss her nominees out of hand.

"I know him," I said, my enthusiasm contained. "I've seen him at school."

"Are you friends? You should invite him over."

"He's older. Second grade."

"You can learn a lot from older friends. Look at me and Dottie. If not for her, do you think I would have had the courage to go for my promotion at work? She's been my rock." Mom and Dottie Lange worked at the Unemployment Insurance Office. They would remain best friends until the day Dottie died, which would arrive sooner than either of them could have expected.

My mother had it wrong, of course. Jack was already a somebody. Best I could claim was envy.

"He's got enough friends," I said.

I was only a year younger than Jack, but still I was in awe. From the first photo I saw of him he struck me as heroic, as if he himself had grabbed the comet's tail, hopped aboard, and chiselled out his prize. It might've been his smile, a cryptic quirk suggestive of more daring feats to come. He was squatting, pointing to the spot where the meteorite had been discovered, yet I would've bet you a million the photographer had tied him down to get the shot, Jack's unruly hair a stirring glimpse of anarchy in a town torn between Brylcreem and brush cut.

The town was Trenton. Still is.

The Ontario Trenton, not the New Jersey one.

Look for Rochester on your map and it's an inch straight up, an aberrant speck of chronic self-deception on the north shore of Lake Ontario, toward the western tip of the Bay of Quinte. Pronounced *kwin-tee*, the inlet is as perfect a *Z* as God has carved. Left to me, it would've been the Bay of Zorro.

The Trent River splits the town up the middle. Three bridges now span the gap, one for rail, two for road traffic. Prior to 1990, drivers and pedestrians relied mostly on the swing bridge on Dundas Street, the main street. Close by, upriver, there was also a footbridge attached to a railroad bridge. But you only took it on dares or if inclined to suicide. Walking under it wasn't a great idea, either, as its 1964 collapse would show.

Trenton is the gateway to the Trent–Severn Waterway. It is popular with boaters, fishermen, and the British Royal Family. Queen Elizabeth has turned up a bunch of times over the years. As a kid, I stood by the roadside and waved to her with the rest of the town and she waved back, though her hand never moved much, like she had a backscratcher up her sleeve.

You might have heard of the town. In 2010, Trenton had a serial killer. The commander of the nearby Air Force base, no less. A colonel. I'm not kidding. The guy had even piloted the Queen's plane a few times. The Prime Minister's, too. Again, I'm not kidding. You can look it up.

The serial killer didn't surprise me. I only wondered what took so long. I have wondered the same about a lot thereabouts—from the dark shit that has come to pass to the dark shit that will.

These days, the Killer Colonel pretty much sums up what most people know about Trenton and this includes the people who live there. I do not hold it against them. Nobody knew much in my day, either. And those who did weren't big on talking. I don't blame any of them. Anymore. Look how long it's taken me to open up.

Every town has its history. Every town has its secrets. Trenton's secret is its history.

THREE

Annie was the girl who believed in things

From the beginning of me I sensed the town would be the end of me, as if my designated bogeyman had vacated his lair beneath my bed, preferring to lie in wait in less patent territory. I saw neither streets nor avenues, only dead ends and dead endings. While other kids made do with stamps and coins and baseball cards, I collected fears. The biggest was that my mother would die and leave me on my own. Not that orphanhood wasn't entirely without appeal. Rusty on *Rin Tin Tin*. Corky on *Circus Boy*. Cuffy on *Captain Gallant*. That mopey kid from *A Dog of Flanders*. Joey on *Fury*. Bomba, the Jungle Boy. Orphanhood was the best thing to have happened to them. I just didn't have it in me to commit. Maybe if I'd had a dog or a horse. A baby elephant.

"Do you ever feel it?" I once asked Annie Barker. It was third grade and I shared my creepy worries with no other. I weighed the pros and cons of everything. I could carry some stuff inside of me for years, the larger part of this story a case in point. "You know, like something is going to get you, except you don't know how bad or how soon?"

Annie was the girl who believed in things. Me, among them, I suppose.

She didn't have any brothers or sisters, so we filled each other's voids. (She filled mine, at least.) She lived with her mom and dad up in The Heights, the new development near Trenton High. I'd never been invited over; we were strictly school friends, like every friend I'd ever had. But I knew her house—127 Pheasant Crescent—and had bicycled by a bunch of times, my focus on the asphalt as I pedalled crazy fast, praying she'd see me, relieved she never did.

"I'm not sure I understand," Annie said. I trusted Annie as much as I did my mother. Maybe more. There are some fears a kid can't confide to a parent. The closer the relationship, the riskier it gets. Had I shared with Mom the terror brewing inside of me, she would have used it against me, upped my cod liver oil, confiscated my jackknife, checked me for worms, banned the scary movies and TV—*The Twilight Zone* and *Alfred Hitchcock Presents*—and put me on a 24/7 death watch.

Annie coaxed me forward in that gentle way of hers. "What do you think is going to get you? Who could possibly want to—"

"I don't know. I just feel it. And there's nothing I can do to stop it. Not anything anybody can do. Like whatever's going to happen is going to happen."

She gaped, suspicious of my motives, like I was out to destroy everything she believed in. "My goodness, no. I do not feel it. No. Not at all. Never. And neither should you." She softened, shook her head with the same forbearance and pity she had reserved for me since first day of first grade. I was and would forever be *her special project*. "Life is a gift. A wonderful gift. Why waste it with silly thoughts? You can't think like that. You just can't. Please."

I could deal with Annie's anger. Her disappointment was the struggle.

"Oh, my Gloomy Gus. Don't you see how lucky we are to live here? There are children in Europe who would give their eye teeth to be in our shoes." Annie was into her Sandra Dee phase then. Sunshine, positivity, and dimples. The Deborah Walley, Hayley Mills, and Patty Duke phases would come later. Whatever. I would not have traded Annie for any of them. (Okay, Tuesday Weld, maybe. Connie Stevens, some days.) "Do you never go to church?"

My church was the Odeon. At home, I prayed at the altar of RCA.

"Does your mother never take you? Have you never read Bible stories— *Daniel in the Lion's Den*? It will do you a world of good. I promise. Have faith."

"I know it." Alan Young, Wilbur Post on *Mr. Ed*, was in the movie. "He pulls the thorn from the lion's paw and later on the lion doesn't eat him."

"Are you joking? That's *Androcles and the Lion. Daniel* is where the angel saves him by locking the jaws of the lions."

"Jeez, Annie. You have any idea how many lions stories are out there? Anyone could mix them up. Tarzan has lions coming out of his ears."

"You drive me crazy, you really really do. Tarzan is not in the Bible, Gus. Who doesn't know their Bible stories? Especially with your name."

"What?"

"If anybody would be a lion expert, it should be you. It's your real name, isn't it? Leo. Leo the lion?"

"That's like saying you should be a barking expert. And are you? Are you, Annie Barker?"

"I'm sorry."

"And don't call me Leo. I'm Gus. Only Gus."

"You don't have to get so mad. I was only trying to help. You get these thoughts . . ."

"I know the story. I forgot, okay? In the end, God feeds Daniel's enemies to the lions and everybody is happy."

"See. That's what I mean. I knew you knew. But you had to act like—I don't know what. Can't you ever be serious?"

"I was serious. I was. You didn't like what I had to say, so I stopped."

"I don't want you thinking bad things. You scare me sometimes. I worry about you, Gus."

"I worry about you, too."

"Me? Why? I go to church. I'm fine."

"I just do."

"Well, don't. Okay?"

"Jeez, okay. I won't."

"You need more friends. That's your problem."

"I got friends."

"Besides me? Who? I never see you with anyone."

"You don't know them. They don't go to our school."

"Well, I hope they're not the ones putting those bad thoughts in your head."

I carried on as before, resigned, the burden of impending doom mine alone. When the time came, I'd save Annie in spite of herself. But everyone else, they'd be on their own. No way I'd become the *Invasion of the Body Snatchers* guy, wailing and flailing as he raced headlong into traffic, warning the unsuspecting masses as they heaped him with abuse. Screw them. Stupid ingrates. Let them learn the hard way. Not that I was anywhere near clear as to what I'd be warning anybody about.

I remain unclear. Yet here I am, on page twenty-three of whatever this turns out to be, racing headlong into traffic. And I am wailing. And I am flailing. At twenty-four frames per second.

# FOUR

The obligatory taxidermy

I asked my mother why we didn't go to church. She was gardening, a smudge of dirt on her cheek, Buffalo's WKBW on the radio in the window. "If you went to church, you would know why," she said.

I met Annie first day of first grade.

Dufferin Street School was a demure Georgian beauty, two stories of quarried stone and priory windows, a mother hen of a building that promised to wrap us up in its wings and keep us safe.

Ask Marion Crane about first impressions, that nice boy Norman Bates.

Oak cabinets flanked Dufferin's every corridor and wall, the best and brightest of Canada's wildlife entombed within. The thriving, threatened, and long gone. Buffed beaks and snouts snuffling up to glass. Eyes glazed, soulless, and unnervingly alert. Gallery upon gallery of feather, fur, claws, and cunning, neither death nor stuffing sufficient impediments to the buffet of grade-school baby fat spread before them. I got the message damn quick. *Study hard. Work hard. Or you're dead meat.* Running would get me nowhere.

Miss Proctor's take was less dramatic. "This way, children," she said. "Let me tell you, you're in for quite the treat." And thus our first grade teacher commenced with our indoctrination. As if my reservoir of fears required topping up.

Eagles, hawks, and falcons. Loons and ducks. A great auk. A passenger pigeon. A cougar. Raccoons, weasels, and ferrets. And overseeing the gutted lot, perched in covens, cabals, and parliaments, the owls. Their bloodless hearts pounded in cahoots and in my ears, the verdict against me unanimous, my complicity in their demise rendered beyond a shadow of a doubt.

In contrast, Miss Proctor was Cinderella preparing for the ball. Chirpy birds and merry mice is all she saw. "Do we have any budding taxidermists among us today? What about other hobbies? Needlepoint, anyone? Wood-burning? You know what they say, idle hands play the Devil's piano. This way, children."

The more messed up the display, the more exuberant our teacher's commentary.

An owl sucking rat. An owl slurping frog.

"Do you know what I enjoy best about being a teacher here, boys and girls? Every day is a walk in the woods and I needn't step an inch outside to enjoy it."

A wolf eviscerating Bambi. A lynx regurgitating Thumper.

Miss Proctor paused, swept her attentive audience with a widescreen wink. She clasped her hands, lowered her voice, divulged the secret. "I can't say if it's true for certain, but I have heard on excellent authority that Mother Nature herself went to Dufferin School when she was little."

Man, the crock she unloaded on us would've made Pinocchio an also-ran.

An hour and three floors later, basement level and its bear cubs the easy winner, we gathered by the cabinet at our classroom door. "So now you see, boys and girls, how fortunate we are to have a zoological repository of this immensity in our very own midst. Never forget how lucky you are to live in this wonderful community and to attend this wonderful school. What did I say? What kind of a walk can we enjoy every day, rain or shine, sleet or snow?"

The halls reverberated with my classmates' joy. "A walk in the woods, Miss Proctor." I lip-synced my part, a fresh dose of dread shooting through my skull. Was she kidding? Were these dopes blind? School was no refuge. The place was a dirt bag shy of graveyard. Had these people never seen a movie? Taxidermy never leads to anything good.

"The red fox, he's beautiful, isn't he?"

"What?" I turned to the honey-haired girl at my side, took in her brown eyes, the crinkling at the corners. Till then, I'd thought *plucky* only happened in movies and TV.

"Him." She tapped the glass of the display case. "The fox. He's so beautiful."

"He's dead," I said.

Her smile stalled incomplete, a younger, cuter Mona Lisa. She couldn't decide what to make of the grumpy lump of asbestos standing before her. Abruptly, she held out her hand how grown-ups do. "I'm Annie Barker," she said. "It's really nice to meet you, Mister . . . uh . . . Gloomy Gus?"

I corrected her. "It's Leo. Leo Berry."

"Like the fruit?"

"That's so funny I forgot to laugh."

"Oh, you are a Gus. Definitely. A Gloomy Gus."

"Did Daddy go to church?" I asked my mother.

"The life we are given is complicated enough, dear, without the added strain of preparing for the next."

# FIVE

The story behind the absent 'n' of Glen Miller Road

Annie's father was the owner of Barker & Sons Lumber out on Glen Miller Road. His dad, the founding Barker, was dead, while the Battle of Britain and the Korean War finished off his older brothers. Mr. Barker shows up later to save my life, among other things. Even so, he's a supporting player and most of what he does occurs off page. I mention him now only because of Glen Miller Road.

You'd think it'd be named in honour of the famous composer and bandleader, seeing as how the town's Royal Canadian Air Force base had been a transport hub in World War II and Miller disappeared in a plane over the English Channel in 1944 on his way to France to serenade the troops, many of whom had bivouacked in Trenton. But anyone who knows the local mindset knows better.

Glen Miller Road honours a mill that used to operate in the glen, and not *Glenn* Miller, his trombone, or his service. The mundane prevails. Always has.

I could extend the benefit of the doubt, of course, assume all the extra *N*s the switch to proper signage would have entailed might have bankrupted the county. I could. I won't.

Outside of active politicians kissing up to former politicians, Trenton has never been big on remembering the memorable.

Glen Miller Road is the least of it. You'll see.

 SIX

I was the boy who wanted things

Jack found the message in the bottle in the sand at Presqu'ile beach in late summer of 1959, the first Sunday after school had begun. "The neck was sticking out," he told the *Record*. "Anybody could have seen it."

The message had come from a crew member of the *James B. Colgate*, a steamer that had gone down in Lake Erie forty-three years earlier.

jbc 20 Oc 1916
high wind wave
good By my Gitte
Harald Nordahl

Here, the photo of Jack, the bottle balanced with care upon his palm, two fingers at the neck, made you wonder if poor Harald Nordahl hadn't passed it directly to him, entrusting the Levin boy above all others. Like the dying soldiers of "In Flanders Fields," the poem teachers hammered into us each November. For the longest while, I thought the point of Remembrance Day was to remind us to memorize poems.

> *To you from failing hands we throw*
> *The torch; be yours to hold it high.*

More than ever, I wanted to be Jack. I wanted to be a finder, too. We'd be The Hardy Boys, Frank and Joe. We'd find stuff together. Solve mysteries. Salvage valuable relics. Rescue cute girls from slavering fiends in derelict mansions. Annie would be our Iola Morton.

I could have told him outright. I saw him around school plenty, walking home, and whatnot. But I was also aware of the risks. One ordinary kid declaring fandom to another is a bad idea any way you slice it. It is going to come off as weird. I would be branded for life. Smart kids nip the inclination in the bud, and I counted myself among them; my mother promoted my genius daily.

Not until the following spring did it cross my mind to stalk him. Serendipity is what it was, and the bell for morning recess. Right time, right place.

We streamed from our classrooms, same as always, and into *The Halls of the Living Dead*. It's what I called them by then. Annie had picked up on it, too, passed it on to her friends. Susan Burgess. Diana Klieg. Bonnie Priddy. They thought I was hilarious, nicknamed me *Igor* for a couple of weeks. I pretended I saw the humour, too.

I'd survived first and second grade by looking the other way, keeping the mammalian and avian zombies at bay. Lapses had been few. Still, the images lodged in my brain, projected onto my ceiling at bedtime. But with April drawing to a close and summer vacation pending, my discipline went out the window. This great horned owl, a feathered demon with tiger-stripe wings flapped into my sightline and pulled me in, her yellow eyes as large as lemons, and who did I see reflected back?—none but Jack, skipping down the stairs from the floor above.

Annie would have gone overboard, had I told her, declared divine intervention. *"Oh, Gus! Oh, Gus! Don't you see, the owl was the angel of the Lord. It's like Fatima. The Miracle of Our Lady of Trenton."*

The owl spoke to me: Jack would never be my friend unless I nudged him into it.

I anticipated his course, positioned myself so we'd bump shoulders. There'd be no way around it. I'd apologize and he'd apologize and then we'd laugh and become great friends. Problem was, he didn't see me. *I stood smack in front of him and Jack didn't see me.* Walked right by. Or was it through? No bump. No nothing. Like I wasn't there. I lifted my hands, warily examined each for symptoms of sudden onset transparency. There'd been morning fog. I would not be the first to be genetically reconfigured by a radioactive cloud. The king-sized spiders in *World Without End*. The king-sized ants in *Them!* Little Joe Cartwright in *I Was a Teenage Werewolf*. The colonel in *The Amazing Colossal Man*. But far as I could tell, my hands were as intact as the rest of me. There had to be another explanation. Could I be invisible *only* to Jack?

We passed fifty times a day and yet he'd never said a word in three years. He found everything else, didn't he? But he couldn't find me? *C'mon, eh!* I was no pipsqueak, either, way easier to spot than some rock from outer space, a bottle in the muck. We needed to be friends, Jack and me. *Best friends.* But how, if I was invisible to him? Sure, I could slap him on the back, make my presence known. He'd see me then—or feel me, hear me, anyhow. *"Hey, Jack, it's me—The Invisible Boy. Yeah, yeah. Over here. No, not there, here. Here. Hey, how'd you like to be friends?"* Anybody try that on me and I'd vamoose damn quick.

I followed ten paces to the rear of Jack and his pals, working their wake, no plan even close to mind. They pushed ahead, out through the Boys doors and into the first warm day of spring. Tight as a posse, they were, *The Magnificent Seven*, and me, the unsung *Eighth*, hot on their trail as they skirted the girls' side and scrambled up the knoll to the softball diamond.

I hung back by the new monkey bars, let the hyperactive cast of dare-devils and crybabies serve as my diversion, should I not be as invisible to Jack as I'd concluded. A bouquet of flowers drooped from the upper-most rung alongside frayed ringlets of cord and brown stems from earlier bouquets.

The old monkey bars had been replaced the previous July after Jimmy Campbell, a kindergarten kid who'd yet to graduate to Dufferin, had pulled them down on himself and crushed his windpipe. Jimmy wasn't heavy by most accounts, though this did not stop the grown-ups and the *Record* from blabbering on about diets for fatsos and playground safety for the better part of summer. The Great Monkey Bar Debate ended after tip-proof monkey bars were installed, steel and concrete anchors at each corner. On the twenty-second day of every month, Mrs. Campbell tied flowers to the monkey bars in memory of Jimmy. Mr. Malbasic, Dufferin's principal, was said to have asked her to stay away during school hours, for fear she'd distress the children. She brushed him off. I watched for her whenever the twenty-second rolled around and let me tell you she was plenty spooky, lidless eyes *Mole People* buggy, her nose a foundry hook, skin as blotchy grey as Dead Jimmy's must have been by then. The woman had a yoke at her neck, sadness in buckets at her side. She'd stare sometimes, like it should have been me in the grave instead of Jimmy. *Any kid but Jimmy*. I felt bad about it, too, had to fight the urge to tell her I was sorry it was not me.

Jack and his gang scattered across the playing field. Dougie Dunwood dug in at home plate. He was TV-kid good looking, curly haired and carrot-topped, with a megaphone mouth and muscles to back it. Dougie was also the town's most famous Boy Scout. The *Record* had done a story on the merit badges he'd accumulated. Most ever for a kid his age. *Pioneering. Paddling. Fellowship. First Aid.* Crap like that. Only badge he hadn't earned was the one he deserved most: *Asshole*. Everybody loved Dougie. Except me. I hated him for the pleasure of it. And watching him play ball effectively enriched my hate. Man, you should have seen the jerk swing a bat, blasting fungos and grounders and line drives till the recess bell cut the other way, and teachers hailed us back to class, whistles shrilling.

"You got a problem?"

I shifted my gaze a fraction right. A fine mist of Dougie Dunwood saliva lubricated my face. He drew a bead on my nose with the fat of his bat. "I catch you staring at me again, I'm gonna bash your teeth in, creep."

"Mickey Mental," I said, without meaning to. Not out loud, anyhow. Or maybe I did. A quick inventory would show I've uttered a lot of stupid shit over the years I would have been better off keeping to myself. The words you're reading now, for instance.

"What did you call me?" He dribbled his bat to my chest, counted down my ribs. I had to admire the dick, his Eddie Haskell routine was more Eddie Haskell than Eddie Haskell.

Dougie was a year older and a haircut shorter. My size tended to protect me from bullies, most figuring I was older, tougher, and stronger than I was. But every now and then there'd be some canny asshole like Dougie who'd put the truth to the physical lie. "I asked you a question. What did you call me?"

I replied with the fawning enthusiasm of an autograph collector. "You got his swing. You know, Mickey Mantle? His swing."

"Hey, Dumbwood," Jack called as he trotted past, and Dougie took off. I was happy to award the guy a new badge: Short Attention Span.

Threats to my dental health aside, I declared my first foray into espionage a success. Recess was fifteen minutes start to finish, and Jack had remained in my sights for all but a few seconds of it. I shivered at the possibilities, possessed by an unaccustomed clarity and calling. I was Superman plying my X-ray vision, zeroing in on answers to questions I hadn't thought to ask.

Again, the owl spoke to me. Marching up to Jack would not make us friends. I had to make Jack want us to be friends. *Want us to be friends.* Only then would he see me.

If I could catch him in the act of finding, I'd be set. By stealing his secrets, the tricks and tools of the finding trade, I'd be on the front page of the *Record*, too. Imagine what Mom would say then, how proud she'd be? Before you knew it, the great Jack Levin would be seeking *me* out. It'd be Jack watching *me* and *my buddies* at recess. And, boy, I'd have a ton. How could I not? *Mickey Mental and me—who saw that coming?*

I honed my craft, brought *The Hardy Boys' Detective Handbook* into play, studied the chapter on surveillance till I could tail myself without detection. My mother, not so much.

"There's something I need to ask you, sweetheart."

"Yeah?"

"Last night, were you peeking into my bedroom?"

"What?"

"My bedroom, Leo. I saw you on your knees, peeking in through my door."

"Wasn't me."

"Really, dear? I'm certain I saw—"

"I was in bed reading when you thought you saw me. Honest, Mom."

"It's normal to be curious about girls, sweetheart. Anything in particular you feel you need to know . . . it's okay, you can talk to me. You don't have to be shy. . . ."

"I didn't do it. I swear. Wasn't me."

If there was a void in *The Hardy Boys' Detective Handbook*, it was a section on plausible deniability.

# SEVEN

Every kid's responsibility

I couldn't track Jack full time. I was—what?—eight, nine during the stretch. I had places to be, Mom to contend with, and no deputy to spell me on stakeouts. But I was on Jack every chance I got, you bet. In the process, I became the son of my mother's dreams. *"My goodness! What's got into you?"* I volunteered to pick up milk and bread from the A&P, aspirin and rubbing alcohol from Simmons Drugs, packages from the post office, and Mom's dry cleaning from Old Man Blackhurst and his dreaded Sure Press—any errand that'd bring me downtown, allow me to detour by the Marquee to check up on Jack.

The Marquee Café was Jack's family's place, a local hangout next to the Odeon. No Jack story in the *Record* was complete without a mention of how he helped out at the diner, all the while maintaining his finding activities and good grades. Quotes from teachers trod similar pap: "Jack is an excellent student, well liked by all and a pleasure to have in my class."

You know those optical illusions where if you stare at the picture one way, you see a tree, and then, if you blink, you see a face? Perhaps I wasn't invisible to Jack, after all, and more an optical illusion, so when he looked my way he saw a tree or something and, given appropriate light and perspective, he might blink and there I'd be. More logical than selective invisibility, no?

Accordingly I took precautions, aimed for inconspicuous as the Hardy Boys instructed. Page 242, *DOs AND DON'Ts*.

Point 2:

> *"Act nonchalant. Most detectives are too conscious of being suspected and therefore act suspicious."*

Point 9:

> *"Look around naturally. Never act furtive or suspicious."*

I regularly spied on Jack through the Marquee's windows, hovering *nonchalant* and un-*furtive* on the penny scale out front of the restaurant.

He was never up to much. At the cash register. At the sink. Clearing tables. Reading comics. Yakking with customers. (Always yakking with somebody, that kid.) None of it was anywhere near interesting, either, though clearly more interesting to Jack than the snoopy kid planted on the scale outside. And yet another theory occurred to me: Jack had lousy eyesight.

I shifted to his house on weekends.

The Levins lived on Queen in a red brick cottage with a screened-in porch, wicker chairs and tables, and a garden overrun with Triffids. St. Pete's Church and schoolyard was across the street, with hedges, trees, and concrete corners tailor-made for surveillance.

Saturday mornings I'd catch Jack heading out with his mom or younger sisters, and not much else. My time was tight on Saturdays. The Odeon matinees got underway at 10, which was where Jack usually turned up anyhow.

Sunday spying was reserved for late afternoon. The highlight was the lowlight, Jack's mom and dad yelling at each other from deep inside the house. I never did make out what was shouted, only that it wasn't good, and imagined Jack and his sisters cowering in closets. Once, I saw Mr. Levin storm out and speed off in his car, Mrs. Levin staring after him from the doorway, posed and composed, like the possessed lady on the poster of *Back from the Dead*, except Mrs. Levin wasn't wearing any flimsy nightgown or holding a fifteen-inch dagger at her hip. And for the first time ever, not having a dad didn't seem to be such a bad thing. As for Jack and his finding expeditions, Sundays were a washout. I seldom saw the guy.

My suspicions ran the gamut.

Jack had access to a secret tunnel, his comings and goings undetected.

Jack was a master of disguise and had slipped by me in the likeness of his dad.

Jack was a shape-shifter with a propensity for stray dogs. Hell, Trenton was the puppy mill of the Baskervilles' dreams. The town's strays were mostly Labs, mostly black, mostly foaming at the mouth, and they'd come charging out of nowhere, chasing cars and bikes and any idiot who'd be idiot enough to run or not run. I couldn't get through a stakeout without having my butt sniffed, my leg humped, my shoes drooled on. Who's to say the strays weren't Jack? Dogs were a natural for any dabbler in the therianthropic arts. I was up on Montague Summers and *The Werewolf in Lore and Legend*. The readable parts, anyhow. *Therianthropes* and *therianthropy* were as much a part of my vocabulary as *to* and *be*. Shape-shifters were at least as populous as mermaids, demons, and vampires. Suspect everyone.

Or what if all along it hadn't been me, but Jack who had mastered invisibility? The slightest breeze, a movement of air, I freaked, groped the space about me, mimicked every dopey mime I'd seen on *Ed Sullivan*. "Is that you? Jack? You there? I won't tell. Your secret's safe with me."

Far-fetched did not enter my thinking. *Far-fetched* is what the soon-to-be-dead assert when dismissing strange explosions on the surface of Mars. It was every kid's responsibility to stay alert. Let the grown-ups deal with the commies. Kids were frontline against The Unknown. And whatever the hell The Unknown would ultimately prove to be, it had me by the short hairs and Trenton in the crosshairs.

# EIGHT

*Crazy shit you look back on in adulthood
and laugh your freaking head off over*

It was Jimmie Dodd of *The Mickey Mouse Club* who'd said, "Get to the bottom of your fears, Mouseketeers, and you'll come out on top of your fears." I took him at his word. Especially on Fridays. My Sure Press Dry Cleaners day.

The dry cleaners had been creeping me out since self-awareness was a novelty, when Mom would lift me in my stroller through Mr. Blackhurst's door, my wide watchful eyes and stupid whimper the enduring takeaways. *Stupid* because—*c'mon!*—this was no butcher shop, no nursery rhyme fricassee of tails and carving knives. This was Sure Press, where cleaning was alleged not to extend to skinning and quartering.

Little kids aren't deceived by the rational. Little kids see what's what, one foot in the world recently departed, one foot in the world currently deployed. Kids can sniff out shit years before it is.

I might have grown less wary of Sure Press over time had it been my nature to let things go. Bad things, anyhow. With Sure Press, the *bad* greeted you on the street outside.

Hercules had Cerberus, the three-headed dog at the gates of Hades. I had the Sewing Machine Witch of King Street.

Tailoring, Alterations & Repairs
Professional Seamstress

She toiled at her cubicle in the window, eyes habitually averted, mantis-like and slate-faced under bun and hairnet, tasked to spin hemlines into gold. "Gassed in the war, they say," Mom often reminded, and tapped the hollow of her throat for emphasis. "Lost her voice box, poor soul."

Compassion was not a trap I readily fell into. The fascination for me was the fried skin that ridged her hollow, four fingernail widths of corrugated red from shadow of jaw to scoop of collarbone. She didn't need to utter a word for me to heed the rhyme she'd spew, her *V*s and *W*s transposed in verse and curse.

> *"Even a man who is pure in heart*
> *And says his prayers by night*
> *Can become a wolf when the wolfbane blooms*
> *And the autumn moon is bright."*

With nothing but proximity to go by, my mother presumed the woman to be both devoted wife and albatross of the long-suffering and insufferable Mr. Blackhurst. Mom never could see the treachery that incubated within the everyday, how the inscrutable duo catered to and fed my intuited anxieties.

The bell above the door didn't jingle on entry so much as *jing*, the opening note of what I took to be the theme of my death scene. My every sense screamed *funhouse*, the floor never quite level, the right angles more and less than right.

Unseen and deep within the shop's bowels vipers hissed. The steam press.

I kept my breathing to a minimum. Sure Press reeked of morgue, cadavers trashed on formaldehyde. Not that I'd been to a morgue. Closest I'd come had been Wilmot Family Funeral Home. And there was the one thing I liked about Sure Press: My father's ghost could stop by at any time, reclaim the cleaning he'd left behind. I hoped I'd be there for it. Hoped he'd know me.

I slung the pillow case onto the counter, shook out Mom's blouses and skirts, and settled in for the wait. Mr. Blackhurst would be in no hurry to show himself. "The British are a methodical people," my mother had explained.

I bided my time, mulled the wisdom of a premature exit.

The Witch moistened a thread, crossed her eyes taking aim at a needle. She swivelled to her side table, sifting, shuffling. Spools. Tailors' chalk. Tailors' tape. Pincushions. A jumble of buttons in a White Owl cigar box.

I cleared my throat. "Is Mr. Blackhurst here?" She poked a thimble onto her finger. Maybe she *was* the Gatekeeper. Maybe the rules had changed and I needed a password. Maybe I was dead and had yet to be informed. The Dead would be the last to know they were dead. God was a smart guy. He'd likely ease you into the Afterlife. You know, start you off simple—trailers, cartoons, comedy short, newsreel—before the main attraction: *Abbott & Costello & You Meet The Heavenly Father.* Wouldn't be the first time I questioned on which side of the firmament I stood.

"It's my mom's cleaning," I said, like she'd switch it up, dance a jig at the news.

I opened and shut the door again, scuffed my heels. My mother disapproved of service bells, said they were disrespectful of hard-working people. But I was hard working, too. Jack could be in the midst of his biggest find ever right then, and I'd miss it all, stuck at the goddamn dry cleaners.

I strained for beseechingly polite. "Excuse me, Miss—" The Sewing Machine Witch accelerated the treadle, her Singer a rocket on the Bonneville Salt Flats.

I tapped the chrome service bell, my tinkle halfhearted. The steam press fell silent, *and the trapdoor beneath my feet dropped open, and down I plummeted, spitting teeth, hitting rock and rock bottom. A slimy green luminescence emanated from the damp stone walls. Houdini's Chinese Water Torture Cell is what it was, the chamber that big or small, minus latches and view. Bones lay strewn about the floor. Human. Rat. Fish. Bambi's dad's antlers. A shiny object beckoned from a corner. A bronze thimble. "Help! Help!" I hollered to an unseen audience, pleas falling short of my own ears. With a bicuspid, I etched a tearful goodbye in stone to Mom. With the thimble, I dug a tunnel, only to wedge myself immobile, joining the ranks of the inexplicably vanished to the eternal dismay of my poor mother.*

The End

BPI

So went the doomsday sequence inside my head. The scenario would have suited me fine, too, in light of all that would transpire outside my head, the turns my actual script would take.

I tapped the chrome service bell, my tinkle halfhearted. The steam press fell silent. Voices trickled forth from the rear of the shop—Mr. Blackhurst and a woman. Hushed and indistinct. Like those whispers that erase your dreams.

"Patience, patience," Mr. Blackhurst bellowed, no rush to show himself. The dry cleaner's accent was high-tea mucoidal, Sheriff of Nottingham snooty, marshmallows for tonsils. Physically he was Little John tall, Friar Tuck wide, and Robin Hood tidy.

"Mr. Blackhurst is one of the good ones," my mother would quietly observe, her glance precise and fleeting upon the man's matrimonial millstone. (My millstone was Mom's Pollyannaism. She thought she was watching out for me and all the while I was watching out for her.) Mr. Blackhurst never failed to be polite and kind to Mom, attentive to the faintest of stains, or to allow me a lollipop of choice, yet I felt vulnerable in his presence, unclear on where to stand, where to keep my hands, where to look. *This was where he wanted me to be.* Oddly, this was also where I wanted to be and why I willingly returned for more. Sure Press was a test. Of what I did not know, could not say.

He shuffled toward me, emerging through the disembodied flanks of men's suits. My father's herringbone swayed among them. My mother had left the suit unclaimed from the week before Dad's accident, as though the woolen bait would one day precipitate his return to the Living. The claim slip remained where Dad had tacked it, to the cork board in our kitchen.

Then something and someone new. *Something and someone I had not seen before.* Behind Mr. Blackhurst in the backlight of his broad wake, as if flickering in silence across a movie screen, a woman, her face framed by and hooded in black fur, collar bunched at her throat, her lips and nails Dragon Lady scarlet, her purple eyes a Technicolor spectacle and dead set on consuming me. *She knew me. Knew more about me than I knew about myself.* A blur was all she was, a wisp within a wink, before the suits closed ranks and the screen went dark.

I angled for a second look, Mr. Blackhurst not helping. I stammered an apology. "I didn't know you were busy with somebody." I rose to my toes, peered beyond his shoulder.

"Alas, my lad, I am occupied only with pleats and wrinkles," he said, and sorted through Mom's laundry.

"But that lady . . ." I pointed toward the suits.

"Lady?" His chuckle patronized. "Oh, you'd be amazed at the wonders I imagine in the folds and creases of laundry. A trompe l'oeil, my lad. No different than lambs gambolling in clouds."

"But I swear I saw . . ." I appealed to the Sewing Machine Witch. She hoed the button box with her nose.

Mr. Blackhurst handed me the ticket. "Tell your mother I'll have the lot next Friday, same as usual."

"I know what I saw," I said. "I know what I saw."

"Anytime after three." He tendered his basket of lollipops. I grabbed and ran. Two lousy yellows and a lousier orange. Served me right.

Nuts, eh? A dry cleaning shop. The crazy shit kids blow out of proportion . . .

5:00 ❷ THE MICKEY MOUSE CLUB—Kids
Insanity and melodrama intersect as
Jimmie helps guest Mouseketeer Gus
cope with his fear of dry cleaning.

. . . The crazy shit you look back on in adulthood and laugh your freaking head off over, your wife or girlfriend teasing you about it, till it's not so funny anymore.

NINE

A cold-hearted obliteration of what was

There's this moment toward the climax of *House of Wax* where the heroine, Phyllis Kirk, fearing for her life, smashes Vincent Price in the face. Except it's not his face. It's the wax mask he's been hiding behind, and as it shatters, the grisly truth is revealed. Phyllis faints. You can't blame her. The psycho's mug is a flame-broiled eggplant.

Trenton is Vincent Price with a chintzier mask and uglier eggplant.

Fires have done a number on the town. Huge, catastrophic fires. Too many in too many years to count. Rip-roaring blazes that have devastated the forests, the fringes, the heart of downtown.

Easter weekend '78, Godzilla dropped in for the night with Hiroshima on his breath. Walk the main street and you'll see, the town never did recover, all claims to the contrary Chamber of Commerce claptrap. There's a charm-less, slapped-together look to the whole. You can't help but wonder if public tenders are extended only to builders schooled on LEGO, and then awarded free rein to masturbate in brick, aluminum, and plastic. Aesthetics. Zoning. Heritage protection. Afterthoughts, if that. Some might argue there's no point in sprucing up tinder. Maybe so. But spend enough time in Trenton and you'll understand, if fire doesn't blacken your soul, the politicians and speculators will.

Mount Pelion rises two hundred feet above the town. It's the highest point for miles. An antique naval cannon sits at the top in commemoration of nothing anybody is clear on. Most days, you can fish beer cans and McDonald's wrappers from the barrel. Explorer Samuel de Champlain and his Huron buddies are said to have climbed Pelion in 1615 to get the lay of the land.

Dufferin Street School went up at the base of the mountain in 1913. Come winter, we'd spend recess on Mount Pelion, sleds and toboggans in tow. Winter 1960, I watched Jack pull a set of car keys from the snow. They belonged to my third grade teacher, Mrs. Beckwith. She'd lost them while on recess duty. Later, she told our class, "Jack Levin is an exemplary young man. By applying yourself with civility and diligence, I believe the same qualities can be found in each of you. Even the girls." The keys were a minor find for Jack and unreported by the *Record*.

They tore Dufferin down circa 2007. Almost ninety-five years reduced to rubble. The city elders had run out of patience, and stopped praying for fire to do their dirty work.

My sentiments ring hollow, I know. Taxidermiphobia notwithstanding, I cannot deny my lingering affection for the school, my attachment shameless and twisted, like nostalgia for a loveless marriage. (And I should know.)

Forget the historical and architectural arguments. It's the calculated injustice that pains me, the coldhearted obliteration of what was, for so long and so many, so dear to heart.

The Past. You'd think it harboured incriminating evidence, the town's aversion to it.

The mountain stands, for now, though passersby can be excused for passing by. The unrestricted width and height of the seniors residence built over Dufferin's grave blocks the view. Sledding is also discouraged, the southern slope overgrown.

In the summer of 2007, a young woman's body was found not far from the cannon. She wasn't the first to die up there, only the most recent. But then I'm getting ahead of myself.

Thing is, the town keeps running. And no one ever stops to ask from what.

TEN

The boy who Peckered himself

"Do you know him?" Annie asked, as we paused to catch our breaths. The snow was deep and fresh. It had come early in November and continued without let-up into February. Hauling the toboggan up Pelion was a trudge, waist-deep in areas.

"Not really," I said. "Except from the newspaper."

"Then why are you always watching him?"

"What? No. I'm not. I don't."

"Yes, you do. Every chance you get. You're doing it now."

"No, I'm not."

"Do you want to be his friend or something?"

"He's got friends."

"You can't spy on him forever. Why don't you go over and talk to him?"

"He'll think I'm crazy."

"But you are, aren't you?"

"Jesus, Annie."

"What's he doing now?"

Jack was kneeling in the snow. "Looks like he found something."

"Something shiny," Annie said. "Keys, I think."

"I've never seen him find anything before."

"So that's why you've been watching him."

"Stop it. I told you. I'm not."

"Do you think he's stuck-up? Bonnie's mom eats lunch at the Levins' restaurant and she says Jack Levin has a big head from being in the paper all the time. Lots of kids say so."

"I don't know. Could be." The speculation was odd, coming from Annie. She never said bad things about people. Not even kids and teachers who deserved it. Once, out in the schoolyard, watching Dougie Dunwood parachute from a swing, I said, "There goes Mickey Mental." As harmless as that.

Annie covered up her smile real fast, swallowed what I could swear was a giggle. "If you don't have anything nice to say about a person, say nothing at all."

"But that guy, he's a stupid jerk."

"You should look in a mirror sometimes."

Annie had found me out. I went cold turkey. Tossed the *Detective Handbook* into the netherworld of my bedroom closet. I had no choice. My cover was blown. I trusted Annie to keep mum, but if anyone else got wind of my spying, I'd be *Peckered* for the duration.

Pecker, aka Doll-Pecker, born Charles Dahl-Packer. He shows up in class, sissy-ass hyphenated name and all, a month or so into second grade, and digs a hole for himself day one. He's come from London—either Ontario or England, like any of us give a hoot. And just as Miss Smeets is winding down her introduction, he feels compelled to interject, "My father and mother are Mr. and Mrs. Geoffrey Packer, the pharmacists—which are as important as doctors, you know—and we own the new drugstore across from the Dairy Queen. Packer Family Pharmacy." Like any of us give two hoots. But then, he goes monkey-ass red in the face when anybody calls him Charley or Chuck, Miss Smeets included, and insists it's Charles and only Charles. Naturally, we call him nothing but Charley or Chuck. And then, first recess out in the playground, he strays over to the girls' side, wanders too close to the swings, and gets kicked in the head by Sally Fritz. A first-grader, no less. Smallest kid in the whole damn school. So small, her friends call her Bitsy Fritzy. And down Charley-Chuck-Charles goes, bloodied nose and mouth, bawling, thrashing about like he's been peppered with buckshot.

Nobody called him Charley or Chuck after that. He was Doll-Pecker and only Doll-Pecker, until the less cumbersome Pecker gained favour. And while ganging up was never my forte, seeing as how I never had anyone to gang up with, I was eager to give it a go. Turned out I had the gift, despite my experience on the receiving end. I got swept up in the thrill, same as Jesse James did when he chose to ride with brother Frank and the snivelling Youngers. Even knowing how the name-calling would cut deep, how the butterflies would gather in Pecker's gut each morning before school, the ache ballooning to his throat and into his head. It wasn't a question of recognizing right from wrong. *I recognized*. I'd been cornered and name-called for the crime of sneezing funny, for the flagrant commission of exiting the school library with the maximum allowable three books under my arm, for wearing a Davy Crockett t-shirt with Bermuda shorts. My shyness could be seen as arrogance, my reticence disdain. Heck, I rubbed some kids the wrong way solely through my concerted effort to stay the hell out of their way. However frowned upon, bullying had credibility, whichever side of the equation you were on.

Bullying was a time-honoured essential of the formative stage and for every *tut-tut* by teachers and *tsk-tsk* by parents, there'd be as many blind eyes turned. I was contributing to the greater good for Pecker's own good. *He'd thank me some day.*

Annie refused to go along. She never called Pecker anything other than Charles.

Unlike Pecker, I'd steered clear of first-graders on swings. And while I'd had my share of run-ins, I approached fourth grade unscathed and unlabelled. I'd been careful, too, had given Mickey Mental a wide berth since our bat-in-the-mouth chat. But *careful* could carry me only so far. By calling me out on Jack and my spying, Annie had saved me from Peckerdom.

I avoided the owl with the big lemon eyes and abstained from Jack with the same tenacity I'd exercised when tailing him. I returned to less perilous obsessions. Comics, *Believe It Or Not!*, *MAD*, and *Famous Monsters of Filmland*. TV, Saturdays at the Odeon, *Hockey Night in Canada*, and the Montreal Canadiens.

The only fallout from my undercover career were the errands. I'd taken my Good Son routine too far. There'd be no shirking.

By fall 1960, I was a full-time civilian again, living the good life, unencumbered by the compulsion that had consumed me. Yeah, as in touch with myself as the alcoholic who gets the idea he can tend bar. Because October comes and Jack goes and finds the damn gold ring and the *Record* goes overboard with the news and my mother goes, "My, oh, my, we haven't heard from him in quite the while, have we?"

By the time I made it to school my brain had turned to Jiffy Pop. I scoured the playground, locked him in my sights, and marched right up. "You're Jack," I said.

"Yeah. I know."

And without additional formality, my three years of self-restraint and scrupulously cultivated anonymity went down the toilet in a sycophantic rush of verbal diarrhea. "I just want to say that uh how I think it's really neat how like how you find stuff like me too uh like five dollars once outside the A&P uh I'm always looking uh Mommy . . . uh my mom . . . uh . . . she said uh . . . uh . . . I mean me . . . you . . . like us . . . we could be, you know, sort of like, you know, The Hardy Boys." *Mommy.* I'd said *Mommy.* My mastery of the awkward was flawless. *Kill me now.* I'd *Peckered* myself.

Silence struck like an executioner's axe.

"Hey, guys, it's the weirdo I told you about. Remember? He thinks I'm Mickey Mantle."

"Yeah, right," Jack said, and he and his pals began roaring, backslapping, arm punching. I was by far the funniest thing they'd heard and seen since Moe last blinded Curly.

They circled me.

"Look at that, Jack. You got yourself a little fairy."

"Hey, pansy! They're calling you back to the girls' side."

"You got a screw loose or what, kid?"

"He's hungry, Jack. Give him a knuckle sandwich."

"You gonna cry, Tinker Bell? You gonna go tell *Mommy* on us?"

"Yeah, he's gonna go tell his mommy at the A&P."

Jack laughed with them, and man, I hated him right then like I'd never hated anyone. More than Mickey Mental himself. "Well, yeah, anyhow," he said, and returned to his friends and their football, jogging long and deep as he signalled for a pass, leaving me behind, alone and, in retrospect, saved from further ridicule.

I was never more than an average student. But when it came to beating up on myself, I was scholarship material from the get-go. Never took much. A minor setback, the slightest slight, and I'd agonize like nobody's business. On those days, I knew to avoid Annie. She'd only try to cheer me up. Good thing, outside of school, we went our separate ways.

Walking home that afternoon, I was well down the slippery slope, nine years old and in the throes of shame. *How clueless could I have been?* As I came upon my street, I wished what I have wished far too often over the years: I wished I was dead. Jack and his idiot pals, they'd be sorry then. I was working on who else might be sorry, cataloguing every best and probationary friend I'd ever discarded or lost, when the footsteps closed in from behind.

"Hey, you. Kid! Wait up. You the Flash or something?"

I did not turn.

"Hey, Speedy Gonzales!"

I did not slow.

"Never mind those guys," Jack said. "They were only pulling your leg."

Poker face. I gave him nothing.

"Well, okay. Good. Glad they didn't get to you. What's your name, anyhow?"

I kept my focus on the straight and narrow, mumbled a miserly and miserable, "Gus." I saw no need to confuse the issue with the truth. Besides, it's who I was by then, Leo consigned to secret identity.

"Hey, I know you. You're the kid who's always weighing himself on the scale outside the restaurant. Yeah, you're the one."

I skipped ahead.

"So, you like finding stuff, too, eh?"

I did not drop so much as a hint of a nod.

"Most people think it's about keeping your head down and your eyes open. But if it was that simple, everybody'd be a finder. The thing you need to know, listening is as important as looking."

I stopped at my house, searched the sky, surveyed the trees, the grass, the sidewalk.

"Well, okay then, Gus, if that's the way you want it." He mock-punched my arm, roughed up my hair till it was as messy as his own, and split, his PF Flyers flying.

I didn't put a comb to my hair for days. Thought the look would improve my finding skills, same as Samson's hair had juiced his strength. Mom got fed up, hauled me off to Seeley the Barber. A brush cut, yet, goddamn.

 ELEVEN

The dad who was blown to smithereens

Jack gave the meteorite to Queen's University in Kingston, the message and bottle to Cardiff Mann, Jr., President of the Great Lakes Mariners Historical Association, and the gold wedding band to Mrs. Edna Bruce, the 72-year-old widow who had lost it 49 years earlier.

Jack's largesse returned him to the front page every time.

LOCAL BOY DONATES RARE METEORITE
JACK THE FINDER DONATES MESSAGE IN BOTTLE
JACK THE FINDER RETURNS LOST WEDDING BAND

Yeah, Jack the Finder. That's what the *Record* was calling him now. Bryan McGrath, the reporter who had taken Jack under his wing, had come up with it. People liked it. Me, too. *Jack the Finder* had a superhero feel about it, a Mandrake the Magician aura.

Queen's put the meteorite on exhibit with a small bronze plaque to credit Jack. You can still see the meteorite in the school's Miller Museum, though the plaque went missing long ago. (I'll solve the mystery for you, soon enough.)

Cardiff Mann, Jr., and the Great Lakes Mariners Historical Association were frauds, of course. The news caused quite the stir.

JACK THE FINDER VICTIMIZED

Jack shrugged it off, expressed confidence Harald Nordahl's legacy would be preserved. "Anyone who'd bother to steal an old bottle is going to look out for it way better than most."

Edna Bruce offered him five dollars in gratitude for the ring. Jack declined politely. "I don't find things, exactly," he was quoted as saying. "It's more like things find me."

The Widow Bruce went on to say Jack's gallantry reminded her of her own son. "I pray it doesn't kill him like it did my Murray." Murray Bruce had lied about his age, enlisted in the Canadian Army at fifteen, fell on Juno Beach at eighteen.

I clipped the Jack stories—I had them all, going back to the meteorite—and stowed them flat between the pages of the biggest book I owned, *Richard Halliburton's Complete Book of Marvels*. I guess I thought of Jack and his finds as marvels, too. The book was the last gift my father had given to me. Not that he gave it in person. And not that I believed the book was intended for me, but rather for the shelves in the den with Dad's other big books. He died at Christmastime in 1954 on his way home from Buffalo, New York. My mother breaking the news is an early memory and easily within my top ten. "You need to listen to me very carefully, sweetheart. Daddy has had an accident. A very bad accident. I'm afraid he has passed away." My father slipped in the bathroom of a Texaco gas station on Highway 2 near Oshawa and cracked his head open on the sink.

Two policemen delivered Dad's car and belongings to our house. They had moustaches Mom described to friends as "utterly droopily mournful." When done, they doffed their hats, and wished Mom well. "Very sorry for your loss, ma'am. A terrible misfortune."

One patted my head. "Sonny."

The other winked with both eyes. "Son."

"He was a good man," Mom said. "A strong believer in life insurance. I'm fortunate. I just never expected—"

"So where is he?" I looked beyond the open door to the police cruiser and Dad's car. I'd counted on a body in addition to the suitcase, briefcase, and bag of snacks—Dad's go-to sunflower seeds and licorice Nibs.

The cops fidgeted with their hats.

"You know Daddy's not coming back," Mom said. "Remember, how we talked about it?"

"But you said we were going to bury him."

"And we will," she said. "Daddy is at the funeral home. That's where people who have passed away go to wait before they're buried. In a few days, you and I and our friends will go there, and we'll bury Daddy."

"With shovels?" I said.

"Yes. With shovels."

"And after he's buried, he can come home."

"He can't. I told you. Not ever."

"But what if he wants to?" I said. "What if he climbs out? What do we do then?" I wasn't playing cute. I understood dead meant dead. It was Mom's reliance on *passed away* that confused me. *Passed away* suggested less than fully dead.

Mom found *Richard Halliburton's Complete Book of Marvels* in Dad's suitcase. There was an inscription inside the front cover:

> Xmas 1954
> To the best son in the world.
> Love you forever and a day,
> Daddy

The handwriting was my mother's. I never did tell her I knew. I mean, what sort of dad would write *Love you forever and a day* to a son?

In time, I would alter a detail or two about my father's death, recount how he was blown to smithereens on D-Day alongside the bold and brave Murray Bruce. Never once did anyone ask how I came to be born seven years after D-Day.

Kids don't get many free passes, but mention a dead parent and you pull an automatic. More dead parents the better.

# TWELVE

The satisfaction to be found
in simultaneous self-preservation and self-destruction

While I was happy Jack had tried to set things right after my schoolyard meltdown, we did not become anything you'd call friends. We'd nod in passing and not much else. The fact I'd rebuffed him had come with a good deal of satisfaction and, however wonky my logic, I kept to myself with renewed determination.

7:00 5 THE REBEL—Western
The Civil War finally ended, Gus Yuma roams the West to escape his troubled past. Friends do not come easy to this sensitive veteran of the Confederacy, but you can bet trouble does.

That was me. Strong, silent, in need of nothing, nobody, nowhere, no time. A hero's life is a solitary life. Mine was, too, until Mom went and got her stupid raise at work.

"How would you like to eat out for a change?" she said.

"Like a picnic?"

"A restaurant."

"I don't know."

"Since when don't you know about burgers and milkshakes and pie?"

"Like at Louie's?"

"Who's Louie?"

"Louie Dumbrowski. Where The Bowery Boys hang out."

Bert and Mollie Levin's Marquee Café was a cubbyhole diner on Dundas at Division. Four tables, sixteen chairs, and nine seats at the counter. A wall of cigars, cigarettes, and antacids. And bins and racks spilling over with chocolate bars, chewing gum, and penny candy—enough to trip up even Hansel and Gretel.

Every second Thursday, on my mother's paydays, I'd meet her at the Marquee.

While Jack wasn't always on the job, he was up to the same old nothing when he was. Tending the cash. Washing dishes. Spinning on a stool. Inevitably, some customer would sidle up and bend his ear. You could see how older people loved talking to Jack. He had a knack for listening, grinning or grim-faced as the drift required. If he was faking it, he had me fooled, his acting chops up there with John Wayne.

As for Jack and me, we kept it cool. Neither of us let on our paths had crossed.

I saw through Mom, too, the Marquee another ploy to round me up a friend. With Jack her prey, I soft-pedalled the pushback.

"I got friends," I assured her. "I just don't bring them home."

"Are you ashamed of me? Our house?"

"I don't want them breaking my stuff," I said.

"Then why don't they invite you to their houses?"

"They don't want me breaking their stuff."

"But you wouldn't."

"They don't know that."

"You have no idea how I worry about you. Some nights, I can't fall asleep thinking about it. You're alone too much. It's unhealthy."

"I told you, I have friends. A ton. I swear."

"Name one."

"Annie Barker."

"A girl? But what about the bo—"

"And Dougie Dunwood."

"Really? The Boy Scout? I hear he's very nice. Good at sports."

"He's the greatest. We play ball and uh—go to taxidermy club—all the time."

Ploy or not, Marquee burgers and club sandwiches were pretty tasty, and every wedge of Mollie Levin pie left you craving your next. Only after the Levins anointed us café regulars did Mom's gloves come off.

"Go. Go, tell him. Tell him, dear. Tell him how much you've enjoyed reading about his exploits in the Record.*"*

"Imagine, the movie theatre right next door. I would not be the least bit surprised to learn he likes movies as much you, sweetheart."

"Why don't you invite your friend Dougie Dunwood over and have Jack come along, too?"

"Leo goes to Dufferin School, too, Jack. He says he sees you all the time, don't you, dear?"

"Leo is a bit of a finder, too. Five dollars once, outside the A&P."

No kid anywhere out-cringed me. Sweaty face and palms. Doubled-over, arms cradling gut. Forehead pressed to cool of table. My prolonged moaning was audible only to me, dogs, and the Shamballan hordes, the mythical denizens of Hollow Earth I telepathically summoned to destroy all surface dwellers.

Mom rose in the ranks, advanced quickly to Levin Family Friend. People were attracted to my mother same way they were to Annie. Although I didn't see it then, I struggle with it now. If I could point to one thing, it'd be the smiles. Yeah, how their smiles would fill their eyes and linger there, just short of or all-out joyful-teary, dimples deep in blush of cheek. The look, you had to see, would break you down before their lips clued in, whether the ode was to joy or melancholy or symphonic variations on each. The thought makes me queasy, Annie and my mom having anything in common. A shrink would have a field day, were I so naive as to allow a shrink inside.

The death blow for Jack and me was when Mom convinced Mollie Levin to get in on the act. They could have cuffed us face to face, airdropped us into the Everglades, and we would have served ourselves up as gator feed rather than submit to friendship. As long as it was what our parents wanted, it would not be anything we wanted. Jack and I, we knew what stunk. That much we had in common.

Mom was off gabbing with Mollie when Jack showed his hand. "I hate when my mother tries to make friends for me. Nothing against you, man. You seem all right, it's just, you know . . ."

"I hate it, too," I said.

"We'd only be asking for trouble."

"It'd be the worst."

"And what's with the name? I thought you said you were Gus."

"Leo is what my mom calls me."

"Like a nickname?"

"She's got a thing for cats. It means lion."

"Gus is better."

"Way better."

We stopped nodding in passing at school.

He stopped coming by our table at the Marquee.

And, man, did I feel good! To have desired something so badly for so long and to have turned it down, moment of triumph at hand, and to have accomplished it not once, but twice . . . That was saying something. Simultaneous self-preservation and self-destruction was no easy feat. I should've been front page of the *Record*. As survival instincts go, mine were relentless. Where I fell short was in the realm of human nature.

With all my looking inward, I had missed what was going on with Jack, the downside of his fame.

While I aspired to share in Jack's adventures, his buddies had a different take. Make the paper once or twice, okay. But turn up so often you're the Montreal Canadiens on another Stanley Cup chase, and you're going to get what's coming to you, and not in a good way.

Schadenfreude is Frankenstein's cousin, twice removed. In small towns, it's once removed.

With every Jack the Finder story in the *Record*, Jack's circle of friends had grown smaller. Before long, his circle was a noose.

THIRTEEN

Eleven shades of suckling on a spit

Charles Dahl-Packer was old hat by middle of fourth grade. He'd cornered the market on victimhood, leaving the usual standard bearers of Wienerdom relatively unbroken and grateful, though no less thirsty for their pantywaist champion's blood. Pecker brought out the bully in the bullied. Good Deed Annie had laid it on the line for the dumb suck. "Don't talk so much, Charles. Don't laugh out loud whenever someone gives a wrong answer. Don't make faces at everything. And your tears, you need to hold them in until you're home. Only girls can get away with crying." For all the *As* on his report card, Pecker was a damn slow learner.

Kids flock on schoolyards for two reasons: Free candy or fights. And the latter is what they were streaming to that morning. Early, I thought. Bullying typically got underway first recess, yet here we were, the starting bell yet to ring. And if this wasn't sufficiently irregular, there was Pecker himself, nowhere near the centre, but giddy with relief to be on the periphery for once, and as merciless in his delight as the most savage of the bunch. The little shit was close to pissing himself, for God's sake. I gave him a shot to the ribs as I elbowed past to ringside.

Jesus! It was Jack. Jack was the new Pecker. And present and oppressing were Dufferin's career bullies and a cadre of promising up-and-comers.

There was Crates. (Yeah, plain Crates, as far as I knew. The single name was his brand. Like Scarface, Bluto, or Ipana.) Isolated, introverted, impassive. Wiry. Light-footed. Human head, mosquito body. You could carry him on your back for a mile and he'd bleed you dry before you knew he was there. I feared him, sure. (Who didn't?) The scuzz was legend. Zen master of havoc, pain, and graffiti. Able to cripple with the twitch of a zit. And while I'd seen the vandalism, pain, and graffiti attributed to him, I'd never actually seen Crates do anything other than look like he might be thinking about doing whatever.

Alan 'Double Al' Allen was the anti-Crates. Your more traditionalist thug. Loud. Beefy. A ganger-upper. *The fightingest bully*. He had no forehead, his hairline an awning for his eyebrows.

Crates intimidated with his presence, Al with his fists, the *Double* as apropos to his brawn as to his name. But he wasn't all brawn. He knew to threaten in the schoolyard and save the beating for the street, beyond Principal Malbasic's jurisdiction. The bugger could make mincemeat of you, use your ribcage for the grinder.

While their styles differed, Crates and Double Al ran neck and neck in visits to Malbasic's office.

Followers and lesser lights included Wayne Trumpeter and the other Waynes—Long-Arm and Dandruff, Vito from Italy, and Lloyd Gonna-kick-u-in-the-nuts.

But they weren't the perps, not this go-round. It was Jack's old pals doling out the justice. Seven of them by my count.

Only Dougie Dunwood stood with Jack and I regretted having judged him unfairly. Unless he had an ulterior motive, saw a chance to earn a Scouting badge for Loyalty. But then Mickey Mental stepped into the box, threw the flats of his hands onto Jack's chest and heaved full-on. And Jack the Finder, that guy, I am telling you, he did not budge. *Did not budge.* He was not the biggest kid by any stretch. Dunwood had the edge in every vital stat. But in this den of thugs, Jack was as hard and resolute as the stone heads on Easter Island.

I gave him credit. I knew how tough it was, the effort required, pretending you don't give two shits when the whole time you surely do.

I also knew what it was like to see friends bail. Unlike Jack, I deserved what I got. Poor Annie, so many times she tried to set me straight. "You're too sensitive, too unforgiving. No one is perfect. You need to give people a chance." Besides my mother, Annie was my only constant. She put up with me no matter how undeserving I was.

"You think you're better than us, Levin." Dunwood's swagger was stop-and-start, his leadership iffy without a bat in his hands. If there was a merit badge to be had for ganging-up, Mickey Mental had his work cut out for him. "You're no better than us, Levin."

Jack nodded, no argument. His hands hung loose at his sides, his fingers flexed mid-way to fists. "You growing a moustache?" Jack said.

"What? No. Shut up, eh? It's chocolate milk, okay? From breakfast."

"If you say so."

"You think you're better than us, Levin. You're no better than us."

Double Al knuckled Dougie in the small of his back. "Get to it, Dumbwood. Wipe the smile off his face. Clock him!" Al's *clock him* confirmed my long-held suspicion he'd earned his stripes under the tutelage of Butch from *The Little Rascals*.

Dunwood wiped his own face before enjoining Jack. "Yeah, wipe the smile off your face, Levin."

"I'm not smiling," Jack said, though I understood how some could think he was. He had an Audie Murphy sort of presence, like in *Destry*. Kill 'em with kindness. Let nothing faze you till it fazes you. *Then blammo!* Me, in his shoes, I would've handed in my badge, let the bad guys loot the town.

"Who crowned you King Shit, Levin?" another ex-buddy piped up, and the cheap shots flew fast and shrill in arbitrary editorial.

"King Shit of Turd Island."

"Too big for your britches."

"Hate your guts, Levin."

"Show-off."

"Stupid jerk."

"Clock him!"

"Thinks he's better than us."

"You're not better than us."

"Your mother wears army boots."

"Wipe the smile off your face, Levin."

"Hey, jackass, kiss this!"

"Kiss this, jackass."

"Clock him!"

The bleachers cherry-picked the sweetest bits and the winning barbs duked it out for dominance, rhythmic *King Shits* and *jackasses* soon supplanted by a finger-snapping staccato of "Clock him! Clock him! Clock him!"

But no one volunteered to deliver the critical first *clock*. A low-level grumbling leached from the mob.

Jack met my eyes, despite my conscious effort to avoid him. I dropped my chin to chest, annoyed and ashamed to have been singled out. I was not part of this. We were not friends. We had agreed not to be. If he was asking for help, I wanted none of it. What the hell did he think I could do anyhow? Now Crates had seen it, too, licking his chops in anticipation of my move.

I edged back, relinquished my space at the front, yielding in cowardly retreat.

Okay, I'd go look for a teacher. That much I could do for him. But then, if anybody saw . . . If Crates or Double Al saw it was me who helped rescue Jack . . .

"Teacher's pet!"

My head snapped up, and there he gloated, mouth wide and wet and chalkboard screechy—Charles Dahl-Packer.

"Teacher's pet!"

Jeez, of all the namby-pamby efforts to energize the jackals, his slander was the lamest of the lame.

"Teacher's pet!"

"Jesus H. Christ," I shouted into his nostrils, and shoved him hard to shut him up. "You think Levin had a say?"

"What?"

I wrenched him toward me just so I could shove him again. "It's what teachers do, isn't it?" I said. "Paint targets on the bright and industrious, groom them as scapegoats?"

"What?" Pecker gawked. "Wha-wha-what?"

I gawked, too. What the hell had I said? Talk about stilted. What kid on what planet would say anything like that unscripted? The voice was mine but the words sure weren't, though I could not say who they belonged to or from where they'd come. It was crazy, I tell you. *I was crazy.* I never knew I had an *industrious* or a *groom* or a *scapegoat* in me, least of all the intellect to string them together in a coherent sentence. Until this moment I had judiciously confined all outward displays of eloquence and precocity to tête-à-têtes with the bathroom mirror.

I tried to bring it down a notch. "Tell me one time Jack has ever milked it. C'mon, one time, you stupid dork."

"Yuck," he said. "Your breath smells like Limburger."

"Shut up."

"Let me go."

"The grief Jack's getting now . . ."

"Stop. You're hurting me."

"He was set up. The teachers. The paper. The whole town . . . Same as if they'd tied him to a powder keg and lit the fuse." My speechifying continued. Like I'd been handed a script and ordered to read the part of the *Lawyer*, the idealistic and earnest dandy newly arrived from the East. "Don't you see? Don't you see? Same as me. Same as you. It's what they do, the grown-ups . . ."

"Cuckoo. Cuckoo. Fartbreath—"

Only after the teachers had pulled me off the dweeb, dragged me up and away by the armpits, did I comprehend what I had done, how I'd backhanded the specs from Pecker's face, kicked his feet out from under him and held him down, pummelled the pussy from gut to scalp and ear to ear, his squeals winning him the allegiance and adulation of the mob, their cheers egging me on, till the tears from Pecker's eyes and the snot and blood from Pecker's nose mixed with the slobber and blood from Pecker's mouth, and Pecker's head swelled black and blue, eleven shades of suckling on a spit.

FOURTEEN

The cowboy who loved leather

Annie once asked me for my idea of life's most peaceful moment. "'When serenity surrounds you and you feel so good inside,'" she said, reading the guidelines for the Sunday School project.

I didn't hesitate. "Right after a building falls down. You know, when the dust has settled, before anybody who's alive has started to dig themselves out or cry for help."

She blinked her slow blink, inhaled a lungful of patience. "For Heaven's sake, Gus, be serious, if only for half a second." She provided examples gathered from more obliging sources. *Babbling brooks. Fishing. Walks in the woods. Sunset from an Adirondack chair. Singing hymns in church. Crickets on a summer night. Grace before dinner, hand in hand with Mom and Dad.* "Clearer now? Something you've actually experienced."

I delved deep, I swear. "Remember the day I punched out Pecker and the two of us were sent to the principal's office?"

"You mean Charles," she said, her annoyance dialled to wary. "Yes?"

"Sitting there, you know, waiting for Mr. Malbasic, looking at Charles and what I'd done to him. . . . The cotton up his nose, in his ear, the blood seeping. Anyhow, this peacefulness came over me. It made no sense, I know. I was in trouble. I knew it. Big trouble. I'd never been in the principal's office before. Even so, I wasn't afraid or worried or anything. Just happy. Really, really happy. Happier and calmer than I'd been in my whole life."

Mr. Malbasic was bowling-pin squat, hairless up top and bulging in the middle. Girdles of neck flab divvied up his chins, the bottommost a baby Blob that grazed on the knot of his maroon tie.

His desk was a Sherman tank under paste wax. You had the feeling it might roll over you at any moment. He rocked behind, his oak swivel stressed to dicey. "Well, now." He tented his hands, a gold wedding band on his left, a Stone Age school ring on his right. His notorious black strap rested inert upon the unspoiled blue blotter. Armageddon in waiting. The strap was eighteen inches long, two inches wide, and a quarter-inch thick, the black worn to tan at either end.

"Your mother, if I'm not mistaken, is that lovely, auburn-haired young widow, is she not?" he said to me, and did his lizard thing, his lips the welcome mat for his tongue.

What? My mother?

"Reminiscent of Gene Tierney, wouldn't you say? *Leave Her to Heaven*. Fine, fine motion picture." He sighed, tracked the daydream passing by outside his window.

"Gene?" I said. "Autry?"

"You'll say 'hello' to her for me, won't you? Her blue eyes and winsome smile have been sorely missed around here of late." He winked. "Perhaps we should arrange more frequent parent-teacher interviews, what do you think?"

I did not think anything. I'd yet to get past *lovely*, *young*, and *winsome*.

"Well, now, Mr. Dahl-Packer." Mr. Malbasic leaned toward the injured toady. "It would appear you emerged the worse for wear. I am most interested to hear your account of the melee."

"I was minding my own business. That Gus kid, he started hitting me for no reason." Pecker sniffled and a bloody wad of cotton shot onto the blotter. The principal waited while Pecker coaxed it back into his nostril.

Mr. Malbasic turned to me. "Is this true, Mr. Berry? Did you strike Dahl-Packer without cause?"

"Dahl-Packer was asking for it," I said.

"Dahl-Packer was not." Pecker winced for effect. "My wrist hurts, too, sir. And my leg where he tripped me. And my glasses, look, they're all scratched up. And bent."

"Alas, gentlemen, numerous witnesses have come forward. Based on evidence procured, it is abundantly clear one of you is a liar. Rather than prolong our hearing unnecessarily, I would ask the guilty party to do the honourable thing. Stand. Proceed before me. And face the music."

I slouched, legs straight out in front, attention riveted to the scuffed tips of my brown Batas.

"The guilty party would be well advised, it will not go well should I be required to ask a second time."

The pasty-faced twerp sat stock still in smug anticipation of his imminent retribution. I'd never realized how small and soft and blond he was. A ray gun set to low, a single blast, and Pecker would be three dabs of Elmer's glue.

The final driblet of peace drained from the aforementioned most peaceful moment of my life. Best I could hope for was an earthquake and the school to crash down on top of me. "Ah, heck. Whatever." I huffed out of the armchair and rounded the desk, dead man walking. *How would I explain this to Gene Autry? My lovely, young, and winsome mother?*

I assumed the assumed position, hands out, palms up, elbows fixed to hips.

"No, no," Mr. Malbasic corrected. "Like this. One hand at a time. That's right. Your free hand beneath the forearm. Like this. Excellent. You don't want me slipping up and breaking your fingers now, do you?"

I needed to get a grip, steel myself against potential tears. I'd never live it down. Not with Pecker invited to the deathwatch, his big mouth champing at the bit. I should have killed the rat and run.

Mr. Malbasic lifted the strap from the blotter and the oak swivel launched him to his feet. The strap came down so hard and fast I had no chance to brace. But it was the snotty grin on Pecker's face that hurt the most.

"Other hand," Mr. Malbasic said. The second blow glanced off my wrist, the sting gone before I felt it. "You may return to your seat."

"What? That's all he gets?" Pecker protested, and I could surely see his point. If my eyes were teary with anything, it was relief. Malbasic and his strap had been overhyped.

Next up, Pecker. Heck, I should have been whistling *Bridge on the River Kwai* for the show that faker gave us. Limping and groaning, like he'd come off shift from building the damn bridge itself. He soldiered up to Mr. Malbasic, his chest out front of his chin, ready for his Purple Heart and the glory to come with it.

"We'll start with your left hand," Mr. Malbasic said.

"Wha—?"

"Or your right if you prefer. . . ."

"But he—it was him."

"If Mr. Berry is guilty of anything, Mr. Dahl-Packer, it is martyrdom. Am I not correct, Mr. Berry?"

"Uh. Yeah? Sure?"

"But he beat me up. It was him. I didn't do anything. On Grammy Dahl's grave, honest to God, sir."

"Reputable witnesses have stated quite emphatically that you provoked Mr. Berry and he acted solely in self-defense."

"But I—"

"Do you deny calling him teacher's pet and doing so repeatedly?"

"Yes, but it wasn't—"

"And was he not walking away from you, minding his own business, when you initiated the altercation?"

"No. What? Sir? What—"

"And most egregious of all, Mr. Dahl-Packer, did you not resort to gutter language—utter the vilest of profanities?"

"Like swearing?"

"Exactly like swearing."

"No. Never."

"Not according to those who recall hearing it distinctly. A four-letter word that begins with the sixth letter of the alphabet and ends with the eleventh. Does this refresh your memory?"

Both Pecker and I performed a quick count on our fingers. Pecker came up with "F-f-fork?" I kept my trap shut.

"Left hand or right. Now, Mr. Dahl-Packer."

"Tell him I never said it. Please, Gus, you gotta tell him. Tell him. Please."

Mr. Malbasic was Whitey Ford, a lefty in full windup. He spared nothing, his tongue the pitcher's tell, from overhead swish to cowhide smacking. Six whacks on each hand for warm-up. Nothing fancy. Fastballs up the middle. And then a pair of sweeping curves: "A seventh for your cowardice, Mr. Dahl-Packer. Neither I nor Dufferin Street Public School can tolerate cowards. An eighth for your abject dishonesty."

To this day, I do not know what to call the funeral that was Pecker's face—the grief, the shock, the tears, the anguish—or the noise that gurgled from the poor sap's throat. It was not crying. It was worse than crying. Closer to dying. Or bagpipes. The wrenching of the weenie's all-abiding spirit.

Mr. Malbasic's patter didn't help. "Quiet now. Quiet now. Take your medicine. Take it like a man. Quiet now. Quiet now. Calm down. Calm down. Be a man. Be a man. . . ."

I sucked it up, blocked out the racket, adjusted the vertical hold that had me blinking blow by blow, my fingers white stripes on black armrests. I was terrified I'd cave, volunteered by guilt to ride shotgun on Pecker's free fall, pouring out my soul in mournful duet.

I sought distraction. The window, the treetops, the clouds. The open door to the storage room. The framed certificates on the walls. The photo by the coat rack—a proud Mr. Malbasic shaking hands with . . . *holy freaking cow!* It was holy freaking Perry Mason. I'd heard rumours they were cousins, but this was the first I'd seen with my own eyes. Raymond Burr of *Tarzan and the She-Devil*. Of of *Gorilla at Large*. Of of *Godzilla*. Like could I meet him? Did he come for visits? What would I say to him? Would Mr. Malbasic let him know I was a bad kid who'd gotten the strap? And who was Raymond's favourite, Lex Barker's Tarzan or Gordon Scott's Tarzan?

Pecker's eighth and last (sixteenth overall) was leather on chicken bone. Smack! Crack! Smack! Crack! The kid was trembling, gulping to corral his runaway breath. Mr. Malbasic laboured, too, deflated into his chair, his face as red as Pecker's hands.

And man, I am telling you, Pecker's hands were a mess, contorted and swollen, a patient of Dr. Moreau, freshly discharged from the infirmary on the Island of Lost Souls. The kid didn't know what the hell to make of the things attached to his wrists, only that the lobster who'd donated them must have fared far worse.

"If you are as fortunate as I, Mr. Dahl-Packer, some years hence, you will have the privilege of testing your mettle in combat. You may be pinned down by mortar or in a gunner's turret over Occupied France. Whichever, you will think of this day and be thankful for your Malbasic training." The principal chuckled quietly to himself. "Now, Mr. Dahl-Packer, there is something you owe Mr. Berry."

Lobster Boy raised his head, his claws pinned to his chest. On his fourth try, he croaked, "I'm sorry," though it sounded to me he'd finally solved the puzzle of the four-letter word that began with the sixth letter of the alphabet.

"It's okay," I mumbled to the floor.

"Do not let me see you in here again," Mr. Malbasic said, and with a pocket-pack of Kleenex as souvenir of the occasion, he directed Lobster Boy to the door, and signalled me to stay put.

"Do you understand the difference between the strapping I gave you and the strapping I gave him?" he said.

I shook my head.

"The strapping I gave Mr. Dahl-Packer was to punish. The strapping I gave you was to elucidate."

I nodded as if I got it. I couldn't stop nodding.

"Martyrdom is admirable, Mr. Berry, but not when the beneficiary of your action is he who is guilty. Stepping forward as you did, accepting blame, is noble, but only when you are, indeed, blameworthy. In future, may I suggest you reserve your selflessness for the deserving."

He smoothed a sheet of stationery onto the desktop, dipped pen into inkwell. Slowest writer on Earth, that guy. *What was he working on, a book? And what was with all his pausing and staring?* At this rate, my record for boredom would be broken—set when Mrs. Beckwith had compelled us to watch a National Film Board epic on herring fishing.

Knickknacks cluttered the perimeter of his desk. A clock and barometer combination. A photo of Mrs. Malbasic wearing a furry dead thing suspiciously similar to the otters in the display case by the boys' second-floor bathrooms. A photo of Mr. Malbasic's daughter in graduation gown and Buddy Holly glasses, eyes as lizardy as her dad's, a glimpse of tongue at her teeth. A paperweight. An owl, *Jesus!* A small brass owl on a black marble base.

At last, he folded the stationery into an envelope, stretched his lips to the frontiers of his gold molars. "It is imperative you give this note to your mother." He flicked his wrist, snagged my hand, and shook. Same hand Raymond Burr had shaken.

"So then, what do you say?" he said.

The guy was a pop quiz that wouldn't die. "Thank you?"

"Don't forget." He tapped the envelope. "Your mother."

I moved to haul my butt out of there real fast, you bet. And I would've, too, had the eight-by-ten sepia by the door not stopped me cold. A young cowboy in a white ten-gallon hat. Fringed vest. Chaps. Hands suspended above pearl-handled six-guns. And at his side, a dance hall dame. Painted face and rose in hair. Ruffled dress and slender waist. Her fingers dainty upon the cowboy's shoulder. Stencilled to the window behind: *DRY GULCH SALOON.*

The giveaway was the cowboy's grin. A gunslinger grin. The photographer had captured his tongue mid-dart.

"Quite something, wasn't I?" Mr. Malbasic said.

FIFTEEN

The boy who was condemned
to an unexamined and undistinguished life

"Did you hurt yourself?" Mom asked.

"Huh?"

"The blood."

"What blood?"

"Here." I followed her finger to the dot on my shirt. I squinted to see it. "Some kid at school had a bloody nose. . . ."

"And what's this? Is this for me?"

I had slipped the envelope into my spelling book, undecided whether to trash it or hand it over. Either way, I intended to read it first. Never failed. The more I had to hide, the more she saw.

She opened the envelope. "What's going on? Did you do something? Please tell me you're not in trouble." I was cornered.

I hung my head, hands at my back, lest they tell the tale. There was no damage to speak of, but I'd read enough Edgar Cayce and others to be watchful for spontaneous stigmata. If Malbasic didn't do me in, The Unexplained would.

* * *

7:30 ⑪ LEAVE IT TO LEO—Comedy
Clued in to her son's crimes by the appearance of spontaneous stigmata, Mom marches Leo to Pecker's house to apologize for beating him up, despite Leo's protestations of innocence and claims of noble motives. Later, at Mom's insistence, the bitter rivals give friendship a trial run. Hi-jinks ensue.

Mom read the note and read it again.

Mom was young, it now occurred to me, compared to other moms. And, I had to admit, sort of *lovely*, as Mr. Malbasic had said. I couldn't see the *winsome*, until after I'd looked it up in Dad's old Webster's. I'd never really looked at Mom before and promised myself never to really look at her again.

She surfaced briefly, frowned or smiled from behind the stationery, and read the note a third time.

"Sit down," she said, composed herself, and read it aloud to me.

Dear Mrs. Berry,

I trust this brief missive finds you well. I am writing you today about a serious matter concerning your son, Leo Berry, a student in Mrs. Crawford's fourth-grade class.

As you know, I take a personal interest and pride in every child who passes through our institution's doors. Indeed, I regard myself a superb judge of character. Alas, it is with deep regret I must tell you, I believe I have gravely underestimated your Leo.

In my previous, albeit limited, observations, I had considered the boy to be an average, unremarkable sort and, though not unworthy, condemned by Fate to an unexamined and undistinguished life. The deficits associated with fatherless children go without saying. Today, however, Leo exhibited behaviour I deem exemplary.

It is evident your effort in raising him alone has been of the highest parental standard. Bravo, Mrs. Berry! Bravo!

Please contact me at your earliest convenience so we may discuss how we might best work together to ensure Leo attains his fullest academic and societal potential.

I remain,

Most sincerely yours,

Mr. Harvey L. Malbasic, B.A., M.A.

Principal

"What did you do that was so wonderful?" Mom crushed the letter against my left ear and my head in the adoring vice of her hands. She pelted me with kisses. "What did my wonderful boy do?"

I was at a loss, groping to couch my act of violence in terms to enthuse. "I dunno," I said. With any luck, she'd break my neck before I said too much.

Ever have the feeling the life you were living was only partly yours, that some of you wasn't you, and some of what you did or said wasn't what *you* did or said?

I have.

All my life I have.

Annie had her own take on what I'd done to Pecker. "I never thought you were like that, Gus. You just stood there and let Mr. Malbasic strap him? How could you be so cruel? How could you not say anything?"

"I got the strap, too."

"You deserved it."

"He started it."

"That's not true, you know darn well."

"No, I don't."

"Still," she said, "don't think I don't know why you did it."

"You do?" How could she know if I didn't? The dweeb had bugged me. I jumped him. Period. Okay, the kid was a pushover. That helped. Anybody else and I'd have thought twice. You won't find a more commonsensical bully than the previously bullied.

"Now don't go telling the world or anything, but I am a little proud of you, too. For what you did."

"You are? What?"

"Jack Levin, he's lucky to have you for a friend. That was quick thinking, Gus, getting those bullies to leave him alone the way you did, creating the distraction."

"It was?"

"And Charles, you didn't hurt him too badly, did you? Not really."

"Nah. Not really."

"Don't let it go to your head, Gus," she said, "but I'm lucky to have you as a friend, too." She kissed me on the cheek and I wiped that kiss off with twice the speed she'd landed it.

Annie was a teacher's pet, too. Like Jack, she didn't milk it. Girls, they can get away with the goody-two-shoes routine, where boys don't have a prayer.

I felt bad about Pecker, though not so bad you'd call it guilt. And not so bad I couldn't sleep. Bad might not even be the right word; my feelings might have been closer to good. There was much to be said for Mr. Malbasic's version of events. Still, I worried the true story might yet reach my mother. Her loss of faith would be tough to bear. Never again would my name be spoken of in the same breath as Alexander Graham Bell or Thomas Edison or Albert Einstein or Walt Disney or Winston Churchill.

And so it was, in the weeks following, to preempt my mother's presumptive disapproval, I strove to tell Pecker how relatively sorry I was. Not that I let anyone in on the effort besides Pecker. It was a balancing act. Going ballistic on him had earned me standing. I was the Wild Man of Borneo. A public apology would destroy the image.

I caught Pecker off the beaten track, just him and me. I was remorseful, too, called after him, "Hey, Charles! Charles, wait up!" No fists. No overt hostility. No cry of *Pecker*. "I just wanna talk, I swear."

The dork wouldn't let me within a hundred yards. Quick off the mark. A four-minute miler. Fast as hell, for a boy who ran like a girl.

I'd done my duty. He had his chance. Two chances, in fact. I was home free.

The Unknown is not the same as The Unexplained.

The Unknown is what's out there waiting for you. The Unexplained is what comes after.

SIXTEEN

The sweetest sound I've ever heard

The creosote plant blew up on a Saturday night at dinnertime, spring yet soggy with winter. The smell of smoke drew Mom and me onto the stoop, joining with neighbours to watch the airborne sludge cremate the sunset. Rumours flew, guesses aplenty as to the source, and whether the flames originated east or west of the river. Mom returned inside, lit a cigarette by the kitchen sink. End times were near. The Du Maurier pack was my red flag, one to three cigarettes per cataclysm. (Like Dad's suit at the dry cleaners, the Du Mauriers were leftovers, two stale cartons in the middle drawer of his desk.)

She extinguished the stub under the faucet. "Well, I suppose, you'd like to go up the mountain."

I grabbed my jacket.

Pelion was the main venue for watching the town burn. So frequent were the fires, a councilman proposed installing benches on the mountainside and charging admission. Might have happened, too, had a *Record* editorial not pointed out how this would attract more firebugs to the region.

Cars crept bumper to bumper up the road defacing the mountain's middle. Mom and I took the footpath, a snaky trail that wriggled to the ceremonial cannon.

There might have been a moon. Hard to say in the thickening gloom. Even so, I spotted the Levins right off. Jack. His mom. His sisters. I slipped into underdrive, hoping to keep us in the dark and apart. Mollie Levin had other ideas. Her jumping jacks and yoo-hoos could have scrambled fighter jets.

Mom hustled to catch up. I plodded behind. Dead weight. Sack of venom. Jack's displeasure synced with mine.

Nothing had changed between us. The guy had yet to acknowledge I'd saved his butt. I didn't want his thanks, merely an IOU. Then again, he might've felt his butt didn't need saving. He was no chicken, clearly. Perhaps he resented how I'd stolen his thunder, upstaged him in the main event. Or it could have been he recognized I was not the rescuer type, and what I'd visited on Pecker I'd visited on impulse, absent Jack's plight.

"Make a mask with your hands, children. Watch me." Mollie Levin splayed fingers over nostrils and mouth. Jack's sisters strived to comply. "The fumes may be poisonous."

Mom added, "Try not to breathe any more than you must."

I fell behind promptly and with purpose, distancing myself from the embarrassment and Jack the Ingrate. And wouldn't you know, he fell behind promptly and with purpose, too.

We plunged our hands into our pockets and sulked ahead, each wishing to be rid of the other. The path worked against us, narrowing as it double-backed, forcing us onward and upward, side by stride. The sky glowed orange above the tree line. Flames lapped at clouds of their own making. Folks cheered the slapdash spectacle.

Jack and I slogged on, sullen in our arbitrary resolve.

Funny how deafening silence can be. We were in a staring contest of the blind, holding out for the other's tongue to blink.

Jack cracked. "Did you hear about my latest find?"

I shook my head, savoured victory in a contest he was unaware had been declared.

"Yeah," he said, "those screws that went loose from inside your head."

"What?" I backed abruptly up and off the path, dug my heels into the mossy incline to let others pass below.

Flashlights were out. Beams danced to and fro the length of the path, bobbing ever closer to the cluster of light at the summit. With night came cold, anonymity betrayed by vapours.

"What did you say?" I said.

Jack scooted up next to me. "The screws that went loose when you beat up Pecker. Why else would you go off on him like you did?"

"It worked, didn't it? I got Mickey Mental and the others off your back, didn't I?"

"Who?"

"Mickey Mental. That jerk Dunwood."

"That's what you call him?"

"That's what he is."

"To his face? You call him Mickey Mental to his face?"

"You call him Dumbwood."

"That's different." Jack laughed out loud. "He's my friend."

"*Was* your friend."

"You, he'll kill."

"Like he was going to kill you? He's so full of it his eyes are brown."

"All those guys are full of it. That's why I didn't need your help."

"I wasn't helping, okay? Pecker asked for it and I gave it to him. You lucked out."

"Yeah. Right. Some tough guy you are. Who you gonna take on next, a girl? Bitsy Fritzy?"

"Guess you'd better give me back my loose screws, then."

"Here," Jack said, his palm extended in offering. I thought he might actually have screws in hand, but he was laughing, and I started laughing, and nothing ever sounded sweeter, Jack Levin and me splitting our guts over dumb shit.

"Thanks," he said. "Even if you didn't mean to save my ass."

"You're welcome," I said. "Even if I did."

I wanted to shout *Geronimo!* We were paratroopers over Germany, Jack and me, fireworks on the ground, flak blistering the skies. We climbed the rest of the way, recapped The Battle that Never Was—Crates slinking and sliming, Double Al's *"Clock him!"*, Mickey Mental's chickenshit indecision, Pecker's wimped-out *"Teachers pet!"* We were as giddy as two friends could be, which made me all the giddier. Sure, I had Annie. But this was different. Jeff and Porky different. Cisco and Pancho different. Paratroopers over Germany different.

People milled about the mountaintop, bodies jostling for vantage. I stuck close to Jack as we wended our way to where he promised our families would be. "It's the creosote plant," Mollie Levin informed us as we trotted up. "Do any of you know what creosote is?"

"Rotten eggs?" Abigail Levin ventured. She was the sister with straight hair and was maybe five or six. "Smells like tar," Isabel said. She was six or seven, her hair curly. (To be honest, I never could get them straight, even when I met up with the younger one years later. At any given time, Abigail could have been Isabel and Isabel Abigail.)

"Very good," Mrs. Levin said. "Creosote is a chemical that comes from coal tar. And does anyone know what it's used for?"

"To preserve wood," Jack said, as though it was common knowledge.

"Bingo!" Mrs. Levin exclaimed, and I shrivelled in the reciprocal glare of our mothers' sweepstake grins.

Jack's soft-spoken aside was for my ears only. "I pick up a lot of oddball facts in the restaurant."

"Like where to find the stuff you find?"

"I don't just find things," Jack said. "I find out things."

I'd grown up watching good parts of the town burn, but nothing to compare to this. One sec, there'd be this inferno ripping across the ground, four football fields of rage that roared up from the river and slammed our eardrums. No sooner would we think we'd lost our hearing than we'd fear our sight had gone, as well, the fire falling inward upon itself, black to black to blackout. And just as the disappointment was setting in, that this was all there was, the dragon roared again, low and slow, razor-thin and foundry-red, layer upon layer of roiling soot, then *sis boom bah!* and *oooo* and *ahhh*, the firestorm renewed, and fireballs exploded *1-2-3*, skyrocketed, stoking the infinite above.

Abby and Issie were bawling their heads off, hands over ears, begging to be taken home. And they weren't the only terrorized kids on the mountain. Could be they knew something the rest of us didn't. It'd be just like the town to keep the truth from us, that Pelion had been snoozing, a volcano overdue to blow. Hell, maybe that's how the fire had started, lava bubbling up from the Earth's core into the creosote works.

There was coughing. *Who wasn't coughing?* And pointing, pointing. Orange fireflies flitted over the river and through the valley, rising as dandelion puffs above the town and up the mountainside.

I won't lie. I was worried, too. And, in my peculiar logic, also comforted by the possibility these were the last days of my personal Pompeii. *This was how I wanted to die*, the whole world going down with me. How else could I be sure I would never miss a thing, that life would not go on without me?

Cinders sparked and spiked. Ash fell plump and greasy, charcoal flakes from a Transylvanian Christmas. The Levin girls and their pleas were heard at last. Our moms dragged us from the mountain.

On the night the creosote plant burned, an old man went down to the river to watch from the best seat in the house. Overcome by smoke, he fell into the Trent. His grown daughter and grown son jumped in to save him.

The old man's body bobbed up next morning, near where he'd last been seen. The daughter washed ashore later in the day, her jacket caught up on a spike in an old railroad tie, the sleeve a tourniquet around her neck. By no coincidence, the tie had been treated with creosote. The son never turned up, which led some to speculate he had exploited the tragedy to exit his troubled marriage and begin a new life elsewhere. The same was said of every Trenton man or woman who had ever gone missing without a trace, whether their marriage was troubled or whether they were married at all. Should you think you might want to make yourself scarce one day, relocate to Trenton. The town will take care of the rest.

The *Record* identified the dead as Russell Coleman, his daughter Margaret, son Kevin. "I knew him," Jack would tell me the next day.

"The old guy?"

"Everyone called him Rusty."

"Like on *Rin Tin Tin*?" I'd never met a live Rusty. Or for that matter a Corky, Cuffy, Cubby, Lonnie, Porky, Chip, Tag, Spin, or Beaver.

"He loved my mom's coconut cream pie. Her liver and onions. And, boy, could he talk."

"Everybody talks to you, Jack."

"Yeah, but there's one story he told me . . . and when you look at what just happened . . ."

"I'm all ears, man."

"Rusty grew up by the Welland Canal, you know, near Niagara. Anyhow, he's out fishing with some pals one day when a ship barges into the locks. Next he knows, water is rushing down on top of them. Rusty gets away, but the others, three of them, drown. He said he never could make sense of it. He fought in the war and everything, too, lost buddies left and right. But those kids, he said, he'd have an empty space in his heart for them till the day he died. Weird, eh, how the water still got him after all this time?"

"Water doesn't forget," I said.

"Wow. Sounds like something I'd say," Jack said.

"It takes a certain crazy to appreciate crazy, I guess."

"We just might become friends, after all."

"So what are you saying? Your screws are loose, too?"

A triple drowning was nothing.

The dying can start ten million miles away—Metaluna, Popocatépetl, Timbuktu, or up the road in Welland—and Trenton will finish it. The lake. The river. The bay. Water, water, everywhere . . . Among local pastimes, only hunting, fishing, and arson rank higher than drowning.

Anyone who's lived five minutes in the town knows somebody who has drowned.

I know four.

SEVENTEEN

Wyatt Earp, The Wild Man of Borneo, and Robby the Robot

"We'll keep them off balance," Jack said. "They won't know what to make of us."

We were a team, all right, Wyatt Earp and The Wild Man of Borneo.

"But I don't know how to be that guy," I said.

"Sure you do. You are as long as people believe you are. Your job is to keep them believing."

I doubted my notoriety would hold. I'd gone after the biggest creampuff in school. Pecker was a joke, and Crates, for one, had been looking at me funny since. Sooner or later it would dawn on Mickey Mental, Double Al, and their flunkies that I was the second biggest creampuff going, the soft target they had always known me to be. Already there'd been inklings, sniping, jostling. "Stare 'em in the eye," Jack said. "Give 'em your mad-dog grin. Make 'em think you're itching for a fight."

"I'm not itching."

"You don't get the choice. The trick is to put enough doubt in their dumb heads, so even if they beat the crap out of you, they'll pay a price—you'll bite their ears or fingers or worse clean off. Wild Man of Borneo, Gus, Wild Man of Borneo."

"They'll kill me."

"You kidding? None of them has the guts for that. Okay, Crates, possibly. But Double Al or Dumbwood, you think they've sent one single person to the hospital, ever? They're too afraid to take it too far. And knowing this, it's like having your own secret weapon. *Because you*, my friend, are *not* afraid to send *them* to the hospital."

I disagreed. The only secret weapon I had was Jack. His friends turning on him was the best thing to ever happen to me.

"What are you afraid of, anyhow? You took the strap and lived to tell. What'd Malbasic give you, three, four?"

"Eight," I said. "Each hand." It wasn't a lie, it was a favour. The truth would only have disappointed Jack.

"Jesus. Seriously? Eight? On each hand?"

"Yup."

"Even better, then. Think about it. How long did you feel it—the pain, I mean?"

"A couple of days."

"Right. So what does it tell you?"

"Um . . . that I have nothing to fear but fear itself?"

"Wow. Yeah. Right. And nobody can hurt you any worse than Malbasic already has. You keep that in your head and you're Superman."

"And if Mickey Mental or somebody shows up with Kryptonite, Jack?"

"Then you're Batman."

We fell into an easy routine. Before school. At school. After school. Our common ground covered more territory than we could have hoped. No one would ever characterize Gloomy Gus a conversationalist, but I was with Jack, I tell you.

"Best movie ever?" he'd say, and we'd be off and running.

"*The 7th Voyage of Sinbad*."

"Best scary movie?"

"*Horrors of the Black Museum* . . . when the girl looks into those binoculars and the spikes shoot into her eyes. . . ."

"Red licorice or black?"

"Black."

"Rin Tin Tin or Lassie?"

"Mr. Peabody."

"You kill me, Gus. You kill me. *Sick*, *Cracked*, or *Mad*?"

"Anyone ever tell you how you look like Alfred E. Neuman?"

"What? My ears?"

"And nose and eyes and mouth. You could be his brother."

"Thanks, jerk-face."

"Okay, maybe not your ears."

"Space movie?"

"*It! The Terror from Beyond Space*."

"Better than *Forbidden Planet*? C'mon, Gus."

"C'mon, yourself. The monster was stupid. A string of Christmas lights with teeth."

"Never saw it that way."

"As soon as you hear adults talking about how great a movie is, you know it's bad. I'll bet your dad loved *Forbidden Planet*."

"We went together."

"And he thought the monster was the best ever, right?"

"He kept asking if I understood the difference between id and ego. He said the story was Shakespearean."

"Jesus. What's that mean? Super-super boring?"

"I'm told we'll find out in high school."

"And you, did you think the monster was all that special?"

"No *Beast from 20,000 Fathoms*."

"You ever see the Tarzan movie where he fights the giant spider? That stupid spider was ten times better than the thing in *Forbidden Planet*."

"At least Robby was good."

"Robots always are."

We talked about nothing, and nothing was everything. Only after our cultural parameters had been established did we up the ante.

"I used to think I was invisible to you," I confessed. "You'd pass me in the halls and it was like I wasn't there."

"Who's to say you weren't invisible, eh? You've got this taxidermy look to you. A bear. Or a Yeti. Yeah, that's you, a Yeti."

"I hate that shit so much. The owls, they're the worst. They set their eyes on you . . ."

"It's the smell that gets to me."

"You smell them?"

"You don't?"

"You're kidding. . . ."

"No. I swear. I'm not sure what death smells like, exactly, but I'm telling you, Gus, it's got to be close to taxidermy."

"Not if you drown. Death would smell different then."

"Think so?"

"I'm just saying. It'd be watered down, wouldn't it? So it wouldn't smell so bad."

"You ever stand next to a wet dog?"

"That's what I'm saying. Different death, different smell."

"But what about after they dried you out?"

"You'd still smell different. Like fish maybe."

"Or seaweed. Yeah. Okay. I can see it."

"There's only one way to die and not smell bad, Jack."

"You've really thought this through, eh?"

"Burn to death."

We agreed to keep the Marquee off limits. We kept a low profile, a nod and muttered mutter. Any display of enthusiasm would unleash a frenzy. Give our moms an inch and we'd die the death of a thousand sleepovers.

And it wasn't friendship, either. We were only on the road. Odds were I'd screw it up long before Wyatt and Wild Man reached the Wild Bill Hickok and Jingles stage.

EIGHTEEN

The day Howdy Doody chased a beach ball into Lake Ontario

Billy Burgess was the first person I knew who drowned. He drowned in June on the last Sunday before the end of our first year of school.

We had played together when we were younger. Billy was fun until he bonked me on the head with a chestnut. I stayed clear of him after he put his foot through the bass of the drum kit my mother's friend Dottie Lange gave me for my fifth birthday. Not that I was Cubby O'Brien or anything; I had overheard my mother giggling with Dottie on the phone. "Leo absolutely loves it, hasn't left it for a second. But he's so much like his father—not a smidge of rhythm in him."

When we entered Dufferin, I lucked out by getting Miss Proctor. Billy ended up with Mrs. Gannon across the hall. I was happy. Gannon was a yeller and Billy would be yelled at plenty.

Billy drowned at Sandbanks Beach near Picton. He chased a beach ball into Lake Ontario and the ball came back without him. It wasn't his ball, either, which did not surprise me. It belonged to the girl he'd snatched it from. When Billy went under, she retrieved her ball and went back to playing.

Billy's family didn't notice Billy missing until packing up for home. When the girl saw them calling for him on the beach, she said, "Are you looking for Howdy Doody?" and pointed to where she'd seen him last. I know this because Annie told me. She was best friends with Billy's twin sister, Susan Burgess.

I could see how the girl mistook Billy for Howdy Doody. Billy and Susan were redheads. Susan had more freckles. She was nicer, too.

The weirdest part for me was how Susan never missed a day of school. This includes the Monday after Billy's last dive.

Years later, when we graduated from Dufferin, Principal Malbasic awarded Susan a certificate for perfect attendance. Afterwards, I saw Susan and her parents sitting in their station wagon outside the school. They were crying. Mr. Burgess, too. "Stop staring," my mother said to me, her voice tailing to shaky.

"But why are they crying now?" I said.

"Why do you think?"

"But Billy was so long ago."

Mom searched her purse for a tissue. "Grieving isn't only about what was. More often it's about what would have been."

Billy's death kept me awake most every night into August. I had questions.

Is it easier to lose a twin who isn't identical, because then you wouldn't have to look at yourself and be reminded half of you was dead?

Or is it easier if you are identical, because then you could look at yourself and it'd be the same as if your other half was still alive? Like half a cherry Popsicle in your hand and half in the freezer. You could eat the half in your hand with no worries, because the exact same cherry Popsicle would be waiting for you in the fridge. And what was going through Billy's head as the water filled him up and took him down? Was he sorry for what he'd done to me? Did he think God was punishing him for the chestnut and the drum? The drum, for sure, Billy had to regret that.

Dottie Lange would become the second person I knew to drown, though she wasn't Dottie Lange when it happened. She was Dottie Swartz, a newlywed at forty-four, bride of thirty-seven-year-old Helmut Swartz, a machinist at Central Bridge and Tuesday-evenings cha-cha teacher at the Arthur Murray Dance Studio, upstairs from Sure Press Dry Cleaners on King.

I once asked Helmut if he knew Mr. Blackhurst.

"He ruined my tux," Helmut said. "But I made him pay double what it was worth. For the inconvenience. And the reefers I'd forgotten in my pocket."

"Did you ever see a strange lady in there?"

"The kooky broad at the sewing machine?"

"No. Some other strange lady. Dressed in black. Hiding at the back."

"I've never met a dame in a dry cleaners who wasn't strange, kid. You'd be strange, too, breathing in them fumes all day."

PRODUCTION _____

DIRECTOR _____

CAMERA _____

DATE ___ SCENE ___ TAKE ___

Second Reel

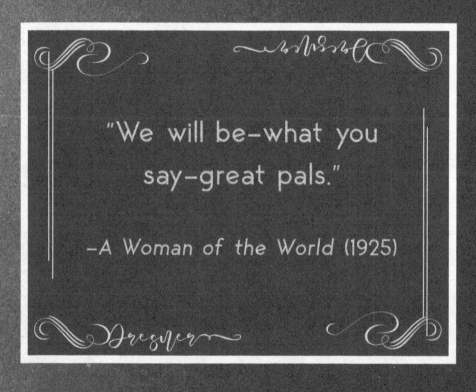

"We will be-what you
say-great pals."

-A Woman of the World (1925)

 # ONE

1988 and I was in an Avis rental
with Jack, my mom, and 13 ghosts

We were in the breakneck dark of a tunnel, light and shadow tripping across the walls, steel rushing steel, locomotive plowing wind, wind thrashing stone, when Jack interrupted the soundtrack: "Sainte-Hilaire, Quebec, 1864. Deadliest rail accident in Canadian history. Guess how many?"

The train hurtled from night into the underwhelming dawn of winter's day.

"C'mon, man. Guess."

I would have preferred a good coma.

"Ninety-nine, Gus. Ninety-nine dead."

He could not help himself.

"Jim Heckenast had railroad stories you wouldn't believe. Worked for CN. Nice guy. Sharp. A Marquee regular. He had a thing for my mother's cherry pie—a big scoop of vanilla on the side. You, too, right? Or was it her apple?"

He wouldn't quit.

"Of course, you and me, we'll always have Trenton and the wreck of '98. A piddling dozen killed, still nothing to sneeze at."

"Enough!" I said, and the Pfizer rep, the golden-haired survivor of Air Canada 797, answered, "You're telling me." She gathered up her belongings and skated down the aisle. We were twenty minutes from Toronto. She couldn't exit soon enough.

* * *

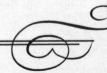

I collected the rental car and left the sprawl of the city behind, connecting to the old road. Highway 2. I was in no hurry. I was on my way home, after all. Like Winnipeg, the best part about getting there was the getting away from there.

This would be my first trip back since 1977, the week my mother died. My *young, lovely,* and *winsome* mother. Dead at forty-four. *Natural causes.* As if there is anything remotely natural in death at forty-four. Let the doctors call it what they will, the cause to me, until I knew better, was terminal despondency. Should be coroner orthodoxy in that town.

On the bright side, Mom didn't drown.

I sold the house, auctioned off the contents. I needed the money. My business card read *Job Applicant*.

Letting go of my father's books was the toughest. I picked through the library, searched for the assorted treasures I'd hidden between the pages, between and behind volumes.

The cardboard ghost viewer from *13 Ghosts* fluttered to the carpet. Unlike the 3D glasses handed out for *Creature from the Black Lagoon* or *House of Wax*, these were double-decker goggles, a rectangle of red cellophane on top through which *to see* the ghosts and, for the faint-hearted, a blue lens below *to not* see the ghosts. I put the viewer to the test, scanned the room for paranormal activity. Detected none outside my head.

The real treasures I was looking for, of course, were the cards. The first turned up in a Hammond World Atlas, between Lithuania and Luxembourg:

Jack and I had buried it in 1962, along with forty-six others, every single one of which I would disinter from Dad's library in the days to follow. But seeing this first card, touching it again, I had to get a grip, memories flooding in, synapses misfiring. All the more reason to tie up the loose ends of my mother's short life and clear the hell out of Trenton for good.

I held on to nine books.

Two copies of *Collected Poems of Robert Service*.

Richard Halliburton's *Complete Book of Marvels*.

Audubon's *The Birds of America*—a 1937 reprint and not the million dollar original.

Orwell's *Homage to Catalonia*. Lenin's *The State and Revolution*. Reed's *Ten Days that Shook the World*. Luxemburg's *Reform or Revolution*. Engels's *Socialism: Utopian and Scientific*.

Plus my *13 Ghosts* viewer. The cards, too, of course. *The intertitles*. No chance I'd let them go.

If you've ever wondered what it would be like to ride a barrel on the Niagara River as it surges toward the Falls, drive a 1988 Ford Tempo sometime.

Avis had provided enough fuel to get me clear of the city, the gauge nudging empty as we hit Oshawa, of all places. Home to the gas station bathroom where my father spilled his brains.

"Whaddya say we go find it?" Jack said. "A Texaco, wasn't it?"

TWO

Straight out of Central Casting

"That night, that fire. You think that fire was something?" Jack had the walk of someone going somewhere, and it didn't feel like school. "That fire was nothing."

"You kidding?" I said. "It was Vesuvius up there."

"Reading too much *National Geographic* will do that to you, kid. That magazine is scarier than *Famous Monsters*."

"I saw the movie," I said. "You know, *Last Days of Pompeii*? Steve Reeves?"

"He looked wimpy without his beard."

"Yeah. But when the volcano blew . . ."

Three weeks in and I'd yet to screw it up, I was approaching a personal high with Jack. While we hadn't attained Wild Bill and Jingles status, the situation was looking good, increasing the likelihood it would soon look bad.

Annie was my confessor, my sounding board. Jack was my buddy-in-waiting and I'd never had anyone like him. With other kids, Mom's recruits, I'd groped for shared intelligence. Hell, I'd hung out with dopes who couldn't tell Tarzan's Cheeta from Jungle Jim's Tamba. But Jack and me, we were on the same wavelength from the get-go. I knew myself too well to pretend it would last. I hoped to keep it going, at least, until I got to see him find something more exciting than lost keys. Another meteorite. Or a magic lamp. Or King Solomon's mines. Or Atlantis. Anything. Before he figured me out.

"How could the fire be nothing?" I said.

"In the scheme of things."

"Scheme of what things?"

"People tell me stuff."

"In the restaurant. Yeah. I've seen. You told me. You don't just find things, you find out things."

"And a lot of times I wish I didn't."

I supposed this was how those dim bulbs on *Concentration* felt, the contestants who couldn't solve the rebus even after the entire board had been revealed. "You wish you didn't what—find things or find out things?"

"The finding out, mostly."

"Jesus, Jack. Stop beating 'round the bush."

"What if I fill your head with stuff you don't want to know?"

"There's *nothing* I don't want to know." I saw my opening. "Especially how you find stuff. You gotta let me tag along one time."

"That's not how it works."

"Then tell me how it does."

"Nothing to tell. Finding just happens."

"Bullshit."

"How long you been waiting to ask me, huh? Is this why you want to be friends? To know my secrets?"

"Yeah," I said, and stopped him in his tracks.

"Wow."

"I told you. I want to be a finder."

"Why?"

"I like neat junk. And I've never been in the newspaper."

"Jesus! Haven't you seen all the good it's done me? Done a head count of my friends lately?"

"Well," I said, a finger raised. "Better than nothing, aren't I?"

Jack gave me the smile generals use when bestowing medals. "You would know, wouldn't you?"

My shrug was modest.

"You're a funny one, Gus. But are you better than nothing? Yeah. You are. Way better, man. You're not nothing. You're something. And any day now I hope I'll figure out what."

We arrived at school as the five-minute warning bell rang.

"Later, 'gator, I will tell you all," Jack vowed, and up the tarmac he dashed for an early morning convening of the Teachers' Pets' Club. It's what I called it, anyhow.

In a distant corner of the playground, Crates lounged with cigarette upon the seesaw. He was watching me watching him. But who the hell had started watching first?

Mickey Mental galloped up from behind, swatted me on the back of the head and cackled past.

At the curb, Annie blew her dad a kiss as he drove off. Partway along the walk, Susan Burgess waited. Annie scurried up to meet her, waved as she hastened by me. A tiny, two-finger wave. She had Teachers' Pets' Club to get to, too.

Down the block, Pecker careened toward the school full tilt, his panicked wheezing a hundred yards out front of him, and a crazy-hungry-unhinged-insane black Lab ten yards behind, and closing. *Jesus!*

10:30 3 ON SAFARI—Nature
A lion mauls a gazelle.
A hyena mauls a zebra.
A black Lab mauls Pecker.

Pecker zigged. Pecker zagged. But he could not shake the demon as it bridled for takedown.

Pecker dodged into the teacher's parking lot. He could see it, taste it—*the Girls entrance and refuge.* The dog lunged, sprung, bloodshot eyes gleaming. And *wham!* A yelp. A crunch. And the hound bit pavement.

The blue Buick Electra reversed.

A second, squishier crunch. A *splorg.*

Mr. Malbasic unloaded his bulk from his car, wagged a fistful of accusation at Pecker, tapped his watch, and motioned for the boy to hurry along.

Pecker circled wide when he saw me, backpedalled a wiggy beeline.

Mr. Malbasic assessed the damage to his fender, then the dog. He reached down, latched onto a foreleg and a hind, and with the stuttered entreaties of a man three months constipated, Dufferin's longest-serving principal cleaned and jerked the carcass to the grass.

Huffing, puffing, perspiring, he fixed his butt cheeks to a hapless birch, dropped his hands onto his knees, and gorged on all available oxygen.

I'd been wise to the taxidermy from the start. I should've seen black dogs with red eyes were ill omens, too.

* * *

Jack didn't show at recess. Not unusual. The pets were often kept back to enjoy random perks. When the badger family was added to the taxidermy collection, for instance, they were given advance previews and got to meet Ranger Clegg, the taxidermist and retired Parks Canada warden. "My grandmother ate badgers during the war," Annie related after the fact. Jack said, "Badgers stink like skunks."

Recess was not a total loss. I got to see Mr. Pennington, the caretaker, wrestle the dead Lab into a trash can.

Jack's absence extended through lunch.

On nice days I ate dessert by the monkey bars, which was where I was headed with three chocolate chip cookies when Mr. Malbasic's office door swung wide, and Pecker and Cruella d' Olive Oyl cut me off at the pass. "That's the boy, Mother," Pecker pointed, and Mrs. Geoffrey Dahl-Packer of Packer Family Pharmacy took my measure with rancid awareness, her eyes black prunes, her lips dry figs, her fragrance Ajax The Foaming Cleanser.

I hustled The Wild Man of Borneo to the rear, ventured a subdued, "Hi."

Mrs. Dahl-Packer was appalled. "Of all the nerve!"

"I told you, Mother."

The woman grabbed me by the ear, surveyed the hall for potential witnesses, and bundled me into an empty classroom. She seized my second ear, held me as she might a sugar bowl, and lifted me to my toes, my nose between her not insubstantial breasts. "How fortunate to have the opportunity to meet in person. Ah, yes, come look, Charles, the breeding is evident. You can see it in his brow, his eyes. Look, Charles, look. Do you see it, the vestige of the Neanderthal? You know what you are, little boy? A troglodyte is what you are."

"I told you, Mother."

"You will not be harassing my son any further, will you?" She pumped my head in furious affirmation. "Because I will make your life a living hell should you so much as sneeze in his direction," she said, and flicked me off as she would a booger.

A week-old bouquet of posies drooped from the monkey bars. I didn't feel much like cookies anymore, anyways.

* * *

Grown-ups fell into four categories. The delirious. The oblivious. The furious. The villainous.

Bullies were all four at once.

Annie, Jack, and me, we were the only real people in town.

But everyone, *everyone*, was straight out of Central Casting.

THREE

Once it's in your head, there is no going back

Life was short and getting shorter. For me, anyhow. I gave my cookies to Jack. "My mom never uses enough chocolate chips," he said. "Tons in these."

"C'mon, man. I've been waiting all day. Tell me what you were going to tell me."

"Creosote is used to preserve wood," he said.

"So I've heard."

"Or paint. What do you know about paint?"

"I don't care about paint."

"A gallon covers four hundred square feet."

My yawn would've made the pages of Guinness.

"Mr. Fox paints houses. He's an encyclopedia of paint."

"Good for him."

"You know the secret to cleaning paint brushes?"

"Throw them out."

"Dish soap and olive oil."

"I don't care."

"You will."

"I won't."

"You remember Mrs. Gibbons, used to teach third grade?"

"Crabby Gibbons. Yeah. I was lucky. The fatty quit before I got to third."

"When she was a kid, she built her own soapbox, except they wouldn't let girls enter the derby back then. So she dressed up as a boy, pretended to be her own brother, and won the whole caboodle."

"What'd she use, a refrigerator crate?"

"Look, I'm telling you what people tell me. But if you'd rather joke around—"

"You're not telling me anything, man. You don't want to? Fine. Don't. Keep your stupid secrets."

"Jesus, what's got into you?"

I had Mrs. Dahl-Packer gunning for me at one end and Jack giving me the runaround at the other. Like they were better than me. Like I wasn't good enough to be a finder, a finder-outer, a human being. What had Mrs. Peckerface called me? A troglodyte. She had me pegged. It's all I'd ever be. Jack was treating me the same.

I swerved into the street and hit the brakes. Double Al, Dandruff Wayne, and a toothy trainee awaited me with open arms on the other side.

"Come. Come. Come and get it," Double Al taunted, as Dandruff Wayne performed his caged-gorilla bit and the trainee mimed my fate should I comply. But then Double Al tripped into the trainee and the trainee fell off the curb, and I broke the cardinal rule, laughed out loud.

Double Al had taken to wearing his boots untied, bows too sissy, and woe to anyone entertained by his frequent stumbles.

I split my sides, strived for the hilarity level of a live studio audience and me the dick they cut to for the rollicking close-up.

I'd had it up to here with the suspense of when and where the bastards would move on me. *They wouldn't kill me. Bullies maimed.* I had Jack's assurance. My suicide would be a partial. Best of all, my blood would be on Jack's hands. By holding out on me he'd forced my hand, led me straight to Double Al.

I hunkered down, *faked them out, exploded from my squat, swift, slick, and lethal, haymakers and windmills. Al, the sap, he never saw me coming. I propelled him into a maple and kindly rearranged his face. Oh, man, you should have seen his buddies run. Gratitude poured in from every corner. By day's end, I'd been hoisted onto shoulders, paraded up and down Dundas, and handed the keys to the city, a statue to be erected in my honour.*

The End

BPI

How I wish.

I hunkered down, readied for the blows to hail. Jack reeled me back onto the sidewalk. And before I could protest, he did the nuttiest thing I'd seen outside a Jerry Lewis picture. He raised a fist, and with his right arm bent to ninety, he gave his bicep two quick chops, and hollered a guttural and fearless, "Vaffanculo! Vaffanculo!"

Hey, think I was confused? Double Al and his bozos were fit to be tied. They were coming for us and they weren't, steps forward, steps back, scuffling on and into each other, arguing, swearing, shoving, and Jack and me shunted to second feature. By block's end, Double Al had socked both Dandruff Wayne and the trainee, and the three had gone their separate ways.

"Holy cow! What was that?" I said.

"Don't you know that about Double Al? He needs to outnumber you by at least two to one."

"No. What you said?"

"Oh, that. Yeah. It's Italian. A curse or something. There's this truck driver, Mr. Canova from Toronto, comes into the Marquee whenever he passes through. He said if I ever needed to put some asshole in his place, see how bullshit baffles brains—"

"It's magic then? Like a spell?"

"I guess. But it only works if you do the arm thing, too."

"Vaffran-what?"

"Culo. Vaf-fan-cu-lo."

"Vaffanculo."

"It's not the word so much, Gus. It could be anything. I told you, it's about keeping them off balance. The less predictable we are to them, the more predictable they are to us. Like when you were laughing, stuff like that, it throws them off somehow."

"That your plan for me, too? Throw me off, keep everything to yourself."

"You don't give an inch, do you? Cool down. Have a little patience. I was getting there, I swear. There's a lot to get your head around. I wanted to ease you in."

"I'm as eased in as I'll ever be."

"Yeah, we'll see."

"Yeah, we will."

"You asked for it."

"Hurry it up.

"Thanksgiving Day, 1918. There used to be this big plant down by the river. It made bombs and bullets and whatever for the war. That's the day it blew up. Thanksgiving, 1918. Took out half the town."

"What are you talking about?"

"Right here. Trenton."

"Bullshit. I never heard about anything like that."

"It's only the tip of it."

"Tip of what?"

"The bad stuff, man. People love telling me the bad stuff most of all." He sped ahead with a tour guide gait and I followed, searching streets and backyards for ruins or whatnot.

"Winter, 1927. Walker Shoe Factory. The roof collapses under heavy snow. Almost thirty dead. . . ." He rattled off the facts and fatalities, revealing the workings of his brain. Jack was a categorizer. He cut through the clutter, broke stories down to relevant components.

I could have been watching *You Are There*, with Jack instead of Walter Cronkite. "October, 1937. Two planes crash into each other over town. Bodies drop out of the sky. Body parts . . . Summer, 1923—"

"Wait. Wait."

"Wait what?"

"Body parts?"

"All over the place. The guy who tells me, he says his son was one of them—a co-pilot. His head turned up in one place, and his middle in another, and his legs someplace else. And then the old man started bawling, because some of his son was never found."

"He cried?"

"Old men cry easy. You should see."

"Jeez."

"Summer, 1923. The circus comes to town. The big top catches fire—"

"And what? Lions and tigers got loose and ate people? Elephants stampeded? I saw that movie. C'mon, eh?"

"Hey, I don't care if you believe me. You wanted to know and I'm telling you. You don't want to listen, makes no difference to me. Look, I know where you're coming from. Some of the people, some of their stories . . . There's this Mrs. Wimmer from Austria. When she was a kid, Adolf Hitler was her babysitter. She says he did things to her."

"What things?"

"When her father found out, he beat him to a pulp—came this close to killing teenage Adolf." Jack put on this old-lady voice. "'Mein fotter vood huf saved da vorld!'"

"I've seen her in the restaurant. My mom talks to her."

"My dad says she's a liar, and she's only trying to cover up her own guilt for whatever it was she must have done in the war."

"But what if her father really had killed Hitler?"

"You're a what-if guy, eh?"

"Aren't you?"

"I'm more what-was. You want more?"

"How much you got?"

"Yesterday afternoon, Mrs. Gibbons is having her tea and calls me over. I figure it'll be the soapbox saga again. But no. 'A story I've never told anyone,' she says. And this one, Gus, I'm warning you, once it's in your head, there's no going back."

"C'mon . . ."

"You were born what—'51?"

"In May."

"Same year. June. Last week of school. A school bus comes down King. Kids packed in like sardines. They're going on a picnic. Except the bus loses its brakes same time a train is going through the crossing at Division. . . ."

"Jesus."

"Mrs. Gibbons is sitting on the bench at the rear of the bus with another teacher. And she thinks the world has come to an end. Crashing. Smashing. Screaming. Glass breaking, flying. So much noise she can't hear the noise. She blacks out. And when she comes to, she's still on the bench. But it's all blurry and smoky and dusty and bloody around her. And the teacher who was sitting with her, she's gone. The whole bus is gone. Nobody and nothing left. Only Mrs. Gibbons on the bench. And there's a foot in her lap. A small foot and it's wearing its shoe. A red shoe. A girl's shoe. Mrs. Gibbons cannot move. The Russians went and dropped the bomb, she's sure of it."

This was better and worse than anything I'd expected. We'd arrived at my house, but I wasn't going anywhere.

"They had to go by the dental records to identify the bodies. . . ."

"Like on TV."

"Except some of the kids had never seen a dentist. There was no telling who was who. And, get this, some were buried with pieces of glass and metal still in them. And they had to have funerals for parts of the bus, because they couldn't get all the flesh and guts out of the twisted and melted parts."

We moved to my stoop. Sat.

"Mrs. Gibbons didn't have a scratch on her. Nothing. Except she shows me this little bump on her arm. I'm the only person she's ever shown it to. It's right here. See. Below her shoulder. A yellowy purple bump. The size of a quarter. She swears there's bits of bus and dead kid in there, because at night, the dead kid, she calls out to her."

"Holy shit."

"I warned you."

"Calling out what? 'Help! Get me out of here.'"

"More like a question. Different words, but always the same. The kid— Mrs. Gibbons thinks it's the girl who lost the red shoe—she wants to know, 'How come a nasty old teacher like you got to live and me and my friends are dead before we started?'"

"No way."

"Swear to God."

"And the girl, it's talking from inside of her? Her arm?"

"Since the bus crashed."

"Like she's haunting herself, almost."

"Mrs. Gibbons wants to kill herself."

"Wow."

"She's wanted to for years. But she worries it'll be unfair to the dead girl inside her arm. She'd be killing the kid a second time."

"She could cut the bump out of her arm, keep the girl in a jar or something, couldn't she?"

"Like in *Donovan's Brain*."

"That'd be so neat."

"I'm not so sure."

"What'd your mom say? Your dad?"

"I asked if they'd heard about the school bus. I didn't go into details. Nothing about Mrs. Gibbons or her arm. My parents have enough problems without thinking their son needs a straitjacket. Truth is, I probably do. I tell you, Gus, some of the stories . . . The old people, it's like they're desperate for me to know. Like they're afraid to go to their graves without sharing the secret. Since the newspaper started writing me up, you'd think I was their best friend. Nuts, eh?"

"Yeah." I saw Jack as my best friend, too, right then. "Nuts."

"Mom said she remembered something about a school bus, but I could see she really didn't. She does that a lot. And then her usual: 'Why can't you think nice thoughts?' I didn't bother with my dad. He'd only tell me I was watching too much TV."

"I get that from my Mom, too."

"So many accidents, eh? Weird stuff. And nobody seems to remember any of it."

"Except the people who tell you."

"And we're just one small town here. I thought maybe it was a *Candid Camera* thing, like they were seeing whose baloney could spook me out the most. So then I asked Bryan McGrath—the reporter at the *Record*, the guy who writes about me finding things. If anybody would know, it'd be him."

"And did he?"

"He laughed, said he wouldn't have a job if bad stuff didn't happen. 'More the better.' I asked if I could go through the old papers. They've got these microfilm readers. He got all serious. Told me if I liked horror stories so much, I should buy *Alfred Hitchcock Mystery Magazine*. Besides, according to him, the *Record* archives only go back to 1955, because of Hurricane Hazel, the big flood and fire."

I knew about Hazel. A branch broke off a tree and shattered my bedroom window. It was the Halloween before my dad got killed.

"And then he warned me, said I'd be wise to take whatever the old coots say with a big grain of salt or I'd end up as empty-headed as them."

"But he didn't say if any of it was true or not."

"That's the thing."

"They gotta be, right? People don't make stuff like that up. Not about dead kids. Nobody likes talking about dead kids. Except kids."

"I'm with you, Gus. Maybe not every story I hear, but most. . . . The way they tell them to me. The look on McGrath's face when I brought up the ammo plant, the planes colliding—like he'd been caught in a lie, like there was stuff he didn't want me knowing."

"Jack, if I tell you something, you promise not to laugh?"

"Not unless it's a joke."

"Since I was little, I've had this bad feeling—"

"As bad as having a dead girl living in your arm?"

"It's hard to describe. It's like something's going to get me and—"

". . . And there's nothing you can do to stop it."

"Jeez, yeah. Like what's going to happen is going to happen."

"Me, too, Gus."

"You swear?"

"On a stack of Bibles. You know *The Twilight Zone* is about Trenton, don't you?"

"Huh?"

"Trenton is *The Twilight Zone*."

"Now you're really kidding. . . ." A whole new bad feeling rose up inside— that everything he'd told me had been a lie, that I'd be the laughingstock of school by morning.

"Rod Serling. He's from Syracuse or Rochester or somewhere." Jack nodded in the direction of Lake Ontario. "He's been here a bunch of times, comes across on his cabin cruiser. I've met him."

"Liar."

"Honest to God, Gus. At the town dock. My parents, they've got these old friends from Erie. He's a doctor and she plays the harp or whatever. Two summers ago, they show up on their yacht. We're over there visiting, and the boat is neat and all, but soon I'm bored out of my mind from hearing about the good old days, so I go out and snoop around the dock. And there he is."

"Rod Serling? *Twilight Zone* Rod Serling?"

"Bending down, checking the lines."

"Bullshit. Bullshit. Bullshit. Up yours, man."

"I'm telling you . . ."

"And you talked to him?"

"First time I only stared."

"First time?"

"Next morning, I went back. He was sitting on his deck."

"Aw, c'mon . . ."

"I said, 'Are you Rod Serling?'"

"And him? What'd he say?"

"'Last time I looked, son.'"

"That's it?"

"That's it. Swear to God. Swear on my sisters' lives."

"Did he know who you were? Did you tell him you were Jack the Finder? Wow! What if he does a *Twilight Zone* about you, Jack? Or Mrs. Gibbons and the girl in her arm?"

"I'm just trying to tell you, he knows the town. And I bet you anything he's gotten a bunch of his ideas right here. Watch the show, you'll see. Some of the episodes, you'll swear, they're documentaries."

"I hate documentaries. You ever see the one on herring fishing?"

# FOUR

Good Deed Gus

"So, you finally have a best friend," Annie said.

"No I don't," I said.

"You're always with him."

"No I'm not."

"I'm not arguing with you. I'm happy for you."

"I got best friends. Lots."

"Has he showed you how he finds what he finds?"

"He will."

"He doesn't talk much, does he?"

"Yeah, he does."

"As much as you?"

"I talk."

"That day, when the park ranger brought the new badgers to school, and a bunch of us got to see them before everybody else, Jack Levin didn't say a word to me."

"Yeah? So? Did you say anything to him?"

"He kept to himself."

"He's not like that."

"He sure knows a ton about badgers."

"I thought you said he didn't talk."

"He did, I guess. But it was more like showing off how smart he is to the teachers and ranger."

"Jack *is* smart. He knows something about everything."

In first grade, Annie sits at the desk behind me. She pokes me in the back to borrow my pencil sharpener, my ruler, my opinions. Usually with her finger. If she's feeling lazy, with her pencil. The eraser end. "Gus, Gus. Psst, Gus . . ." Miss Proctor tells Annie to mind her own business once a day. Miss Proctor never sends anyone to the office. She doesn't have it in her.

Next year, Annie sits to my right. She bites her lower lip when she draws in art class. She taps the tip of her nose when adding and subtracting. This is all new to me.

Come third and fourth, she takes the desk ahead of me. When she turns to talk, it's sometimes part way around, more often all the way. Depends on the urgency of her news, jokes, observations, the temper of her counsel, her psychotherapy and editorials. It's the way she turns I love the most, the movement of her hair, shoulder to shoulder, the shape of her lips the instant before she whispers, and how her eyes conspire with her whispers. I was supposed to hate girls. And all I ever wanted was to hug her.

Our shared sense of doom is where Jack and I truly bonded.

My breakfast with the *Trent Record* went from daily chore to daily obsession. I combed the pages, scoured the obituaries and in memoriam notices. My aim was to expand Jack's list or, at least, lend credence to the stories he'd been told. My mother, in her doting oblivion, was thrilled by how I'd bolt for the paper as it smacked the stoop. She was forgiving when I whined for sections or accused her of hogging. The scissors and notepad I kept at hand awed her no end (though clippings and notes of any substance amounted to none). Mom never had to say a word. Her pride was her corsage: Young Churchill's mom would have begged to have been so blessed.

I could have robbed a bank and Mom would have seen a rosy future in finance for me. As it was, I started breaking into houses.

The *Record* pickings were slim. The town was going through a fallow period. Accidents were run of the mill. Cars. Tractor spills. Incidents and tragedies small scale and unremarkable. Three with one blow was our assigned minimum. Four or more would be saying something.

One night after dinner, I was watching TV when the doorbell rang. Mom called to me as she went to answer. "Leo, it's your friend, Douglas Dunwood."

I peeked out through the venetians. The angle of the living room window was pretty neat; if you stayed to the right, you could see who was at the door without them seeing you back.

"Leo, it's your friend," she called again as she opened the door. "Do come in, Douglas. Leo should be right out."

He was wearing his dopey Scouting outfit, merit badges up the Mickey-Mental ying-yang. He took off his stupid hat, flashed his baboon Mickey-Mental teeth. "'Good evening, Ma'am," he said, and launched into a prepackaged spiel. "The Boy Scouts are conducting a paper drive in your area next Saturday. Should you have papers to donate, please bundle them neatly and deposit them on your stoop. We will be by to pick them up between the hours of eight in the morning and seven in the evening. If you are elderly or infirm, we will be pleased to assist you. On behalf of Scouts Canada, thank you for contributing to the well-being of our community.'"

"I don't know where that boy is. Leo. Leo. Are you coming? Douglas is waiting." And then to Dunwood: "He tells me you're in taxidermy club together. If only you could get him involved in Scouting, too."

Dougie said something I didn't hear and plugged his Mickey-Mental head back into his Mickey-Mental hat.

"He'll be so sorry to have missed you. Leo, Leo, Douglas is leaving."

This was when the idea came to me. Old newspapers would be filled with disasters and crimes. Old newspapers would allow me to pull my own weight, give me the heft to compete with Jack. Never mind the *Record* archives being lost, I'd create my own archives.

Jack got his stories from the old and living. I'd get mine from the old and dead.

I confined my crimes to houses of the freshly departed, the 60-plusses, where "widow of" or "widower of" or "predeceased by" factored large in the *Record*'s obituary. Houses you could bet were vacant.

Old people didn't draw much attention to begin with. Lights out on Halloween. No jack-o'-lanterns or candy. *What did they expect?* And in the immediate aftermath of last-corpse-out, their houses drew less attention still. Until the will turned up, that is. I prowled the buffer between after-death and before-heirs.

And it wasn't precisely breaking in. Unlocked windows and doors were routine, which made it walking in or climbing in, and there was nothing criminal in that. And when the place was locked up, I didn't push it, simply moved on to the next obit.

In spring and summer I carried hedge trimmers. In autumn a rake. In winter a shovel. *Good Deed Gus,* for all to see. You'd be amazed how a smile, a friendly wave, can derail a nosy neighbour. Direct challenges were met by a forlorn, "I miss my grammy/grampy." Worked like a charm.

I'd guessed right about the elderly. Old newspapers were as plentiful as doilies, dust, Q-tips, and Ex-Lax. In stacks. In boxes. Sealing drafts. Lining drawers and cupboards. Wadded into shoes. Wadded around glasses, cups, saucers, and heirlooms.

I kept it brief. Riffled through pages with a trained eye. *I knew what I was after.* Tore out whatever tickled. And skedaddled. I never took anything more, I swear. Okay. Once. A *Mighty Mouse* comic book in 3D from 1953. But that was it.

A few stories touched on some of what Jack had been told, though details were sketchy and follow-ups scarce. You had the sense interest petered out fast. Or glossing-over horror had begun early on.

As for bad stuff of consequence, I came up with a couple I thought might qualify. Still, I was in no rush to share. The finds were of a different nature than Jack's. I didn't want to come off stupid, like I'd missed the point and murder had no place on our list.

⟁FIVE

On alternate Sundays, Dottie Lange dropped by our house on her way home from church. My mother would make finger sandwiches, while Dottie supplied date squares or brownies. The lunch was their "square meal," a little joke between them. Dottie was a Betty Boop soprano in her early forties, a Miss Clairol blue-black with Cleopatra bangs. She wasn't old enough to be Mom's real mom, but she was a reliable surrogate. My mother had no family. None she spoke of, anyhow. Among the photos in the drawer of Dad's night table (so called long after it had ceased to be), there was one of baby me in my mother's arms. Standing with us, a lady I had never met. On the back, in dull pencil and Mom's hand:

July 1951
Leo (2 mos), Emily Eden

Mom and Eden could have been twins, had Mom's hair been longer, had Eden been happier.

"Who is she?" I asked.

"Someone who used to matter," Mom said. "In time you'll see, people like her turn up a lot in old photos."

I do not know the age at which deceit begins to contaminate a kid's brain. Don't know when exactly darkness chokes off the light or skepticism subverts assumption. But I do know this: The captain of the *Titanic* had a better handle on icebergs than any grown-up has ever had on any kid.

Mom poured Dottie's tea. "I read his letter to you, didn't I?"

"Once wasn't enough," Dottie said. She plopped two lumps into her cup.

"I'm telling you, Dottie, Mr. Malbasic's confidence in him is already having a positive effect. I can't wait to tell him when we meet."

Dottie tipped the creamer, stirred the white to beige. "What have I been telling you about Leo all along, Emily? The quieter they are . . . Special. He is special." She patted my hand. "You are special."

"Sometimes I see him as the little boy he is. Other times . . ."

"Man of the house."

"Yes. Yes."

Their belief in me, their optimism, does not in any way diminish the warm memories of those Sunday get-togethers.

The thing no adult could be allowed to see was how Jack and I found joy in death and hope in destruction. Every qualifying accident, crime, or disaster logged—past or present—was cerebral confirmation of worse things to come. Our watchword was *impending*. God, we loved the word. *Impending* gave us purpose.

It helped, too, how we were both into *Ripley's Believe It or Not*, though it was my frequent and casual mentions of Elsie Hix, Frank Edwards, Rupert Furneaux, Edgar Cayce, and Charles Fort that cemented my potential as a viable sidekick. I'd wager we debated the merits of every unexplained mystery and phenomenon known to man.

The *Mary Celeste*. Or, as Arthur Conan Doyle had misnamed it, the *Marie Celeste*.

"You'd think Sherlock Holmes would have pointed out the error."

"Or solved the mystery."

The Abominable Snowman.

"Hillary found a Yeti scalp on Everest."

Death by spontaneous combustion.

"You could be walking home from school and next you know you're a cherry bomb."

The Loch Ness Monster.

"There's one in Lake Ontario, too."

"But it's only a prehistoric earthworm."

Lost worlds. Atlantis. Lemuria. Mu.

"I bet you could find them all, Jack. If anybody could."

Houdini's secrets, which according to page 129 of my *Reader's Digest Junior Omnibus*, would be revealed in their entirety on April 6, 1974.

"I hope I'm still alive to see it," I said.

"Me, too," Jack said.

The Nazca Lines of Peru.

The vanishing lighthouse keepers of Flannan Isle.

The Tunguska flying saucer explosion of 1908.

The Dropa Stones.

And Oak Island, the Nova Scotia treasure pit engineered by Captain Kidd himself. It intrigued me like no other, and spooked me the same, instilling a lifelong fear of being buried alive. In quicksand. In a landslide. In a coffin. In my lies.

"I wouldn't hold my breath," Jack said. "They won't find anything on Oak Island till it wants to be found."

His certainty could be so damn aggravating. "Things don't *want* to be found," I said. "They *get* found."

"If that's what you want to think. But I'm telling you, when something is lost, it lets you know when it's ready to be found. Like hide-and-seek, when you're still under the bed an hour in, you sure as heck want to be found, right? You show yourself. You catch an eye. You make noise. Like that."

"Is that why you haven't found anything since Mrs. Bruce's ring? Because nothing's ready?"

"I've found plenty. Just nothing to brag about."

"You gotta show me. Please." He couldn't refuse his best friend. Annie had recognized it, after all. Jack must have, too.

The Levins' garage stood remote and perpendicular to the house, concealed at the end of a grass and gravel driveway—a misplaced country lane, really—that wound between a stand of overzealous pines. The roof was a patchwork of bare plywood, weathered tar, and fractured shingles. The wood siding thirsted for a fresh coat of white. It was a fitting postscript to my surveillance of Jack and the disappointing answer to why my Sunday stakeouts had turned up nothing. The garage was obvious if you knew it was there; not so much if you didn't. I'd neglected to cover off the underlying principle of Hardy Boys detective work: *Get the big picture, clodhopper.*

Jack fished a key from his pocket. "You got to promise you won't tell anyone about this. Ever."

"I promise." I couldn't think of anyone who'd be interested, besides Annie. "I'm good at keeping my mouth shut."

"I need you to swear, Gus. Dumbwood or some of the others, they get wind of what I've got here and . . . well, you know what they could do."

"I won't tell. I swear."

"Even if we stop being friends and hate each other. You need to swear you'll keep this to yourself, so help you God."

"I swear. So help me God. Even if we hate each other."

"You Catholic?"

"Mom says we're between religions."

"Well, cross your heart or something anyhow, for extra insurance. That's what you do, right?"

"Cross my heart." I ran a plausible sequence from navel to throat and twice from tit to tit. I stopped short of "and hope to die" and "stick a needle in my eye."

"All right," Jack said, and we shook on it. "'Rich or poor, a man's word is the most valuable thing he's got.'"

"Roy Rogers or Gene Autry?" I said. Had to be one or the other.

"Joey the Clown." He bent to one knee and popped the lock. "*Circus Boy.*"

"Oh, yeah," I said, unconvinced.

Jack gripped the handle. "Well, you asked for it." He straightened and the garage door rose with him.

4:30 5 SUPERMAN—Adventure
Gloomy Gus, cub reporter for the *Daily Planet* newspaper, visits Superman's Fortress of Solitude.

SIX

X, N, and K

"You're the first and only friend I've let in," Jack said. "Except for Mr. McGrath, once."

Homemade shelves lined the walls to my left and right, boxes on unpainted planks. Centred on the wall ahead was a bulletin board with newspaper clippings, and surrounded by maps on all sides. Notes, pushpins, and coloured wool dotted and crisscrossed the lot, suggesting rhyme to Jack's reason. Atom-Age linoleum overlaid the floor, blue and red starbursts on a faded yellow universe. An 8 x 4 work table held down the middle of the floor, sawhorse supports at either end and a too-logical arrangement on top: Gilbert microscope, Gilbert chemistry set, magnifying glasses, transistor radio, spiral-bound notepads, a Woody Woodpecker mug stocked with pens and coloured pencils, and two yards of hardcovers and paperbacks strung upright between Lone Ranger and Tonto bookends.

"Where do you want to start?" he said.

He took me through his unpublicized finds, as he called them, the artifacts stored in empty chocolate bar and chewing gum cartons scavenged from the restaurant.

Indian arrowheads.

Fossils.

Shell casings. Bullets.

The brass hands and face from an old clock. (An upside-down 2 filling in for a 7.)

Shards of dishes and pottery.

A Howdy Doody glass, a chip in the rim. (It had begun life as a Welch's grape jelly jar.)

Forks. Knives. Spoons.

Tin boxes, rusty or very rusty, with lids and without. Rowntree's Cocoa. King George Coronation '1937 Souvenir' Tea Biscuits. Ivory Soap. Macintosh's Toffee de Luxe. Cracker Jack. Shawmut Seidlitz Powders, whatever the heck that was.

Jars and bottles.

Doll heads. Tin soldiers. Dinky Toys.

Coins. Military buttons.

Where more than one item was in a box, they would be separated by dividers and wrapped individually in Saran or, if tiny, in frosted envelopes, the ones stamp collectors favour.

Stickers indicated the name, date, and place of the finds, with Jack rating the items according to quality. *X* for *Excellent*. *N* for *Neat*. *K* for *Okay*.

"Show me something good," I said. "Like the bottle you found. Or the meteorite."

"The *X* finds."

"Yeah. Them."

"They're tough to come by, man. And the ones I have found, well, you know what happened . . . you read the paper."

"I just thought . . ."

"Not as exciting as you expected."

I approached the maps.

"I keep track of where I find what. Occasionally patterns develop. Like over here. See. Most of the buttons and bullets turned up by Keating Woods—the open field between the orchards. Mr. McGrath figures it was the site of a skirmish. But he didn't write it up. He worried people would start digging the place up and ruin what was left. I found some bones there, too, but I covered them up."

"Like human bones?"

"Don't forget, you promised to keep all this to yourself."

"Hanna Park, too." I moved to another map. "You've found a bunch out there."

"Mostly *K*s, though."

"You gotta take me with you, Jack. You got to."

"Damn it, Gus, how many times do I have to tell you? I don't go looking for anything. Swear to God, I don't. Whatever I find comes looking for me. You found money outside the A&P once, right?"

"Five bucks."

"Did you go looking for it? Did you? Or did you look down and it was there?"

"I guess."

"Exactly. It called to you. Think how many people walked by before you did. And how many never noticed."

"My mom, she didn't."

"Right. The five bucks chose you."

"Yeah, but everything else chooses you. Why not me?"

Jack groaned, steered me to his work table. "I thought you'd understand. You're here because you're the only one who would." He ran his hand from Tonto to the Lone Ranger. "Some things cannot be explained."

The books were arranged alphabetically by title. I recognized most by the spines alone. I owned them all, save four or five.

The Art of Thought Reading
Atlantis: Found!
The Book of the Bizarre
The Book of the Damned
Boys' Book of the Supernatural
Confounding Coincidences
Developing Your ESP
Extra-sensory Perception
Haunted Houses
Lo!
Lost Treasures of the Ancient World
Lost Treasures of North & South America
Lost Worlds
Mysteries of the Ancient World
Mysteries of the Unexplained
On Mysteries of the Mind
On Reincarnation
On Secrets of the Universe

Past Lives
Real Ghost Stories
Reincarnation and Karma
Strange as It Seems
Strange but True
Stranger than Science
Strange World
Strangest of All
Supernatural! Unnatural! Actual!
Unexplained Mysteries
Unexplained Phenomena
World's Stra⋯ges⋯ Mysteries
Weird, Wei⋯
The Werewolf i⋯
You H⋯

"Why not you, Gus? Why not you?" Jack said. "Hey, *why me? Why me?*"

I had no answer.

He showed me his *Mad* magazines. It was no match for my collection. But he had me beat on comic books. Three huge boxes. I'd barely cracked the lot when I turned up *Detective Comics 225*, the first appearance of J'onn J'onzz, *The Martian Manhunter*.

I didn't bring up the finding again until it was time to go. I was cautious and disarming. Stuttered a little. "Maybe if we hang out more, I was thinking maybe, you know, your finding powers might rub off on me."

He laughed, relented. "Okay. Sure. How about this Saturday, we go to Hanna Park and see what happens?"

"Yeah. Yeah. But after the Odeon, okay? No way I'm missing *13 Ghosts*."

"Me, neither," he said.

The wicked witch from *The Wizard of Oz* was in *13 Ghosts*. So was that kid from *The Boy and the Pirates*, hands down the best pirate movie ever made. But the best thing about *13 Ghosts*, the reason I associate it with Jack and that day, was the ghost viewer they gave to everybody who showed up. You couldn't see the ghosts without it. (Well, actually you could, but you wouldn't know unless you broke the rules and removed your viewer during the ghost scenes.)

Jack saved his viewer. I saved mine, too.

# SEVEN

Death from above

Jack was true to his word. Heck, he was better than his word. Hanna Park was only the beginning. We did Keating Woods and Creighton Farms and the back slope of Mount Pelion. We went everywhere and anywhere he had ever found a thing and places he'd never set foot. And we did everywhere and anywhere again. Saturday mornings, we'd catch the matinee at the Odeon and afternoons we'd be on our way.

Sometimes I'd get the chills, be reminded of a story I'd found during my burglaries. But doubts remained and I stayed silent.

I'd like to tell you Jack and I found Noah's Ark. I'd like to tell you we found the Patiala necklace or the *Awa Maru* treasure. I'd like to tell you I found the lost Zippo lighter I borrowed from the top drawer of my father's bureau the day after he was buried.

We found nothing.

"I'm the cause," I said. "I'm the reason you've been coming up empty. I've jinxed you." We were a few weeks into our Saturday routine when I got around to owning up. The matinee had just let out.

Jack was hesitant to answer. He started and stopped, then sighed like the guilty do on the downslope to confession.

"You been holding out on me?" I was no stranger to betrayal.

"You're no jinx, okay?"

I clammed up. I didn't make it easy for him.

"Just come with me. Okay? Please."

I embraced my latest grudge with open arms, same as I might an old friend were I ever to fluke one off.

Jack was repentant and persuasive. Still, I gave no ground.

I dragged my feet, maintained my silence, let the traitor stew. I followed, my curiosity and animosity at loggerheads.

He scoped out his front yard, then marched ahead to the expanse that sided the driveway. "See that," he said. Upturned grass. Grey dirt. A shallow hole. "Last Wednesday, after school, I saw this crazy Lab digging up the lawn. I chased him off, but when I went to take a closer look . . . well . . . you'll see." We rounded the path to his Fortress of Solitude. My second visit.

I fired off a fresh round of blasé. I could not care less. Given the chance, I'd grab his *Detective Comics 225* and take off, never to see the prick again. Serve him right.

He removed a Dentyne carton from the shelf. "There are some finds, you need to understand, Gus . . . sometimes I feel . . . I dunno . . . like a grave robber."

He'd marked the carton with a big red *X*. My disinterest faltered, replaced with a twinge of empathy. Perhaps I'd been too quick to react.

He dangled a gold bracelet from thumb and forefinger—an oval medallion suspended between two chains. "This was where the dog was digging." He snaked the piece into my palm.

A blip of colour adorned the centre of the medallion, a severely shrunken heraldic shield, something a leprechaun might carry into battle. At the top, a red and gold crown was fixed upon concentric blue circles. Some Latin words. And in silhouette, a gold eagle, wingspan exceeding the circumference. On the scroll at the base: Royal Canadian Air Force.

Numbers were engraved above the badge and a name below:

LEBEL, S.E.

"What is it?" I said.

"Flip it over."

On the back, another engraving:

LOVE, IRIS

"It's what they call a sweetheart bracelet. During the war, wives and girlfriends gave them to flyers for good luck."

"Neat. When's it gonna be in the *Record*?"

"I've been feeling sick inside since I realized what it was."

"Because it makes you feel like a grave robber. . . ."

"Remember the story about the planes colliding over town? Bodies dropping from the sky? The old man who told me . . ."

"The guy who cried."

"Right. Well, his name was Lebel—"

"Holy cow."

"Yeah. And the son who died, the copilot, his name was Simon."

"'Lebel, S.E.' Jesus." I fought off the heebie-jeebies, tossed the bracelet back to Jack. "Just like the wedding ring you dug up."

"Difference is, this came from the sky."

"You gotta give it back to the old man. You got to."

"You think I wouldn't have already if I could? He died months ago. But I've done some checking. His son's wife, Iris, she still lives in town. The only Lebel in the book, anyhow. Across the river, up on Tompkins Street. I've been nervous about going over there, afraid of how she might take it."

"It'd be like Simon coming back from the dead. Every so often we get a package or something addressed to my dad. Or a phone call for him. It hasn't happened for a long time. I mean, he's been dead for years. But when it does, my mom, you'd swear she's seen a ghost. She'll go into her bedroom and not come out for hours. Not a word. Not a peep. Not even when I call her. Once, she didn't come out even for work, and her friend, Dottie, she had to come over."

"See. I knew you'd be good at this, Gus. You've got experience in this sort of thing. You're why I've been waiting. How about we give it back together?"

"She'll thank me, right, like Mrs. Bruce thanked you?"

"We're square, then? I'm forgiven for holding out?"

"It feels good, right, when people thank you?"

# EIGHT

Amnesiaville

Trenton's wrong-side-of-the-tracks moldered east of the river. Up Dundas. Through the downtown. Over the swing bridge. The side where the creosote plant burned. Where Central Bridge built its boats and Helmut Swartz worked when he wasn't teaching Dottie Lange the cha-cha. Where Seaway ships docked. Where coal was dumped. Where steel drums went to rust.

Tompkins wasn't like the circles and crescents up in The Heights, Annie's neighbourhood, with its modern prefabs and putting-green grass. Or the venerated Queen, King, and Victoria, with their turn-of-the-century Edwardians—long-ago manors of railroad execs and robber-baron yes-men. Tompkins fell into a third category of street. Hodgepodge.

There were the older, wartime houses, single story toolsheds inspired by the architectural stylings of the Three Little Pigs. These were dwarfed by newer, larger dwellings, the dreams-come-true of incurable insomniacs. Nothing matched. Nothing jibed. Except the mats out front and the cats curled upon them—a feline DEW line. They raised their eyes in listless la-di-das as Jack and I passed. Iris Lebel lived somewhere up ahead.

"Henry Comstock was born on this street," Jack said, off-the-cuff and unsolicited as was his custom. A rougher, tougher, less inquisitive me, and I'd have punched him in the mouth, already. There's not a landfill on Earth without a substratum of putrefied know-it-alls. But Jack was so damn unselfconscious in his eclecticism, the particulars never jarred. This was the issue with the Double Als, the Mickey Mentals, and the Waynes. Crates, too, I guessed. They were synonym-challenged, Jack's earnestness taken as conceit.

A crack on a sidewalk. A brick in a wall. A random remark. *That signpost up ahead . . .* Triggers were everywhere. Jack soaked up the trivia in his stride, and I assimilated the best of it in mine. He knew stuff; *I wanted to know stuff,* if only to fulfill Mr. Malbasic's prophecy—the attainment of *my fullest academic and societal potential.*

"The Comstock Lode—that Henry Comstock?" I said. "He's from here?"

"Born and bred."

"Then why isn't it Comstock Street?"

"His mom's name was Tompkins."

"God, it's like they don't want us to know anything about anything."

Trenton cranked out future NHLers, dime a dozen. Kids who could skate and shoot a puck were gods, which accounted for the large numbers of godless among the rest of us. But Henry Comstock, this was news. And the latest chunk of town history censored by the resident brain trust. It baffled more and more, I tell you.

"Why's everything so cool so secret?"

"Could be there are no secrets," Jack said. "Could be people just forget."

"Like amnesia . . ."

"An epidemic of it."

"And only grown-ups catch it."

We weren't precocious. We watched TV. We went to movies. We absorbed. Any kid who watched Westerns was up to snuff on the Comstock Lode. *Nevada* with Robert Mitchum. *Bonanza* did a whole episode. *Death Valley Days* ran a dozen. It was the first big silver strike in America—Nevada's rush of '59. And Trenton's very own Henry Comstock was its namesake. Sure, Ol' Pancake was alleged to have been a claim jumper and moralizing dickwad. And, yeah, he died penniless in 1870 from a self-inflicted bullet to the head. But did this make him all that different from Trenton's other favourite sons? Really? I mean, we're talking Comstock Lode here. The richest vein of silver the United States of America has ever seen, compliments of yours truly, Trenton, Ontario, Canada, for crying out loud. And nobody knew? Except Jack the Finder, the old coot who must have told him, and me. C'mon. This was certifiable. This was Amnesiaville.

# NINE

The deliriously grateful widow of Tompkins Street

If the wartime houses on Tompkins were postage stamps, Iris Lebel's was postage-due. The bungalow belonged in a hobby shop window. *Made in USA by Lionel.*

Iris was at her door, locking up. She was small, thin, and sized right for easy storage, her home made to measure.

Jack and I held back by the gate, aware of the emotional bombshell we were about to drop on the unwitting widow.

She high-stepped around her cat with a polka move she'd probably seen on *Lawrence Welk* and landed hard when she glanced us idling. She rummaged in her purse with haste, juggled Marilyn Monroe sunglasses onto her face.

"I know her from somewhere, maybe," I whispered to Jack.

"You sure?"

She was elegant in her way. Kewpie cheeks and Revlon lips. Pale green kerchief over an Audrey Hepburn cut and an ankle-length beige trench with broad lapels. She raised her collar to rouged cheeks, cinched her belt.

"Miss Lebel?" Jack said. He smiled. I smiled.

She wrangled a shopping buggy from behind a hedge and onto her crumbling walkway. "I know who you are," she said.

"You do?" Jack said.

"I am sorry. I cannot help you."

"I don't think we're who you think we are," Jack said

"I don't think," she said, "I know." She spoke lilt-free, passion run through a wringer. Like authors who give public readings in what they presuppose the voices inside their readers' heads to be—narcoleptic and hung over.

I added my two cents. "But we've brought you something really neat."

We stood aside. She barrelled through.

"Wait. Please," Jack called after her, jingling the bracelet. "It's this. It's yours. Please, Miss Lebel."

"Missus," she corrected without slowing.

"But he's Jack the Finder," I shouted. "He found your bracelet."

"The sweetheart bracelet. Simon's bracelet."

She faltered, turned, her eyes narrowed with uncertainty. None of the blubbering appreciation Jack and I were expecting. Not yet.

"It was in a hole," I said. "I helped him find it."

She abandoned her cart, inched closer, her purse secured between bosom and crossed arms, our integrity to be determined.

She examined the bracelet without touching it, appraising, verifying, as Jack dangled it before her.

Damn right I knew her. And now I knew *from where.* Her high collar could not hide the scarring—the strip of fried skin beneath her jaw and tapering downwards.

Oh, man! Could this get any better? Or worse? Iris Lebel was two weirdos in one. If this wasn't a portent, what was? I wanted to run and I wanted to stay. *Hell, I had to stay.* Wherever this was going, I couldn't skip the ending.

"And his arm?" Iris said. "What have you done with it?"

"What?" All Jack and I could do was gape. My gaping encompassed both the scars on her neck and a renewed suspicion Jack had held out on me again—Simon Lebel's arm on a shelf somewhere in his garage. "Ma'am?" Jack said.

"His left arm. The bracelet would have been attached."

Jack shook his head. At a loss.

"It is, however, twenty-five years. To expect flesh *and* bone is asking too much. Bone alone will do."

"I didn't see any," Jack said.

"Me, neither," I said. "But we could let you know if an arm turns up, couldn't we, Jack?" I was helpful, hopeful, debating whether I should let her know I knew who she was. "Or fingers, too? There could be finger bones."

My resourcefulness did not go over well. Her eyelids clattered with the rat-a-tat of busted blinds. She reached abruptly for the bracelet, missed, and watched it fall. It lay on the sidewalk, a small, almost perfect triangle of gold, the medallion at the base. "How appropriate," she said, swooped up the jewellery and flung it into her purse, forgoing the anticipated fanfare, gushing gratitude, and cash reward.

She reassumed command of her shopping cart and whipped down the block, her trench flapping at the heels of her flats.

"Blackhurst's," I said.

"The Sewing Machine Witch," Jack said.

TEN

Mothers and other strangers

After Iris dipped below the horizon, we stayed with her afterimage. We had the look you get after you've spotted a UFO, incapable of turning away for fear you'll miss the second flyby.

"I didn't think she could talk," I said.

"Or walk. You ever see her out of her chair?"

Coincidence. Contrivance. Red herrings. *Deus ex machina*. If you've never seen your life as a movie, you've never seen your life. The editing is nonexistent, of course, so you'll need the wherewithal to sit through the excess of boring parts to the end. It can be any genre, too. Western. Monster. Mystery. Adventure. Drama. *Except Comedy*. (Comedy only works in shorts, fifteen minutes max. Never feature length. Never in real life. In real life, fifteen minutes of comedy is a stretch.) The trick is to see how you figure in the story. Lead, supporting, or extra. Hero, sidekick, or bad guy. Just because it's your life is no guarantee you'll survive beyond the opening credits.

"She seemed younger," I said. "Not so witchy."

"Night and day, man. A different person."

"As soon as I saw her neck . . ."

"No wonder cops love scars."

"She got them in the war. Poison gas."

"I don't think so," Jack said.

"It's what my mom says."

"Not according to Mr. Blackhurst. That circus fire I told you about—the big top going up in flames?—that came from him. And when he saw I maybe didn't believe him, he said all the proof I'd ever need could be found at the sewing table in his window."

"The scars, then—that's how she got them. . . ."

"Yup."

"Did he marry her before or after?"

"What? Blackhurst and Iris? Iris Lebel? The witch? You kidding? You think he could fit in that dollhouse with her? One fart and he'd blow the walls out. He's got some big old house across the bay. Lives alone, far as I know."

"Or maybe the lady I saw is his wife."

"Who?"

"At the cleaners, one time. She was hiding at the back and watching me. But when I asked Mr. Blackhurst about her, he said it was nobody, that I'd imagined her."

"Maybe you did. Not everything's a mystery, Gus."

"She was pretty. She wore a fur coat. Movie-star pretty."

"Sure it wasn't the witch in her Iris outfit?"

"I know what I saw."

"Could have been your mom."

"What's that supposed to mean?"

"She's movie-star pretty."

"No, she's not."

"You blind?"

"Shut up, eh? She isn't."

"Okay, calm down. Your mother is not pretty. Okay. I agree. She's not pretty."

"Jesus, Jack, leave her out of this. I'm trying to tell you something."

"So you saw this woman . . . and she was looking at you."

"It was how she was looking. Like she knew me."

"Who's to say she didn't? I'm sorry, Gus, but for an unexplained mystery, it's not exactly Stonehenge. This is a small town. Lots of people know us even if we don't know them. You're trying too hard to make something out of nothing."

"I know what I saw."

"A woman at the back of Sure Press. Big deal. Could be Blackhurst does have a wife. Or a daughter. Or sister. Cousin. A part-time pants presser. Ever consider that?"

"But why would he say I didn't see anybody when I know I did?"

"She could've been his girlfriend and he wants to keep her secret. Your mom, for instance."

"Cut it out."

"You need to ask yourself the right questions. Jumping to conclusions or jumping off a cliff—same thing. Most mysteries can be explained away in nothing flat. The ones that can't, they're the ones you bother with."

"Like the amnesia epidemic."

"Yup."

"Still, if you would have seen her . . ."

"Iris probably knows. You could always ask her," Jack said, one feeble yuk-yuk ahead of me. "Now that she's so grateful to us and all . . . loves us so much."

Jack had nailed it. Until determined otherwise, a woman who looks at you from the back of a dry cleaning shop is not a mystery; she is a woman looking at you from the back of a dry cleaning shop. Odds are, she's also pressing pants.

I wish I could tell you it was a lesson I retained.

My concern was not that Iris (or her alter ego) wouldn't tell me about the lady in black, I worried she would.

What if Old Man Blackhurst did have a girlfriend? And she really did turn out to be my mother?

Principal Malbasic had put Mom's looks in my head and I'd hoped the fact would stay between him and me. Now the cat was out of the bag. Jack had seen it, too. And no telling how many others. Mom *was* movie-star pretty. No denying. I just would have preferred not to know.

I was happier when Mom was the same as every other mom.

Jack's mom wore an apron, baked pies, and made you feel at home, even if you weren't in anybody's home. She had fat hands and fat cheeks.

Annie's mom was almost Annie. Same eyes, same nose, same lips. But not my Annie. Mrs. Barker was Granny Annie. Hair grey. Teeth grey. Somebody who drank tea and ate Peek Freans Digestive Biscuits. She was the oldest of all the moms.

Mrs. Dahl-Packer was College Mom, Pharmacist Mom, Ominous Mom, and Pecker's Mom. Her face was soap in my eyes.

My mom could have passed for my big sister. The big sister in an orphan movie. The sister with Hollywood ambitions. The sister who gave up her dreams to raise her younger brother. That sure as hell should have taken the pretty out of her.

I didn't ask Iris anything. Who would I be asking, anyhow, that reticent slip of a woman we now saw increasingly about town, *Photoplay* her fashion bible, or the working witch she molted into, who saw not, heard not, spoke not?

Last thing Jack and I expected was Iris to come to us. In her way, of course. And not that I can point to any good it did us. Her warnings would be too cryptic and Jack and me too thick.

ELEVEN

Toward the fulfillment
of my academic and societal potential

My mother had said she'd walk home with me after her meeting with Mr. Malbasic, if the timing was right and they didn't need her to rush back to work. When she didn't show up after class, I was relieved for all the usual reasons walking anywhere near school with a parent entails. Until I got home and found the police car out front.

The last police car to come by our house had delivered Dad's belongings. The one before had brought the news of his death.

"My mother's dead," I said to Jack, and went inside.

Mom wasn't dead. She was in the armchair by the television set. She was smoking, the Du Maurier pack open on the coffee table.

Two men sat across from her on the sofa. A policeman in uniform, his cap in lap. A detective in brown jacket and grey pants. He had an *M Squad* hat propped on a knee, but he wasn't Lee Marvin.

"Who's dead?" I asked.

"Get your snack," Mom said, "and take it to your bedroom."

"But you don't like me to eat in my bedroom."

"Today's an exception." Her smile was fake. Her smiles were never fake. She tapped ash into the ashtray. I counted four butts, lipstick stains on the filters. The police had been talking to Mom for a while.

"Tall for his age," I heard one of the cops say as I poured my milk. "Soon be taller than you, Emily."

"Gets it from his father's side," Mom said.

I wrapped some Arrowroots in a napkin.

"Close the door behind you, sweetheart," Mom said, as I tramped up the stairs.

I kicked the door shut so they'd hear, set my snack on my desk, and dropped to the floor. I pressed an ear to the hardwood. The living room was below. Some nights I fell asleep on the floor, listening to *Playhouse 90*, *Bat Masterson*, *Alfred Hitchcock*, *The Untouchables*, *Jack Paar*. The nights my mother couldn't sleep were the best TV-listening nights for me.

"I'm not accusing you, Emily. As I said, it's something you need to be aware of. First, your husband dies from a blow to the temple and now Harvey Malbasic suffers the same. We've got a pattern here."

"What pattern? I was a hundred miles away when Alex had his accident."

"I'm just saying, these are coincidences the Court will look at should Harvey succumb."

"He assaulted me, Ken. He assaulted me." She must have known the policeman to have called him by name. I did not know how she knew him.

"It's your word against his. He is the school principal, don't forget. Well respected. Unblemished record. Military service. And it's not as if you didn't have motive."

"Motive? I didn't have a motive. I went to see him because of the letter he—"

"Revenge, Mrs. Berry."

"What are you talking about?"

"He did strap your son, after all."

"What? When? Leo never said—"

"Leo, it would appear, has earned himself a reputation in recent weeks. And hardly desirable. Seems it's not only his height he gets from his father's side. From what I hear, your husband was quite the hothead in his day."

"No, he wasn't. That's ridiculous."

"According to some . . ."

"They told you wrong."

"We're not here to accuse."

"Then why are you here?"

"All we want is to set the record straight. One more time, from the beginning, tell me exactly what happened."

There was a long pause. Long enough to eat my cookies and drink my milk. My mother might have been lighting up another cigarette, too, ruminating on her strategy.

"I gave you the letter he sent home with Leo. You read it."

"You realize it's dated the same day Leo received the strap?"

"What's that supposed to mean?"

"You tell me."

"How? The first I heard about the strap was five minutes ago."

"Okay. Fine. You didn't know your son was strapped. Mr. Malbasic wanted to see you. Go on."

"Because he wanted to help Leo."

"Right. The letter."

"Like I told you, he put his hand on my shoulder and as he ushered me into his office, he asked if anyone had ever told me how much I look like Gene Tierney."

"The actress."

"Yes."

"I can see that. You do a little. Well, in her heyday, I imagine. And had anyone?"

"Anyone what?"

"Told you this before?"

"Yes. *He had*. Mr. Malbasic had. Several times. I reminded him and we laughed."

"So you liked it?"

"Yes and no. It was very flattering. But it also made me uneasy. Like he was flirting with me."

"But you didn't discourage him. . . ."

"It was just his way, I thought. You know, being complimentary. But this afternoon was different, Ken. The moment he shut his office door he grabbed me—grabbed me right here."

"On your behind? Would that be accurate?"

"Yes."

"A grab or a squeeze? Two times ago . . . let me see . . . ah, yes . . . here it is . . . you called it a squeeze."

"Either way, he did it intentionally. It was firm. His whole hand. I could feel his fingers."

"A grab then. Not a squeeze."

"It was both. It started out as a grab but ended up as a squeeze."

"Uh-uh. I see. And then?"

"I jumped, of course."

"That's all? Earlier, you said you spoke out."

"I cried out. From surprise. He'd never been so forward before."

"You're saying this wasn't the first time you'd been intimate with him, then?"

"No. I am not saying that at all. It was the first time he'd ever touched me."

"Surely, the two of you had shaken hands."

"Yes, other than that, I mean."

"And then?"

"He could see I was flustered. He laughed, winked at me like he'd meant no harm. I laughed, too. Perhaps he hadn't."

"You stated earlier that you also winked at him?"

"Only to put him at ease. In case I'd misunderstood. You know, over-reacted? He wanted to help Leo. I was afraid I'd jeopardize that. It's easy to read people the wrong way. I didn't want to make a mountain out of a molehill."

"How do you think he interpreted your wink?"

"He didn't see it. His back was turned. He was taking his seat. And I took mine. He opened a file folder and started talking about Leo."

"He had a lot to say about your son."

"Yes."

"Good things?"

Mom made a clicking noise with her tongue and lips. Far as I could tell, she lit up another. "I can't remember. I was too distraught to listen."

"So you *were* angry at him, then?"

"Not angry. Ashamed. I couldn't stop thinking how he'd touched me. It wasn't an accident. It was a blatant pass. He's a married man. I was embarrassed. For myself. For him. For his family. For my son."

"Your son wasn't present."

"Of course not. But I was there because of Leo. And Mr. Malbasic had suddenly made it about me."

"And this is when you picked up the paperweight and struck him in the head."

"I never hit him with anything."

"There was blood on the owl."

"I didn't hit him."

"But you shoved him, did you not?"

"I didn't realize he'd stopped talking. It felt like hours. But when I looked at the clock on his desk, it was no more than ten minutes. He was calling my name. 'Emily? Emily?'"

"Are you sure it wasn't 'Mrs. Berry, Mrs. Berry,' Mrs. Berry?"

"Were you there, Officer? Were you? Because it seems to me you're far more interested in your version of events than mine."

"Continue. Please."

More silence. And then: "He wanted to know what I thought of his plan. 'So, what do you think?' he said. 'Does it sound reasonable for young Mr. Leo? Something we could work on together? Bi-weekly sit-downs, perhaps, you and me, to monitor his progress—work out the kinks?' I thanked him. Told him I would need to think about it. I stood to leave and next I knew he had his arms around me and was sticking his tongue in my mouth. I tried to get away and he fell. I screamed. His secretary came running in. The ambulance came. I went home. And now you're here, as if the entire fiasco was my fault."

I watched the policemen leave from my window. Jack was still outside, on the sidewalk, in the same spot I'd left him almost an hour earlier. I shouted down to him. "She's not dead."

"You didn't tell me Mr. Malbasic strapped you," my mother said.

"Are you going to jail?" I said.

TWELVE

The Justice League of Angels

Mrs. Crawford put Susan Burgess, Annie Barker, and Charles Dahl-Packer in charge of our class's get-well card for Mr. Malbasic. They were given a large sheet of white Bristol board, which they folded in half. The card was almost done when Pecker coughed glue onto it.

"Were you eating glue?" Mrs. Crawford asked him.

"It was an accident," he said.

Pecker was relieved of his duties and sent to the bathroom to wash his mouth and chin. Susan and Annie started over with a sheet of yellow Bristol board. They were not happy, but it was the only colour Mrs. Crawford had to offer.

Susan was the best artist in our class. On the front of the card, she drew a picture of the cannon on Mount Pelion, with flowers and *GET WELL SOON!!!* shooting from the cannon. Each word was a different colour and each succeeding line was larger than the line that came before it. Inside, she drew more flowers and used green pipe cleaners for stems. Annie came up with the poem.

We're sad you fell.
We hope you get well.
Come back to school soon
And please visit our room.

Yours truly,
Mrs. Crawford's 4th Grade Class

I thought it was pretty good and told Susan and Annie so. I liked how the pipe cleaners intertwined with the poem. "Pecker thought of that," Susan said. "Too bad he had to go and eat the glue."

Mrs. Crawford instructed Annie to bring the card from desk to desk, so everyone could sign their name. "Neatly, children," she said. "Principal Malbasic frowns upon poor penmanship. He'll see your name and know who was careless."

As Annie began her rounds, Mrs. Crawford whispered in my ear. "It's best for all concerned if you don't sign the card. You can pretend to write, so you don't feel singled out, but don't actually, okay?"

I didn't want to sign it, anyhow. And I didn't pretend to, either. Annie couldn't believe it when I handed the card right back to her. "But—but—"

"Keep moving, Annie, honey," Mrs. Crawford said.

At recess, Annie asked me why I didn't sign the card.

"Do you ever wish you had a different mother?"

"How can you think such a thing?"

"You're lucky your mom is old."

"And you're lucky your mom is young. You'll have her a lot longer than I'll have mine."

"Old mothers are better. You don't have to watch out for them so much."

"You watch out for her?"

"People have been telling me I'm the man of the house since I was five."

"If my father died I'd never stop crying."

"Do you think my mother's pretty?"

"What?"

"My mother. Do you think she's pretty?"

"You're acting really weird, Gus. What's going on?"

"I wish she wasn't."

"Can't you be happy about anything? Anything at all?"

"Nothing bad ever happens to you."

"You sound as if you wish something would."

"Mr. Malbasic thinks my mother is pretty. That's why he's in the hospital."

"You're making even less sense than usual."

"Never mind."

"You don't know anything. You really don't."

"Oh, yeah? Really, Annie? I know stuff you wouldn't want to know."

"Think so, do you? You think you've got it so hard. Poor, poor Gloomy Gus. I've got news for you, Mister, you're not the only one. My mother had nine babies before she had me. And every single one of them died. You think nothing bad ever happens to me? Nine dead babies happened to me. Do you know what it's like to be the only one who didn't die? Do you know how hard it is? Do you know the first thing I remind myself every single morning? 'Don't die, today, Annie. You'll kill your parents if you do.' I told my dad once. And do you know what he said? He said he was disappointed in me. He said I should feel privileged, because God had chosen me to live my brothers' and sisters' lives for them. And I shouldn't ever worry, because I had nine little guardian angels watching out for me."

"But that's good. They'll keep you safe."

"No. It makes it worse. It's not only Mommy and Daddy I can't let down, it's my nine angels, too. Do you know what my mother calls me? Her 'sweet gift from God.' She says the others were meant to die so I could be born— that everything they were, and ever would be, is wrapped up in me. It's my job to live a long, long life in their honour. And it's their job to protect me so that I do."

"Do you know what they're protecting you from? Did your mom say?"

"Of course not. She doesn't know. Do you know what you're protecting your mother from?"

"Sort of. Well, not exactly."

"If having a pretty mom is the worst thing in your life, Gus, you don't know how lucky you are."

"I didn't sign the card because of my mother. Mr. Malbasic tried to kiss her and when she tried to get away he fell down and banged his head. My mother might go to jail."

"Oh, Gus . . ." Annie touched my arm same way she'd stroke a kitten. Her eyes glistened. "I think you and your mom need my angels more than I do, right now. I'll pray for her, okay? I'll pray Mr. Malbasic gets better and I'll pray your mother doesn't go to jail."

"Maybe you could pray for her to be less pretty, too."

She groaned. "I pray for only good things, Gus. Not bad."

"It'd be a good thing for me."

"Your angels, Annie. The nine of them. You think they're like the Justice League of America?"

"Are there girls in the Justice League?"

"Wonder Woman."

"They could be, then."

"The Justice League of Angels."

It may not sound like it from what I've told you so far, but I think of Annie as often as I do Jack.

How can I not?

❤THIRTEEN

God save our gracious Gus

I got the mumps and missed two weeks of school. I'd planned on a leisurely binge of comic books and game shows, until Mrs. Crawford and Mom conspired for Jack to bring my homework to the Marquee, where my mother picked it up after work. A couple of days in, Jack slipped a note into my speller.

Gus, I found something really neat in Hanna Park.
How are your mumps?
Are you eating Jell-O?
See ya!
    Jack

The Monday I returned to school, I saw Mr. Malbasic in the parking lot. It was his first day back, too. Annie's prayers had worked. For him, at least. The jury was still out for Mom and me.

I scurried ahead, made sure he didn't see me. I had prayed plenty, too: *Please make the bump on Mr. Malbasic's head give him Trenton amnesia. Please make Mr. Malbasic forget about Mom and me. Please make my mother look like other mothers, just not like Pecker's mother.* I would have prayed for Mr. Malbasic to die, but then Mom would have been up on murder charges.

An assembly was held in the school basement to celebrate the principal's return. Dufferin didn't have a gym or an auditorium, so Mr. Pennington, the caretaker, would set up folding chairs. For the stage, he'd drag together eight plywood platforms to create one big platform.

Jack, Annie, and a bunch of dorks—that somehow included Mickey Mental in his Scout uniform (*are you kidding me!*) and Pecker (*what the hell!*)—went on stage to present Mr. Malbasic with a wolverine for the taxidermy collection. The wolverine was poised on all fours on a base of sparkly fake snow. A fleshy, bony, bloody thing was clamped between its jaws. Ranger Clegg, the taxidermist, gave a brief lecture on wolverines and showed us a National Film Board of Canada documentary about the Edmonton Eskimos of the Canadian Football League, after which he apologized for bringing the wrong movie, but hoped we enjoyed it, regardless. Janet Barstool, a brainy first-grade girl with glasses and two yards of pigtails, read the inscription that accompanied the wolverine:

> *February 1961*
> *To Principal Malbasic*
> *for his tenacity of spirit.*

Mr. Malbasic thanked us for our prayers and well wishes. "My mishap serves to highlight the need for caution in the most humdrum of daily pursuits . . ." My thoughts wandered to his tongue and its failure to dart, if bumping his head had cured him of the habit. The Unexplained thrived on miracles triggered by blows to the brain. People who could suddenly speak Chinese or predict the future or sing opera or draw like Jon Gnagy, the guy who taught art on TV in fifteen-minute lessons.

"Would Leo Berry please stand up? Leo Berry? Leo? Leo Berry . . . is he here? Leo?" Mr. Malbasic's words didn't click until the kids around me started laughing and pointing and Mrs. Crawford hollered from the aisle for me to stand the hell up. I obeyed, an A-bomb in my belly, Mr. Malbasic's grin the detonator. "If not for the quick thinking of Mr. Berry's mother in summoning assistance, it is entirely likely I would not be with you today. What do you say? Three Dufferin cheers for Leo Berry and his mother? Hip hip . . ."

My ass was back in my seat before the whole goddamn school completed their goddamn first hurrah. And in the midst of the hoopla and applause, the one word I had resisted for so long formally, officially, and everlastingly entered my lexicon.

Fuck.

The fucking noun, adjective, adverb, and verb in all its fucking permutations. (Or the nine I was aware of, that is.)

Fucking.

Fuck you.

Fuck me.

Fucked-up.

Fucker.

Fuckers.

Fucked.

Fuckface.

Fuckin' eh.

More hand-clapping and cheering followed, and the piano started playing, and the whole school leaped to its collective feet, and everybody sang to God to "save our gracious Queen." I didn't care how noble, victorious, and glorious the Queen was, I didn't have it in me to even hum. Far as I was concerned, God would be better off saving nobody.

In closing, Mr. Malbasic volunteered volunteers to help Mr. Pennington put away the chairs. "You. You. You. You. You. You. You. And you."

Lloyd Gonna-kick-u-in-the-nuts. Dandruff-Wayne. Crates. Wayne Trumpeter. Long-Arm Wayne. Vito From Italy. Double Al. And Leo Fucking-fucked-up-fuck-fuck Berry.

I rasped to Mr. Pennington: "Sir, I just got over a deadly case of the mumps, sir." I palpated my glands with delicacy, impressed upon him the fragile nature of my recovery. "Sir?"

"Start with this row," he said. "Stack 'em there."

I'd never thought of chairs as weapons before. But I didn't blame my fellow volunteers. The raps to my knees and ankles, I had them coming. On top of all previous transgressions, I was now the dumb fuck who had saved the life of the most hated school principal in the history of Dufferin Fucking School.

"I want you to know I didn't cheer when Mr. Malbasic did that to you," Annie said.

"I saw. You and Jack were the only ones."

"To be a teacher's pet is hard enough, but principal's pet . . . Oh, Gus, that was so mean of him. And then, to make you clean up with Alan Allen and the others . . . It must have been awful."

"*Daniel in the Lion's Den*."

"Yes. Exactly."

"At least my mom's in the clear."

"You've got to tell her what he did to you today."

"And have her go see him again? Uh-uh."

"You're very brave, Gus. You really are."

"I wish I was dead."

"Why do you always say that? Come to church with me. Just once. You'll see, there are better ways to handle things."

"Like how? Wish harder?"

The school was a block behind us before Jack commented on the limp I'd made no effort to hide. "Those guys did a number on you, eh?"

"Folding chairs are the switchblades of furniture," I said.

"Malbasic really set you up, eh? Guess he's still got it in for you for punching out Pecker. That was my fault. I mean, you did it for me and all. I should tell him. . . ."

"Nothing to do with you."

"It's about your mom, then?"

"What about my mom?" I'd told Annie and only Annie about Malbasic's crush.

"Our mothers are friends, Gus. They talk. I hear stuff."

"Well don't, okay?"

"And there you go, again. Friends help friends. Friends listen to friends. But you . . . It's like you're the only one who's got stuff going on. You don't care anything about anyone except yourself. You're an asshole, man. A real asshole, sometimes."

"You been talking to Annie?"

"Why? Your girlfriend call you an asshole, too?"

Sure, Jack and Annie had their worries. Every kid did. Only Richie Rich was spared. But for Jack and Annie to put me in the same boat with them . . . Their dads weren't dead. Their moms hadn't been jumped by the school principal. Their moms hadn't been on the fast track to Sing Sing. They didn't have Mrs. Dahl-Packer gunning for them. I'm not saying I held the exclusive on misery. Not by a long shot. There was this school book we had—*Visits in Other Lands*. Bunga lived in the jungle, ate melons, and didn't have a shirt to his name. Netsook, the Eskimo kid, froze his nuts off and chewed blubber. Hell, not having TV was the least of these kids' worries. I got it. But I had my burdens, too, and they were as valid as any. Bunga. Netsook. Suvan of the Steppe. Simba of the Congo. Pedro of the Andes. *Visits in Other Lands* could just as easily have had a chapter on Gus of Trenton.

"Whatever is coming is coming, Gus. It's like Chicago before Mrs. O'Leary's cow kicks over the lantern. Trenton has a cow, too. Except we don't know where it is or what damage it's going to do. So stop with your 'poor me' bullshit. It's 'poor us,' man. 'Poor everybody.' Something is coming. I feel it. You feel it. More than ever, we need to stick together."

"And if we're wrong?" I said.

"Disappointing, sure. But we'll get over it."

"We'll grow up, you mean," I said accusingly.

"Like you think you got a choice?"

Anyone who claims he never once in all his life didn't wish for disaster is a liar. Jack and me, we did more than wish. The town's DNA had us banking on it. An uneventful life had no place in our futures.

I was going for the big mope when Jack shifted gears. "So, are you ready?" he said.

"For what?"

"To be a hero."

FOURTEEN

There goes Marilyn Monroe

"Tell me, Gus, you ever hear something so crazy you put it out of your head without a second thought? And then, later on, could be days or weeks, something happens that puts the crazy thought right back?"

With Jack, my fallback face was nothing but attentive, while my brain was often happy to settle for the gist. "Yeah. Sure." The slack in my jaw would've done a Morlock proud.

"A couple of months ago, Mr. Blackhurst traps me in the Marquee. You never know when he'll come out with another circus fire, so I'm always sure to listen. And this time, out of the blue, he says he used to be in pictures and his wife was an actress and they made movies—get this, man!—right here in Trenton. A big studio near Hanna Park."

"Home movies, more like it."

"Yeah, I know. Totally loony. And then he says, they called the town Hollywood North."

"Hey! Look! There goes Marilyn Monroe."

"Thing is, Mr. Blackhurst might not be so nutty. This thing I told you I found . . ."

A car passed. Mrs. Proctor, my old first grade teacher, in the passenger seat. She waved. Another car, a station wagon, kids' noses on the windows. And then Mr. Malbasic and his Buick, his hands at ten and two, observing us as he coasted through the stop sign and rounded the corner.

Jack prodded me beyond the reach of prying eyes into a small clearing between a thicket of cedars and a leafy hedge. The watchtower of a rickety Victorian looked down upon us. "The Malbasics live there," I warned.

"Don't worry," Jack said, and we crouched low at the base of the hedge, branches scratching at our backs.

Jack took a breath, released it slowly, giving me the once-over, as if my fidelity might be in question. And with a here-goes-nothing shrug, he pulled four cards from his canvas schoolbag. Each was about the size of a shirt cardboard.

He revealed them one by one.

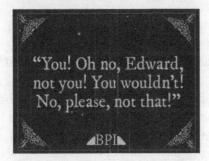

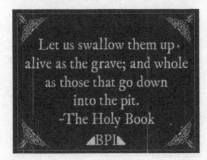

Meanwhile, upriver,
bitter Fate deals a
dastardly hand . . .

BPI

"Neat. They're like what you see in old-time movies," I said.

"Second I saw 'em, I thought of Mr. Blackhurst's story."

"It's true, then?"

"You tell me. He said the movie studio had been near Hanna Park. That's where I found them—the swampy stretch by the train tracks."

"I've been there a zillion times. You and me, we were there together."

"That's how it is with lost crap, man. Once it's made itself known, you wonder how you ever missed it. This old metal box was sitting under leaves and deadwood, but not like anybody couldn't see it. And the cards inside— every one as good as these, Gus. Forty-seven of them."

"Show me. Show me."

"There's something I'm going to want you to do."

"I don't care. Just show me."

My limp had miraculously vanished as we arrived at his garage.

Jack had wrapped the individual cards in Saran and stored them on his shelves, divided among a half-dozen candy cartons. It felt strange to hold them, the cardboard weightless, yet heavy in hand. I shuffled them endlessly, reading, imagining.

A boy chases his dreams.
A girl follows her heart.
A boy searches his soul.

BPI

"Been over them so many times," Jack said, "I know most by heart."

"And that down there—the BPI—what's that?"

"Part of the mystery."

"You're gonna be in the paper again, Jack. You gotta be. They're amazing. This one. Look at this one. What are you waiting for?"

"Yeah, well, the paper—that's what I wanted to talk to you about. I'd like it to be you, Gus."

"Me what?"

"Act like you found them."

"You crazy?"

"You'll be doing me a favour."

"Why? Because you don't want to lose any more friends. And you figure I don't have any to lose. Is that it?"

"Hey, c'mon. You know I'm not like that."

"Anybody can be a jerk."

"Yeah. Even you."

"I'm just saying . . . And she's not my girlfriend."

"What?"

"Annie. Before. You called her my girlfriend."

"Friend. Girlfriend. What's the diff?"

"You know darn well what the difference is."

"Man, you're an idiot. Look, if you really want to know, my mom and dad aren't getting along so well lately, okay? That's all there is to it."

"Your dad shouts a lot."

"What? How do you know?"

"I just do."

"Yeah. Right. I guess you heard him when you were hiding out across the street. When you were on my tail every other second. You think I didn't see you? You think I didn't know? And you accuse me of being a jerk. . . ."

"I didn't—"

"I would've had to be blind. I thought you'd break the damn scale outside the Marquee you were on it so much."

"I was just—"

"I don't give a crap what it was. You're a weirdo. A freak. Think I don't know? I'm a weirdo, too. And if I'm able to give your stupid spying ass a pass, the least you can do is give me a pass."

"Does he hit you?"

"What?"

"Your dad."

"It's not like that. Just him and my mom. They're always fighting or whatever. And, these days, well, it's . . . I dunno."

"I'm glad I don't have a dad."

"Me, right now, making a big deal out of something I found, well . . . I mean, my sisters and all, it wouldn't be good. Like all I cared about was myself. You'll be helping me out. You'll be helping us out—getting to the bottom of these cards—the Hollywood thing."

"It'd be lying."

"Like you're not the expert. . . ."

"Shut up."

"It'll be fun, Gus."

"Why not wait till your parents aren't fighting? Tell everybody about the cards then."

"If I had fifty years, maybe. The other night, Mom was talking about divorce."

"Like divorce divorce? Like Elizabeth Taylor?"

"Imagine how your mom will feel, seeing you in the paper and all. Think about it, Gus. How proud she'll be. And Mr. Malbasic, once you're in the paper, you'll see, he'll be nicer. They'll treat you special. You'll be a hero. It's what you've always wanted, isn't it?"

"What do I have to do?"

"Nothing to it. Put on a good show. Act like you found them. And have a good time."

"I'm not so sure."

"Look, the cards aren't going anywhere. Think about it, okay?"

"And if I decide I won't, you gonna be pissed off?"

"There's your biggest problem, Gus. You think everyone thinks like you. I'm not you. I don't waste time moaning over every stupid thing. We're friends. I don't see that changing for anything, even if you do."

FIFTEEN

A bad week

Tuesday, with Jack at the dentist and me alone, four coworkers from Monday's assembly showed up to host a celebration of their own. The kid whose mother had saved Mr. Malbasic's life was the guest of honour. I knew it was coming, just not so soon.

Double Al and Lloyd blocked the path ahead, Long-Arm Wayne and Vito from Italy behind.

"I'm just getting over a deadly case of the mumps," I said.

"Don't kiss us, then." Double Al could be funny, though no Buddy Hackett.

"Vancouver," I said, racking my brains for the Italian curse the truck driver had given Jack. I made the *L* with my arm, chopped my bicep. "Van Johnson."

They hustled me through the cedars and into the small clearing where Jack and I had been twenty-fours earlier.

"Yep, Coffin Canyon.
One way in.
No way out."

BPI

The bozos didn't take the precautions Jack had. Should Malbasic look down from his watchtower window, he'd have the best seat in the house. Knowing him, he'd relish every jab, hook, and uppercut. I took some satisfaction in the image; his huffing and puffing up all those stairs to the watchtower. With his barn-door butt and roadhouse gut, he'd be dead before he made it to the top.

"All set, Charlene," Double Al called out, and Pecker came stumbling through the bushes he'd been hiding behind. He righted himself, charged, and swung his schoolbag at my head. I ducked, took a glancing blow off an ear, leaving Vito to catch the leather smack in the kisser. The maniac was at Pecker's throat in a flash and might well have choked the miserable weenie had Double Al not pulled him off.

"Fists, Charlene, fists. The deal was, we hold him, you punch him. Don't go swinging that thing, again. You could hurt somebody."

Pecker apologized, and Vito spit in his face. "Vaffanculo."

Aha, that was it! Vaf-fan-cu-lo. I reined in my smile, knowing it would make it worse for me. Inappropriate smiles were magnets for fists. Jack suffered the same malady, but he had the fighting smarts to back it up.

"You think it's funny?" Pecker said. "We'll see how funny you find it when I'm done with you. We'll see how you like it." He punched me in the hip, though I think he was aiming for my gut. Or my nuts, knowing him.

"Not so fast, bud." Again, Double Al intervened. "First, you pay up."

Pecker unsnapped his bag and shook the contents onto the grass. Candy, chewing gum, peanuts, chocolates, chips.

Double Al squatted, sifted through the stash. "Where's our smokes?"

Pecker dropped to his knees, plucked out two cigars. "I got these."

"Cigarettes, Charlene. Three packs each. That was the deal."

"But look, guys, look. See. See. I doubled the candy. Look. Chocolate covered peanuts. Ju jubes. Boston Baked Beans. Bridge Mixture. Charms. Everybody likes Charms."

"That wasn't the deal, Charlene." Double Al and his cronies closed in.

"Where my Camels?" Lloyd snarled.

"My Players," Wayne added.

"Wasn't my fault. My Dad was watching. Next time, though. I promise. I'll get them for you next time, I swear. I will. You'll see. But this is good candy. And the cigars, look, see, they're Muriels. That's good, right?"

"No, Charlene. Not good."

"Stop. You're hurting me," Pecker said.

I capitalized on the contract dispute, took off like a shot.

In the back pages of the Wednesday's *Record*, there was a small piece about Mom and how "her quick thinking saved the life of beloved, long-time Dufferin School Principal, Harvey Malbasic." Mom's refusal to be interviewed for the article was attributed to "the comely widow Berry's characteristic humility."

Mom trashed the paper without checking out the sales.

Later, talking to Dottie on the phone, Mom said, "Better for him than the truth, I suppose. Yes. You're right. Better for me, too." I'd never heard my mother more dejected. I felt sad for her. Wished I could help.

On Thursday morning, as I waited on the corner for Jack, a shiny black Cadillac pulled to the curb and the window rolled down. I figured the man at the wheel was looking for directions, until I saw the woman in the passenger seat.

"You just won't quit, will you?" Mrs. Dahl-Packer said.

"Jesus, no," I said, under my breath, both swearing and praying.

"We have decided to send Charles to private school in Port Hope," Mr. Dahl-Packer said. (Or was he plain Mr. Packer?) He parted his hair in the middle. His eyeglasses were thick with a tinge of pink. He sat on a wood-beaded seat cover. "My wife tells me you are the boy responsible for Charles's spate of difficulties. You have made his life utterly wretched, it would seem. Are you proud of yourself, young man?"

"I'm just getting over a real bad case of the mumps," I said.

Mrs. Dahl-Packer grabbed my ear and twisted till I faced her. *Cripes! How'd she pull that off? I hadn't seen her get out of the car.* As before, she hoisted me up till we were nose to breast. "I know your mother. I know her type, the frivolous small-town flirt who married the handsome ne'er-do-well—the local Billy Bigelow. . . ."

"Alexander. His name was Alexander."

". . . and, tragically, discarded by the wayside to raise his misbegotten progeny. The apple does not fall far from the tree, I am afraid." She smelled of orange juice and spearmint. "You and your mother share a sickness that festers in the mind till it manifests in the physical. Serious illness is inevitable. It is written all over you." She released my ears, placed her hands on my shoulders. "But I want you to know, Leo Berry, my husband and I will be waiting. We will do everything in our power to ensure that you and your dear mother receive the exact dose and type of medicine you both so richly deserve."

"My mother didn't do anything," I said.

"Evidently. Your breeding and belligerence attest to the fact."

On Friday, after lunch, Janet Barstool interrupted our class to give Mrs. Crawford a note. (Janet was the office monitor of the week, a privilege never before extended to a first grader.) My teacher popped three fingers over a truant whoop, and happily zeroed in on me. "Leo! Mr. Malbasic wants to see you. Right this minute, dear." Any more joy and you would've sworn she'd just won a Whirlpool washer on *Queen for a Day*. She was under the impression untold delights awaited me down the hall. I was, after all, the lovely boy whose courageous mother had saved the life of the revered Mr. Malbasic.

Mrs. Miller, the school secretary, and Janet Barstool applauded me when I came into the office. Mrs. Miller also said, "Splendid."

Mr. Malbasic guided me to his office, his arm a cobra on my shoulder. He shut the door behind him, steered me past his desk and into the storage room attached. He shut this door, too.

His tongue darted. Clearly, I'd jumped the gun on the bump on his head and the loss of his tic.

"Do you have any idea why you are here, Mr. Berry?"

I searched the space, the shelves of stationery supplies, the mimeograph machine. "To count pens, sir?" I said, holding out hope mindless tasks were in store.

He chuckled. "My goodness, you are a card. Unfortunately, I was remiss during your previous visit. I neglected to give you your due. Silly me." He pulled the strap out of thin air, a sleight of hand I could have done without. "Today, we are going to make up for my oversight. Your hands, please, Mr. Berry. How many is it I owe you? Ah, yes, allowing for the one from our previous session, that would be seven on each for a grand total of eight on each."

"I'm just getting over a deadly case of the mumps, sir."

"Left or right, first?"

I held out my left and the strap flew down. This wasn't going to be easy. He was putting way more behind it than he had before. I began to offer up my right but he grabbed my wrist, held the left in position. "Not yet, you don't." And he hit the hand a second time.

"I see confusion," he said. "Let me explain. Since my mishap, I have suffered the occasional bout of what doctors call diplopia. Double vision, perhaps? More familiar? The good news is, it comes and goes. The bad news is, it has come at this inopportune moment. So, in order to be certain, it's best I strike twice—the hand I see and the hand I imagine I see."

"But you didn't miss, sir. Look. It's red. You hit me square on. Both times."

"Oh, yes, another thing. While this room is quite soundproof, I would be most appreciative, nonetheless, if you would refrain from excessive drama. Undue howling, screeching, bellyaching, or similar incivilities. The others, Mrs. Miller and Miss Barstool, you wouldn't want to let them down, now, would you? Or Mrs. Crawford? Indeed, the entire school has been led to believe you're quite the peach—that your mother saved my life. I can't imagine where they got that idea. Can you?"

I did a quick calculation: 7 x 2 x 2 = 28.

Twenty-eight, Jesus.

Who'd ever survived twenty-eight?

12:00 ❸ THE KENTUCKIAN—Western
Walter Matthau bullwhips the hell out of Burt Lancaster for four senseless minutes, but does Burt give up? Uh-uh.

I would not cry. I would be Burt. On my feet and fighting back. Okay, maybe not fighting back. Going at it with your school principal was a one-way ticket to Boys Farm. But I would be on my feet, at least.

By the fourth (or eighth, depending), I was Jell-O in a loose caboose, my legs no sturdier than Twizzlers. And that peculiar noise ricocheting off my teeth and cheeks, it was not crying. I can't say what I was doing, but *I was not crying.*

By the sixth (or twelfth, depending), tears filled my eyes. Rolled down my cheeks. Salted my lips. It might have looked like crying. Might've felt like crying. It wasn't crying. I was not crying.

By the ninth (or eighteenth, depending), my hands were dead. But not the rest of me. And I was not crying.

By the fourteenth (or twenty-eighth), I promised myself, first chance I got, I'd kill the bastard. And sobbing, by the way, is not crying. Sobbing is mourning. Because you take fourteen on each, you know by instinct some part of you has died, your hands the least of it.

"There, there. That wasn't so bad, now, was it? No worse for wear. Now clean yourself up. Dry your eyes. Attend to the swelling. And I'll return when you've regained your composure." He handed me a box of Kleenex and a bottle of witch hazel. He exited the storage room, shutting off the light, closing the door.

I shrivelled to the floor, the cold metal of the cabinet against my back. Splashed witch hazel over my hands. Splashed witch hazel over everything. And waited in the dark. Waited. A couple of hours, easy. Until the bell to end the school day had rung. And then some. Before Principal Malbasic checked back in, removed me from solitary.

He sat me at his desk. I would have grabbed the brass owl paperweight and pulped his head, had I been capable of grabbing, and pulping. He'd beat Pecker's hands to lobster claws. Mine were plump red pillows.

"Do you know what this is?" He cleared a space and placed a sheet on the desk before me. "This is your school record. It will follow you for the rest of your empty life. Go ahead. Read it. Take your time."

I didn't read it. Didn't need to. The words he wanted me to see popped from the page like neon on a dark road.

troublemaker **_remorseless_** **_malcontent_**

slow **_deficient_**

reckless

unpredictable

violent **_unfit_**

"I am not an unreasonable man, Mr. Berry. I want only the best for all my students. Yes, you included. If anything, I have been assured I am an excessively fair-minded individual. It is why I am, again, requesting you take a note home to your mother. I would like nothing more than for her to reconsider working with me, so that we may expunge the most grievous offences from your record and successfully foster your scholarship and tenuous humanity."

Heck, how many bad people did this town have? And why were all of them out to get me?

I knew the type. (Mrs. Dahl-Packer was another.) The villain who blabbed too much. Bandied about fifty-dollar words, sentences engineered from the nuts and bolts of an Erector Set. Jack was long-winded, too, but he used his powers for good. Malbasic was long-winded with malice. Malbasic. Dahl-Packer. They could saw you in half with their smiles.

He came around to my side of the desk, motioned me to my feet. He bypassed my useless hands and slid the envelope into my hip pocket. He patted my butt, winked. "Fear not. It will all come out in the wash."

I'd kill him. I'd get a gun and kill him. I'd kill them all. Dahl-Packer, she'd get hers. Double Al and Mickey Mental. The Waynes. Even if they weren't long-winded, I'd kill them, too.

Do not feel sorry for me. Sympathy is pity with an extra syllable. Above all, do not start liking me.

I am not a good person.

I could have been.

I wanted to be.

But I am not.

SIXTEEN

The woman who went fishing from Dam 1 on the Trent–Severn

I didn't read Malbasic's note. It was blackmail, I knew, my future the trade-off. I ripped it up, double-flushed the pieces.

I hid my crippled hands from Mom. I would not give her cause to go anywhere near the school. I sat on them. Pocketed them. Crossed my arms and buried them in my armpits. Practised the military *at ease*, wrists stitched to backside. And when I had no option, I willed them to function. To grip a glass. To twist a fork. To turn the TV dials. Even so, Mom would have noticed the swelling and redness soon enough had Dottie's death not offered up distraction.

Dottie Swartz, formerly Lange, drowned on the Saturday morning after my Friday drubbing. My mother got the news late in the afternoon. I was upstairs in my room, reading, when the phone rang.

She cried out. The same heartbroken shriek I'd heard when I was three, the policeman at our door with news of Dad. She fell to her knees for Dottie, too, her forehead pressed to the rug in the living room.

Dottie took a header off Dam 1 into the Trent–Severn and was swept downriver. She'd bounced off a concrete buttress as she tumbled and, according to husband Helmut, "Went out like a light before she hit the river. Swallowed up like a Raggedy-Ann."

She and Helmut had been fishing from the dam. They'd been married two months to the day. Her wedding was the first I'd been to. My mother was her best man, or so she and Dottie joked.

Dottie had given up on love and marriage, when Helmut came wooing. He'd relocated from Kitchener, Ontario, to take a job at Central Bridge. She'd met him on a Tuesday evening at Arthur Murray Dance Studio, where Helmut taught the cha-cha. But you knew most of this, already, if you've been paying attention.

The wedding was fun. Pigs in blankets. Chicken livers in bacon. Deviled eggs. Party sandwiches—tuna, salmon. Spam with pineapple. Rainbow Jell-O molds with tangerine. Vanilla wedding cake with buttercream frosting.

Dottie and Helmut danced up a storm. Mom and Dottie badgered me to dance, too, wouldn't leave me alone, but I'd have none of it or them. Three dumbest things on Earth: Neckties, earrings, and dancing.

The day after Dottie drowned, I told Jack I'd be his front, claim I found the cards in Hanna Park.

Mom was deep in the dumps and sliding deeper. I wasn't sure she'd ever climb out. But I had to give it a shot. Seeing me in the paper. A hero. Gus the Finder. *Okay, okay—Leo the Finder.* That'd put a smile on her face. And Mom and me, we'd be sticking it to Malbasic, too. He'd hate to see any good come from us.

"Once we show Mr. McGrath . . . You've got to promise you won't tell him or anybody it was me. I'm warning you, not ever."

"Okay. Fine."

"Swear to God."

"I swear to God."

"Swear on your mother's life, Gus."

"C'mon, Jack. What's the big—"

"Forget it, then."

"No. Wait. Stop. I swear." I mumbled a wobbly, "On my mother's life."

"Don't you forget."

I nodded with vigour. Proving myself a worthy sidekick could be exhausting. A never-ending audition.

PRODUCTION —————————————

DIRECTOR —————————————

CAMERA —————————————

DATE   SCENE   TAKE

Third Reel

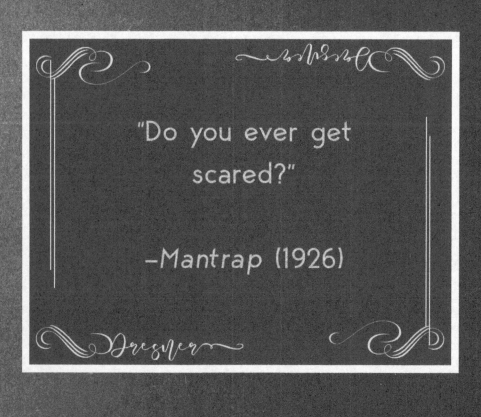

"Do you ever get
scared?"

−Mantrap (1926)

# ONE

1988 and I was at a Texaco in Oshawa
to confront the sink that killed my dad

A 1988 Ford Tempo does not turn on a dime. But it came close as I swerved into the Texaco on the other side of the highway.

I couldn't say definitively it was my father's fatal Texaco, though the cranky pumps and peeling paint gave me cause to believe it could be. I surveyed the grounds, saw no wreaths, decaying bouquets, or point-of-interest marker:

ALEXANDER BERRY,
HUSBAND OF EMILY, FATHER OF LEO (AKA GUS),
CRACKED OPEN HIS SKULL ON THIS SPOT IN DECEMBER 1954

I checked out the restroom for old times' sake, unzipped at the urinal, contemplated the sink. *"You can trust your car to the man who wears the star . . ."*

Standing there, soaping up, I concluded it was more likely the toilet that killed Dad, the cops figuring death by sink a softer blow for Mom and me.

Night comes early in January. Darker and dirtier, too. It was cold, though nowhere near as dark, dirty, and cold as Winnipeg. Trust me, I'd have found a way out of the city if I didn't hate it so much, if I didn't believe we deserved each other.

Jack perked up as we entered Port Hope, an hour east of Toronto in good weather and light traffic. "This is where Pecker's parents sent him to school after you punched him out."

This wasn't news.

"Trinity College School. Founded 1865."

Snow was falling.

"Peter Jennings went to Trinity. Think Pecker met him?"

I switched the wipers from low to medium.

"He anchors the evening news on ABC."

Like I didn't know.

"And Joseph Scriven, he writes *What a Friend We Have In Jesus.* No shit, right here in Port Hope, he writes it. And then up and drowns himself."

It wasn't a blizzard, not yet, only the makings of one.

"But why not, eh? Back in Ireland, the guy's bride-to-be drowns, so he runs away to here. And what happens? His next bride-to-be croaks, too. I mean, you got to figure, Jesus wasn't all that good a friend."

On that 1977 visit, clearing out my mother's house, I came across seventeen drug prescriptions in her name. Seventeen. I couldn't tell you what half were for, only where they'd been filled. Packer Family Pharmacy. I put them in a bag, got in the car, and headed straight over. I didn't stop to think. Pushed right up to the pharmacy counter.

"Yes?" Pecker said. He wore a white coat. The prick was a fucking pharmacist.

"You killed my mother," I said.

"Pardon me? Who are you?"

The contents of my bag clattered across the countertop.

He caught a plastic bottle on the rebound and read the label. "Mother," he said with urgency. "Mother." The pills rattled in his hand. "Mother, I need you now."

Mrs. Dahl-Packer poked her head from the dispensary, sidled serenely up to Pecker. She wore a white coat, too. "Yes?" She looked to her son, then to me, and blinked. Pecker handed her the bottle. She read the label. "Oh, it's you," she said.

"You poisoned her."

Her smile took its cruel sweet time to cover the distance, left corner of her wizened mouth to right. "So sorry for your loss."

# TWO

Unicorns in stables

The best lies are unplanned. My forte was the throwaway. The one-liner no one would question, but allowed for backpedalling when someone did. *"What did I say? No, of course not. What I meant was . . ."* The doubt set in only after Jack signed me up to his scheme. "You'll be dealing with a newspaperman, Gus, not some feeb on the playground. And not your mom, either. Mr. McGrath suspects for one second you're pulling the wool over his eyes and he'll strangle you with it. I'm telling you, he can smell bullshit before the bull farts."

Jack put me through the paces, drilled me backwards and forwards on his story. I was sold on it, too, almost believed I *was* the finder, until the Friday we turned on to Quinte Street. "Let's say we found them together, okay?"

"C'mon, Gus, not now. You can do this. It's going to be a cakewalk."

The *Trent Record* was no *Daily Planet* and, his horn-rimmed glasses aside, Bryan McGrath was no Clark Kent.

Hatrack tall and coat-hanger thin, the senior reporter looked nothing like the headshot that ran with his hunting and fishing column; he was a good twenty years older, his hair greyer, eyebrows wilder, mouth meaner. He wasn't anybody I'd ever want to go hunting or fishing with. Or, I suppose, it could've been my recent interactions with local villains had me anticipating the worst from everyone. He came across friendly enough, slapped Jack on the back and glad-handed me short of paralysis. "So, Jack tells me you're a finder, too. Gus, is it?"

"Yes, sir," I said, and with a nod to my mother, relented: "Leo, actually, sir. Leo Berry. Gus is what my friends call me."

"Well then, I'll call you Gus, too. How's that? Jack here tells me you've got something special. I'm eager to see."

He led us from the reception area and into the fog of the newsroom. Clouds of smoke veiled the fluorescents overhead. Cigar stink masked cigarette stink. Three rows of desks, nine desks in total. The clack-clack and ding of Remingtons and Underwoods. Reporters. Those who weren't smoking were chewing. On pens, pencils, toothpicks. Men typing. Men on phones. Men with their feet up. A woman fiddling with her typewriter ribbon. They waved or winked at Jack as we passed.

The woman said, "What's cookin', handsome?"

"Hi, Miss Bridgeman," Jack said. Mary Bridgeman was the society columnist. I hadn't recognized her without the dead fox on her neck.

An old guy covered the mouthpiece of his phone and said, "What'd you dig up this time, son? The Holy Grail or the Lost Dutchman's gold?"

"Neither, sir. But my friend here has a doozy."

"I sure doozy," I said, feeling at ease with my imminent celebrity. I felt so good, in fact, I didn't feel like me.

"Your friend's a regular Jack Benny, eh?" McGrath said.

Yeah, McGrath was all smiles and chuckles as he brought us into his office. I beamed with confidence, as rehearsed. I set the Manila envelope on his desk and slipped out the old-time-movie cards *I'd found*. And, Jesus, McGrath's face ruptured in dumbstruck fury; he was goddamn freaking Dracula and I'd just pulled a crucifix on him. "What the hell. What the hell."

He shut the door to his office with a heavy hand, rolled ink-stained shirtsleeves up ink-stained arms to scabby elbows. He lit a cigarette, tossed the match, glanced at Jack, inhaled, scowled at me, exhaled, contemplated the floor, inhaled, exhaled, picked tobacco from his tongue, stared out the window, inhaled, and sprang—marched me across the floor, behind his desk, and up against the wall, plowed his forearm hard across my chest, and exhaled into my face. Fumes. Threat. Extinction. "Where did you— where did you get these?" I cowered weak and inconsequential, *The Incredible Shrinking Man* astray in the cellar, fresh meat for the resident black widow. "Who gave these to you?"

The heat of his cigarette singed my cheek. Any closer and my left eyebrow would be a three-alarmer. If only I hadn't sworn on my mother's life.

Jack came to my rescue. "Nobody gave them to him," he said. "He found them. Hanna Park. Wasn't it, Gus?"

I blinked frantic confirmation.

McGrath gritted his teeth, waited a beat, and backed off. "Who else has seen them?"

"What's going on?" Jack said. "Sir?"

McGrath cleared two overtaxed ashtrays from a corner of his desk and sat. He took a long, thoughtful drag of his cigarette, examined the length of ash at the tip.

I slunk toward the door, begged Jack to heed my telepathic plea to follow. "Sir?" Jack said. "Mr. McGrath?"

As if all this wasn't cuckoo enough, McGrath chose this moment to regale us with poetry, his delivery hoarse and laden with menace. "'There are strange things done in the midnight sun by the men who moil for gold; And the Arctic trails have their secret tales that would make your blood run cold. . . .'"

"Pardon?" Jack said.

"It's 'The Cremation of Sam McGee,'" I croaked. "Robert Service." It was the only poetry I liked, outside of "Casey at the Bat." Not that I cared much for it in the moment.

"Jesus H. Christ! Can't you see I'm speaking metaphorically? I'm making a point here, boys." McGrath stubbed out his cigarette, crumbled the unfiltered butt between thumb and forefinger. He spun from his perch, pressed a fist to the window, his forehead to his fist. "Not a place on Earth doesn't have its secret tales. Given time, not a place you'd go that wouldn't make your blood run cold. This town . . ." He came at me again. "I'm telling you, this find of yours, let it go. Trust me. For your own good."

"But why?" Damn that Jack. The idiot didn't know when to quit. "We'd heard they used to make movies here. Right? And we were thinking these cards are from back then. They could be, couldn't they?"

"Who filled your head with that hogwash, Levin? Same clowns who told you the town was disaster central? Movies? Trenton?" He slapped his side and guffawed.

"Nobody told me," Jack said.

"Pulled it out of thin air, did you?"

"I heard, that's all. We heard. Gus and me. Right, Gus?"

I said nothing.

"Yeah, and there used to be unicorns in stables across the road, too. Jesus Christ, boys! The two of you, you need to stop now. Cease. Desist. Shut the hell up. They're gonna put you away, you keep mouthing off nonsense. What are you gonna come to me with next, Levin? Hubcaps from a flying saucer?" And to me: "You. The cards—that the lot of 'em?"

"What?" I'd yet to get my head around the unicorns.

"The cards? How many you got?"

"What was it you told me, Gus?" Jack maintained the sham. "Forty-something?"

"Where are they?"

I'd forgotten the answer we'd rehearsed. Fortunately, Jack hadn't. "My garage."

"Ah, the world famous museum of the unexplained, eh? Figures."

"We thought they'd be safer there."

"Yeah. Well. *Safe* doesn't begin to tell the story." McGrath switched it up, a yellow finger, locked, loaded, and aimed between my eyes. "Listen and listen well. You're gonna pack them up, these and whatever else you got. And you're gonna burn every last one. All 'forty-something.' You read me?"

"Yes, sir." My throat was tight. My voice Mickey Mouse. I'd take Malbasic's *twenty-eight* any day over whatever the heck McGrath was dishing out. The principal was out to maim. McGrath was out to God-knows-what.

"No, sir. No." And there was Jack, mouthing off again, like he was debating bedtime with his mom or dad. "Not without a good reason."

"You're mighty protective of something you claim you didn't find, son."

"Gus found them. Hanna Park."

"Then why's it you with all the answers, Levin?"

"You're not being fair. You can't tell us to burn them for no good reason. I won't do it."

"What do you know about fair? Some shit deserves explaining. Some shit doesn't. Plain as that. Explanations won't change a thing. Sometimes there is no explaining. You, Levin—you're gonna help your little pal, make sure it gets done right. Capiche? And then the two of you are gonna forget you ever saw 'em or that we ever talked about 'em. You're gonna walk out my door. This never happened. You got that? I'm not kidding. You were never here."

"But why?"

"But but but. But but but . . . I'm warning you, Jack—you and the Boy Wonder here—you need to stop finding shit. You need to stop asking shit.

You need to stop listening to shit. You need to stop thinking shit. You don't have a clue, the damage you can do." He weaved back and forth between us, poking, prodding, shadow-boxing. "You love your folks? Your mother, your father? Do you, boys? You love your brothers and sisters? Your puppy dogs? Your parakeets? Please. I said *please*. Do what I'm telling you. Because it'd be a crying shame otherwise if you brought anything bad down upon any one of them. I'd hate to see it and, I'm telling you, you will hate it a good lot more. Burn them. We on the same page? Burn them. It's not a request, it's an order. You do what I say. Or else."

"Just like that?"

McGrath collided with Jack, bumped his chest into his chin. "Just like that. Close. Cover. Before. Fucking. Striking." The guy should have been spitting bullets, he was wound so damn tight. He was trembling, too, from rage or fear or both, which made the moment all the more incomprehensible to us.

And Jack, that stubborn ass—same as when he took on the school bullies—he did not budge. "And if we don't?"

"Goddammit, Levin. There is no *if*." McGrath thumped him into the wall as he'd done to me. "How many times you going to make me ask? Do you love your family?"

"Of course."

"Me, too," I volunteered.

"Then do what needs to be done. I'm not your enemy here, boys. I am as far from an enemy as a friend can be."

"Okay. Okay."

"Smart boy." McGrath eased off, nodded relieved. "Agreed?" he said cheerfully. "Agreed?" He proffered his hand, and the two of us shook in turn.

"Uh-huh," Jack said.

"Agreed," I said. His hand was cold *and* sweaty, which flew in the face of the grade school science I'd acquired to date.

McGrath reoccupied the corner of his desk, lit up another smoke, vowed he'd be watching us, and burst out laughing. "Gus, is it?"

"Yes, sir."

"You've got the handshake of a dead fish."

THREE

Cha-cha teachers at large

"Jesus, Jack, why'd you make me lie? Now he thinks—"

"You wanted to be a finder, didn't you?"

"We need to kill him."

"What are you talking about?"

"Before he kills my mom. We need to kill McGrath." Scaredy-cats are nothing if not practical.

"You weren't listening, Gus. He's not going to kill anybody. And neither are we. He was talking about circumstances. Don't you see, he was trying to scare us? The look on his face when he saw the cards. He wouldn't touch them. He was more frightened than you, Gus."

"Of what? Cardboard?"

"I haven't the foggiest. Could be the cards are worth something. Like stolen diamonds. And the thieves who lost them will try and steal them back."

"Or maybe it's what the cards are made of. Maybe it's not cardboard, but diamond dust or sheets of platinum or uranium. . . . Or what if they're atomic secrets? How to build the bomb? Or what if they're cursed and whoever finds them . . . Jeez."

"Your guess is as good as mine, man. But I know who can set us straight on one point—where we should've gone first."

"Or we could just burn them," I said.

"Spend five minutes on a stool in the Marquee. Adults tell you all sorts of dumb shit. You ever sift flour for your mom? It's like that. You got to shake out the crud. The day you see me believing and doing everything I'm told, put me out of my misery. And then run like crazy. Because it'll be a sure sign the Brain Eaters have landed—and you're next."

"I'll keep it in mind."

"I'm not joking."

"Jesus, Jack."

"You know what I'm saying. Like you're some goody-goody? Don't give me that. I know you, Gus."

"What Mr. McGrath said . . . I'm afraid."

"You think I'm not? But I'll tell you this, it's a whole lot better than being bored. There's only one thing we need to be afraid of. And that's growing up, ending up like McGrath, flying off the handle over nothing, sticking your head in the sand."

"I know. Growing up changes everything."

"And not in a good way, not that I've ever seen."

Jack was on fire. He strode ahead. I simmered behind.

Solving mysteries was risky. California's Lost Ship of the Desert. The Oak Island Money Pit. Many good men had lost their lives in the pursuit of riches. I could understand. Gold and silver could turn poor saps into rich pricks. But the Trenton Movie Cards were different, the payoff far from clear. And there had to be a payoff, damn sure. McGrath's madman routine made that plain as day. I skipped ahead, caught up with Jack. "What if the cards are code for something? What if they tell a story, where to look for something?"

"Like a treasure map."

"Or some big secret."

"Like a message from outer space."

"And all we have to do is put them in the right order."

"McGrath. He's afraid we'll figure it out. That's what it is. McGrath's afraid we'll find out what *he* knows—what he doesn't want *us* to know."

"Thinks we're dumb kids. Thinks he can throw us off, keep whatever it is for himself."

"Burn 'em, eh? My ass! You don't get to the bottom of a mystery by destroying your clues."

"I'm in, Jack. I'm all in."

"Never doubted it for a second, pal."

As we made our way from the *Record* to King Street, I looked again to The Hardy Boys and their *Detective Handbook* for assistance—summoned what I recalled about shaking off tails. "You're crazy." Jack laughed, glanced left and right, and over his shoulder. "Relax. McGrath's not following us."

"Yeah, right. Coming from you, the guy who said the cards would put me on the front page. . . ."

We stuck to my roundabout route, the sudden turns and about-faces, and reached the dry cleaners without picking up any suspicious types. Far as we could tell. The five-minute walk took ten. A costly ten.

We were too late. Sure Press was closed. Fridays, 8:00 a.m. to 4:30 p.m. I should've known. We peered through the glass. Jack tapped on the window. No sign of anybody.

"Hey," I said, pointing. In among the buttons of the cigar box on the witch's table was Simon Lebel's sweetheart bracelet.

"Jeez, shows you how much it meant to her. . . ."

"It's an omen," I said.

"You think?"

"Feels like it."

"Good or bad?"

I had no answer. Either the world was getting crazier or Jack and I were. For now, it was a toss-up.

We decided to try Blackhurst's again on Monday after school. Just then I heard my name. Helmut Swartz was crossing toward us from the police station on market square. He wore a bandage the size of a sleeping bag on his hand. Story was, he had tried to save Dottie. Had the injuries to prove it. Cut himself up bad, smashed the glass to get at the lifesaver. "Hi, Leo," he said. "How are you, kid?"

"Okay," I said. "You?" He didn't look great. He could have used a shave and a haircut. Dark circles ringed his famous blue eyes. They were black and beady, sunken within the dark harbour of his skull. Dottie had raved to my mother about Helmut's eyes, how they made her swoon.

He held the door to the dance studio ajar. "Blackhurst closes early on Fridays. Everybody's open till nine, but him. Lazy old coot."

"Yeah. We know."

"I miss her terribly. I want you and your mom to know, Leo. Because some folks, well, they're saying I don't. They're saying terrible things." He looked over to Jack, nodded an aggrieved howdy, and the door carried him inside.

Jack exhaled. "They used to come to the Marquee a lot—him and her. Haven't seen him since she drowned."

"I don't think you're supposed to go to restaurants after somebody dies. At least until after they're buried." The funeral had been delayed. The police were holding onto Dottie's body.

"They're saying he pushed her in?"

"Honest?" I said. "Did he?"

"That's what they're saying."

"But he's walking around. Like he's normal. Like anybody."

"Like you and me," Jack said.

And I looked about the street, at the people going by, men, women, kids, window shoppers and window washers, jaywalkers and loiterers, people with purpose and people with none, and I wondered. *Wondered*. If what Jack had said was true of Helmut, it had to be true of others. People you pass everyday as you go about your life. People who have murdered with no one the wiser. People who have murdered and gotten away. People who had murdered, served their time, and who were hankering to kill again. People who had killed by accident. By negligence. By stupidity. There had to be hundreds. Thousands. Walking around like they were you and me. And if this was true of Trenton, it was true of everywhere. You couldn't help but pass a murderer or two or three or fifty every day of your life. And every one as free as Jack and me and Helmut Swartz.

"Jack," I said, "there's something I need to show you."

I went home to get the clippings, then met him at his garage.

"How long you been holding onto these?" he said. He used tweezers to examine the clippings, the paper brown and brittle.

"A bit," I said, looking back over the months to my first burglary. "I worried they might not be what we were looking for. Not enough dead, I mean."

"Are you kidding? Murder? The numbers don't matter when it's murder. These are great. Old papers, eh?"

"In our cellar." The first rule of lying is to keep your answers concise.

"Were there follow-ups? Did they catch who did it?"

"None I could find."

"Great work, Gus. Really."

I tell you, seeing him add my finds to our list felt damn good and I regretted my delay in bringing them to him.

1933 – Two girls stabbed to death on Mt. Pelion, first body found in May, second in August

1950 – Bodies of a boy and girl found under the water tower on Pelion—police torn between "lover's leap" or "foul play"

"Maybe you got a knack for this, Gus," Jack said. "Could be your specialty is murder. On Pelion."

"I'm just getting started," I said.

But then, in short order, murder proved to be Jack's specialty more than mine, and our list grew longer still.

1919 – Four bodies found after barn burns down, pitchfork wounds evident

1926 – Two sisters beaten to death on Pelion

1930 – Family of three stabbed to death in Hanna Park, father, mother, toddler

No denying, he took the wind out of my sails. What was the point? I ended my burglary spree. The dust had been getting to me anyhow, like I had a permanent cold.

# FOUR

Mom in mourning

Mom would apologize whenever I'd catch her crying in the first couple of weeks after Dottie. She'd pluck up, put on her brave face, and give me the life-goes-on baloney, the dying-is-a-natural-part-of-living baloney. She never gave me the she's-in-a-better-place baloney, though I hoped she might. A sunnier outlook, however fuzzy, would have done me good. Living life without a net was wearing us down. Mom's brave face was sadder than her sad face. (Sadder sights were in store for me, of course. But her early Dead Dottie days would remain among my top-five saddest.)

Her going through the paces was the part I couldn't bear. She'd mope along half-human, half-robot, fixing breakfast, making her bed, watching TV, only to go over the top with delight or joy at the drop of a hat, over nothing I could see as delightful or joyful.

I observed her closely, waited till she had both feet in the Land of the Living before telling her how I'd bumped into Helmut. "He said he misses her, no matter what people are saying about him."

"I would hope so." Mom gave the potatoes a final mash and brought the pot to the table.

"Do you think Helmut pushed Dottie into the water?" I said.

"What?"

I repeated the question.

She froze, the spoon and potatoes suspended above my plate. "All that matters now is what people want to believe." The potatoes fell, buried my meatloaf.

"But do you think he could have?"

She wiped a tear from her cheek. "You remember how flighty Dottie could be." She dolloped potatoes onto her own plate and sat, elbows propped, utensils in hand. "She tripped. She fell. She drowned. It's what I was told. It's what I prefer to believe."

"Mr. Swartz looks different now."

"You think so? How?"

"Like he could have done it."

The light in Mom's eyes flickered. "You're saying he looked guilty?"

"Tired. Nervous, maybe."

"My God, who wouldn't be, Leo? That makes him human, not guilty."

"I'm just saying, you know, because people are saying."

"Well, don't. Don't ever. People say many things. They've said things about me. About you. Doesn't make them true."

"You don't think he pushed her, then?"

"It is what it is. Nothing can bring Dottie back. She loved Helmut and that was good enough for me. Perhaps she rushed into it. It was quite the whirlwind. If I've said two words to the man . . . But I will tell you this, the more you get to know a person, the more you will find to dislike. It's why I hope, now—especially now—I never do get to know Mr. Helmut Swartz."

Later, I'd come to see Mom's theory worked in other ways, too.

The more people got to know me.

The more I got to know myself.

Helmut was too distraught to speak at Dottie's funeral. Mom was going to tell a funny story about Dottie, but the minister didn't feel it was appropriate, so Mom just spoke about their friendship and Dottie's kind heart. As we walked home, I asked Mom if she missed Dottie more than she missed Dad.

"It's different."

Mom did not specify how it was different and I didn't follow up. I missed Dottie more than I'd ever missed my dad. I was afraid Mom felt the same. I wanted Dad to be at the top of her *missing* list. Because who else was there to miss him, if not her? And if Dad wasn't missed, he'd be forgotten. And to be forgotten meant you never were.

* * *

I do not know if Mom missed my father till the day she died. She did miss Dottie, though. No other friend fully filled the void. Or, more accurately, was permitted to. Not even in Mom's post-Dottie world where her career path would see her corner the market on friends.

It's good to lose a parent when you're young, I think. Maybe not both. But one, for sure. Age five is the cutoff. Three-and-a-half worked for me. The fewer your memories, the less significant your loss. Don't get me wrong. I felt bad for my dad, but I didn't know him long enough to miss him badly enough. I missed him for what he missed out on by dying, not for any bond I could recall between us. Memories of my father were spare and suspect, manufactured from photos and fables and counterfeit sit-downs, Dad as Ward and me the Beav.

"Every kid needs a dad" is a myth. You've got to have a dad before you can need one and the degree of need depends on the dad you had.

But losing friends. Your peers. I could see why Mom took Dottie's death so hard. A dead friend could just as soon be you.

# FIVE

Novices on the front lines of puberty

The Sewing Machine Witch was coming down the block as we were scurrying up, and somehow transformed to Iris before our paths crossed.

"Hey, hi," Jack said. He hoped she'd yet thank us for the bracelet.

"Stay dry," she said, gathered her cardigan and sprinted past.

"Huh?" I said.

"'Stay dry,'" Jack repeated.

"What's that mean?"

"Rain is coming?"

The sky was clear, clouds token.

We'd cut it close. Mr. Blackhurst was twisting the OPEN sign to CLOSED. Jack rapped on the window. The old man pointed to the sign. Jack pulled a long face, laid it on thick. "Please, sir. Just this once."

I hung back as Blackhurst let Jack in.

"Gus!" Jack snapped, and I followed him inside, watchful, guarded.

"I told your mothers I shut the door at five. No exceptions."

Jack wasted no time. "You told me they used to make movies here. Were you pulling my leg?"

Blackhurst hitched up his pants. "What's this about?"

"Show him, Gus."

I tapped the cards from the envelope. The look on Blackhurst's face, well, you would have thought a cherished old friend had dropped in to chew the fat. His caterpillar eyebrows arched with devious glee. Slowly, reverently, he reached out. "May I?" he said, and lifted the cards from my hands.

"Sir?" Jack said. "You know what these are?"

"Intertitles," Mr. Blackhurst said, more to himself than to us. "Never in all my days did I presume to touch the likes of these again." His accent was hoity-toity gravy, and thicker by the word. Wherever the cards were taking him, he was game for the ride. *Blackhurst down the rabbit hole and through the looking glass.*

"My friend found them." Jack urged me forward, his hand at my back, and I shot him a dirty look. I was disinclined to repeat the lie without a sense of how it might go. McGrath had plowed me into a wall. Blackhurst could steam-press me to death.

"Ah, this one," Blackhurst sighed. "I so fondly remember this one."

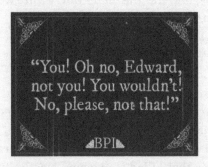

"I wrote it myself for *The Black Ace*. Nary an iota of lurid violence, yet you should have heard the audiences scream." He shut his eyes, basked in the memory. "Wholly terrorized, chilled to the marrow, they were. It was marvellous. My magnum opus. Yet it was the infinitely inferior *The Lodger* that won the accolades. How unjust is that! And only recently, Hitchcock, you know, the man is shameless—the shower sequence in *Psycho*, stolen frame for frame from *Black Ace*. The scoundrel thought no one would know, thought sufficient time had elapsed. But I know. We know."

"And this down here?" Jack said, indicating the logo.

"Blackhurst Pictures International, of course. My production company. Alas, as ill-fated and lamented as the others—Canadian National Features, Adanac, Pan American Films . . ."

"So it's true, then—they *did* make movies in Trenton," Jack said, and my excitement was every bit as palpable as his.

"Hollywood North, right, Mr. Blackhurst?" I said, eager now to be a featured player. "I found them. It was me who found the intertitles. I've got a bunch of them, you won't believe."

"Thing is," Jack said, "Mr. McGrath, over at the *Record*, he told us we needed to burn them. Why would he—"

"I beg your pardon? McGrath? Bryan McGrath?"

"Yeah. Like he was scared of them."

"It was really, really weird," I said, thriving on the upswing.

"McGrath, the great saviour. Why in Heaven's almighty name would you share a discovery of this magnitude with a knave? A more egregious overreactor I have never known. Burn them? Quintessential McGrath. A nervous Nellie of the first order. A mediocre and malodorous screen scribe transmogrified to mephitic muckraker. My dear lads, your intertitles are but memories of a bygone era. The man's worries are woefully misplaced."

"So there *is* something to fear, then, sir?" Jack said.

"Isn't there always, my boy?"

"You're telling me," I said with a laugh. By now, I was fully on board with the new, enthusiastic version of me.

"Can we see the movies?" Jack asked. "Do you have them?"

"Norman." We turned to the rear of the shop and the voice of a woman.

Mr. Blackhurst hastily drew us back. "She will tell me I have said too much. Alas, to you, I will have said too little. No matter what you may hear, it was not the talkies that killed Hollywood North, it was indeed, as you have surmised, the fear."

"That's enough, Norman. Enough."

"Perhaps a close-up now, gentlemen, a wistful glance to the right, focus soft, and cut to the intertitle. 'He had dreams, you know. Hail the Revered Masters! F.W. Murnau. D.W. Griffith. C.B. DeMille. And if not for ignorance, delusion, and myth, the redoubtable N.K. Blackhurst.'" He winked at me. At Jack. And aged ten years in ten seconds. The cards sailed to the floor and some of his brain, too. His expression went from blank to black, Dr. Jekyll awakening to find Mr. Hyde's bloody cane in his hands.

"Sir?" Jack said, but the man had hopped the fast freight to *Voodoo Island*. In dull retreat he dragged his feet and exited behind a curtain of cleaning.

I dropped to my knees to gather up the cards. Jack skirted the counter in pursuit.

"Let him be," the woman said, gentle, then assertive: "Let him be."

I rose gingerly to my feet. *Holy cow. And wow!* It was the woman. *It was her.* Minus the fur.

She stood square with Jack, ravishing and resolute, a vision to behold in black silk and pearls, with raven curls falling softly to slight shoulders. She was Helen of Troy relocated to a dry-cleaning shop in Trenton, Ontario, Canada. A cruel twist of Fate, for sure, even discounting the lousy winter weather.

Jack edged away. I'd never before seen him anywhere near flustered. His footsteps were jittery in keeping with his stammer. "You must be Mr. Blackhurst's daughter . . . uh . . . um . . . wife . . . uh . . . daughter . . . uh . . . Jesus help me, I'm so sorry, so sorry, Miss, Missus, Ma'am, Missus, Ma'am, Miss . . ."

The lady was either the youngest old person I had ever seen or the oldest young person. Whatever, she was way too pretty for this town. Hell, a dream come true, she put my mom to shame; next to her, Mom was a beard shy of sideshow. This woman was nobody's mother, nobody's sister. *And it was her, all right. The woman I remembered. It was her.*

"Excuse me." I raised a hand, thinking this an opportune moment to impress. "Did Mr. Blackhurst tell you? It was me. I'm the one who found them, aren't I, Jack?"

She folded her arms, slender fingers and scarlet nails extended to opposing shoulders, and raised her chin in expectation. *The expectation we would leave.*

"Do you remember me?" I said. "I saw you one—" And those blue eyes of hers, goddamn, way bluer than any blue was meant to be. I swallowed. Could not stop swallowing.

We did not want to leave. We wanted to stare.

She observed us with contained impatience, bending us to her unspoken will. And those heels of hers, goddamn, they must have run halfway to Heaven.

Poor Jack and me, drawn and quartered, mere novices on the front lines of puberty. And those red lips of hers, goddamn, way redder than any red was meant to be. We could not breathe.

The door jangled shut behind us. The shop went dark.

We lingered outside the cleaners, in no rush to shake her spell. Whatever it was she'd stirred in me was nothing I wanted to end. When our legs got around to moving, it was more a result of the Earth's rotation than a desire to move on.

"That was her," I said, stating the obvious. "The lady I told you about. In the fur coat. The woman who acted like she knew me. I told you she was real."

"She sure didn't act like she knew you now, did she?"

"Do you think she's his wife? She could be his wife."

"And Mr. Blackhurst, what he said, the movies, Hollywood North . . . He was telling the truth, you could see."

"He loved the cards."

"But McGrath, and now her, getting all worked up over . . . Over what, man?"

"History isn't supposed to be a secret."

"And it isn't supposed to be forgotten. At least not by the people who only just lived it. Not this quickly."

"Your mass amnesia theory makes more sense by the second."

"Nah. Nothing makes sense, man. Not without the *why*. We know about Champlain and the Indians climbing Mount Pelion. They taught us that much, right? That sort of history. So it's not everything. It's the more recent stuff."

"The bad stuff."

"The accidents, sure, but why the movie cards? A movie studio? Where's the bad in that?"

"Makes you wonder how much more they're hiding from us."

"Hiding? Or forgetting?"

"Could be both. Like dogs who bury their bones and next day can't remember where."

"We need to keep our eyes open. And we need to be careful. I mean, what if you and me—what if we start forgetting, too?"

"I won't forget her, that's for sure."

"She was something, all right."

"I told you, man. I told you."

SIX

Mom on the move

"Movies?" Mom stifled a giggle. In the wake of Dottie, anything resembling happiness was cause for optimism. "A studio? Here?"

"A long time ago. Mr. Blackhurst was telling us. . . . His wife, she was there, too."

"Don't tell me the sewing machine lady has finally spoken?"

"Not her. Another lady."

"What other lady?"

"And Alfred Hitchcock—"

"He was there, too?" Her giggles ran fast and loose, now.

"No. No. But Mr. Blackhurst knows him. He's friends with him. Okay, not friends, because Alfred Hitchcock stole from—"

"My goodness, sweetheart, what are you going on about?"

I caught myself, realized how I must have sounded. I replied softly, "Nothing. I guess."

"Are you feeling all right? It hasn't been easy lately, I know. For either of us." She patted the top of my head, squeezed me tight, as if the nonsense inside of me was ketchup. "Mr. Blackhurst is a very nice man. But he can also be rather odd. I would not put it past him to make up the occasional tall tale. He was only teasing you."

I laughed convincingly. "I know. You're right."

"The whole idea is so farfetched. If it were anything more, we would have heard, don't you think?"

"Like there'd be historical markers or something."

"Exactly." Her grin remained on standby. Again, I was glad to see it, yet also hated when she humoured me; to her I'd be three years old forever. "It's important to respect seniors, Leo, but to believe everything . . ."

"I know he was being silly. I just thought—"

She perked up, bustled me to arm's length. "Hey! I've got news, too." More and more, she was returning to her old self, moving beyond Malbasic and Dottie. "I quit my job. I'm going to be an Avon Lady. What do you think of that?"

The office was cluttered with too many memories, work no longer fun without Dottie, though I never saw how work at the Unemployment Insurance Office could have ever been fun.

"You'll be ringing doorbells?" I said.

"'Avon calling!'" she chirped.

"You sound like the TV commercial."

"You think so?"

"I swear, Mom. You're going to be good at this. Bet you anything."

SEVEN

Another unexplained mystery to call our own

Frank and Joe Hardy. Damn right we were.

All week long we collected cardboard, whatever we could find—from shirts and whatnot. When the stack equalled the height and volume of the forty-seven movie cards, we burned the cardboard and divided the ashes between two Kit Kat cartons. Jack labelled them same as he had the other finds on his shelves, by content, date, and rating. He gave them an *X*. And then, to make the lie complete, he added:

MOVIE TITLE CARDS X
Found by Gus, Hanna Park, April 1962

"We need to leave them where McGrath can see them. Easy, but not so easy he'll see we've set him up."

Jack cleared a spot next to the box where the meteor had been stored, before he donated it to Queen's University. All he'd kept were photos of the meteor. And meteor dust. "Alphabetical order," he explained.

We waited till Saturday morning when my mom was at the A&P and Jack's parents were at the restaurant to make our next move. We secured the cards beneath the false bottoms of two board games, Risk and Concentration, and smuggled them from Jack's garage to my house. We figured they'd be safer there. McGrath didn't know me from a hole in the wall, not like he knew Jack. Besides, he rightly suspected it was Jack who'd found them. We saw that.

The worry he'd kill my mother had subsided. Mostly, anyhow. Jack had put me at ease. "Me and my family are way better targets." McGrath was a Marquee regular. "If he's going to hurt anyone, he'll start with us." The trick was to make him believe he'd scared the crap out of us and we'd destroyed the cards. Jack was certain he'd come snooping, follow up on us.

We pushed back the coffee table, the armchairs, and sofa, and spread all forty-seven across the living-room floor.

We spent a good couple of hours, struggling to make sense of the words, come up with a coherent sequence.

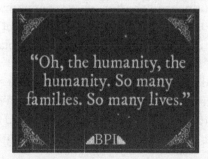

We reordered the cards every which way. Read them aloud two, three, four times, listening to each other for clues, searching for a breakthrough. Some went together more than others, raising our hopes.

The Spanish Main, 1522

BPI

Little did Captain Snow know the treasure he would come to cherish most awaited him west of Hispaniola, where X marked the spot of a fetching young maiden's heart....

BPI

But try as we might, we could find no red flags to justify why McGrath went psycho or why the Blackhursts had circled the wagons. No Rosetta stone to pave our road to fame and fortune.

"The answers are in front of our noses," Jack said. "It's going to come, you'll see, when we least expect it."

"If we could see the movies . . ." I said.

"Till then, another unexplained mystery to call our own."

We buried the forty-seven among the books of my father's library. I slipped the last between the slippery pages of Lithuania and Luxembourg in a Hammond World Atlas.

"Pull up! Pull up!
Good God, ol' chap,
pull up!"

BPI

"You sure your mom won't find them?" Jack said.

"My dad was the reader."

"A big one, too, from the looks of it."

"He died in the War. On Juno Beach."

"Wow. Like Mrs. Bruce's son. You know, the old lady whose wedding ring I found."

"My dad and him, they were friends," I said.

# EIGHT

Cause for optimism at last

While Jack and I were burying the cards, a speedboat smacked into the concrete pier at the town marina during time trials for upcoming races. The driver of the speedboat died on impact. They had to scrape him off the dock with squeegees. Six bystanders were injured by flying debris. Five would be dead by month's end. The sixth lost her eyes and an ear.

The driver was Dr. Cornish. "He was my dentist," Jack said, and added the accident to our timeline.

"Do you think we'll forget?" I said.

"That this happened?"

"It's how it should work, if we're like everybody else. . . ."

"I hope not."

"But we wouldn't know, would we?"

"That's what forgetting is. Not knowing. And not knowing is as good as never happened."

"What if one of us remembers and not the other?"

"It'd be like half of us dying."

"Or half of us gone crazy," I said.

NINE

Into the din and the glare

The Thursday after that eventful Saturday, Mom and I were having dinner at the Marquee. Mom had reason to splurge. In the two weeks she'd been at it, her Avon business had taken off faster than anyone could have anticipated. She was loving it. "It doesn't feel like selling. It's more like chatting."

I'd just pulled the toothpick from the second quarter of my turkey club when Jack gave me this anxious look and the restaurant door swung open.

Bryan McGrath hailed Jack's dad as only a café regular can. "What's cookin', Bert?"

Mr. Levin fired back from his post at the grill: "What's the scoop, Mac?"

"Five cents and you can read it in tomorrow's *Record*." McGrath chuckled and settled in at the table by the window. You would've sworn he owned the damn joint.

He summoned Jack with a curt two-finger wave and the grizzled specter of Robert Service reared its head once more, the lines reeling ominously through my skittish brain: *When out of the night, which was fifty below, and into the din and the glare, There stumbled a miner fresh from the creeks, dog-dirty, and loaded for bear.*

Mom was yammering on about my school day, about her day at work, her lunch, her customers, her district manager, her best-selling shade of lipstick, and this wonderful article about what's wrong with TV she'd read in *Reader's Digest*, but my focus was Jack and the reporter. Not that I could hear a word. I had to wait for Jack to fill me in.

"You talked to Norman Blackhurst."

"I brought my dad's shirts in for cleaning."

"Don't lie to me."

"I'm not."

"What did the old fool tell you?"

"Thursday. He'd have the shirts on Thursday."

"You think I'm an idiot, Jack?"

"I'm not thinking anything, sir."

"That man, he's not right in his head. Imagines things. Hallucinates. You best forget whatever it was he told you."

"But my dad already picked up the shirts."

"Now you're a comedian, eh? You disappoint me, Jack."

"What is it you think he told me?"

"Ha! You're good, kid, I'll grant you that. You and your pal take care of the business we discussed?"

"I can show you the ashes."

"Neither of you tempted to keep a souvenir?"

"Swear to God," Jack said. He crossed his legs at the ankles to ensure God's forgiveness for implicating Him in the lie. God would understand, survival at stake.

McGrath clicked his tongue like he'd just cocked a six-shooter. "Always knew you were a bright boy."

And for no reason he could explain, Jack cracked: "I know about Hollywood North, the movies. Why's it all so secret?"

"Blackhurst. I knew it." McGrath's mouth withered dry and small. "Demented old fuck." The sinews of his neck skewered his skull. He dragged his eyeglasses the length of his nose, folded them into his shirt pocket. He was shaking, his every word a hardened turd: "How 'bout you fix me a nice slice of your mom's apple pie? A wedge of cheddar. Cup of joe. Black. Three sugars."

Jack's chest was heaving as he passed our table. "I'm so glad you boys have become friends," my mother said.

"Me, too," Jack and I said in unison.

Jack filled McGrath's order, set the pie and coffee on the table. The reporter clamped wiry fingers onto his wrist and from behind the cover of a

Karloff grin, he said, "Let's you and I go hunting one of these days. I'll set it up with your dad. I got this elephant gun—what a beaut!—same weapon Frank Buck favoured. You know Frank Buck, don't you? Big-game hunter. Crack shot. Ice water in his veins. Could take a rabid rhino down at twenty paces and never break a sweat." McGrath called across the floor to Jack's dad. "Hey, Bert, Jack here wants to know if you'll let me take him hunting one of these days. What do you say?"

"It'd be an honour," Bert called back. "He couldn't ask for a better teacher."

Jack faked a smile, said, "I don't know what you want me to say, Mr. McGrath."

"Look, son, a person digs up the past, next he knows—no future." He let the message sit. The threat was direct and left Jack speechless. "I know you love your family, son. But what about this town? You love it, do you?"

"What?"

"Trenton? Do you love it?"

"Sure. It's okay."

"I'm on your side, son. I see kids playing with dynamite, I take away the matches. You need to understand: sometimes the truth is less credible than the lie. You let it out of the bag, they stick you in a straitjacket. Need be, they put you down like a mad dog. Am I making myself clear?"

"Yes."

"I am telling you for the last time, stop before you're sorry. Because you have no idea how sorry sorry can be."

McGrath lightened his grip. Jack reclaimed his hand, and retreated before forced to go another round.

He secluded himself at the sink, washing and scrubbing, beating up on dishes. Glanced over. His face blank. Caught my eye. Mouthed: "Oh, shit." And not ten seconds later, a shake of his head and a larger: "Oh, shit." The worries I'd suppressed boiled to the surface. Was McGrath about to make good on his earlier threats?

The reporter polished off his pie, smoked, nursed his coffee, kibitzed with Bert and fellow regulars. *Everyone knew Bryan McGrath. McGrath was a good guy.* Like Dougie Dunwood and Vlad the Impaler were good guys.

My stomach made a break for my throat. The guy was waiting for Mom and me to finish up so he could follow us home and finish *us* off. I was sure of it.

I ate slower.

Way slower.

We were getting to our desserts when McGrath stood to leave. *Without warning, he lunged for our table, slid across the surface, and plunged his fork into my mother's heart, so deep it went clear through to her back, emerging below a shoulder blade, a morsel of apple pie undisturbed on the tines.*

In some ways the reality was worse.

We were getting to our desserts when McGrath stood to leave. He ambled to the door, hummed as he circled behind me. I figured I was in the clear, but then he turned 180, pulled a spazzy double-take. "Hey, I know you."

I bowed my head, excavated the Suez through the meringue of my lemon pie. But good ol' Mom, she would not stand for it: "Don't be rude, Leo. Mr. McGrath is speaking to you. He writes for the newspaper, you know?"

My head weighed a ton, the neck hydraulics seized up.

"I do indeed, ma'am. But your son . . . Am I right? Aren't you the boy who's friends with that nice little girl—what's her name?—Annie, is it? Annie Barker?"

"He is," Mom said. "Tell him you are."

"I know her family well," McGrath continued. "Dad owns the lumber yard out on Wooler Road. Gone hunting with him once or twice. Fine people. Sweet girl. You be sure to say hello for me next time you see her, will ya, Leo?"

I sent my fork to the bottom of my pie and shovelled half into my mouth. I did not chew or swallow, held the pie in the recesses of my cheeks, vacuumed up the remainder from my plate and packed it in, as well.

"What are you doing? Slow down." My mother shook her head, amused and confused. "And since when are you so shy?"

"Boys will be boys, eh?" McGrath said.

I breathed through my nose, my cheeks expanding, saliva infusing the lemon filling.

"Won't you join us?" my mother said. "I've enjoyed your writing for years."

"I'd be delighted to," the psycho said, and signalled for Jack to bring him another coffee. "And one for the lady."

"So nice of you," my mother said.

The lemon pie liquefied, trickled into my gullet, the flow intensifying as my mother emptied the vault. Who we were and where we lived. Where I went to school. Where she had worked and what had befallen her best friend, Dottie Lange—or Swartz—and what she was up to now.

"'Avon calling!'" McGrath said, a playful wink for her, nicotine smarm for me.

"I never would've believed I'd enjoy it so much," she said. "Had I known, I would have started with Avon when I was younger."

"How's that possible, Emily? No way you're a day over twenty-one."

"Oh, you are a charmer, Mr. McGrath." *Charmer, my ass.* Hadn't Malbasic taught her anything? Letting her guard down with an old fart came to no good. Yet, here she was, flirting to beat the band. You would have thought Cary Grant himself had picked up the tab for her coffee.

"Leo isn't your brother, then?"

Mom was not naïve. She knew when a guy was on the up-and-up. So I can only conclude she was starved for something beyond the scope of what twelve-year-old me could offer. Bryan McGrath's corn, I guessed.

He turned thoughtful. "A career change motivated by tragedy. There's a story there, Emily, if you'd care to have it told. I'm just saying, of course, professionally speaking. No obligation."

"You must be joking." Mom was as coy as I'd ever heard her, and hoped to never hear again.

I gagged. Fought the reflex. Popped out of my chair. Charged to the door. "What's got into you?" Mom cried after me.

"Math homework," I lied, and the last of the lemon pie hit my gut.

I pushed through the door, the kindly voice of Mr. McGrath on my tail: "Don't forget, son, you be sure to say hello to Annie for me."

TEN

From Kingdom Come to Brigadoon

I raged into my bedroom, grabbed the first thing that meant anything to me. The Aurora Wolf Man I'd assembled with glue and care and painted by hand. Busted off his head. Stomped him to Kingdom Come, Plastics Division.

McGrath walked Mom home. I could hear them jabbering outside, caterpillars cocooning in my ears. *What was wrong with this picture?* I dove onto my bed, face in pillow, pillow baled about my head. He was old enough to be her grandfather. My great-grandfather. *What the hell was wrong with my mother?* Only then did the pattern occur. *Her penchant, Jesus. Bride of Dracula. Bride of Frankenstein.* My dad had been an old guy, too. Born in '05. Dead by '54. More than a quarter century older than Mom. Those fragments of muffled conversations made sense to me now, Dottie consoling Mom, Mom bemoaning fate and family.

"*They couldn't accept him, Dottie. . . .*"
"*. . . Alex's age was just the tip of it.*"
"*. . . the biggest mistake of my life, they kept saying.*"
"*. . . him or us, Emily.*"

Alexander Berry. Harvey Fucking Malbasic. Bryan Fucking McGrath. What was the point of trying? I could not protect my mother from anything or anyone, least of all herself. She might not have slugged Malbasic with the bronze owl, but I wouldn't have put it past her if she had. Who next, Old Man Blackhurst?

Mom poked her head into my bedroom. "Did you get your homework done?"

"Yeah," I muttered sullenly. "I did the math, all right."

"You want to talk about it?" she said.

"It all adds up."

"Seems a little early for you to be in bed."

"He's a great guy, Mom. Great guy. Best ever."

She did not take the bait. She never did, bless her heart, which I knew to be a good heart. Her brain was the problem. She began to shut the door and stopped. "What's that on the floor?" She knelt by my bureau. "Oh, Leo, you didn't? Why?" she said, as she picked up the pieces of my Wolf Man.

> *"Even a man who is pure in heart*
> *And says his prayers by night . . ."*

McGrath broke into Jack's garage the same night. He didn't bother to cover up. He left the two Kit Kat cartons on Jack's work table, ashes spilled and scattered.

"He wanted us to know he was here," Jack said.

"Do you think he fell for it?" I said.

"We'll know soon enough."

Jack and I backed off on the cards after this. Openly, anyhow. McGrath was a hovering constant in our lives. Perhaps he'd always been and we'd never noticed. We hadn't given up on the mystery; we revised our strategy, maintaining a low profile until we had a better grasp of the situation or McGrath dropped dead, whichever came first.

If we didn't have to bother with our parents' dry cleaning, we would have avoided Mr. Blackhurst, too. Still, we kept it businesslike and when the old guy would show up at the Marquee, Jack made himself busy. Not that Blackhurst appeared to notice. Regulars talked among themselves as much as they foisted themselves upon Jack. Somebody, anybody, to talk to. As though the Marquee was the one place in town they were free to be their *old* selves. It was harder on Jack, by far. Hollywood North percolated in our imagination, our speculation, relentlessly stalking our conversation. Hollywood North was our Brigadoon, without the sappy singing, the heather on the hill.

Jack gave his time to the house painters and truck drivers, the A&P cashiers and railroad men, the fishermen and office workers, with their facts and stats and trivia, their regrets and anecdotes of minor interest.

Bet you didn't know the main ingredient in ketchup was originally mushrooms.

Bet you didn't know hitchhikers in Europe walk with their backs to the oncoming traffic.

Bet you didn't know locomotives have ice breakers up top to clear icicles from tunnels.

It was the old-timers, though, who came through as always, spurred Jack and me upwards and onwards with their inexhaustible reminiscences, the fun-times they had and the horrors they had lived. They kept The Unknown on the table, our disaster file alive.

We weeded out the ho-hum fires and drownings. By the end of May, any doubts we were onto something were erased for good.

1918 – AMMO PLANT BLOWS UP

1919 – BARN FIRE AND PITCHFORK MURDERS, 4 DEAD

1926 – TWO SISTERS MURDERED ON PELION

1927 – SHOE FACTORY CAVES IN

1930 – FAMILY OF THREE MURDERED IN HANNA PARK

1933 – TWO GIRLS STABBED TO DEATH ON PELION

1937 – PLANES CRASH (SIMON LEBEL FALLS TO EARTH IN PIECES)

1934 – CIRCUS TENT BURNS

1944 – 51 POISONED, 22 DEAD AT RCAF DAY PICNIC, NO CAUSE FOUND, NO BLAME PLACED

1950 – BOY AND GIRL LEAP FROM PELION WATER TOWER

1951 – SCHOOL BUS CRASH

1962 – SPEEDBOAT CRASH, 6 DEAD (INCL. DR. CORNISH)

While Hollywood North remained out of bounds, at least openly, we continued to pursue our other mystery—the disaster and the amnesia. Why didn't anyone remember? Asking anyone outright prompted condescending chuckles, amusement at the musings of youth. Worse, when Jack approached those who had related the stories to him in the first place, most denied both the incident and the telling. Jack tried the hypothetical route. "Say there was this town and something really bad happened, like an earthquake or an explosion, and a bunch of people got killed. But then, a few weeks or months later, when you ask around, hardly anybody knows what you're talking about. Like the thing never happened. How's that possible?"

Only Mrs. Gibbons, the lone survivor of the school bus accident, provided anything resembling coherence. "Because what happened today crowds out yesterday. And personal memories crowd out the impersonal. Look at yourself, Jack, what would you say occupies your thoughts—what you did this morning or what you did in first grade? *What-is* triumphs over *what-was*."

"I see," he said. "So, then, things like the school bus crash, they're what-was?"

"What school bus crash?" she said.

Behind closed doors, we also puzzled over the intertitles. McGrath had cowed us, not paralyzed us. We were stubborn little pricks. We'd periodically pull a card or two from the shelves, hoping the answer might leap out, enabling us to expose the threats and lies and diabolical doings McGrath and the town had been up to.

I transcribed the intertitles onto foolscap, a carbon copy for Jack, so it'd be easier to review the cards on our own. I daydreamed the heck out of them, too, imagined myself in the rapture of *Eureka!*, rushing down Henry Street to bring Jack the thrilling news. Only to have McGrath hunt me down, bleed me, dress me, strap my carcass to the hood of his truck. Then Jack's carcass. Then Annie's. Then Blackhurst's. Then my mother's.

You fixate on anything as long as we did, expect your unconscious to twist the knife. Weird dreams got weirder. Personalized intertitles flashed with unwelcome regularity through the minefields of our REM. We pledged to report as much as we remembered to one another (taboos and shame permitting) and never speak of same again. We were kids. Subtle we were not. No dream dictionary needed.

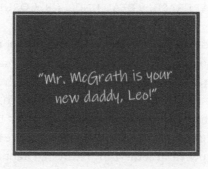

"Mr. McGrath is your new daddy, Leo!"

> "WHO WOULD DO THIS TO THEM? MY SISTERS NEVER HURT A FLY."

> "So I drink their blood, sweetheart, what of it? The older they are, the younger I become. Ha-ha-HAAAA!"

> THE BOY'S INNATE SKILL HAD DETERIORATED SO SWIFTLY HE COULD NO LONGER FIND EVEN HIMSELF.

The dynamics of our walk-and-talks changed, too. For starters, we invited Annie to come along. Or, as she saw it, we inflicted ourselves upon her.

Outside of the privileges accorded Dufferin's goody-goodies, Annie and Jack operated in separate spheres and I'd been happy to keep it so: Annie, my school friend; Jack, my after-school. But with McGrath's threat to do Annie harm looming large, Jack and I felt obligated to protect her. "Not on our watch," we pledged. Her dad drove her to school most mornings, so that was covered. (Unless McGrath was into car bombs.) So the walk home fell to us. It was the least we could do. Our duty. *My duty.*

We did not tell Annie why, only that we thought it'd be fun. "You know, hanging out with us."

"Doesn't sound like fun," she said. "You're off your rockers. You know where I live—up in The Heights? It's blocks out of your way."

"We don't mind," we said. She had her friends to consider, though they branched off early along her route. "We'll walk with them, too."

Mostly, Annie confided, she was wary of the famous Jack the Finder. "He's so full of himself. So conceited. He has never once said hello to me. And now he wants to walk me home? No, thank you."

"You ever say hello to him?" I said.

"I've been friendly."

"And when I hear kids complaining about you, saying how snobby you are, does it make it true? Are you? Just because somebody thinks something?"

"They say I'm snobby?"

I lowered my eyes, self-effacing in my deep regret. She didn't need to know I'd never heard a mean word spoken of her. "Thing is, Annie, he wants to get to know you."

"Honest?"

Her excited flip-flop caught me by surprise. I retracted my poor choice of words. "Yeah. Well. I mean, not like that."

"Like what?"

"Like how you're acting."

"How am I acting?"

"Like you're thinking it's about being more than friends or something."

"What does that mean?"

"You tell me."

"Tell you what?"

"We want to walk you home from school. All there is to it. And, maybe, if you want, you can come to the Odeon with us. A Saturday matinee or something. We might even take you finding sometime, if you want."

"I get it, Gus. I get it. We're all going to be friends together."

"Exactly."

"Why now?"

"Why not?"

"You've never even tried to be friends with me on your own. Never."

"But we are friends."

"I've seen you ride your bike past my house a hundred times and you've never once knocked on my door. We've known each other since first grade, yet outside of school you run the other way. I've invited you to my birthday parties, my cottage, and in all the years you never came. Why now?"

"It's time?" I ventured, feeling the heat in my cheeks.

"I guess it is. I never did understand why you didn't want us all to be friends to begin with." Her dimples betrayed a willful mischief. "But are you sure you're up for it, Gus—handling two friends at once? It's going to be a whole new experience for you."

# ELEVEN

The scare of '62

In August 1962, fourteen-year-old Jimmie Orr flew with his family from Sao Paolo, Brazil to New York City. Jimmie was feverish and headachy and had been for some time. From New York's Grand Central, the Orrs boarded the overnight train home to Toronto. Within days of arriving, Jimmie was diagnosed with smallpox and quarantined. The East Coast of Canada and the U.S. spiralled into a tizzy. Pundits and know-nothings screamed epidemic.

Trenton doubled-down on the tizzy. Fifty-five Air Cadets camping out at the base had come into contact with Jimmie, somewhere, somehow. An airlift of vaccine began. Trenton Community Gardens was converted from hockey rink to emergency inoculation centre.

Jack and I waited in the arena together, the going slow, the lines long and mobbing up. How Iris Lebel found us was anybody's guess. "Shots won't stop what you got," she said, and a riptide of arms and elbows swept her back to wherever she'd come from.

"She's losing it," I said.

"Or trying to tell us something," Jack said.

The smallpox scare of 1962 did not make our list. No one died. No one got the disease besides Jimmie Orr. Still, Jack and I saw the silver lining. The Unknown had given us a heads-up. Before too much longer, we'd have The Unexplained on our hands.

TWELVE

Friends in a Franklin W. Dixon vein

You know by now I was no expert on friendship. My specialty was hate—a prodigy of the art by six, could've-been author of the how-to by twelve. Would've been a perennial bestseller, too. Like *How to Win Friends and Influence People*. Like *The Power of Positive Thinking*. Dale Carnegie, Norman Vincent Peale, and Gloomy Gus—the self-help triumvirate.

I knew hate when I saw it. Hate was what Annie had for Jack and Jack for Annie. Don't tell me you would have seen it any differently.

Annie's practice was to walk home with Susan Burgess and Diana Klieg. On Fridays, Bonnie Priddy came along, too. Bonnie was the tallest girl in school. She wore a leather brace on her left leg and carried a crutch; she'd had polio. Bonnie visited her grandmother on Fridays. "She makes the world's best meatloaf," she'd say. I had no grandmother. Could only imagine what a grandmother could do to meatloaf that my mother could not.

In the beginning, Jack and I lagged behind, parrying the girls' snickers and barbs. Our presence was cause for debate and hilarity. We were *their* unexplained mystery of fifth grade, a Trojan horse dragging up the rear. Annie instigated, too, alternately laughing off the attention or irritated by it. She was different with friends close by. Always was. This was not my trusted confidante, the sympathetic ear. These were the moments I liked her less, though she would predictably reverse course in private, carry on as if she'd done nothing to offend, and I'd come out the other end liking her all the more.

Jack and I accepted the abuse, unwavering in our mission, truck drivers in *The Wages of Fear*, Annie our nitroglycerin.

Susan would peel off first. Diana next, along with Bonnie. It'd be another half-block before Annie would drop back to walk between us, or Jack and I moved up to escort.

First day out, Annie set the snotty tone with Jack: "Haven't seen you in the paper much. Guess you don't find things, anymore, eh?"

Jack played shocked to the hilt. "You read the paper?"

"What makes you think I don't?"

"I didn't expect you'd have the time, seeing how you're always playing with your hair."

"Try combing yours for once, why don't you! It's like I'm walking *The Shaggy Dog.*"

She would have been nicer, I guessed, had she known we were out to save her life. I worried, too, she'd put Jack off, cause him to leave the body-guarding to me alone. Jack, to his credit, did not let the sniping interfere with duty. Week three, in fact, he invited her to his Fortress of Solitude. *Yeah, just three frigging weeks.* I didn't get it. Me, it had taken months.

"You're the first girl I've ever let in," he told her. "Not counting my sisters."

"I'm sure your sisters don't count you, either." Annie maintained form, impassive and unimpressed.

Jack would laugh at her insults. Not always, but often. Another thing I never quite got.

They couldn't go two sentences without taking a shot at each other. I should've worn black and white stripes, carried a whistle. "Cut it out, you guys. C'mon, eh?"

"She started it."

"Did I? Really?"

"Yes. Really."

"Did not."

"Did, too."

"C'mon, you guys. Please."

"Shut up, Gus."

"Yeah, shut up, man."

They had a knack for being nice to each other, without being too nice.

At some point, Annie took note of the Lone Ranger and Tonto bookends. "So what are all these, then?" she asked.

"Um," Jack said. "Books?"

"I'd never have guessed," she snarked.

"Mysteries," I said, aiming to defuse. "Unexplained phenomena. Ghosts. Lost worlds. UFOs . . ."

"Interesting." She looked to Jack. Her sweetie-pie face. "May I borrow a couple?"

"I don't lend books."

"I'll be careful."

He put her to the test. "Do you dog-ear the pages or use a bookmark?"

"Bookmark."

"Always?"

She dumped the *sweet*. "Occasionally I tear off the cover and make ori- gami butterflies with it."

I laughed, elbowed Jack in the ribs. "That's a good one, eh?"

Jack didn't find it funny. Could be he didn't know what origami was. To most, Japan was Pearl Harbor, tin toys, and Sessue Hayakawa. "Swear you'll bring them back." Had he owned a lie detector, he would have hooked her up.

"Why wouldn't I?"

"I don't want them getting lost."

"Why would I lose them?"

"You'd better not."

"What do you recommend?"

"They're all great," I said. I was Johnny Appleseed, casting joy wherever I went.

Jack grabbed a Hix and a Ripley. "Start with the easy stuff."

She rebuffed him, crouched for a closer look at the titles. "This one," she said. "And, uh, this one."

Atlantis: Found! and *Weird, Weirder, Weirdest!* "Good choices," I said, though any would have been.

Jack added his original recommendations to hers, opened a notepad, marked down the titles and the date.

Annie smirked. "Will I be fined if I return them late?"

Jack never did collect on late fees. Annie returned the books and borrowed more. After the third lot, Jack stopped keeping a record.

She loved the books as much as we did. "I can't get some of these out of my head. The boy with the clock eyes, for instance . . . So weird. Are they true? Do you guys believe them all?"

"Not all," I said.

"Most," Jack said.

"They don't teach us any of this in school."

"Another unexplained mystery," I said.

"But Oak Island. You'd think we'd learn about Oak Island. It's in Nova Scotia."

"Mahone Bay," I said.

"Or the ghost stories. Some of these have to be real. So many of them."

"The Marfa lights."

"Raining cats and frogs."

"Divining rods."

"You try asking adults about this stuff and they look at you like you're nuts."

"Most religious people don't believe in the supernatural unless it's in the Bible," Annie said. "I think they should, though. The more strange things that happen in this world—like in these books—the firmer a person's faith should be, don't you think? God is supposed to work in mysterious ways, isn't He? Everybody says so. Your books—there's enough there to persuade the dumbest nonbeliever."

Theirs was not real hate. I saw soon enough. Real hate is easy to keep up. Done correctly, it'll follow the hated into their grave, allow you to dance a little.

Whatever Jack and Annie had against each other, it ebbed and flowed. I never could put my finger on it. Stopped trying. I wanted the three of us to get along. Nothing more. Frank Hardy, Joe Hardy, and Iola Morton—a *Franklin W. Dixon* friendship. Spanky, Alfalfa, and Darla. Clark Kent, Lois Lane, and Jimmy Olsen.

"Show me the best thing you've ever found," Annie said.

The garage had become our de facto clubhouse, the status official when Jack added a third chair for our newest inductee. A folding lawn chair.

"The best thing isn't here," Jack said, too quickly for our own good. And hers.

I matched his recklessness with my own. "Why don't we show her already, Jack?" And then to Annie. "They're at my—"

Jack hissed through bared teeth. "You lost your mind?"

"Your fault," I told him. No way he was going to pin this on me.

He backtracked for Annie: "My best find ever was stolen. The message in the bottle from the *James B. Colgate*."

I took the cue. "It was a ship that sank in Lake Erie."

"A sailor from Sweden wrote the message. It was to his wife."

"He drowned," I said.

"In 1916."

Annie was awed and moved. "That's so sad."

"Yup."

"Yup."

"Who stole it?" she asked.

"Some jerk," Jack said. "Called himself Cardiff Mann."

"Junior," I added.

"You can read about it over there." He directed her to the bulletin board. "The clipping on the bottom right."

Annie read enough to get the idea. "That's terrible."

"No sense crying over spilled milk," Jack said, the unassuming hero.

Annie scanned the other clippings. "Bryan McGrath writes about you a lot. Him and my dad are friends. They go hunting."

Jack and I didn't know what to say. Hearing Annie speak the reporter's name gave us the willies.

"Yeah, that bottle was so neat," Jack said.

"One time I put a message in an Orange Crush bottle and dropped it into the bay," I said.

Annie gave us a skeptical once-over. She dropped her hands to her hips, recast them as fists. "I am sick of you both. I am fed up with you treating me as if I am stupid. If you want to be friends with me, you had better stop. I want the truth and I want it now. What was it you wanted to show me?"

Jack gulped. "That was it."

"Yeah, the bottle." My smile was so massively fake my lips should've ruptured.

"Peas in a pod. *Rotten* peas in a pod. You, Jack Levin— you're as bad a liar as Gus."

Dragging Annie into the mystery of Hollywood North was what we'd been looking to avoid. Alluding to the cards was dumbass, and I kicked myself for it. Even if Jack was mostly to blame. Keeping Annie in the dark was how we kept her safe. Or so we hoped. Jack and I were in the dark, too. But Annie's was a darker dark. Her best defense was ignorance. And it was here she put herself at greatest risk. Because ignorance was not anything Annie settled for. Sure, skeptics might've scoffed, pointed to her faith in God, Jesus, and her nine sibling angels as proof of her ignorance. But not me. Not ever. Annie came to her own conclusions. I've thought about this often over the years. Her belief in a Higher Power was not ignorance; it was conviction arrived at from what she called "faith-based evidence"— sunrises, sunsets, first breath, and last. To Annie, faith synthesized the deductive and the inductive. Miracles were not an abstract; reality itself was the miracle. *"How can anyone not see?"* Faith was the absolute and binding logic that Science, in all its blinding logic, was too rational, too pedantic to see.

Annie's belief gave me the strength to question my disbelief.

Annie did not back down. Anytime and anywhere, her demand was as reflexive as *hi* and *bye* and *God bless you*: "Show me the best thing you ever found."

Jack and I had slipped up.

"Show me."

She saw right through us, knew we were hiding something. "Show me."

She persisted and we resisted.

"I told you, Annie."

"We told you, Annie."

"I'll stop asking when you two stop lying."

The girl was out to wear us down.

"Show me."

THIRTEEN

McGrath on the hunt

Annie was one of us now, and we wrestled with the unfairness. "She's either full-fledged or she's not," Jack said. "We should tell her. McGrath hasn't been on our backs for weeks."

"You think he's gone away?" I sputtered. "He's coming for Sunday dinner. To my house."

"Your mom really likes him, eh?"

"She doesn't know him. Not like we do."

"Soon you'll be calling him Daddy."

"Shit, you think I'm not worried?"

"You can't let him into the den—your father's books . . . If he starts snooping around . . ."

"Jesus, Jack, I'm not stupid."

"I enjoy his company. He's an interesting man." My mother assured me they were friends and nothing more. "Bryan is old enough to be my father. Grandfather."

"When has that ever stopped you?" I said.

"Pardon me? What did you just say?"

"I don't like him."

"If I listened to you, I wouldn't have a friend in the world."

"I liked Dottie."

"How does that have anything to do with Mr. McGrath? One does not cancel out the other."

"He smells like tobacco."

"If I based my friendships on who smokes, I'd eliminate ninety percent of the people I know."

"I don't like him."

"Oh, my! You won't let up, will you? You get so angry when I choose friends for you, but it's okay for you to choose for me?"

"Jack's mom is nice. She can be your new Dottie."

"Mollie Levin and I are friends. Good friends. But it's different. Different with Mr. McGrath."

"He's not your friend."

"You can't have me all to yourself, Leo. I have a right to a life, too. I'm warning you, you be polite to him. He's a writer. You can learn from him. Didn't you say you wanted to be a writer, too?"

"I want to be what Dad was."

"You don't have a clue what Daddy was. I barely know."

This was a revelation. "I thought you said he was a . . . a . . ." *Jesus.* In all these years, I'd never asked and she'd never stepped up to say. His books, his age, the freaky circumstances of his death—this was the sum total of my knowledge of him, the material on Alexander Berry so lacking, my mother had been unable to build a convincing mythology. She'd left the job to me, and the bio I'd concocted didn't go much beyond blood on a toilet floor.

"He did something," she said, floundering as I floundered. "Something to do with insurance. Or importing and exporting. He was vague—what can I say? Your daddy was not a talkative man. He preferred to read."

"He wore a suit to work. A tie. Right?"

"Always. You've seen the snapshots."

Okay, then. All was not lost. He wore a suit, a tie, and did something. My father was a TV dad.

"He was a good provider, Leo. He didn't leave us high and dry like so many men do to their families."

"He fought in the war, too, didn't he?" Ward Cleaver had been in the Navy. The Seabees. Mind you, I'd seen no pictures of Dad in uniform.

"Of course. He was very active. I'm sure he was."

* * *

Dinner began with hollowed-out oranges carved into baskets and filled with fruit cocktail. Then cream of tomato soup, Swedish meatballs, mashed potatoes, green peas, and red cabbage mixed with something redder.

Mom asked Mr. McGrath about his work.

"Did you see the piece I did on that old lady? Incredible. A hundred years old and square dances every Tuesday."

"I should be so lucky," Mom said.

"You're perfect the way you are," McGrath said, and I harpooned three Swedish meatballs with my fork.

"Did I mention Leo is friends with Jack Levin—the boy who's always finding things?"

McGrath slapped a thigh. "Well, isn't that interesting! Jack's a fine boy—though his finding days would seem to be behind him. A long while since I've heard from him, though I see him at the restaurant often enough. Hard worker, he is."

"The Levins are wonderful people."

"And what about you, Emily? How goes the door-knocking?"

"I can barely keep up, I'm so busy."

"I told you, one of these days I'm doing a feature on you. Beautiful young widow becomes a cosmetics tycoon."

Mom blushed. "Stop it. Just stop it."

"Yeah. Please," I said.

"Aha, Silent Sam speaks. So, your mother tells me you want to be a writer?"

"You should show Mr. McGrath the story you wrote for school—the one about the forest fire and the wolf."

"I threw it out," I said, and jumped up from the table in search of ketchup.

"Lovely. Just lovely, Emily. Haven't had a home-cooked meal this superb in years. A man could get used to this." McGrath's wink was for my benefit, as I returned from the pantry.

"I'm so glad you enjoyed it." Mom beamed.

"I'll bet you could work wonders with venison."

"I could certainly try," Mom said, "if I knew where to get some."

"Oh, I might be able to arrange the occasional tenderloin." Now the asshole winked for Mom's benefit.

"You ever watch *The Real McCoys*?" I said.

"Can't say I have, son." McGrath's brow furrowed with interest.

"You remind me of Grandpa McCoy." I gave the bottom of the ketchup bottle three hard whacks. "You know, Walter Brennan."

Mom kneaded her forehead, smiled with all her teeth and gums. "Give me a few minutes to clean up. We'll have dessert and coffee in the den. Show Mr. McGrath the way, Leo. I am sure he will have much to say about the books."

"Books?" McGrath pushed back from the table. "Now you're talking."

"Why can't we have dessert here?" I said. "Or the living room?"

She glared. "Because it will be nicer in the den. Dear."

I walked a fine line. If I protested too much, he'd sense I was covering up and sniff out the cards in a flash. I had to be protective, just not overly or obviously. *Where the hell was Jack when I needed him?*

Our den was a drunken hexagon. No two walls shared the same dimensions, which made the room something other than a hexagon. Oak bookshelves were built into five of the walls, the sixth a leaded bay window. Dad's walnut desk dominated the study. Two pedestals, nine drawers, and a writing surface inlaid with gilded leather. Behind the desk, a leather chair on rollers. In front, two leather armchairs dotted with brass studs. A Persian carpet of red, blue, and gold flowed from under the desk, traversing the dark hardwood floor to within a yard of the door. A sparse array of relics took up the perimeter of the desktop: Dad's circular pipe stand, five pipes and a humidor in the centre, his silver letter opener with the ivory handle, a pewter ash tray, and a desk calendar forever flipped to December 1954.

"Lord love a duck!" McGrath squawked, and bounded toward the widest shelf. "Quite the collection." He tilted his head to align with the spines. "Would you look at these!"

"They're my dad's," I said, conveying lineage, ownership, possession, caution. "They're my dad's."

"A voracious reader, indeed. Wish I'd known the man. We would have had a considerable amount in common, your mother notwithstanding. Ah, look at this, a John James Audubon—"

"Don't touch it. I told you, they're my dad's." I improvised on the fly, invoked my *Village of the Damned* persona, segued to the toxic *Twilight Zone* kid—the boy who turned a neighbour into a Jack-in-the-Box for playing a Perry Como record. I'd enlist the pigtailed murderer from *The Bad Seed*, too, should it come to that.

I edged toward the desk and letter opener. Plotted. I'd drive the blade into his neck. Or his heart. Or his brain. *Yeah, straight through an eye and into his brain.* I'd claim he tripped, recycle Mom's alibi from Malbasic and the bronze owl incident. "They're my dad's," I repeated, hardnosed and hardline. I squared my stance, hands on the desktop behind me, feeling my way to the letter opener.

McGrath swirled his tongue from cheek to cheek, assessing me. His hand wavered over the Audubon. I couldn't tell you where every intertitle was buried, but there was one in the Audubon, damn sure. I'd slipped it between the birds myself.

"Here we are, then," Mom trilled, arriving with a tray.

"In the nick of time," McGrath exclaimed, and winked his bullshit wink yet again, his *nick* dangling between me and dessert. He unwound into the nearest armchair. I took Dad's seat behind the desk. Mom sat in the armchair kitty-corner the prick.

She poured coffee, while I claimed the chocolate milk, a facile attempt to placate; she never let me have chocolate milk with dessert. *"Too much sugar and the flies will eat you up."*

She spooned apple crisp into cut glass bowls and topped each with whipped cream.

I had no appetite, toyed with the mush, sculpting, digging.

"You've outdone yourself, Emily."

"Easiest dessert ever." Mom was way too happy in the moment and I worried for her. A fall was coming. It had to be. McGrath or me, one of us would knock her from the peak.

"You were so right about the books," he said. "Love to get my hands on some of these."

"They mean a great deal to me," she said, transitioning to wistful.

"That Audubon could be worth a tidy sum. A first edition a sizeable fortune. Indeed, several of these would have value to collectors."

"I'd never sell. I couldn't."

"It'd be important to know. At the very least for insurance purposes. Be a shame should something happen and you came away with nothing."

"Who'd have thought?" Mom said, raised an eye, flared her nostrils, her way of saying, *"I told you so, Leo, he is a decent man."*

McGrath stroked his chin, returned to the shelves, perusing and pondering. *But he didn't touch,* which was all I cared about. He squatted, occupied with the doings on a lower shelf. "Whoa, whoa," he said. "What have we here?" And I thought uh-oh.

"Another bankable Audubon?" Mom said cheerily.

McGrath swung up and about with a suddenness I'd only seen from TV lawyers. "Was your husband a Red, Emily?"

"What?" Mom said, uncomprehending.

"A communist?"

"Alex?"

"I'm not accusing, only entertaining. Were his views what you might call radical?"

"I'm not sure I—?" She'd gone pale, which took some doing. In the fairest-of-them-all rankings, Snow White wouldn't have had a prayer against Mom.

"Several of these—this shelf particularly—have a distinctly pinko bias." Clean, snatch, and jerk, McGrath finessed the books onto the desk, a full house of sedition.

Homage to Catalonia by George Orwell
The State and Revolution by Vladimir Lenin
Ten Days that Shook the World by John Reed
Reform or Revolution by Rosa Luxemburg
Socialism: Utopian and Scientific by Friedrich Engels

My stomach rear-ended my tonsils. My worst fear realized. Pressed to the back of the shelf from where he'd taken the books, as plain as the nose on Jimmy Durante's face, was an intertitle. *A fucking intertitle.*

Were I at the Odeon I would have snorted aloud at the implausibility—any plot in which any villain, no matter how self-absorbed, could have missed the card.

"Alex never spoke of politics," Mom said, and I feared she might cry. I was stressed enough, without her tears stoking the anxiety.

"Alex. Alexander. Not an uncommon name in the Soviet Union. As for the Berry, now, I wonder . . . Bershov? Berezin? Berezhnoy?"

But my mother did not cry. Not a tear. "This is idiocy," she said evenly, angrily. "Where are you going with this? Why are you doing this, Bryan?"

"Now, now, Emily. Please. Please." The scheming bastard was beside himself. "I have upset you. This was certainly not my intention. Oh, my dear, I am so terribly sorry, you must believe me."

I loved it. McGrath had showed his true self sooner than I could have hoped.

He perched on the edge of the desk nearest my mother, lit up a cigarette. Like he'd done to Jack and me at the *Record*. He gathered her hands into his. "My intent was never to point fingers. I was merely intrigued at the possibility. I am first and foremost a journalist, don't forget. I am confident, if anything, your late husband's interest was academic. At worst, he was a fringer—a fellow traveller. Trenton has its share, trust me."

My mother bit her lip, withdrew her hands.

"But then how many real commies own Audubons, eh? Let me see if I can't brighten your day, find out if yours is as valuable as I suspect. You could be a very wealthy young woman, Mrs. Berry."

His back was momentarily to Mom and me as he searched for the Audubon. No way he wouldn't see the commie shelf and exposed intertitle. *No way.*

My arms an oval upon the desk, my head resting upon a shoulder, I corralled the letter opener, glimpsed my mother's state of being, witnessed her destiny in the glisten of her eyes, *and over the desk I leaped, by God and Country, and pumped and pumped and pumped that letter opener into McGrath's neck till his head was bobbing from a fleshy thread.*

The End

BPI

Oh, boy. How I could've.

My arms an oval upon the desk, my head resting upon a shoulder, I corralled the letter opener, glimpsed my mother's state of being, witnessed her destiny in the glisten of her eyes, and initiated my unplanned plan B.

I stuck two fingers down my throat and the Krakatoa of my gut erupted. Hell, I thought I'd lose my teeth, the velocity of the vomit surging upwards and outwards with a force I've not encountered since, a tsunami of Sunday dinner, waves of red cabbage and what might've been red berries.

Into my apple crisp.

Onto my father's desk.

Onto my mother's lap.

Into McGrath's coffee and onto McGrath's shirt, trousers, shoes. *I'd snuffed his cigarette!*

"Oh my, Leo." Mom dodged as I spewed, rushed to my aid, a wad of napkins at the ready, mopping and blotting.

McGrath was on his feet, flicking the barf from his hands, stomping it from his feet, helpless as the ooze descended into his waistband.

"I'm sorry, Bryan." Mom didn't sound sorry. "You should go now. Really. I'll pay for your dry cleaning."

"The boy is disturbed, Emily. He belongs in boarding school. A military academy. I'm telling you, for his own—"

"Yes. Thank you. I'll be sure to give your suggestion all the consideration it deserves. Now, if you don't mind . . ."

After Mom had gone to bed and the house was quiet, I put some distance between the intertitle and Dad's commie books, transplanting the card to a higher shelf and *The Voyage of the Beagle*. On the off chance Mom came around and forgave McGrath, I didn't expect he'd have much interest in a book about a travelling dog.

FOURTEEN

Annie in the Lois Lane

Jack grabbed my shirttail as Annie and her pals sprinted ahead. "She doesn't want us walking with her. She's sick of us treating her like a girl."

"But she *is* a girl," I said, confused why she'd suggest otherwise—and when and where Jack had spoken to Annie without me around.

"She's fed up with our lying to her. I came this close to telling her what's what."

"Not after last night. You can't. I told you, McGrath is as bad as ever. You should've seen him. He shook my mom up good. . . . One second he's Rock Hudson with Doris Day, next he's calling my dad a commie."

"Your dad was a commie?"

"I dunno. Maybe. McGrath said some of his books—"

"Wow, like a Russian spy?"

"More like Herb Philbrick, I'm thinking."

"A communist for the FBI."

"Yeah, but then the commies found him out and killed him."

12:00 4 I LED THREE LIVES—Espionage
FBI counterspy Alexander Berry, family man insurance salesman, and importer/exporter, infiltrates the American Communist Party, foiling Communist plots and unmasking those who would destroy America.

"I thought your father died on D-Day."

"That's what they wanted us to think."

"Who?"

"It's top secret, man."

"You are so full of it, Gus, it's coming out your ears." That was Jack for you. Robert Ripley and his cohorts could issue any manner of outlandish claim, but mine he pooh-poohed.

"Yeah, well, this isn't about my dad, okay? We're talking Annie, remember? And say we do tell her about him, the intertitles, Hollywood North—then what? She tells her dad, her dad tells McGrath, and McGrath . . . Jesus, who knows what?"

"You're sure he didn't see that card?"

"How many times I gotta tell you?"

"Must have been a sight—your puke all over him. . . . McGrath is more batshit crazy than the old coots he warned me to be wary of."

"So what are we going to do?" I said.

Annie looked to see if we were following, wrinkled her nose in annoyance, threw up her hands and waved us off. What could Jack and I give her, satisfy her need to know without putting her in any more danger? How much did Clark Kent tell Lois Lane, for instance, to allay her suspicions he was Superman?

A Variety Pack of neuroses collected mold in the pantries of our brains. *Sugar Frosted Death. Rice Creepies. Nabisco Shredded Guts. Cap'n Crunch Your Bones.* Neat little boxes of assorted anxieties, and plenty to spare. "What if we threw her a few bones," I said, "without bringing McGrath into it?"

We waited for her friends to go their separate ways and sped ahead before Annie had the chance to flee. Nose up. Chin out. Jaw set. She would not look at us. "Get lost."

"We're going to show you," I said.

"You need to understand," Jack said, "it's not anything we've found that we've been keeping from you, it's something we've found out."

"We didn't want to scare you," I said.

"That's what I hate about boys. Because I'm a girl, you think I scare more easily than you. Tell that to Joan of Arc. Or Amelia Earhart. Or Florence Nightingale. Or . . . or . . . or Marilyn Bell. I'm no more frightened of anything than you. Probably less."

"We'll see," Jack said.

"You will," she promised.

"Annie Oakley was pretty brave, too," I said.

"It's in the name," Annie said, and fired off a broadside of Annies, Anns, and Annes, three of whom I'd heard of: Ann Blyth, Ann-Margret, and Anne of Green Gables.

FIFTEEN

Sideshow for the darker plan afoot

"You wanted to see the best thing I've ever found," Jack said.

Annie stationed herself by Jack's garage door. Her schoolbag hung from her shoulder.

"Except," I said, "we don't know why it's the best."

"Not yet," Jack said.

"But we will," I said.

"Get on with it or I'm leaving," she said. Earning our way back into her good graces would take some doing.

Jack flipped to a page in a spiral notepad, passed it to her, and returned to his work table.

She read. Pondered. Frowned. Double-shrugged. Clung to her suspicion like it was a life raft. "If you ask me, you guys spend too much time at the Odeon. I've never heard about any of this."

"Us neither," I said. "Until we did."

"These things, Annie, they happened here, in Trenton," Jack said. "All of them."

"So what?" she said. "Accidents happen everywhere. Crimes."

"Yeah, but everywhere else they remember the bad stuff. They talk about it. Put up memorials or whatever."

"I don't understand."

"Neither do we," I said. "Not yet, anyhow."

"You do realize what you're saying," Annie said, and huffed. "If what you claim is true, and no one remembers these things happening, how is it you do?"

We explained what had been going on, how we came to make the list and our inability to connect the dots, the so-called amnesia.

She was adamant. "People do not forget things like this. They just don't."

"Unless they *just do*," Jack said.

"It's The Shadow," I said. "He's come to town and clouded everybody's mind."

"Except yours, of course. And Jack's," Annie said. "'If a tree falls in a forest and no one is around to hear it, does it make a sound?'"

The front legs of Jack's chair slammed to the floor. "Our tree does."

"We don't need to hear it falling, as long as we find it after," I said.

"Neither of you is making any sense whatsoever."

"Jesus Christ, Annie." Her stubbornness was getting on my nerves. "You've read the books. You know how unexplained shit goes. Nobody knows nothing. That's why it's unexplained. These accidents, disasters, murders, damn it—this is Trenton's *Believe It or Not!*"

"Stop shouting. Stop swearing at me. My goodness, Gus."

Jack scratched his head, stood, and paced. "You know Father Gurney, right? You go to St. Pete's."

Annie softened. "He was the nicest of them. He's senile, now, poor man."

"Well, he wasn't always senile, that's for sure. He's who told me about the Walker Shoe Factory. He'd just moved to the parish. Had been in town maybe a week when the roof fell in. In that one day he gave last rites to more people than he had in all his previous years combined."

"You swear on your life, Jack? You swear it was Father Gurney who told you?"

"You think I'd make that up? I swear on my life about everything I'm telling you."

"Me, too," I said.

Annie shifted her bag to her other shoulder. She chose her words carefully. "Father Gurney told me something, too, once. It's silly, really. My mother told me to ignore him, you know, because his memory was failing . . . but then, today, what you're saying . . . I wonder . . ." She examined our list again, sighed with a shiver. "He said 'Trenton is the Devil's playground.'"

I would have laughed had she and Jack not looked so damn serious. Adult-face is what they had.

"There's more," Annie said. "You know all the fires around here, the people who drown?"

"Billy Burgess," I said.

"Helmut Swartz's wife," Jack said.

"Father Gurney says 'they're the Devil's stepping-stones, the sideshow for the darker plan afoot.'"

"Holy shit." I was spooked, excited, spooked, and redeemed. "Holy, holy shit. I knew it. I knew it."

"Did Father Gurney say what it was?" Jack asked. "This 'darker plan'?"

Annie bit her lip the way she did in art class, tapped the tip of her nose like in math.

The schoolbag slid from her shoulder, the last of her acrimony slipping away with it. "I've got a story for you, too," she said. "One more for your list, maybe."

SIXTEEN

The all-you-can-eat buffet of The Unexplained

"You know the new houses they're building on Creighton Farms?" Annie said.

"Jack and I went finding up there. Before they started digging."

"And what did you find?"

"Nothing," Jack said.

"Nothing worth anything," I said.

"Did you look near the farmhouse?"

We hadn't.

She folded her hands into her lap, stared down, prepping from imaginary crib notes. "My father is supplying the building materials for the project. Lumber and nails. Drywall. Like that. A few days ago, I heard him telling my mother how they had to stop construction because of something they dug up out there. I couldn't hear what, but Mom's face, she was really shook up. But when they saw me watching, they changed the subject, put on their happy faces. It was all so fake."

"I know the look," Jack said, his empathy goosed with a shot of glum.

"Me, too," I said, not to be forgotten.

"They've been walking on eggshells ever since, always on the lookout for me, shutting doors, extra quiet so I won't hear. They're working so hard to act normal, it's like living with robots. It's worse now than when my grandmother got cancer and they tried to hide it from me. I couldn't stand it, so I asked my mother straight out what was going on. 'Oh, just one of your dad's silly work things,' she said, all sing-songy, so I knew for sure she was hiding something. 'No worries, dear. No worries.' And then she started talking about her friends and their bird-watching group and how—'*Did I tell you the news?*'—they'd spotted a Kirtland's Warbler and their names were going to appear in some birding magazine, and me—I felt I had ants crawling all over me."

"You want a cream soda?" Jack lifted the lid of the cooler parked beneath his table, "Drink Pepsi-Cola" in script on the side. It was the newest of his Fortress's amenities. He passed me a bottle and snagged one for himself. Annie wasn't thirsty. She only sounded thirsty.

"I've turned into you, Gus," she said, "the spying I've been doing. Last couple of nights I put a glass to the wall so I could hear what they were saying."

She paused. We waited. Her breathing dipped to rocky shallows. "Graves," she said. "They found graves. Under the farmhouse and out behind. Bones. Skeletons. And I don't know what else. Too many to count the first day. And I don't know how many since. My dad is scared. He's never scared."

"People used to bury their families on their property," Jack said, but it was way too level-headed to put the skids on Annie's story.

"Some of the people they found—" She had to stop and start over. "Some of the people they found, my dad says they weren't—they weren't dead."

We'd hit the jackpot. Burial grounds were the all-you-can-eat buffet of The Unexplained, the dead, the undead, and the better-off-dead. There'd been the devil heads of Bradford County, Pennsylvania—human skeletons with horns sprouting out the top of their skulls. The Chase Family Crypt in Barbados—where heavy lead coffins flew like matchboxes whenever a fresh corpse was interred. The Lake Delavan skeletons—ten-foot-tall giants in the heart of Wisconsin. The vampire skeletons of Bulgaria—iron stakes protruding from where their hearts had been. Now it was Trenton's turn, *oh boy!*

"How not dead?" Jack said.

"Vampire and zombie not dead?" I said.

"That's all I know. Except my dad thought they should call in the police, but Mr. Moroney—he's the builder—he doesn't want to delay construction. And my dad, well—Mr. Moroney gives him tons of business—so he's afraid to rock the boat."

Jack and I set our empty bottles on the floor.

"I want to see for myself," Annie said, appealing to us with her big brown eyes, like there was a snowball's chance in hell we wouldn't go along. "Before Mr. Moroney plows it all under."

"He can't do that," I said.

"He's going to. Any day now, from what Dad says."

"Tonight, then," Jack said. "I'll bring my camera."

Annie reached into the cooler. Popped the cap. Swigged. "Flashlights. We'll need flashlights."

SEVENTEEN

Night of the living dead

I was the first to arrive at Pilots Hall. It was nine sharp, as planned, and I worried the others had copped out, or been caught sneaking out.

I imposed a fifteen-minute deadline for Jack and Annie to show, and bided my time, tapping my foot to the music blaring from inside the squat white building. "The jukebox is the only good part," somebody said, and there was Mickey Mental himself, not six feet behind me, propping up the building, knee bent behind him, sole of his boot flat against the stucco. "Hey."

"Hey," I said.

"Come for your dad, too?" he said.

"What?"

"Your dad? He inside, too?"

"My dad is dead," I said.

"Oh," he shrugged, and I guessed it was off-hours for bullies.

The field behind Pilots Hall was a trailhead of sorts to Creighton Farms. The location was also a safe bet on a school night, unlikely to arouse suspicion. You'd often see kids thereabouts after hours, peering through the smoked windows, checking up on their dads at their mothers' urgings and, if need be, hanging around to escort, as Jack's mother once put it, "the drunken good-for-nothings home." Pilots Hall members were former longshoremen, Great Lakes sailors, and airmen. The Hall's professed values aligned with the Lions, Kiwanis, and Kinsmen. The community service the Pilots was most famous for was cheap booze. (In 1968, it would become the only service club in town history to be shut down by local authorities. Today, an auto parts dealer and a tattoo parlour occupy the building. Only clue to the past is the Pilots coat of arms engraved into the cornerstone. A winged anchor rising from what is either stormy seas or a head of beer.)

Jack turned up a moment after Annie, surprising us with his sisters in tow. "If I didn't let them come, they would've squealed."

"We brought our own flashlights," Abby said, and Issie shone hers in my eyes.

"Hey, Levin," Dougie called from his post.

"Hey, man," Jack said. "Your dad off the wagon, again?"

"Yup. You?"

"Nothing special."

"Keeping late hours, eh?"

"Not really."

"Off finding, are you?"

"Just hanging out."

"Well, see ya, I guess."

"Good luck, eh?—your dad and all."

"I hope he drops dead," Dougie said. "Like Gus's dad did."

"My dad was killed in the war," I said.

Annie welcomed the girls with affection, corralled them to her side, and moved us on out with a *Wagon Train* wave. We rolled through the Pilots parking lot and into the field behind, the grass gone to seed, knee-high to either side of the path.

Annie was her upbeat self, and you'd never know by the show she put on we were marching to a graveyard. The act was for the Levin girls, of course, reaching its dramatic peak with a balletic sweep of her hand that arced from countryside to sky. "'The wind was a torrent of darkness among the gusty trees, The moon was a ghostly galleon tossed upon cloudy seas, The road was a ribbon of moonlight over the purple moor, And the highwayman came riding—riding—riding . . .'" Not a line was sung, yet this was the closest I'd come to life as a movie musical. I wanted to run up to her, hug her, bury my face in her hair and, for God's sake, kiss her. *Hug? Kiss? Jesus!* What the hell was with me? I banished the corny thoughts from my head, promised I'd never think such stupid shit again.

"Wow," Abby said. "That was so good, Annie. Is there more?"

"I like poems," Issie added.

"'The Highwayman' is the most romantic verse anyone has ever written."

"I hate poetry," I muttered, reclaiming my self-esteem. "Except for 'Casey at the Bat,' a couple others."

Despite my grumbling, Annie's assessment wasn't far off. The wind was gusting. Clouds were gathering, though nothing you'd call a sea. And the moon was full, without being ghostly. If luck was with us, the *ghostly* was up ahead.

Jack came to a sudden stop. "We're being followed." We doused our lights, cocked ears.

"Mickey Mental?' I said.

"Could be anyone," he said.

I shortlisted my probables. You know their names by now. We'd be sitting ducks. Not a day went by some Ontario kid didn't turn up dead in some field. We'd be five more.

To our left, a hairy swoosh of grass. We crouched. And black against black tore across our "ribbon of moonlight," and we exhaled relief and laughter. Just another berserk Lab. Not one of us couldn't identify the slosh of tongue, the frenzied panting.

At Keating Woods, Jack took the lead from Annie. He knew the territory. "The bullets and buttons I showed you, found most out here," he told her.

I won't dwell on the owls. Nor the hobo we came across, his campfire and lean-to, how he asked if we had something for him to eat, how Annie materialized an orange and tossed it to him. No point, either, in going on about the Ford Fairlane parked without a road in sight, doors open, and a naked boy and girl rutting on the front seat, how Annie situated herself between Abby and Issie to block their view, how she shoved the mesmerized Jack and me to move on, and kept shoving until we did.

At Creighton Farms, Annie pointed to where she believed the farmhouse used to be. Flashlight beams duelling, we began our final leg across furrowed ground. Maintaining our bearings wasn't as easy as we'd anticipated. The windbreaks that had once protected the fields and crops had been uprooted. Luckily for us, workers had thrown up a fence around the main construction site, a haphazard assembly of saggy chicken wire and wooden posts, bicycle reflectors affixed here and there. In the foreground beyond the fence, a yellow backhoe sat idle. Here, too, along with the Creighton homestead, the land had been cleared of centuries-old oaks, elms, and ash.

We cast our lights onto the excavations. The ground was flat, with man-made mounds rising to and fro, deep valleys between. A schoolyard diorama of the Rockies.

We were on to something, all right. The signs confirmed it. As if we'd ever doubted.

"I know Mr. Moroney," Annie said. "He's done things. . . . He means what he says."

"You can stay back here and wait, if you're afraid," Jack said. Annie socked him so hard his flashlight went flying, and the fence came down as he staggered to break his fall.

"Sorry," Annie said, as she scampered merrily over Jack and the chicken wire and onto the site. Abby and Issie shadowed Annie's every move and expression. Gung-ho, they were.

I helped Jack to his feet. "Good thing it wasn't barbed wire."

"She's dangerous," he said.

"No need to tell me."

"Oh, my," Annie cried. "Over here, over here." And Abby and Issie echoed, "Over here, over here."

I asked Jack if he'd explained to his sisters where we were going, what we hoped to find. "Yeah," he said, "but I don't think the *dead* and *graveyard* parts sank in."

The bones were everywhere. Hell, they were as plentiful as the dirt that had been dug up with them. Big bones. Little bones. Fragments. Slivers. Confetti. Resting atop and about the mounds. Poking out from the mounds. All over the mounds. And in the pit at our feet, a garden of bones.

"How many you think?" I said.

"Too many," Annie said.

"Are they people bones?" Issie asked.

"Over there." Jack's beam strayed a ditch farther up, the light reflecting off the shiny surface.

"Watch where you walk," Annie cautioned.

You could see a few bones here and there, but you could tell the second pit had been excavated with greater care. It was square, thirty by thirty, and shallower, four feet deep at most. Plastic tarps were laid in sections across the bottom of the pit. Jack ordered his sisters to hold the fort up top. He did not ask Annie if she wanted to wait with them. "Here goes nothing," he said, and the three of us slid down the dirt walls into the pit.

The tarp was secured with iron spikes. Unlike the sloppy workmanship at the fence, they'd been driven deep. We had to tug and jiggle before a corner came loose, and then another and another, and the wind whipped under the tarp and wafted it upwards, a pterodactyl taking flight. Four smallish skeletons greeted us, each wrapped in ragged and weathered shrouds—dirt, bug turds, and what a runaway imagination might conclude was dry blood.

"Like Jesus and that Shroud of Turin thing," I said.

"Look closer," Annie said. "It's cheesecloth."

"What my mom uses to make blueberry syrup," Jack said.

We stayed close, moved to the next tarp. Here, three crude wooden coffins, lids unsecured and askew. Jack lifted each in turn, examined the undersides. As feared, the narrative was the same as those buried in shrouds.

"Drag marks," I said, pointing my light at the dirt. "They've been moved from where they were dug up."

"Back there, too," Jack said.

"So they could use fewer tarps," Annie theorized. "Grouping them together."

We braced ourselves for the third tarp, though I didn't see how it could be any less horrifying, but then Abby and Issie were at our backs and in our ears and freaking and screaming and hollering to high heaven, thrashing to get the hell up and out of there. And for a couple of seconds, we were freaking and screaming and hollering to high heaven, too, not knowing who the hell or what was up.

"I told you to stay back. I told you," Jack yelled. "Happy now? Think you'll ever get that out of your heads? You'll never get that out of your heads."

Annie calmed Jack down and, with her help, the girls calmed, too.

"What are they?" Issie asked. "Who are they?"

"I want to go home," Abby whimpered.

"Don't you dare move again," Jack said, guiding them to a corpse-free corner of the pit.

"Listen to your brother," Annie said. "You've got to."

None of us were going to let a couple of baby-faced interlopers blow our opportunity.

By the fourth tarp, we'd had enough, seen enough, yet we pressed on, if only for the stomach-turning perversity of it all.

The first had clued us in on Annie's dad and his concerns. The second, third, fourth, and fifth showed how low Mr. Barker was prepared to go to hang on to Moroney's business. He must have needed the money pretty badly. By the sixth we more than understood why Mr. Barker had said the people they had found were not dead. By the seventh the revulsion weighed so heavily upon us, we could barely move, barely talk.

The dead had been buried in makeshift shrouds, cardboard boxes, or crude wooden coffins. One had been folded into an apple crate. We could only guess the ages, a good many looked to be kids, borderline or early teens like us. But not all. There were several adults, too. And none of this, I tell you, was the worst of it.

Skeletons don't frighten. Skeletons are fun. It's what we'll all be someday. What frightens, what isn't fun, are the hideous routes some of us will take in becoming one.

"All of them," Annie said. "They're like that poor girl. That poor girl in those books of yours."

"The Woodstock girl," Jack said.

I referenced the source. *"Weird, Weirder, Weirdest!"*

Woodstock, Ontario is two hundred miles southwest of Trenton. In 1886, a fifteen-year-old girl became sick, died, and was buried. Days after, her folks had second thoughts and decided to move their beloved daughter closer to home. It was a decision they likely regretted for the rest of their messed-up lives. When the body was exhumed, the girl was discovered balled up and shockingly fetal, an arm thrown back behind an ear, face aghast in breathless agony, fingernails and fingertips worn and torn, her burial shroud clawed to bloodstained tatters.

"What could be more horrible than waking up in your own coffin?" Annie said.

I tried to make her feel better. "How about having your eyelids cut off, honey poured on your head, and buried up to your neck in an anthill in the desert?" She did not see the humour. "Without a hat."

"People don't get buried alive anymore," Jack assured her.

"They did here," Annie countered. She swung her light to either side and then out front. "Look how many. Look how many."

"These are old graves," Jack said. "From a long time ago."

"Not all," Annie said. "You saw . . . you saw. There was flesh on some of those bones."

"Catgut," I said.

"Still pretty old, though," Jack insisted.

"One more," Annie said. "One more tarp, just to be sure."

"We are sure," Jack said. "More than sure."

There was no stopping Annie. She was dowsing death the way she covered off that pit, zigzagging through the tarps to select her final one.

Nothing changed.

The last tarp told the same story as the previous seven. One coffin, two shrouds. Misshapen skeletons, calcified corkscrews of cartilage, porous bone, and hair. Faces contorted and distorted, a death worse than death. Silent screams reverberating into The Eternal. Shrouds hand-shredded to streamers. The undersides of coffin tops clawed and scored.

Another thing, too. The extremities of the skeletons. In every case, a hand or a foot, though never more than one, was missing. Chopped. Lopped. Whatever. For whatever.

The fifteen-year-old Woodstock girl had nothing on the corpses of Creighton Farms, may she rest in peace.

"Who'd do this?" Annie said.

"'Who knows what evil lurks in the hearts of men?'" I said, my attempt at deep.

"What evil lurks in your head?" Jack snapped. "You think it's funny, this hellhole?"

"Funny or not, Gus asked a good question," Annie said. "What evil does lurk?"

Jack mumbled a grudging sorry and changed the subject. "I'd better get those pictures in," he said, and swore as he patted down his pockets. "No, no, no. No. The flashbulbs. I forgot the goddamn flashbulbs. If it wasn't for my stupid sisters distracting me . . ."

We aimed our five flashlights at the best of the dead, or worst, I suppose. Our batteries had weakened by then. Jack could not guarantee the photos would turn out. He cursed himself again for the flashbulbs. He'd stopped blaming his sisters, though the pair kept their distance.

We returned the tarps to their places. The ones that hadn't blown away, anyhow, and used rocks to hammer down the spikes. Rain was falling as we finished, so there wasn't any need to cover up our tracks. Mud would take care of it. We raised up the trampled section of fence and set off the way we'd come. To ration our batteries, we kept it to one flashlight at a time.

"I don't want to be buried alive," Annie said, as if anyone besides Houdini ever had.

"Aimee Semple McPherson had the right idea," I said. "She was buried with a telephone in her coffin."

Annie perked up. "You can do that?" She didn't ask who Aimee Semple McPherson was, but then Annie would know. In the '20s and '30s, McPherson had been a big-time radio evangelist, preaching Christianity to America. She went on to found her own church, before croaking under mysterious circumstances during the war.

"*Believe It or Not!* is full of safety devices for coffins—escape hatches, alarm bells, oxygen tanks."

"I'd be cremated, if my parents would let me," Annie said. "It's our souls that matter. Our bodies are only vessels."

"Me," I said, "I'm going to live forever, that's all there is to it."

Annie ignored my declaration of immortality, and returned to the scene none of us would ever fully leave behind. "Someone knows what went on back there. One person didn't do all that."

"If it was a person," I said.

Jack ended his brief silence, shared what he'd been mulling. "Creighton Farm is over a hundred years old, easy. Whatever the people who lived here were up to, it was passed on, from father to son, mother to daughter."

"A family tradition of killing," Annie said.

I asked the obvious. "Know any Creightons?"

"Crates," Jack said, his mouth dry. "He's a Creighton."

"He is?"

"First name or last, not sure which. Don't know if he ever lived on the farm, though."

I squinted into the dark, behind, ahead. Crates could be on us before we knew it, slit our throats, slice off a souvenir limb, and shovel us under in the grand Creighton tradition. Either way, he'd be at school next day. Like Susan Burgess, he had a perfect attendance record, though he never received an award for it. Malbasic was said to deduct a day from his "stellar attendance" for every hour Crates spent in the principal's office. My guess, Crates was so far into negative territory he'd never dig his way out.

"He works for my dad in the summer," Annie said. "Dad would have let him go, too, a long time ago, because of how he sneaks up on people—how he's nowhere to be seen, and then he's standing right next to you."

"It's the moccasins," I said. "He's always wearing moccasins."

"But then Dad put him to work on the grinder, sharpening tools and knives. That's all Dad has him do now. Dad says Crates is the best sharpener he's ever had. Especially scythes and mower blades."

We picked up our pace as the rain intensified. At Keating Woods, Jack again: "Aimee Semple McPherson was born in Ontario. Did you know?"

We didn't. Nor did we care much at this point.

"A town called Salford. And Salford, if you want to know, is only ten miles from Woodstock where that girl was buried alive. . . ."

"Jesus," I said.

"Stop talking," Issie said.

"Please," Abby begged.

Annie put the light to her watch. "My parents will kill me if they catch me out this late." She started jogging and we jogged with her. We ran all the way to Pilots Hall. And it didn't have a damn thing to do with what Annie's parents might do to her, either.

We didn't see the hobo and his campfire on our return pass. We saw the peel of the orange Annie had tossed him. The Ford Fairlane hadn't moved, though the doors were shut, the windows fogged over, the chassis creaking.

Owls. There was no shortage of owls.

Annie's house came first. The lights were on. All the lights. She didn't know what to say to Jack and me, touched our arms, hugged Abigail and Isabel.

"Well," she said, her laugh caustic and unexpected. "'It is a far, far better thing that I do, than I have ever done . . .'"

"What?" we said.

"Nothing," she said, and consigned herself to the longest mile.

The front door swung open. Her dad yanked her inside, muddy droplets splashing, shooting stars under porch light.

Jack and I stalled at the crossroads. "So?" he said. "*Premature Burial* or *Tales of Terror*?"

"*Creighton Farms*," I said. "Vincent Price will play me."

"Guess I'm stuck with Peter Lorre, then."

"There's always Ray Milland."

"I'll stay with Lorre, thanks."

"Debbie Reynolds can play Annie," Issie said.

"Hayley Mills is better," Abby countered.

"Annie can play herself," I said. "She's good at that."

"Sweet dreams, Gus," Jack said.

"In whose lifetime?" I said.

EIGHTEEN

Heavenly luxury with a two-car garage

The interrogations were intense. If anybody was going to squeal about our ghouling, you'd have expected it to be Abigail and Isabel. "Annie Barker isn't going to tell and neither are we," they swore to their brother. "Annie's so nice."

The punishments varied. Two weeks with no Saturday morning TV for the girls. A month of hard labour at the Marquee, and no TV or Odeon for Jack. Two weeks of early bedtimes and three Hail Marys daily for Annie.

I'd come in through the back door. I could hear Mom laughing. *The Tonight Show.* The new guy, Johnny Carson, had been growing on her. She called to me in the kitchen. "Is that you, Leo?"

"Thirsty. Came downstairs to get a drink."

"Do you know how late it is, sweetheart?"

I waited for another round of laughter, dashed behind Mom's back and up the stairs without her noticing I wasn't in my pajamas.

We shared our nightmares, hoping to purge the carryover. My nightmares were as petrifying as anybody's. And I lied about them all. I had no dreams about the farm. No dreams about any part of that night. I thought this was a good thing, made me stronger than the others, though not so good and strong I could admit my deficiency to Jack or Annie.

Look, the episode was pretty messed up any way you looked at it. And nightmares were small potatoes. Five kids in a graveyard playing footsies with the living dead. We should've been traumatized numb and dumb. Abby and Issie, especially. And none of us spilling the beans, telling parents, police, anyone. I have no explanation, other than us being Trenton kids born and bred. We saw horror with a softer focus, somehow. The night on Creighton Farms was as real as it could get without ever becoming as real as it should have been.

Mr. Moroney stuck with his building plans. The afternoon after our expedition, the land was plowed under and over. "'Every godforsaken bone pulverized,'" Annie heard her dad say. "'People had been snooping around. Moroney blew a gasket. No, there's no point in telling anyone. God, no. Anybody who's anybody is in his pocket.'"

Next day, a Wednesday, the *Record* reported a body had been discovered during "recent excavations at Creighton Farms." Although only one body was mentioned, the three of us were smug in the certainty *body* would be revised to *skeletal remains* and the total increased way way upwards. The burial grounds would be exposed, the guilty punished.

Thursday, the paper updated the story. "I seen this black dog sniffing 'round and then I seen a hand sticking out the dirt," said the backhoe operator who uncovered the body. The victim was "a fourteen-year-old boy who had failed to heed multiple warning signs and breached the high-security barrier surrounding the construction site." The dead kid was Douglas Dunwood of Windsor Street in Trenton.

"You think he followed us?" I said.

"I don't want to think about it," Jack said. "People drop out of our lives like flies and there's nothing we can do to bring them back."

"Dead is only a word, Jack," Annie said. "Douglas has gone to a better place."

"He was my best friend," Jack said, "until he turned into a jerk."

"It's a sin to speak ill of the dead."

"I always liked him," I said.

On Friday, a special school assembly was held. Reverend James James from the Dunwoods' church led the school in prayer and a minute of silence in memory of Douglas. Dougie's uncle represented the family. He gave a short speech, thanked us for loving Dougie, and showed us the clothes Dougie would be wearing for his eternal rest—Scouting hat, shorts, shirt, and hodgepodge of merit badges. The school erupted with clapping and cheers. A lady from the Red Cross presented a National Film Board movie about the dangers of children playing at construction sites, with an emphasis on blasting caps. Mr. Malbasic then paraded us outside where he announced Dufferin's *Elmer the Safety Elephant* flag would fly at half-mast until the new school year in September, whereupon Dougie's Scoutmaster lowered the flag and saluted the school.

A week after our nighttime foray, the *Record* ran an artist's rendition of the "greatly anticipated" Creighton Farms subdivision. The caption: *Heavenly luxury with a 2-car garage.*

"What's so funny?" Mom asked.

"*Hi and Lois,*" I said.

The graves never made the *Record*.

Jack's photos came back blank.

"That seals it," he said, and pounded his fist against his garage door until Annie and I went rodeo on him, and bulldogged his arm.

The less you like a dead kid, the tougher it is to get your head around the death. We wrestled with guilt, Dougie's passing somehow our fault, which it was to some degree. If he hadn't seen us outside Pilots Hall . . .

"How do you think he died?" I said. "Bet you it wasn't an accident."

My speculation rankled Annie. "Didn't you watch the movie? You know how dangerous construction sites are. He's gone. What does it matter?"

"I heard they found him under a ton of dirt," Jack said.

"I heard nothing of the sort," Annie said.

"That'd be the same as him being buried alive," I said. "Like the others."

"Or perhaps he just fell," Annie said. "Simple as that."

"You really think so?" Jack said.

I offered up another philosophic gem. "The only good part about dying, I figure, is you get to stop being afraid of dying." That set Annie off, all right.

"My goodness, Gus. If you attended church, you'd know there is no reason to be afraid."

"But you were afraid out there on the farm. You're saying none of this—all those bodies—has shaken your faith?"

"Only in my fellow man. Not in God. And no matter how terribly their lives ended, they're with Him now."

"But it was God who let it happen."

"Is that what you saw—God's work? Poor you. I saw only the Devil's work—what Father Gurney said, the 'darker plan afoot.'"

"So God only does good things and the Devil only bad?"

"That's a question only the Devil would ask."

"Something else about Dougie," Jack said to me, when we were alone. "He was missing a foot. The police aren't saying, but the guy who drives the cement truck was talking in the Marquee and he said it looked like an animal had eaten it."

Whatever else was going on, there was no dismissing Annie's contribution to our cause. She was owed her due and we gave it. Since the events ranged over years, and the years were vague, we debated where on our list Annie's find belonged. The top, as it turned out:

18?? TO 19?? – THE 'BURIED ALIVE' OF CREIGHTON FARMS

"I'm honoured." Annie smiled wanly, her sincerity riddled with anguish. "I can't fall asleep without thinking about it. Those poor people, and the murderers scot-free. And then, what happened to Douglas."

I shared my favourite theory. "Tons of murderers get off scot-free. Bet you anything we pass a bunch every day of our lives. Going to dance hops. Laughing at knock-knock jokes. Killing kids on Mount Pelion. Eating club sandwiches. Bowling with buddies. Pushing wives off dams. Dancing the cha-cha. Eating popcorn in the Odeon. Going—"

"Stop. Does your brain not have an off switch?" Annie was going through one of those periods where she didn't have much patience for me. "Why must you say such awful things all the time?"

"Because they're true."

Jack's change of subject didn't help. "I had another bad dream last night. Running out of air. Trying to claw my way out. . . ."

"Me, too," I said. "Me and Mickey Mental in the same grave. And Crates with a big shovel."

"Well, anyhow," Jack said.

"Uh-huh," Annie agreed. "Yeah. Well."

"What is this, a funeral?" I said cheerfully. "Look at us! We're here. We're alive. We're in one piece." I had my moments, I tell you, loopy though they were.

We celebrated, popped cream sodas, clinked bottles. To Annie and her find. To Mickey Mental, may he rest in peace. To our bright futures. To happier days ahead. To good times, safe times. To friends forever. You'd think I would have paid heed, shuddered at the flagrant foreshadowing.

5:00 10 THINGS TO COME—Science Fiction
During Christmas celebrations with friends and family, businessman John Cabal (Raymond Massey) dampens the holiday spirit with talk of doom and gloom. Minutes later, the whole planet goes kablooie, with war droning on for the next umpty-hundred years.

I was mighty bugged, too. Bugged there'd been no celebration for me. Bugged by my own massive failure. No one raised the issue. Never crossed their minds, I'll wager. Jack and Annie were never like that; they had a Three Musketeers mindset—one for all and all for one and all that goody-goody malarkey—and I tried my damndest to have it, too. Still, Annie had leapfrogged me with Creighton Farms. My dead were nowhere near as good as their dead. I'd contributed—what?—all of four bodies to the list, and two, the kids who fell from the water tower, iffy entries at that. Even should the day come and I did have a whopper to offer, I could never overtake Annie. What could be better than God-knows-how-many buried alive, severed extremities to boot?

Jack the Finder. Annie the Finder. Gus the . . .

I relapsed, went B&E again. Dead oldsters. Vacant houses. Yesterday's news. Missing persons is what I was after. I'd piggyback on Annie's find, put names to the bones on Creighton Farms.

Jack the Finder. Annie the Finder. Gus, *Kid Crimesolver of the Year*.

I don't know the rate at which people disappear in small towns. But from the numbers I came up with, I'd bet you a thousand bucks Trenton set the per capita pace. I'm not talking run-of-the-mill runaway husbands, wives, and kids, either. I'm talking honest-to-goodness hole-in-your-heart gone.

I didn't bring the clippings to Jack. No point, I realized, a few days in. There was nothing left to tie them to. The new houses were going up fast and nobody was going to tear them down. Grave markers is what those houses were, and what they are.

As for Robert Ripley, Elsie Hix, Frank Edwards, and company, our enthusiasm for their chronicles of the unexplained was no longer what it had been. We were spooked. Burnt out. *Dead tired*. How else can I put it? We did not sit and plan. Never discussed or plotted. Our decision to leave well enough alone arrived by osmosis.

Ironic, too. Thanks to the Creighton Farms mystery, McGrath was finally getting his wish. We were backing off. By taking Jack and me deeper into The Unknown than we'd ever gone before, Annie might also have saved her own skin.

What was it McGrath had said in the restaurant? It had been one of Mom's payday dinners. *"Some shit deserves explaining. Some shit doesn't. Plain as that. Explanations won't change a thing. Sometimes there is no explaining."* Jack and I could see it now. Plain as that.

Our priorities were shifting, as well. Jack would be moving up to Trenton High come fall. While Annie and I would only be a year behind, it would be measured in kid years—and kid years were triple the length of any adult year. No telling the shit that might happen. (For all I knew, *both* Jack and Annie would be leaving me behind. For sure, Malbasic had a surprise or two in store for me. How many black marks would he have scribbled into my file by then, how many synonyms for troublemaker in my school records?)

So it was, Jack, Annie, and I withdrew to safer, less troublesome ground.

"Best superhero?"

"J'onn J'onnz, Martian Manhunter."

"What?"

"You heard me."

"You're kidding?"

"Who, then? Superman?"

"Herbie Popnecker."

"Who?"

"*Forbidden Worlds*. The tubby kid with the glasses? The lollipop? He's at least as good as your dumb Martian Manhunter."

"Not to me."

"*Famous Monsters of Filmland* or *Screen Thrills Illustrated*?"

"*Find the Feathered Serpent*—you ever read that book?"

"Hot dog or hamburger?"

"Hot dog."

"Larry, Moe, or Curly?"

"Shemp."

"He's dead. So is Costello."

"Abbott and Costello's Costello?"

"Yup. Hardy, too."

"The fat one?"

"Sorry."

"Curly, then, I guess. The old Curly, not the new Curly."

At first, Annie only listened, as Jack and I dazzled with our profound knowledge and extraordinary taste. But soon, she came around, brought her own spin to the game, giggling her head off . . .

"Best Paul Anka song?"

"Troy Donahue or James Darren?"

"Best Elvis movie?"

"Beehive, bun, or ponytail?"

"Gidget or Tammy?"

. . . as Jack and I drew sputtered blanks. And no, we didn't mind for a second. Not even Jack. The sarcasm and nasty shots between the two had ended long before. It had happened so gradually, I'd hardly noticed, almost forgot Jack and Annie hadn't been friends from the start. Like me and Annie. Like me and Jack.

"You guys are a riot," Annie would say, and in my head there'd be my plaintive reply, "I love you, too, Annie Barker. So goddamn much." And shuddered at the unexplained mystery that caused me to think such a hokey thing.

Jack, Annie, me, we kept it going until June of 1963.

The 20th.

A Thursday.

The day Jack Levin disappeared.

PRODUCTION _____

DIRECTOR _____

CAMERA _____

DATE _____ SCENE _____ TAKE _____

Fourth Reel

"Feast your eyes
-glut your soul on my
accursed ugliness."

-The Phantom of the Opera (1925)

 # ONE

1988 and I was in Cobourg
with Jack, Marie Dressler, and Aimee Semple McPherson

The roads were icy. Last count, seven cars in ditches.

Then eight.

Then nine.

Snow was blowing in from the lake, the wipers struggling, the headlights useless in the whiteouts. The visibility was closing in on zero as I inched into Cobourg. I knew what Jack was going to say before he said it, and beat him to the punch: "Marie Dressler was born here. Won the Oscar for *Tugboat Annie*."

Jack cut me with his smirk. "*Min and Bill*, idiot. She won for *Min and Bill*."

"I was testing you," I said.

"Don't give me that. You've lost whatever it was you had. Accept it. Get over it."

"We could go to her house for dinner," I said. "It's a restaurant, you know?"

"Of course, I know. I know what you know."

After Mom was gone, I swore I'd never go back home. Yet here I was, eleven years on and on my way, at Death's behest again. It could be habit-forming, I thought, once a decade, give or take.

I should have told the lawyer he'd dialled the wrong number, got the wrong guy. Should have said Leo Berry was dead. But I had guts, right? Jack had told me that. "You got guts, man," he'd said so long ago.

"The visit will be in your best interest, I assure you," the lawyer assured me. I could hear the money in his formality. Greedy pig, that's what I was, between jobs again. At least my exes had remarried, leaving me free and clear on the support, though I doubt either wife would call what I provided as that, exactly. I will not embarrass them by naming them. Aside from their poor judgement in marrying me, I take the blame in full. *You try living with me.*

Nope. No children. The world didn't need a Gloomy Gus II.

"Quick!" Jack said. "Scariest movie motel ever?"

I dug deep. "Raven's Inn. *Horror Hotel*. Christopher Lee. Venetia Stevenson." That shut him up, all right. No Hitchcock. No Perkins. *Ha!*

"You guys are a riot," Annie said from the back seat. I turned to look. She wasn't there.

Thirty-five miles to go. Might as well have been a thousand in this weather. Snow blanketed the sign, but *otel* and *Vaca y* were enough. I plowed through the drifts into the lot.

Only thirty-five miles. I was in no hurry. I've told you.

Once, at a motel in Grand Forks, North Dakota, I found a five dollar bill in a Gideon Bible. I have thumbed through every motel and hotel Bible since. In Cobourg, the Holy Book yielded a bookmark, colourful images of fire, brimstone, roiling seas, and Aimee Semple McPherson, magnanimous in grainy black and white, her thoughts expressed in C.B. DeMille calligraphy:

"THE SEA SHALL GIVE UP THE DEAD WHICH ARE IN ITS DEATH AND HELL SHALL DELIVER UP THEIR DEAD AND THEY SHALL BE JUDGED, EVERY MAN ACCORDING TO HIS WORKS."

—THIS IS THAT (1919)

Grand Forks wasn't the first time I found money in a Bible. The week after Mom had passed, I pulled a dusty basket of *Redbook* and *Good Housekeeping* magazines from the crawlspace in the cellar. At the bottom of the box was an oversized New Testament, bound in white with a golden bookmark, and dedicated by hand on the flyleaf:

September 1945
To our beloved Emily,
Love you forever and a day,
Mother & Dad

Scattered among Matthew, Mark, Luke, and John were American dollars, British pounds, Polish zlotys, Turkish lira, and Deutschmarks. There were also three passports, American, British, and German, the identity pages torn from each.

# TWO

Dear Gus

Annie waved her friends on ahead. Susan and Diana complied with misgivings, eyeing me as I approached, separating from Annie with reluctance. "It's your funeral," Diana said.

"What's up with them?" I said.

Annie had bad news on her face. She wanted to be anywhere other than where she was. "Jack isn't coming."

"Okay." I hadn't seen him all day. It was the week before summer vacation. "Teacher's pet business to wrap up?" I said.

"His parents are splitting up."

"Yeah?" I said, faking it now, till I had a handle on where this was going.

"You knew it was coming, right?"

"What was coming?"

"His parents. They're getting a divorce. His Mom's taken him and his sisters to Montreal."

"Montreal?"

"They've got family there."

"What? Wait. You're saying he's gone?" Confusion gave way to disappointment. I'd expected more from Jack, a vanishing to rival the lost colony of Roanoke, for instance. Or Angikuni Lake and the Eskimo village that went poof.

"It wasn't like he kept it a secret," she said. "Still, the suddenness, I suppose."

"But he'll be back, right?"

"Maybe. Sometimes. I hope. I mean, his dad is here, the restaurant . . ." She fumbled with her schoolbag, fished out an envelope. "He left you this."

"What is it?"

"Um . . . an envelope? Probably with a message inside?"

I didn't want to touch it. "What's it say?"

"Gosh, how should I know?" She grabbed my wrist and slapped it onto my palm. "Honestly, Gus, sometimes . . ."

"Why you? Why didn't he give it to me?"

"What difference does it make? For goodness sakes, stop staring at the thing. Read it."

I tore open the envelope, unfolded the three sheets of pale green paper. His mom's stationery.

Annie glued herself to my side, reading along. "What's Hollywood North?"

"Nothing." I turned a shoulder, held the pages closer to my chest.

"Be like that." She simmered, spun hair with her fingers.

Jack's first two pages were a sprawling whirl of hoops and loops and curlicues, syllables in cartoon clothing.

Dear Gus,

I've been doing lots of thinking about Hollywood North and the accidents and the cards and everything.

What if it's not amnesia, but more like THE TIME MACHINE? How the Morlocks took care of the Eloi, fed them, gave them clothes, made them think everything was great. And then the Morlocks ate them.

What if that's what's going on? What if there's something out there like the Morlocks and they're making everybody think life is hunky-dory. It'd sure make it easier to pick people off like they've been doing, wouldn't it? You know, make it look like accidents or murders. But hiding something bigger.

What if everybody in Trenton is like the Eloi? That'd make us Eloi, too. But who are the Morlocks? Space invaders? Escaped Nazis? Russians? Nikita Khrushchev said WE WILL BURY YOU. What if the Reds did all that on Creighton Farms?

Look, I don't have the answers, but I'll bet my life Mr. McGrath and Mr. Blackhurst's wife (or whoever she is) are working for the real Morlocks and we got too close to the secret and they had to scare us off. I'm telling you, we figure out the WHO and the rest falls into place. Could be the secret is in the cards.

Think about it Gus. Keep your head up and your eyes and ears open. And watch your back. Don't end up like Dougie.

Yours truly,
Jack L.

The third page was our list, neatly printed. Or now, I guess, *his* list.

Here's what we've got so far. Some new ones, too. Customers have been super chatty lately.

18?? TO 19?? – THE 'BURIED ALIVE' OF CREIGHTON FARMS
1898 – GRAND TRUNK TRAIN WRECK
1918 – AMMO PLANT BLOWS UP
1919 – BARN FIRE AND PITCHFORK MURDERS, 4 DEAD
1922 – TOUR BOAT BURNS AND FLIPS IN BAY
1923 – FOSS BROTHERS CIRCUS BURNS
1926 – SISTERS MURDERED ON TOP OF PELION
1927 – WALKER SHOE FACTORY ROOF CAVES IN
1929 – SCOUT CAMP FLASH FLOOD KILLS 7
1930 – FAMILY MURDERED IN HANNA PARK
1933 – TWO GIRLS STABBED TO DEATH ON PELION
1934 – FOSS BROTHERS CIRCUS CATCHES FIRE (IRIS LEBEL BURNED)
1937 – PLANES COLLIDE OVER TOWN (SIMON LEBEL)
1938 – MOUNT PELION LANDSLIDE CRUSHES 4 HOUSES
1942 – DUCK HUNTERS MISTAKE FISHERMEN FOR NAZI INVADERS, 5 SHOT DEAD
1944 – RCAF DAY PICNIC POISONS 51, KILLS 22
1950 – COUPLE JUMPS FROM PELION WATER TOWER (POSSIBLE MURDER)
1951 – TRAIN HITS SCHOOL BUS
1962 – SPEEDBOAT CRASH, 6 DEAD INCLUDING DRIVER

"So?" Annie said. "Nice letter? Happy now?"
I crumpled the pages, buried them in my pocket along with my fist.

"Aren't you going to let me read it, at least?"

"He said goodbye to you, didn't he?" I turned my back and stomped away.

"Gus, stop. What are you doing? Please . . ."

And that fist in my pocket, I tell you, I held it clenched until I'd made it home. Had to will my fingers to unwind.

What the hell was I supposed to do with his stupid letter, anyhow? What was I supposed to do now?

The Hardy Boys were dead. Iola Morton, too.

THREE

Ambushed!

The town was down one celebrity. Nobody gave a crap.

Trentonians had better things to occupy themselves than some big-headed puke who made their small-headed pukes look pukier. Grand openings of a Canadian Tire store and an A&W Root Beer Drive-in. Donkey Baseball at Legion Park. Wrestling at the Community Gardens. The annual Air Show at the base—always good for a close call or two, if not a crash.

Jack the Finder had been yesterday's news since McGrath ceased to make him news.

I wallowed in my bitterness, brooded over how he'd given Annie the low-down on his leaving and not me. I vilified Annie for it, too. When did she become more important to Jack than me? And that so-called latest theory of his, how he'd kept it to himself? He didn't own the mysteries. They were *our mysteries*.

Why should I care, anyhow? Train wrecks. Plane crashes. Dead school kids. *Read a newspaper, why don't you? Watch Huntley and Brinkley.* Like McGrath had told him, bad stuff happened *everywhere*. And those dumb movie cards—I *never* gave a crap, not even when I did.

Who'd he think he was? Who'd she think she was?

I'd show him. I'd show her. I'd put up a wall, dig a moat, stock it with piranhas.

I didn't need anybody. Not him. Not her. Not anybody.

* * *

Mom intercepted me at the door. The Avon Lady gig was working for her. Working for me, too. She was hardly ever home after school. Leaving me free to watch TV, read comics, or whatever. But that day, of all days, she was all over me.

"I guess you heard the news about the Levins," she said.

"How long you known?"

"A few days. A couple of weeks, perhaps. He did tell you, didn't he?"

"He told me, all right."

"It's normal to be upset, your best friend moving—"

"He's not my best friend."

"I'm sure he'll be back to visit. Mollie suggested we could arrange for you to go to Montreal for a few days this summer. How exciting would—"

"I'm not going anywhere near that dirty double-crosser."

Come July, Annie would be off to her family's cottage at Barcovan Beach near Carrying Place, the zag end of the zigzag Quinte. I'd be done with her till school resumed in September. But in the week leading up to her departure, my redemption was her mission. Never once in the years I'd known Annie had she come by my house. Not even for birthday parties. Of course, I'd sabotaged my mother's good intentions every year, supplying no names to invite. I'd heard of kids who'd planned parties where nobody showed and I vowed early on I would not be that kid. Then, too, there'd been the Shirley Temple movie where news arrives during her party that her father had been killed in some war, leaving her penniless and at the mercy of the bitchy-faced boarding school mistress. Next Shirley knows, she's Cinderella, accused of stealing blankets and locked up in the attic.

A kid absorbs. A kid learns.

Who was Annie now, anyhow? She looked the same, yet she wasn't the same. She showed up at my door at least twice a day for a week and ambushed me here and there about the same.

"You're being silly. C'mon, Gus, please. You don't throw away a friend for no good reason. You know I'm your friend. Your best friend. Your oldest friend."

"This is crazy, Gus. C'mon. Stop it. Let's go back to the way it was."

"Jack didn't mean to hurt your feelings. He didn't know how to say goodbye, that's all. He thought the letter would be better."

"I don't know what I did that was so wrong, but you can see I'm sorry. I'm so so sorry. That's got to mean something."

"Please, Mrs. Berry, make him talk to me."

"I wish I could," my mother said. "If it's any consolation, he's not talking much to me, either."

Annie followed me home on the last day of school. Her last chance to make it right. She was half a block behind when Double Al and Lloyd jumped me, bulldozed me through the cedars and onto the grass.

Long-Arm Wayne and Vito hauled me to my feet, twisted an arm behind my back, and screwed me into a headlock.

My heart should have been beating a mile a minute. I should have been hurting. I should have been scared. Instead, I was bugged by their lack of originality. Was the space between the cedars and Malbasic's big green hedge the only option for ambushes in this town?

"Still think everything's a big joke, eh?" Double Al said.

I coughed, and Vito eased up on my neck. "Don't you guys watch movies? TV?"

"We got unfinished business with you."

"Why always here? No abandoned warehouse around? No place with girders and chains so you can string me up while you beat the shit out of me?"

"What did you do with that Charles kid?"

"Huh?" This was weird. "Pecker?"

Vito gave up on the headlock. He allowed me to straighten before twisting my left arm behind my back to overlap with my right, currently held by Wayne.

"The drugstore kid," Double Al clarified.

"Where have you been? It's over two years," I said. "His parents sent him to boarding school. Port Hope."

Lloyd delivered four sharp pokes to the chest. His fingernails needed trimming. "I want my Camels."

"And the cigs the little shit owes me." Wayne's tongue was purple. His breath smelled of grape Kool-Aid. But then everybody's tongue was purple. An hour earlier, we'd been living it up in our classrooms, Dixie cups raised in toast to summer vacation.

"How am I supposed to do that?" I said.

"That's your problem," Double Al said. "You shouldn't got rid of the little fucker. Now you owe us."

I gave logic a shot. "Pecker will be home for the summer. I'm sure he'll keep his promise to you then."

"Yeah, but we want you, smartass." Double Al punched me in the stomach and as I doubled over, he waved their shopping list in my face. They were after a hell of a lot more than smokes.

> *4 transistor radios*
> *1 can of Player's chewing tobacco*
> *6 packs of Wrigley's Spearmint*
> *1 bolt cutter*
> *1 glass cutter*
> *Kiwi shoe polish, black*
> *1 duffel bag*
> *8 packs of Ramses*
> *4 Gillette Right Guards*

"What are Ramses?" I asked, which they thought was hilarious.

"He's never used a rubber." Double Al stomped on my foot, kicked me in the shin. "The Boy Scout said you were the sneakiest bastard he knew. Said we should keep an eye on you. Swiping this shit, c'mon, it's gonna be a breeze for you. You steal shit all the time." He stuffed the list into my pocket. "Think nobody's seen you going into them dead peoples' houses?"

"My grandmother lived there."

"How many grandmothers you got?"

I caught a glimpse of red among the cedars. The ribbon in Annie's ponytail. She was watching. I'd give her something to see, all right. And went for broke. "Too chicken to swipe it all yourself, eh? Bigger the mouth, bigger the pussy."

Double Al didn't hold back. His elbow hit my throat, laid me flat. Vito dropped onto me, pounding me. Wayne stood over me, kicking me. And there was Annie in her gingham party dress, pink and white and panic, yelling, "Get off of him! Get off of him!"

I didn't feel a thing. Swear to God. They weren't going to kill me, so how bad could any of this be? A busted arm? Dufferin bullies didn't kill, Jack had said. Heck, the assholes had barely touched my face. A few swats in the mouth, but with floppy fishy fists, and I had to smile at that. Fact was, I couldn't stop smiling. Made sure to keep my smile in place even as pain began to give notice. And, oh man, my smile, it drove them wild, a razor-blade grin and razor-blade eyes, the look Crates had working for him.

Annie tried to pull them off. They pushed her down. She went back for more, screeching at the top of her lungs, *Help! Help! Help!* in every colour and variety you could imagine.

And somewhere in the midst of this, I saw Mr. Malbasic at his watchtower window, raising the blinds, his tongue darting as he peered down on the scene. I laughed. And, sure enough, the halfwits thought my laugh was meant for them. And their fists closed up, dime bags of cement. Two black eyes. Yeah, I'd come out of this with two black eyes. Two swollen ears. A swollen jaw. And for the rest of my life I would wonder how Malbasic—*pop a bonnet onto the fucker's head and he'd pass for Dumbo's mom*—how Malbasic had had it in him to climb the thousand stairs to the peak of his big old house.

It was therapeutic, I tell you, letting him see yet again how I was a boy who could take it. Malbasic the analgesic, that's what he was to me. Until he raised his window, bellowed down, "You, there! Stop that. Stop that, this instant. I know who you are. I know every last one of you hoodlums. The police. I'm calling the police."

The rats scattered.

"Are you badly hurt, Mr. Berry?" Malbasic called. "Do you require assistance?"

I cranked myself to sitting.

"Do you want me to call your mother, Mr. Berry? She was here not two hours ago."

"What?" *What did he say?*

"Your mother, do you wish me to call her?"

"No. I'm fine," I croaked, churning saliva to dilute the taste of the blood. A grape Kool-Aid would have been welcome right then, I tell you.

I stood, rubbed where it hurt, which was everywhere.

Mr. Malbasic nodded approvingly and lowered the window. He continued to watch from behind the glass.

"Your nose is bleeding," Annie said. "It might be broken."

"I don't need you. I don't need anybody."

She was trembling, fighting tears.

I shooed her hands away and then brushed past her. I did not look back. I did not want to see her tears. I would not fall for her tears.

She was sobbing, a sound as mournful as my mother's on her worst days. "Nothing more I can do," Annie said, rejected and dejected. "If that's how you want to be."

It wasn't anywhere near *how I wanted to be*. It was how I was.

You know what bugged me most? You know what I couldn't stop thinking about? Double Al. Vito. Lloyd. Wayne. I hadn't laid a hand on any of them. Hadn't thrown a goddamn punch.

I am a bad person. If you didn't believe me before, you'd be wise to believe me now.

FOUR

Heaven is for real

And yet again, Mom fretted in the open doorway. Would I never be permitted to suffer in solitude? "My God, what's happened to you?" She'd known I was coming. She'd been waiting and watching. More than once I'd told Jack her ESP was worth investigating.

And I was a sight, all right, a metamorphic mass of black, blue, and blood. An Alamogordo amoeba after an A-bomb test. Two mesas to the left of the mutant ants of *Them!* But I had something more on my mind. "Why were you at Mr. Malbasic's house?" I said, determined and grim. Talking hurt. My lips were balloons, the sort clowns twist into sausage dogs.

Mom met me on the walk, her gentle hand at my back.

"Tell me," I said.

"You first."

"I fell off my bike."

"Your bike is in the garage."

"I fell down the stairs at school."

"Tell me who did this to you."

"Is Mr. Malbasic your new boyfriend?" I said.

She sat me down on a stool at the kitchen sink, dabbed at my split lip and slit eyebrow with warm water and soap. She blotted the blood from my nose, stuffed a nostril with cotton, and swabbed me with witch hazel, calamine, iodine, and Bactine.

"I can get their names without any trouble. Mrs. Malbasic phoned. She told me everything. Her husband saw it all. He knows who they are."

"They didn't kill me."

"Thank God for that. But next time, if those boys—"

"They won't. I'll take care of it."

"What do you mean you'll 'take care of it'? You can't fight them. Look what they did to you."

"You should have seen what I did to them."

"But it was only you—they were four."

"The Battle of Thermopylae—three hundred Spartans held off a million Persians." And trust me, getting *Thermopylae* off my tongue was pure torture.

Mom failed to hide her grin, her dubious pride. She planted a kiss between a welt and a bruise. "You didn't start the fight, did you? Mr. Malbasic said you appeared to be defending a girl. Is it true? Was it Annie Barker?"

"I did what I had to do."

"Well, whatever it was, I hope it's out of your system. The way you've been behaving lately . . ."

"What way?"

"Angry. Always angry at something. Is it because of Jack? Or me? Have I done something wrong?"

Were I to run down the reasons, there'd be no stopping. "Isn't Mrs. Malbasic mad at you because Mr. Malbasic likes you so much?"

"So that's it?"

"Some of it."

"Florence Malbasic is my biggest customer. Mr. Malbasic has been on his best behaviour since the afternoon he came home to see me in his living room, sitting on his loveseat, reviewing the Avon brochure with his wife. He insisted she buy one of everything. Florence and I laughed. And then she did buy one of just about everything. How's that?"

"Wow," I said.

"And if you're worried about him giving you any more trouble at school— if that is what's been upsetting you—it's over. I promise. He told me to my face, he's going to do everything in his power to ensure you achieve your 'fullest academic and societal potential.'"

"He said that?"

"Who else would say something so pompous? But I have no doubt he'll keep his promise, now that I have his wife's ear. The more immediate question is, what are we going to do about you?"

"You don't have to worry about me."

"But I do, sweetheart. I haven't stopped since the day you were born. I won't stop till the day I die."

A few days later, Mom was hanging laundry when she came across Double Al's shopping list. It had gone through the wash. "Is this yours?" she asked. "I hope it wasn't impor—oh, my!" She covered her mouth, recoiled from the note, and gawked at me, a sudden stranger.

I peeled the damp list from her hand. One word had survived the wash: *Ramses.*

"They're supposed to be good rubbers," I said.

Mom became Trenton's top Avon Lady. And then the county's. In her first year, she ranked number twelve in the province and had a gold pin to prove it. A letter from head office declared her rise "meteoric and unprecedented." In her second year, she ranked number three.

Between house calls, she'd host makeup parties in our living room.

"Your look is so natural, Emily," the ladies would tell her.

And Mom, conspiring and inspiring, would say, "As natural as Avon and the miracles of modern cosmetology science." Genes never entered the conversation.

I'd shut my door. Blast my transistor.

Mom worried about my behaviour. I worried about hers.

Success made her more confident. You could see it in her hair, her eyes, her clothes, her shoes, her walk. She liked herself more. I liked her less. And don't think I didn't hate myself for it.

Twice a week, at least, she would take out the TV tables and we'd eat dinner with *6 O'Clock Movie* on channel 4. One night *Leave Her to Heaven* came on. It was the Gene Tierney movie Mr. Malbasic had been so keen on. In two minutes flat I saw all I never wanted to know. I skipped dessert, went up to my room. It was the last *6 O'Clock Movie* Mom and I would ever watch together.

I would leave Dufferin without a black mark against me. I didn't thank Malbasic. Didn't thank Mom. I thanked Dottie Swartz. *"Thank you for drown-*

ing, Dottie." Closest to sincere prayer my thirteen-year-old self had come.

Thank you for drowning, Dottie. Mom would never have left the Unemployment Insurance Office and become an Avon Lady, if you hadn't.

Thank you for drowning, Dottie. Mom would never have become friends with Florence Malbasic, if you hadn't.

Thank you for drowning, Dottie. Mr. Malbasic would never have recognized the errors of his ways, if you hadn't.

I would have liked to have told Annie, if only to ridicule her holy-rolling. "What have I been telling you, Gus?" she would have said. "Heaven is for real."

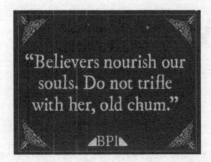

"Believers nourish our souls. Do not trifle with her, old chum."

BPI

FIVE

Life without Jack
(July 1, 1963 to June 17, 1966)

EPISODE I

Jack would have loved the dogs and the baby. The sucker would have been all over it.

One sunny July morning, a baby carriage sat on the veranda of a Tompkins Street house. It was an older, larger home, easily dwarfing Iris Lebel's shed farther down the block. Three black dogs came marauding up the middle of the road. They passed the house by, peed on an abandoned tricycle, sniffed each other's butts, caught wind of a fresher scent, and reversed in pack formation.

The lead dog nudged open the unlatched gate of the grey picket fence and the dogs loped into the yard and up the four steps to the porch. They knocked over the pram and the baby rolled out.

The baby's mother screamed onto the scene and a dog took her down by the head.

The baby died on the spot. The *Record* left details to the reader's imagination and rumours filled in the blanks.

The baby's mother was given rabies shots and hospitalized for shock. She also required reconstructive facial surgery, which led to a series of fundraising efforts over the next few months. Bottle drives. Bake sales. Car washes. Sock hops.

A bounty was placed on the heads of the dogs, local hunters invited to participate.

By month's end, twenty-two dogs were dead. Eighteen were black Labs and two chocolate. The carcasses were strung up in market square, as they came in, and left to hang until a provincial health inspector intervened. The Springer Spaniel and Miniature Poodle killed in the hunt were not displayed.

Three hunters were also shot, none fatally, though a man who worked at the Black Diamond Cheese Factory lost the use of his legs, which was when the town called off the hunt.

EPISODE 2

Mom's maternal shortcomings were mounting. The Marquee mitigated her guilt. "It's as close to eating home as eating out can be," she told me, as if this was a good thing.

Then, too, there was Bert Levin. With Mollie out of the picture, it didn't take long for him to pay more attention to Mom. Two weeks, if that.

Bert was a handsome guy. Tall. Solid. Reliable. With a dash of bad boy, courtesy of his Clark Gable mustache. His apron might have deterred some. Not Mom. She saw a man at ease with his masculinity.

If you needed a bite to eat or a few bucks to carry you through, you could count on Bert Levin. The *Record* had run stories on his grab bag of kindnesses. A lonely widow saddled with a teenage sad sack was right up his alley.

In the years prior, Bert had been friendly within limits. Now he was quick to sit with Mom and me, nurse a ginger ale, munch chips. "Dessert's on the house from now on," he told Mom.

His generosity had been a bone of contention for Mollie. According to Mom, she'd accused Bert of frittering away Marquee profits. "No matter how kind Bert is, Mollie played a big part in those earnings. Her pies, my goodness. If they serve apple pie in Heaven, you know it's going to be Mollie Levin's."

I'd been half-listening, coaxing a long grey hair from my layer cake. "She's dead?" *Had Jack crossed a line? Had McGrath and his elephant gun paid a visit to Montreal? Would Mom be next?*

"What? Mrs. Levin? No. No." Mom overcompensated for the confusion. "It's just an expression. Mrs. Levin is fine. Absolutely fine."

I went for broke, figured I'd never have a better opening. "When you die, will you promise to contact me from the Beyond, same way Houdini promised Mrs. Houdini?"

She inundated me with mush. "With every ounce of my soul, I promise." I ducked under her hugs and kisses, knowing she'd carry on twenty minutes past unbearable.

Mom composed herself, cast her attention to the open kitchen and Bert. "Still, his heart is in the right place. With the right woman, I suspect he'd do just fine."

EPISODE 3

Two weeks after the attack on the baby, I was standing in Sure Press with the latest batch of Mom's dry cleaning. For the first time in memory, Iris wasn't there. "She sick?" I said.

"Funeral today," Mr. Blackhurst said.

"Hers?"

"Dog baby's."

Helmut Swartz, who now owned the Arthur Murray Dance Studio, and doing quite well by all accounts—dance instructor *and* wife killer an irresistible combination to Trenton women—was unlocking his door when he saw me exit the cleaners. "You know what they're going to say about the mother, don't you, Leo? They're going to say she fed her baby to the dogs on purpose. You watch. You'll see."

Not five minutes later I crossed paths with Crates. I was at Division below St. Peter's Church, observing the funeral crowds heading up the hill. I didn't know he was on me until he was at my ear. "Too late to grab a good seat." He wore a white shirt and a solid brown tie with a silver Pilots Hall clip.

"What?"

"You're the Ramses kid, eh?"

"Me?"

"Ramses. What Double calls you."

Downright disheartening. Seven years in school together and he didn't know my name.

"Waiting for the funeral to start, are you, before you break into the dog baby's house?" He had this whoosh to his voice, reminded me of fly casting.

"Who, me? I wouldn't do that."

"So you're going, then?"

"Where?"

"The funeral."

"Of course."

"You should have a tie."

"I forgot it," I said.

We sat in the nosebleed pews, most distant the pulpit. Crates smelled of sawdust. "The boys worked you over good," he said.

I laughed it off. "I can handle them."

"Pay your taxes."

"What?"

"Every tax they collect they gimme a cut, so they don't *get* cut. Smokes. Rubbers. Sen-Sen. You don't pay up, you get cut. I can do it right here, right now. You can be the next funeral."

"I'm not Catholic," I said.

"But you're friends with that Jack the Finder kid who's got the store."

"Yeah, but he's gone away."

"Starting next Friday and every Friday, we cut out the middleman. You pay me direct. Down by the tracks, same time and place as today. Smokes. I'm easy. Any kind. All you can get. Got it?"

"But I'd have to steal them. Mr. Levin won't let me buy—"

"Green Chiclets, too."

Downside aside, it was a breakthrough. A historic moment. Crates had actually spoken to me. When the congregation jumped up to hymn it up, I slunk out, understanding in full, at last, why Mom and me did not go to church.

EPISODE 4

Okay, so I did give a crap about the movie cards. They were my refuge. Spent hours poring over them. It was me who found them and it would damn well be me who got to the bottom of them.

My persistence would pay off. *Had to.*

... Thus, the cruel hand of Fate rang the opening bell.

◢BPI◣

Not everyone saw the Big Dipper first try, either.

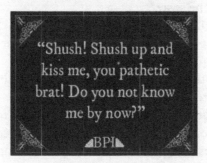

"Shush! Shush up and kiss me, you pathetic brat! Do you not know me by now?"

◢BPI◣

EPISODE 5

Lifting cigarettes from the Marquee was a breeze. You wouldn't think so, but big and klutzy kids can get away with shit the agile and coordinated cannot.

The main shelf was behind the cash and inches from the pop cooler, so when reaching deep for a soda with my right hand, I'd throw my left onto the cigarette shelf for balance, never failing to send a few packs onto the floor. "Ah, jeez. Sorry." As I stooped to gather them up, I'd press up against the cooler and drop a pack down the front of my pants into my Jockeys, before returning the remainder to the shelf.

The Chiclets were a nickel. I paid for those.

Crates was satisfied with one pack of smokes a week. He was generous that way.

I wasn't happy paying taxes, though. Wasn't happy stealing from Bert Levin. Wasn't happy knuckling under.

EPISODE 6

My shame and bruises were my license for revenge.

I channelled Randolph Scott in *Seven Men from Now*. I'd corner the culprits alone, take them down one by one. Double Al and his gang. Crates, if it came to that.

Screw contingencies. To overthink would be to chicken out.

I honed my combat skills. Sparred with the mirror on the back of Mom's bedroom door. Beat up pillows, punched out trees. Scoured my comic books, the pages of *TV Guide*. Studied with the masters. Chuck Connors. Clint Walker. Gary Cooper. Jimmy Stewart. John Wayne. Alan Ladd.

A guy who speaks with his fists. I'd be that guy. Songs would be written. Frankie Laine would sing.

Vigilante! Vigilante! The Vigilante Kid.
From Trenton he came, dark side of the town,
Dynamite in his fists, his soul vengeance-bound . . .

EPISODE 7

On July 22, 1963, Sonny Liston kayoed Floyd Patterson in two minutes, ten seconds of the first round of their Las Vegas rematch. The very next Saturday, Movietone delivered the blow-by-blow, direct from ringside to the Odeon screen.

I ran to Simmons Drugs right after and bought *The Ring*, Sonny pounding Floyd on the cover, no less. That magazine might as well have been two ten-ounce gloves, the swagger it gave me.

EPISODE 8

You don't start at the top. You work your way through the fodder, wade into the vengeance. A couple of rounds with Wayne, any Wayne. Take Vito out in the third or fourth. Toy with Lloyd fifth through eighth. Double Al nine, ten. Finish off Crates in the twelfth, if it came to that.

I was riding my bike to nowhere when I saw Crates tramping out of the west, along the tracks and through the crossing where the locomotive had flattened the school bus. It wasn't a Friday. Wasn't a tax day. And it was nothing I'd planned. Least of all stepping into the ring in Bermuda shorts. Canary yellow. (Mom's idea, not mine.)

I was fed up and hating myself more than usual is what it was.

I could have pedalled away, Crates none the wiser. But then I'd never unstreak my cowardly streak. I was ready, two issues of *Ring* in my head by then. And don't forget Randy Scott in *Seven Men from Now*, to whom I'd added Kirk Douglas in *Last Train from Gun Hill*.

> *Vigilante! Vigilante! The Vigilante Kid.*
> *Bowie knife a-gleaming, Crates blazed a bloody trail,*
> *Showdown in the offing, Gus leapt onto the rail . . .*

I parked my bike under the *Stop On Red Signal* and gave chase. I stuck with the grass, arcing towards Crates from around and above. He wouldn't know what hit him until it hit him.

I recognized the momentousness. Succeed, and I would never be forced to be *me* again. I took note of the rolling green hill to my right, the shaded path to the rectory and convent, the red brick of the church and school on high.

Crates was coming from his job at Annie's dad's lumberyard. He'd be tired. But then how tiring could knife-sharpening be? Especially for "the best knife sharpener" Annie's dad ever saw.

I frisked him from afar. He was bare from the waist up, shirt slung from shoulder and flapping as he hopped from tie to tie. The guy was skinnier than the steel underfoot and as hard or harder. Biceps. Triceps. Bone. If he was carrying a blade, it'd need to be thinner than thin.

I welcomed my fears. *Nerves were good.* Rocky Marciano himself had said so in *The Ring*. And how many fights had Rocky lost? Not one. In his entire professional career.

Plus I had the element of surprise working for me. Surprise was worth ten men. Twenty. It was either Elfego Baca or Texas John Slaughter who'd taught me that.

I padded up behind him, grabbed a fistful of his shirt, my right raised to deck him when he turned. But the fucker did not turn. The fucker spun. And by default, I spun, too, and the shirt rolled up and around my neck as Crates reeled me in. A goddamn Cheerio Champ, the bastard. He yanked, and I spun out the other way, a freaking two-bit human yoyo.

I bailed. Rapped a knee off a rail. Tore up my hands in the gravel ballast.

Crates scratched at his stubble. He'd been shaving since kindergarten. "What the hell, Ramses?"

I rocked on the rail, hugging my knee, applying pressure, thinking fast. "I know what Ramses are." I'd finally done my homework. "I buy 'em all the time. I just wanted to tell you."

"Oh, okay. Sure. I can see that. Sneaking up behind me. Grabbing my shirt. Sure, had to be it." Crates's laugh was channel 3 on a busted antenna. "Now what? Just gonna sit there and kill yourself?"

My knee had swelled up fast. I saw the merit of his proposal. "I'm not paying taxes anymore," I said.

He lofted his shirt onto his shoulder. I flinched, forearms protective of my face. But Crates didn't slug or slash. He nodded back toward the way we'd come. "Train."

The hum ran up the rail and buzzed my butt. I heaved backwards off the track, rolled to my belly, chin in grass.

Red lights flashed. Crossing bells clanged. My bike twitched. My bike rattled. My bike danced away from the *Stop On Red Signal*, seesawed upright onto the rails, and sacrificed itself before the cowcatcher.

"Yours?" Crates asked, as the 4:20 freighted the wreck past us.

"I'm not paying taxes anymore," I repeated, figuring he'd missed it the first time, which was why I wasn't bleeding.

Crates squatted, his knee on my throat. The good humour vacated his face for the bump and grind of his Adam's apple. "You think I give a fuck about your taxes? I got more taxes than bees got honey." He flicked his wrist and the sun winked upon a five-inch blade. "But you creep up on me again and I'll send you home with your ears in your pockets."

Vigilante! Vigilante! The Vigilante Kid.
Danger is his bloodline, vengeance is his biz,
Came the final battle, the blood was solely his.
Now off into the sunset, lo his mournful bellow
Vigilante Kid—Bermuda shorts of yellow.
Yippie, yip, yo. Yippie, yip, yellow.
Yippie, yip, yo. Yippie, yip, yellow.

EPISODE 9

Susan Burgess intercepted me on my way out for lunch. "Talk to Annie. Please, Gus."

"She appoint you peacemaker or something?"

"She doesn't know. Honest."

"Leave me alone."

"She misses you. Life is too short for silly fights. My brother knows better than anyone."

"Billy is dead eight years," I said. "Billy knows diddly-squat."

"You're an idiot. An even bigger idiot than Annie says. I hate you."

She walked away and Long-Arm Wayne stepped into my path and I punched him in the gut as hard as the Vigilante Kid could.

"Sir. Sir," he retched. "He hit me. Ramses hit me."

I deflated. *Shit*. I had failed to see Mr. Malbasic skulking by the wolverine cabinet. The principal's tongue darted from Long-Arm to me and back. "You hit yourself, young man," he said, and crossed the hall to the recently installed turtle exhibit.

EPISODE 10

On the day President Kennedy was assassinated, they sent us home from school early.

I wondered if Dallas was like Trenton, in that bad things happened and people forgot them.

I wondered if Lee Harvey Oswald might have been born in Trenton, like Henry Comstock of Tompkins Street and Comstock Lode fame.

I wondered how much more Annie hated me after I saw her crying and hurried by pretending I didn't.

EPISODE 11

Mom gave her life to Avon Beauty Products and Avon gave Mom the good life. "The lipstick life," she quipped. "I should write a book. It would make a good title, don't you think?"

"I wouldn't read it," I said.

"You're not who I'd be writing for."

Mom was home less and less. And when she was home, she was somewhere else. I didn't complain. Most kids would kill to have a single mom preoccupied with career. The latchkey lifestyle was *my* good life, easing the return to my loner roots, erasing my wasted time with Jack and Annie.

Friendship was great, if you were cut out for that sort of thing.

EPISODE 12

The footbridge that ran alongside the railroad bridge fell into the Trent River in February of 1964.

Confirmed loss of life: a woman and her dog.

The casualty was Mrs. Roger Campbell of Truro Avenue, mother of the late Jimmy Campbell, the kindergarten kid who was killed years earlier on the Dufferin playground, when the monkey bars crushed his windpipe. Last I'd seen her had been on the morning of the day Kennedy was shot, tying what might have been her farewell bouquet to the new monkey bars.

Witnesses said Mrs. Campbell often walked her dog on the ice near the footbridge. The dog was a beagle and his leash was frozen to Mrs. Campbell's hand when they carried her from the ice.

Two additional victims turned up when they cleared the debris. Both males. Transients from parts unknown. People talked more about them than they did about Dead Jimmy Campbell's dead mom.

Jack would have been all over this, too.

EPISODE 13

Four weeks and talk about the old footbridge was done. People wanted only to hear about plans for the new footbridge. Like there had never been an old footbridge.

How did good news push out the bad? Did bad news have an expiration date, like cottage cheese? Or did bad stuff come with a countdown clock, same as stunts on *Beat the Clock*? And who decided what and when?

I put Bert Levin to the test, aimed for subtlety. "Too bad the old footbridge fell down, eh?"

Bert flipped to page 3 of the *Record* to show me the illustration. "They say the new bridge will be covered. That'll be welcome come winter."

With Mom, I went for the heart. "I can't stop thinking about poor Mrs. Campbell and her dog."

"Who?"

"The lady who got killed when the footbridge collapsed."

"I thought you meant Evelyn Campbell. Only this morning she God-blessed Avon for the improvement in her complexion."

EPISODE 14

First day of high school, Annie saw me the second she came into homeroom. She scoped out the classroom and swung into a seat six rows over and six desks up, as far from me as any seat could be.

We'd made sure to sit near each other in every class since first grade.

"Like I care," I said to nobody and loud enough for everybody.

EPISODE 15

The lady in black starred in my dreams with increasing regularity. She did things to me. Strange things. Good things. She was remaking me, I thought. Into what I wasn't clear. I couldn't step into Sure Press without looking for her, wishing for her. I was at the cleaners more than ever, too. Mom competed with Doris Day, the frequency of her costume changes.

One day, spur of the moment, I spoke to Iris. My mouth opened, words spilled out. "Remember a long time ago when I was here with my friend and we were showing Mr. Blackhurst some cards and that lady came out from the back? Was she Mrs. Blackhurst?"

Mirthless. Disinterested. Dedicated to her craft. That was Iris.

I talked. She sewed. "You're neighbours with the lady whose baby got eaten by the dogs, right? Did you ever—"

"How many sides to a triangle?" she said, without looking up.

I stopped, swallowed. "Three?"

"You'd be wise to remember."

"I would?"

She repositioned a hem. "You know what happens in triangles."

"I've read about pyramids."

"The Triangle Shirtwaist Factory fire. One-hundred-twenty-three girls burned up. Twenty-three men burned up."

"Here? Trenton?" This would be the all-time winner on the list, surpassing Annie and Creighton Farms. A fire to beat all fires.

"New York City," she said. "My mother was there. She jumped with me inside her. The curse followed." She craned to the right, put her neck on full display.

"Oh," I said, enthralled by the close-up, disappointed the factory fire had not been local, and failing miserably in my responsibility as an investigator of The Unexplained.

"Bad things happen in threes."

EPISODE 16

Mr. Blackhurst idled on the corner stool by the payphone. "Where's the young lad?" he said to Bert.

"It's a long story, Mr. Blackhurst."

"He's a good listener."

"Jack is good at a lot of things."

"I wish to speak with him."

"I can pass your message along, if you like."

"Three hot dogs," Mr. Blackhurst harrumphed. "Mustard."

The old man ate his hotdogs in nine bites. Three per dog.

On his way out, he paused by our table, rested a hand on Mom's shoulder. "My dear sweet lovely miss, you ought to be in pictures. Has anyone ever told you?"

"You, sir. Many times."

"Where have you been? You don't visit me."

"Busy. Busy. My son has been helping me out." She gestured toward me. "You see him often enough, I'm sure."

Mr. Blackhurst was slow to recognize me, and less than convincing when he did. "Ah, yes. One of the boat children."

"What boa—" I began to say, but Mom signalled me to let it go. I let everything go when it came to Blackhurst. I'd been wanting to remind him just about forever how I was the boy who found the intertitles. Hell, it should've been me he wanted to talk to, not Jack.

EPISODE 17

McGrath blew into the Marquee with his usual shtick. "What's cookin', Bert?" he said, and stopped cold at the sight of Bert sitting with Mom and me. The batteries of his brain ricocheted out his butt and down his pant leg. "Well, isn't this cozy!" he said, and blew the hell out as abruptly as he blew in.

It came to me then, exactly how I'd exact my revenge on Jack.

7:30 **4** THE COURTSHIP OF LEO'S MOTHER—Comedy
A boy conspires to find a suitable spouse for his widowed mother, setting his sights on the father of a former friend.

EPISODE 18

I had stopped paying taxes. I didn't stop stealing cigarettes. Not a lot. Maybe two packs a month. I restricted my efforts to the red Du Maurier packs.

EPISODE 19

"I like Bert Levin," I said. "He's a great guy."

"So you keep telling me," Mom said. "You like him. I get it."

"I do. I really do."

"I'm glad. I really am."

EPISODE 20

A homeowner on Creighton Farms dug up some bones while planting a garden. First reports said the bones were human.

Second reports said the bones were not human. There were no third reports.

EPISODE 21

Bert was at the grill and out of earshot next time McGrath pulled his shit.

"Slut," he coughed into Mom's ear. "What happened, Emily? Lose your taste for old peckers?"

EPISODE 22

"Jack Levin will be visiting for Thanksgiving," Mom said.

"No skin off my chin," I said.

"Bert wanted me to warn you, Jack may not have time to see you."

"Good."

"Bert has a lot planned. Probably best, too, under the circumstances, we don't go by the Marquee while he's in town. Bert feels they should spend time alone."

"Bert doesn't want Jack to know you're his girlfriend. Jack would hate that."

"Girlfriend? Where did you get that idea? Bert and I are friends. Nothing more."

"Then how come I hear him sneaking into the house at night and sneaking out in the morning?"

EPISODE 23

Jack does not call me on Thanksgiving. He does not come by my house.

"I like Mr. Levin," I tell my mother. "He's nice to me."

EPISODE 24

My mother could have been a model in a Ford Thunderbird ad, the way she was preening in her new convertible. Wire wheels. Sportster Hump. The whole shebang.

Her lips were pink. Her dress was pink. Her kerchief was pink. Her T-Bird was red on red. And Mom was a bona fide Avon superstar.

"What do you think?" she said.

What did I think? What did I think? The mother I had known and loved was lost to me for good, that's what I thought.

"Come. I'll take you for a spin."

A car like this in Trenton. Driven by a woman like her. The attention it attracted. Forget Gene Tierney, Doris Day. Mom was full-blown Jayne Mansfield. *"I can't promise Avon will give you tits like mine, nor am I promising they won't."* Jayne Freaking Mansfield, the Avon Lady.

"What next, Mom? You gonna dye your hair blonde?"

"When will you stop being so mean to me?"

EPISODE 25

Bert sitting with Mom got to McGrath every time. "Careful, Bert," he bleated, "she invites you to Sunday dinner, expect a main course of blue balls."

Bert crumpled his bag of chips, pushed up from the table, smoothed his lawman mustache, and marched up to McGrath. "I'm sorry, Bryan. You've been a good customer, but unless you can be civil, you are no longer welcome here."

McGrath drew deep, consigned a .45-caliber ember to the ash tray. "Tell me you're joking, Levin."

Bert pointed McGrath to the east. "There's always the Skyline," he said, referencing the larger diner up Dundas.

"I hate booths. Jukeboxes. I'm at home here." Loss. Despair. It was strange to hear the likes of this from the likes of McGrath.

"Apologize to the lady."

"I'm only watching out for your best interests, Bert."

"Apologize, Bryan."

McGrath's eyes roved from his coffee to his pie to the steadfast Mr. Levin to Mom, radiant in her embarrassment. "I apologize, Mrs. Berry." There was a sadness to his sincerity.

When McGrath had gone, Mom thanked Bert. "We were never more than friends. Bryan has no cause to be jealous."

"Well, Emily," Bert said, "and I don't mean to put you on the spot, but I would be most honoured to give him considerable cause."

EPISODE 26

The Courtship of Leo's Mother was into its third season, no end in sight. "Marry him," I nagged. "I'd like to have someone to call Dad at least once before I die."

Mom laughed, set aside her paperwork. "I'm fine the way things are. We both are, thank you."

"Is it because you're waiting for another old man to come along?"

"Pardon me?"

"You like old men. Dad was an old man. Mr. McGrath. Is that why you won't marry Mr. Levin? Because he's only a little older than you instead of a lot?"

"You think you know it all."

"I got eyes."

"The Levins never divorced. And the way things are going, they probably never will. How about that?"

"There's always Mr. Blackhurst waiting in the wings."

"You manage your relationships, I'll manage mine."

"I don't have any relationships."

"Exactly. Now you know how much I value your opinion."

EPISODE 27

Bert popped a Tab, took me aside. "A fellow I know, Clyde Neil, he's looking for a couple of boys to help run the town marina this summer. You interested?"

"What'll I have to do?"

"You any good at flirting with girls?"

Annie's friend, Diana Klieg, passed by outside. Since moving up to high school, she wore her caramel tresses to the middle of her back. I sat behind her in geometry. I was flunking geometry because of her hair.

I needed the practice. My love life had not progressed beyond the lady in black and my right hand.

"Best part is, you'll be working with Jack. He's coming home for the summer."

EPISODE 28

"What are you doing in here?" I said. The den had been mine, pretty much.

"Work stuff." Mom ripped the page from the typewriter.

"I don't want the job," I said.

"Mr. Levin went out of his way for you."

"I'll find something else."

Mom gathered up the papers on the desk and shoved them into the top drawer. "Whatever problem you have with Jack Levin, get over it. You are taking this job or else." She locked the top drawer, put the typewriter in its case, and pulled open the middle drawer of the desk. She tapped a Du Maurier from its box. "The strangest thing," she said, lighting up. "The more I smoke, the more cigarettes there seem to be in here. It's the *Shoemaker and the Elves* story, but with cigarettes."

"Or else what?" I said.

"No allowance. No TV. No Odeon. No books. No comic books. No records. No anything."

EPISODE 29

I poked a paperclip into the lock, jiggled, and the desk drawer slid open. Mom's "work stuff" sat on top. Pages of it.

> Lipstick Life
> by Emily Berry
>
> Chapter One
>
> The best thing to have happened to Eloise Benson was her husband dying while she was young and beautiful. All married women deserve to be so blessed. Love, hate or indifference, no first husband is a keeper. Nor is a first child, for that matter, she thought, and frowned with displeasure at her reflection in the dresser mirror. So lovely on the outside, so callous on the inside. She loved her son. But Eric, a strange child in many ways, was resentful of her happiness and she, in turn, was resentful of him.

I threw the papers back into the drawer.

EPISODE 30

I followed Lloyd Gonna-kick-u-in-the-nuts and Vito from Italy out of the Odeon. I was far from my peak, my *Ring* magazine days behind me, but my rage was no less diminished.

The Great Escape was the best movie I'd seen since *The 7th Voyage of Sinbad*. I missed Jack right then. We'd have sat through two screenings, damn it. Steve McQueen and his motorcycle—*oh, man!*

I watched Lloyd and Vito ride off on their bikes, and brought wire cutters to every matinee thereafter.

Come Saturdays, I'd sit in the window of the Marquee before each showing and wait for Lloyd or Vito or any of the other bullies to show. *For a Few Dollars More* flushed them out. Double Al and Vito, anyhow. Crates was an unexpected bonus.

I could hardly believe the day had come. I dashed out and around to the side of the building. Coast clear. Six bikes in the rack. Four boys. Two girls. I cut through the spokes on the wheels of the boys. Clean cuts, as practised. Unlikely to be detected. Two spokes on each rim left intact. I didn't touch the girls bikes.

I was late getting into the movie, but plodded out with the rest of the audience when the end credits rolled. Took my time, too, my popcorn to finish.

Double Al and Vito lifted their bikes from the rack, and wouldn't you know, Crates's bike was a girl's, damn it. Still, there was much to entertain as the wheels collapsed, Al crashing onto Vito, Al's face into the pavement, Vito's face into the bike rack. They were hurt. Hurt bad. Al spitting blood and teeth. Vito down for the count, no sign of anything. And Crates, he was laughing so hard, you'd have thought he was watching *Gomer Pyle*.

People crowded around. Cars pulled over to watch. And I was happily one of many, munching my popcorn, as laid back and steely-eyed as Clint Eastwood would've been had he popcorn to finish.

And then the third and fourth kids retrieved their bikes. I didn't know the boy, but the girl was Bonnie Priddy. Annie's friend. Bonnie the polio girl, who at the beginning of tenth grade announced she was free of her leg brace, her friends cheering, and Bonnie doing a goofy dance in response. *What the hell was she doing with a boy's bike?*

I wanted to warn her. But Crates was still laughing and Double Al was still bleeding and Vito was still down and adults were rushing to help and I wasn't stupid.

EPISODE 31

Charles Dahl-Packer won the 1966 Ontario Science Fair. Big shiny medal. Big fat scholarship. Big news in the *Record*.

"His mother is one of my best customers," Mom said.

EPISODE 32

Sometimes a kid just knows things.

The cards were going to change my life.

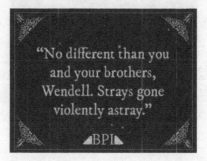

My certainty was as much a mystery as the cards themselves.

When a kid knows, a kid knows.

Sunset bled across
the waters,
an open wound
poisoning the bay.

BPI

The change would be for the better, at least.

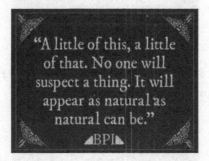

"A little of this, a little
of that. No one will
suspect a thing. It will
appear as natural as
natural can be."

BPI

Couldn't get any worse.

PRODUCTION _____

DIRECTOR _____

CAMERA _____

DATE _____ SCENE _____ TAKE _____

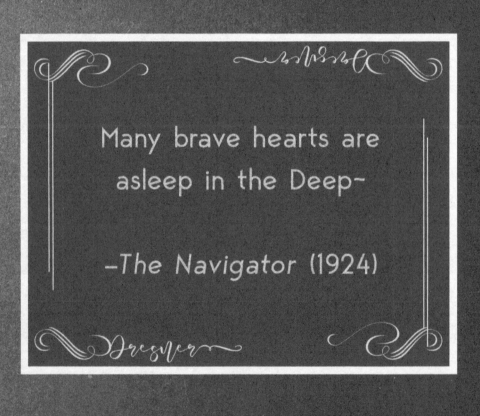

Many brave hearts are
asleep in the Deep-

-The Navigator (1924)

 # ONE

"Jack?" I called, but he was gone, pulled what I'd come to call his Orson Welles exit. Like Michael O'Hara in *The Lady from Shanghai*. Rita Hayworth, lovely, blonde, and duplicitous, lies bleeding to death on the floor, and he walks out the door.

I parked the Tempo in the lot of Loblaws supermarket, where the rail freight office used to be. Around the corner from the *Record*. Within shouting distance of the Odeon. Except the Odeon wasn't the Odeon.

From what I gleaned later, the theatre was bought out in 1978 and renamed the Centre, the Marquee Café squeezed out to make way for more screens. This being Trenton, no one protested, I surmised. Least of all the Levins. They'd been gone longer than any of us by then.

The last Levin I'd seen in the flesh had been in Ottawa in '80 or '81. I was in the city with hopes of landing a government job, writing pamphlets on topics I had no interest in. I had a couple of hours to kill before the interview and was browsing the shops of Byward Market when a young woman approached. "Excuse me," she said, her voice soft, apprehensive. "Your name wouldn't be Gus, would it?"

She was tall and slim and bubbly, long dark hair under a tartan tam-o'-shanter, matching scarf at her throat. I tried to place her but could not. "I don't get called that much, these days," I said.

"Oh, my God!" she cried, like she had a fairy up her butt, and the fairy catapulted her into my arms. "I'm Abigail. Abby Levin. Jack's sister. Jack's sister. Oh, my God, it's you, it's really you."

"And you," I said, taking her measure, comparing her to the bratty kid stored in memory. "All grown up. I'd never in a million years . . ."

I asked what brought her to Ottawa ("*Law school.*"), how her parents were doing ("*Good days, bad days.*"), how her sister was ("*Issie just got married!*"), if she'd been back to Trenton ("*Not for a dog's age.*"), and as many other questions as I could dream up to keep her from asking any of me. And when I'd exhausted all avenues, I fed her the line about my urgent meeting, parading my sad regret.

"I can't believe it's you. You're going to laugh, but my sister used to have the craziest dreams about you—something about a graveyard and being chased by skeletons." Abby lowered her eyes, her cheeks redder. "I had dreams about you, too. The funniest, strangest dreams. Like I was looking at you through cheesecloth, the kind my mother used to strain berries for syrup. Kids, eh?"

"I'm really sorry, Abby. I wish I could—"

"What about later? Do you think we could meet up? Please, Gus, please. There are a thousand things I need to ask."

"Sure. Why not? I'll be free after four. Name the time and the place."

She did. Some Italian hotspot nearby.

"Oh, Gus, this is so wonderful. I can't wait to tell my parents. They are going to be so happy. Imagine, after all these years, Jack's best friend." Abby hugged me tight, kissed both my cheeks twice.

I skipped the interview. Skipped dinner. Skipped the hell out of Ottawa.

Head down, collar up, I toured the town, grateful for the biting January cold, how it kept people indoors and out of my face.

Went by Dufferin, the snow too deep for climbing Pelion. By Hanna Park. By my old house, impressed by the makeover. By Jack's house on Queen—a greenhouse where his Fortress of Solitude had been. Across market square, up King. Arthur Murray Dance Studio gone. Sure Press gone. By the *Record* building and the marina. Over the bridge. Up Marmora to Tompkins—

Iris Lebel's happy hovel supplanted by a mammoth architectural Escher. Looked down on the creosote plant by the river. Back across the bridge to the lawyer's office on Dundas, near where the Gilbert Hotel stood, before the fire. "It'll be worth your while," the lawyer had said, as if anything could or ever would be.

Issues of collective memory aside, I prayed to God there were some who remembered Jack Levin. Surely, dear God, Annie Barker was not forgotten. Not by all.

Me. I hoped to God no one remembered me.

I'd keep the visit short. Quick in. Quick out. Get the will over with. Never to be seen or heard from in these parts again.

Love story. Horror story. True story. I wished I knew.

I said I know four people who drowned. I told you about Billy Burgess and Dottie Swartz.

Jack and Annie, they're the other two.

# TWO

Damn you, Jack Levin

The Trenton Marina was a weather-beaten slab of mausoleum concrete at the mouth of the Trent–Severn Waterway and in the shadow of the old swing bridge. No larger than a softball infield, it was tucked into a corner off the main street, behind a couple of restaurants and a dress shop. There was a single gas pump at dockside, with bollards and cleats alternating up and down the right angles, interrupted only by a twelve-foot boat ramp down to the water. There were no slips. Overnighters berthed parallel to the wharf.

I showed up first morning intent on keeping mum. I'd make Jack regret every rotten thing he had or hadn't done to me. I'd freeze him out, same way I'd punished Annie.

Jack trotted right up to me, damn him, mock-punched my shoulder, messed with my hair. "*Spiderman* or *Fantastic Four*?"

I was a model of self-restraint.

"Ginger or Mary Ann?"

Of all the people to have a beef with, Jack was the lousiest.

"Kinks or the Stones?"

I missed this most, the back and forth. I held firm. I would not confuse missing with forgiving.

"*Dr. No, From Russia with Love,* or *Goldfinger*?

I turned my back, shuffled to the ancient picnic table by the canteen. We'd been told Clyde Neil, our boss, would meet us here under the tree.

He knew Jack a little from the Marquee, but he'd hired me sight unseen on Bert Levin's reference.

Jack persisted. "Leafs or Canadiens?"

"Goddamn, you know the answer. Canadiens. Canadiens." They'd just won their seventh Stanley Cup in eleven years. It wasn't because they were hockey's Yankees I liked them. I liked the Montreal Canadiens because every other idiot in town loved the Toronto Maple Leafs. And when the idiots in this town loved anything en masse, I ran the other way.

"Wow. I thought for sure you'd cave without me. Mighty daring, Gus, a solo Habs fan this deep in Leafs territory. You got guts, man. I always knew." And just like that, the grudge I'd nurtured for three crappy years showed signs of cracking. I wanted nothing more than for his assertion to be true. *You got guts, man.*

"You just left on me," I said.

"You got my note."

"You told Annie."

"C'mon! My list wasn't better than some corny goodbye?"

"All the times you visited your dad—"

"Once, I swear. Two days. It was my dad who always came to visit us."

"You could've told me to my face. You should've told me. Before Annie, at least."

"It was sudden, Gus. Honest."

"Not so sudden. No way."

"What do you want me to say? 'I'm sorry?' Okay, I'm sorry. I thought for sure the list and letter would do."

My own sorry stuck in my throat.

We stewed in our respective pots atop the picnic table, feet on the bench as we gazed out upon the silky fabric of the Quinte, seagulls on patrol, mewling high and low. The dock manifested an odd sort of quiet in the days leading up to summer, the ambient sounds of traffic, industry, and nature blended into Muzak. This didn't change, not even when July brought the tourists. The dock was The Bermuda Triangle of cacophony.

"So, any luck?" he said.

"With what?"

We'd arrived at the truce. Negotiations for the peace had begun.

"Our mystery?"

"Which one?"

"Take your pick."

"McGrath hasn't gone anywhere, you know?"

"Still giving you trouble?"

"I keep out of his way. Dirty looks is about it—since your dad put him in his place."

"My dad and McGrath? Really? They're like friends?"

"McGrath had been giving my mom a hard time. Your dad made him back off."

"Wow. Good for my dad."

I was leading him up the garden path, set to drop him hard, sucker-punch him with the news his dad had been sleeping with my mom.

"Let that jerk start up with us again. Let him try. It's different now, Gus. You're bigger, I'm bigger. You're smarter, I'm smarter. Did you hear, I got my brown belt in judo?"

"That supposed to impress me? Like your dopey Beatles haircut?"

He sniffed. "Annie warned me. She says you've been a misery the whole time I've been gone."

"Yeah? When she tell you that?"

"You might as well know, Annie and me, we've been writing letters."

"What now, you're boyfriend and girlfriend?"

"You have a problem with it?"

"Not as long as you got your brown belt in Judo," I said, and Jack nearly split a gut. I hadn't meant it as a joke. I mulled who to kill first, him or Annie.

"Hey, take it easy. I was teasing. Annie and me, we're good friends, same as you and me. Same as I hope you and Annie will be again. What do you say, Gus—time to move on?" He threw out his hand, and I fell for the ploy, snagged it firmly in mine (consciously unfishy) and we shook, not like we were sixteen and seventeen, but like men—any two of *The Magnificent Seven*. Except Lee, the crazy weenie. The Robert Vaughn part. Before he got his balls back and went to work for *U.N.C.L.E.*

"I hear Crates is out of our hair, too," Jack said.

I nodded.

"What was it he did? Cut bike spokes or something? Freaking nuts."

"He thought it was a big joke, too. You should have seen him laughing."

"You were there?"

"It was a Saturday. After the matinee. Hard to miss."

"And Bonnie Priddy—what'd she ever do to him?"

"She was lucky. Lost a few teeth. Broken wrist. But Vito, they say he's still learning to walk and talk again—smashed his head so hard. He's why Crates ended up in adult court. Be a long while before we see him again."

"Crates was always scary, but never thought he had that in him."

"A couple of summers ago, I was riding my bike down Division. He comes out of nowhere, flashes a switchblade, and pushes me in front of a train."

"Jesus Christ."

"You should've seen my bike."

Think whatever you want. Crates deserved what he got. Look at the stuff he'd gotten away with over the years. Pulling Double Al's strings. Collecting taxes from good kids. He was going to cut my ears off, don't forget. Justice is justice. Any which way it's served. And there was no dismissing Creighton Farms. No telling how big a hand he'd had in that.

I told Jack about the footbridge collapse, Mrs. Campbell and her dog, the two other guys.

"My dad only said they were building a new one, nothing about an accident. So it goes, huh? The past never more than five minutes old."

"And the dogs—you must have heard about them, the baby?"

Again, he had not.

"On Tompkins Street," I said.

"Where Iris Lebel lives."

"Yup." And I brought him up to date on my chat with her, too—how she'd been tight-lipped on the lady in black, gaga over triangles. "If she was cuckoo before, she's cuckoo and bananas now."

"My mom, she had an aunt who died in the Triangle Shirtwaist Factory fire—1911, I think."

"But in New York, not here."

"Right, that is weird. Before she was born, too, eh? And then, later, the circus fire. What if—Jesus!—what if it's her who started the fires?"

"Wow. Like a firestarter even from inside her mother?"

12:00 ⑪ PYRO . . . THE THING WITHOUT A FACE—Horror
Barry Sullivan is out to kill Martha Hyer,
his beautiful ex-mistress who torched his
house with his wife and daughter inside.

"She said something about bad things coming in threes. What if she plans to set another?"

"Or what if she's been setting the fires all along?"

We added the footbridge and baby-munching dogs to the list. Felt like old times. And God, I was torn. The work I'd put in, building my walls, warehousing my antipathy. As much as I wanted it to be over, I couldn't let it go without a bit more fight. "Your dad's been sleeping with my mom," I blurted.

The old, matter-of-fact Jack replied. "Yeah, he told me."

"He did?"

"And my mom's been sleeping with my judo teacher. Sensei Sol."

"Holy cow."

"At least Mom and Dad don't yell at each other anymore. There's the bonus."

"That's good."

"We're almost brothers, now, Gus. That's good, too."

"I like your dad. He's really nice to me."

"That's his problem. He's nice to everybody. Anyways, I always liked your mom. She still as pretty as ever?"

Weak is what I was. Worn out and worn down. Sick of the isolation. Sick of fuelling my rage. Sick of reminding myself what the hell my rage was about.

We waited the whole day for Clyde Neil. He never showed. But Annie did.

THREE

The best single moment of my life

Annie arrived at the tiller of a small wooden outboard, puttering in from her family's cottage at Barcovan Beach.

I toed the line between preoccupied and distracted as Jack greeted her at the dock. I hated how she pecked him on the cheek, how her hand lingered in his. And then she spotted me and her Ellie-May-Clampett smile faded to caution. She looked to Jack before approaching, tentative and coy, in blue jeans, orange-striped T, and black Top-Siders. "Good to see you, Gus," she said, daring me to disagree. "Friends?"

My victories have been few and, in their limited wake, any satisfaction fleeting. The hug she gave me remains the best single moment of my life. And as her tears wet my cheek, I convinced myself they meant far more than the measly kiss accorded Jack.

She was the Annie I'd ached for, though not the Annie I'd left behind. A new Annie. A lithe and loving Annie who'd climbed down from a movie screen to melt into my arms. I'd changed, of course, during my exile; but I'd never thought in terms of Annie changing, too. Sure, I'd seen her often enough at school and wherever, but only out the corner of my eye, and quick to look the other way. And now I didn't want our hug to end. Wanted to tell her how stupid I'd been. Wanted to confess how much she meant to me.

"I've missed your gloom," she said, dimples deep and plunging deeper.

I tread my emotions, lips stitched to silence.

I do not sentimentalize Annie Barker. I do not idealize her. She is the only girl I forever strive to remember as she was in reality and not in my imagination. The catch in her voice. The bounty in her laughter. Her long brown hair, her bangs. Her ponytail. *God, I loved her ponytail days.* Her eyes, the displays of happiness and hurt, anger and forgiving—the steely glare she'd use to put me in my place, to save me from myself. Her fears and her faith. Her knowledge and her knowing.

The longing never leaves me.

How beautiful she was. How beautiful she would have been.

The Hardy Boys and Iola Morton were back in business.

You'll never know how light a body can feel until you've shed three years of fury. *Sunshine, Lollipops and Rainbows*— that was us, all right. The Athos, Porthos, and Aramis of a Lesley Gore anthem.

FOUR

Boys of summer

The learning curve for the job was low. Good thing, because teaching wasn't Clyde Neil's métier. He turned up a day late, a cockamamie excuse on his tongue and paranoia in his eyeballs. "Greenwich Mean Time. Since the war, throws 'em off." He opened his arms to embrace the watery horizon. "Landing craft. You never know. Nazis, boys. Japs, '42, hunter pal of mine shoots five on our shores. On our shores. Hushed-hushed and covered up. Keep your eyes peeled, boys."

Clyde owned Clyde's Auto Body on Water Street. The Town, after routine elimination of all qualified candidates, named Clyde the wharfinger. Bert Levin was the first to make mention of the title. I'd thought he was talking about the sequel to *Goldfinger*.

Wharfinger was a fancy word for dock manager. Not that Clyde did any managing. Five seconds into showing us the ropes, he was sweaty, winded, and ready for a nap, then spent the next two hours downing Cokes, guzzling from his silver flask, chain-smoking Export "A," and guffawing over how much he hated water, how he swam like a tire iron, how he couldn't tell a *yawtch* from a *cata-meringue*, how his folks got vapourized in the big tanker truck smash-up of 1948, how his grandpa dropped the *O'* from O'Neil to speed the spelling, how he wished he'd had a penis that swelled up and stuck—"You know, like a collie's. Wouldn't that be the cat's meow!"—and how he hoped we'd be good boys, wouldn't cause him grief.

Jack was in top form. Missed nothing. "Tanker truck smash-up? What was that?" he said to Clyde.

"That punk Jim Geary, murderin' chiselin' bastard, haulin' for Supertest, comes round the bend out by Marmora, and ba-ba-boom!" Clyde swallowed hard, head flung to the sky, as if God had drained him sober. Got to his feet, almost pitched over, and staggered to his pickup.

"But Mr. Clyde . . ."

"C'mon now, don't go girly on me. You twos will do jim-dandy." He floored the truck, whipped off the dock hell-bent for leather, through the stop sign at Dundas, horns slamming his intrusion.

"Tanker truck explosion," I said to Jack.

"Check," he answered. It was music to our ears.

We saw Clyde irregularly after our *training session*, which was the only way to see him. He'd beep his arrival, call us over to his truck, and hand over our pay. "Everything on the up and up?" he'd ask, and never once hung around to hear if everything was.

Jack and I were on our own from sunrise to after sunset, seven days a week, and that was fine by us.

"Raquel Welch or Brigitte Bardot?"

"Brigitte speaks English, right?"

"Like it'd matter?"

We'd berth the boats, the ritzy and the dinky, pump gas, haul ice, grill hot dogs, toast up frozen pizza and, when Annie wasn't around, flirt like mad with the girls who'd come sailing in—a good many fresh out of a Beach Boys song. Jens and Patties and Candies and Sandies and Lauras and Lindas and Cathies and Connies from Rochester and Syracuse and Toronto and Cornwall and Buffalo and Alexandria Bay. And, jeez, the moms, too. Some days we'd swear Ursula Andress herself, curves and white-bikini-hot, had quit on James Bond to hook up with Trenton's boys of summer. "Are you guys brothers?" they'd ask, and Jack and me, we'd grin, no desire to clarify. *Brothers* worked in our favour, though neither Jack nor I could fathom why. And just about everyone chatted up Jack, like in the Marquee, minus the revelations. "Mostly it's about the boat they had before and the one they're gonna buy next. Stinkpotters knocking blowboaters, blowboaters knocking stinkpotters."

One Sunday afternoon a Chinese river junk rippled onto the horizon, sails furling and the engine kicking in as the thirty-footer navigated the buoys. We'd seen nothing like it and we weren't alone. Sailors watched from their decks, passersby from the bridge and shore.

"This ought to be good," Jack said.

There had been a certain sameness to the yachts and crews to date, girls and bikinis notwithstanding. Not that we were complaining. But the junk conjured adventure on the exotic side, until the fucktub pulled astern.

PHARMASEA
TRENTON, ONTARIO

At the helm was Pecker himself—fucking Charles Dahl-Packer in white pants, blue blazer, and captain's hat—and tossing the lines to Jack and me from starboard were his fucking mom, his fucking dad.

I kept my head down, willed myself to be one with the concrete, as I tied the lines to the cleats.

Pecker had shot up in height, Plastic Man stretched two ways from the middle. He was now taller than either Jack and me, though nothing you'd call improved.

"Well, look what the tide washed up!" Mrs. Dahl-Packer announced, and while I hoped she didn't mean me, I knew she did.

"Hi," I said meekly, bygones and all that. "Nice boat."

Pecker pranced ashore, motioning me to keep my distance. "Do you think for one moment we'd trust the likes of you?" He knelt by the cleats, untied and retied my hitches. His Mom elbowed his dad, and Mr. Packer carbon-copied his misbegotten scion in the make-work.

"Are you going to stand there all day? Make yourselves useful." Pecker clapped his hands. "A block of ice. Chop-chop."

Jack inserted himself between me and the Dahl-Packers, backing me toward the neutral corner of the canteen. But I shoved him out of the way, *grabbed Pecker by the throat and his dad by the hair and smashed their heads together, dumped the dazed fuckers into the bay. And then I grabbed a line, jumped aboard the* Pharmasea, *and strung Mrs. Dahl-Packer up from the yardarm, whatever the hell a yardarm was.*

The End

BPI

Tell me you wouldn't have wanted to do the same.

Jack inserted himself between me and the Dahl-Packers, backing me toward the neutral corner of the canteen. "Yes, sir. Right away, sir," he said.

After counting sixty-five cents into Jack's hand for the block of ice, Pecker tossed him an extra nickel and winked.

Jack bowed. "Hop Sing thanks you humbly, Master Cartwright."

"It's Packer," Pecker corrected. "Dahl-Packer. And you are most welcome."

The *Pharmasea* would come and go, the Dahl-Packers thorns in our sides for the season. But we had plenty of good going on, too. Days earlier, our first Monday on the job, Mr. Blackhurst had cruised in from his house across the bay.

# FIVE

Beluga

"Great to see you, sir," Jack said, and together we hoisted the dry cleaner dockside. A beluga would have been less unwieldy. Mr. Blackhurst had put on a few pounds, his butt as flopsy-dropsy as elephant ears.

Mr. Blackhurst tucked in his shirt, adjusted his tie. He nodded to each of us in turn, though the specifics of his acknowledgement were typically sketchy. I was accustomed to it. But Jack—the *Jack Levin* whose ear he'd bent a hundred times and, last I heard, was eager to bend again—it was like he'd never seen him before.

Blackhurst wobbled, palmed our shoulders to steady himself. "Now, lads, take note. I prefer not to chew my cabbage twice," he said, his jowls flouncing. "Longevity of marriage is more often evidence of not happiness—rather complacency."

Blackhurst could've given Chairman Mao and his *Little Red Book* a run for his money had I been prescient, capable of seeing his non sequiturs as anything other than screwy.

Jack took the Earth-to-Blackhurst approach. "Remember me, sir? Jack Levin. Bert Levin's son. The Marquee. You and me, we used to—"

"My dog, it should be sizzling by now." He shifted his attention to the canteen and his amphibious girth followed in ponderous sway, his belly essential to the locomotion.

And thus the morning ritual was begun, Blackhurst's words of wisdom a pillar.

Crack of dawn, five days a week, we'd hear the engine sputter to life, the drone carrying from across the bay. Jack and I would drop whatever we were doing. One of us would throw a hotdog onto the grill while the other headed down to dockside. Right on schedule, Mr. Blackhurst and *Evie III* would come splashing into view, the nineteen-foot Chris Craft at once elegant and arrogant as it spanked the early morning waters. She was a pampered beauty, that runabout, lacquered mahogany and polished chrome, with red vinyl seats that put shame to leather. If ever a boat was a woman . . . Or vice versa.

There's this *Little Rascals* episode where rich twit Waldo steals the affection of Darla from Alfalfa, impressing the fickle little vamp with his kid-sized yacht. "She's a very trim craft," he tells her, and Darla asks why he calls his boat a *she*. And Waldo, over the top on the pomposity meter, sends her swooning with his reply: "Things of beauty, grace, and speed are usually referred to in the feminine gender." *Evie III* was all of this and more.

Mr. Blackhurst could've been Waldo all grown-up, commodore's cap and ascot. As a movie director, if his claim was true, he could have pulled off jodhpurs, boots, and beret with equal aplomb. In the years I'd known him, however, his attire never varied: white shirt, paisley tie, suspenders, brown trousers with double pleats and two-inch cuffs. His socks were uniformly brown. ("A man who purchases socks of the same style and colour will eliminate a year, at minimum, of superfluous decision-making from his life." —Chairman Blackhurst)

The canteen was set back from the dock, diagonally opposite the gas pump, under a buggy willow and up against a high grey fence built to conceal the backside of the Chinese restaurant on the main street. The structure was ten by five, at most, a clapboard and tin affair—the tin generously provided by tobacco and soda pop companies to advertise their wares.

PLAYER'S PLEASE.

PALL MALL – OUTSTANDING . . . AND THEY ARE MILD!

CANADA DRY – LET'S HAVE A PICNIC!

RC COLA – THE FRESHER REFRESHER

A padlocked chest freezer—*Ice Blocks & Bags*—braced the short end of the canteen. The picnic table creaked out front.

A hotdog was Mr. Blackhurst's standing order. "My breakfast chaser," he'd say with a gravelly chuckle, and a healthy sprinkling of sheepish. Three quick bites, never varied.

He'd hitch up his trousers till foiled by overhang, and with a snap of his suspenders propel himself in the direction of King Street and his day of dry cleaning ahead.

Never once did he acknowledge Jack as Bert Levin's boy or me as the kid who had brought him the intertitles. Forget movie-making or Hollywood North.

I pushed Jack to go for it. "You got your brown belt. What are you afraid of? Let's get him talking again."

"It's been what—a week? We don't want to scare him off."

"At this rate, he'll be dead and buried before we get any answers. He likes talking to you."

"And what answers do you expect, Gus? So he tells us more about Hollywood North. So what? As long as no else buys into the story, it rings as true as Goldilocks or Peter Pan."

"It can't hurt to try. We'd know. At least."

"Know what? What more do you think there is? If they really did make movies in Trenton, that's great. History. Case closed. And if they didn't, if it's all bullshit, tell me one thing that changes. The mystery is not Hollywood North, Gus. The mystery is why this town knows nothing, remembers nothing, cares about nothing."

"Donkey Baseball brings out the crowds," I said.

Jack's laugh was bleak. "I stand corrected."

"Thing is, Jack, what if Hollywood North is a symptom of the same disease? Same as Creighton Farms or dogs running wild and eating babies? Solving any one mystery could unlock all the other mysteries. The bad stuff. The crazy stuff."

"Then you try, Gus. You ask him the questions you think need answering."

"I'm nobody to him. But Jack the Finder . . . Jack the *Finder-outer* . . . C'mon, man. What's with you, all the hot and cold?"

"Everybody is nobody to him, these days. Can't you see, he's lost it?"

"No. You're wrong. He hasn't. He hasn't, Jack." I was calm, logical, and aware my brain might well have swapped places with Jack's. "Blackhurst is an actor. He turns it on and he turns it off. He always has. He's no different than he's ever been."

"Except fatter, older, balder."

"Think about it. That day, when he told us about the movies he'd made, he was sharp as a tack. Until the lady in black stepped in. If not for her, I bet you we'd have had the whole story."

"So what are you saying?"

"We sit him down, show him the cards again. Just you, me, and him. Right here."

"Jesus," Jack said, his look akin to sighting Jesus. But it sure as heck wasn't Jesus.

McGrath had made his grand re-entrance, his stage the marina. Like the Cyclops lurching out of the cave and onto the beach in *The 7th Voyage of Sinbad*. A sense of timing this good, you had to be born with it.

 # SIX

Cyclops

The *Record* building was on Quinte, corner of Creswell, a lobotomized back-street any normal town would have relegated to the fringes. Businesses were so shady here, legit storefronts would have killed business. The dock was a convenient escape route to Dundas and the east bank of the river for winos, drifters, resident ne'er-do-wells, and reporters who populated the area. Bryan McGrath was at the midpoint of the square.

Five seconds, no more. He did not speak. Did not gesture. Did nothing but stand and stare. And the fear Jack and I had believed we'd left behind came rushing back in demoralizing spades. McGrath's impassivity reeked of a familiar and sickly menace.

I might as well have been pinned to his office wall again, his forearm pressed to my chest, his cigarette at my cheek. And the look on Jack's face, I tell you, he was that kid at the table in the Marquee, the reporter's wiry fingers clamped to his wrist, Frank Buck's elephant gun between his eyes.

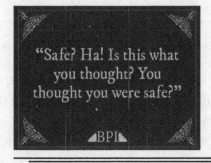

"Safe? Ha! Is this what you thought? You thought you were safe?"

BPI

As quickly as the fear had filled us, the fear was gone. I can't explain it, except to say those two terrified twerps were not us. *Threaten me six thousand times, shame on you. Threaten me six thousand and one, shame on me.*

"Still feeling brave?" Jack said, as we watched the skinny old prick slink off.

"More than ever," I shot back, my backbone on short-term loan from every overeager, skin-crawling child actor who'd ever destroyed an otherwise good movie for me. "I've had enough. That guy, it's like running in circles. One day we're scared shitless, next we're laughing him off. Once and for all, Jack, let's end it."

"Who'd have thought? You really do have guts."

"We don't show Blackhurst those cards again, we'll hate ourselves forever."

"Fear is a funny thing, eh?" Jack said, and my eyes glazed over in anticipation of another Jack Levin moment of reflection. "In the city, living in Montreal, you get accustomed to the sirens. Police cars. Fire trucks. Ambulances. Night and day. Death has lots of business and lots of choice there, so the odds work in your favour. But coming back here, small town, if the sirens aren't coming for your neighbour, they're coming for you."

"You're telling me you're scared?"

"Always."

"Like what we used to talk about, then. Something bad is going to get you. . . ."

"But before, when I lived here, I never felt it as much as I have since I've come back."

"And whatever it is, you think it'll be coming from McGrath?"

"You saw. The guy's a stick in the wind. We could take him easy. It's something else. Something I can't put my finger on."

Mr. De Grote, my biology teacher at Trenton High, had said the human body is composed of sixty percent water. He never said what the other forty percent was. My guess was apprehension.

Rare was the afternoon McGrath didn't amble through the background of our foreground. Some days he'd torch us with the death rays of his eyes, other days he gave the impression he couldn't care less. Little did he know the feeling was mutual. We exercised restraint, fought the urge to give him the finger, hurl epithets, exact revenge for all he'd put us through.

Canteen traffic slowed in the afternoons. I was restocking the chocolate bars when I heard Jack calling. He was down at dockside, pumping gas into a sleek twenty-seven-footer flying a U.S. flag. I hoped maybe Rod Serling had shown up. Or, more likely, knowing Jack, another all-American goddess sunning on a deck.

Jack pointed me toward the swing bridge and the voices raised in anger.

Holy frigging cow. Together again for the first time, Blackhurst and McGrath were going at it. Nose to nose and toe to toe, no small feat considering the difference in their sizes. *Hardy versus Laurel.* Red in the face. Gaskets blowing. Vessels bursting. Perspiration flying. Finger-wagging. Hand-waving. Fists-pumping.

We never did learn what they were arguing over. Didn't matter. We'd procrastinated with the cards too long. The reality hit as we helped Mr. Blackhurst onto *Evie III.* His face 12-gauge red. With rats humping in his shirt pocket—you would have sworn that's what it was—the *Sturm und Drang* of his stale-dated heart, blood sluicing to the path of least resistance.

"Tomorrow," Jack said.

"Crack of dawn," I said.

SEVEN

In a borough abustle with simpletons and sycophants

I pulled three cards from the library and slipped my random selections between the pages of yesterday's *Record*. Habits born of fear die hardest.

I met Jack before sunrise under the maroon awning of the Gilbert Hotel, a three-story throwback to the glory days of rail. Spittoons in the lobby. Crushed velvet, brass, and mahogany. And guests soaked to the gills in whatever was their pleasure.

Bert Levin had sold the house on Queen the year before. Mom had offered to have him board with us, but he opted for a room in the Gilbert. Five nights out of seven he was sleeping with her, anyhow, so the room was mostly about propriety. When Jack came back, Bert squeezed a cot into the room. He also stopped sleeping with Mom.

"For God's sake, Emily, I'm not hiding it from him. I told him we were seeing each other. And he was absolutely fine with it. Jack likes you. He likes Leo—or Gus as he calls him. But anything more between us right now, I'd be throwing it in the boy's face. It's only a couple of months, Em. C'mon. We cool it till September and pick up where we left off. Where's the harm?"

My mother lit up six consecutive Du Mauriers and boycotted the Marquee and Bert. "It's my decision," she told me. "You're free to do what you wish." Mom's independence had been a source of personal pride, especially as she climbed the Avon ladder. She'd given a good share of it up for Bert and was now determined to reclaim her losses. "If that man thinks he can come and go as he pleases, treat me like his little side dish, he's in for a surprise. Oh, I'll cool it till September, all right."

The streets were quiet as Jack and I drifted toward the marina, cones of yellow from the streetlamps overhead, moths coming off nightshift. A wino asked if we knew where he might buy buttermilk. We told him we didn't know. A cop car cruised by. The cop knew Jack from the Marquee, asked if the wino was giving us trouble. We told him he wasn't. A black Lab snored in the entranceway of Woolworth's. We tiptoed past.

To hear *Evie III* hum to life that morning was a relief, I tell you. And seeing Mr. Blackhurst come ashore surely added to it. He was in better shape than we'd expected in the aftermath of his set-to with McGrath. The old guy was exuberant in fact, babbling on about his beloved *Evie III* with more than the usual rapture, entering the homestretch with his tip of the day for Jack and me. "Life, you'll find, is infinitely simpler, your wife and mistress sharing the same name."

We thanked him as part of the routine, the lesson gleaned beside the point.

Our intention was to reintroduce him to the cards gradually, but Mr. Blackhurst had opened another door and we could not resist.

Jack kept it casual, tried not to pry. "*Evie III*, is she named after your wife, sir? The lady we saw in the dry cleaners. You remember?"

"The day we showed you the intertitles," I said. "Alfred Hitchcock, you don't like him, do you?"

He patted his hotdog bun, gave the dog a quarter spin. "Evangeline August. My Evie. She had the world at her feet, that girl. Mary Pickford, Lillian Gish—none shone brighter. And to think she gave it up to be with the likes of me."

"She was a movie star, sir?"

He poofed, eyes magnified by three. "In a borough abustle with simpletons and sycophants, what else would she have been? Good Lord, an extra?"

"Sorry," Jack said, and I mumbled a semblance of the same, unclear as to what we were apologizing for and where we ranked between simpleton and sycophant.

"You lads, of all people, should know. Does it not take one to know one? From the moment Evie laid eyes upon you she possessed nary an iota of doubt. 'Stars,' she called you. 'Stars.'"

"Us? What?"

"Pardon, sir?"

"If you have *it*, lads, you have *it*."

"I'm not sure we get *it*, sir," Jack said. "If you could just expl—"

"Dear God, you inform me now, the denouement at hand? For Heaven's sake, you have your roles. Am I your wet nurse? Follow the bloody script. And the girl? Where is the girl? Why isn't the girl here?"

His last bite was rocket fuel, the speed he took off, his belly his nosecone. Like where was the real Mr. Blackhurst and who the hell had taken over his body?

The intertitles would have to wait another day.

# EIGHT

The best job I ever had

You know those questions you hear in bars, when the small-talk peters out, before the quiet turns to disquiet? The one book you'd want if shipwrecked on a desert island? Your last meal before they fried you in the chair? *The best job you ever had?* All these years later, it is only the last I can answer without hesitation: Take away the lunacy that came after and you couldn't beat the first three weeks of the summer of 1966. Hanging out with Jack, the give and take. I didn't need to be me, free to hone the fantasy of a better me. *You got guts, man.* That's what Jack had said. Said it twice. *You got guts, man.* If only.

NINE

The day after Richard Speck

Jack had a theory as to the nature of Evil, how it manifested itself in vapours, windborne and guided by whim. "Trouble with Trenton," he said, "the vapours linger." He could be a dramatic son of a bitch. Half the time I'd wonder if half the stuff he said wasn't swiped from movies and books.

But there was no denying the malignancy in the air. The day before, news had come from Chicago, 600 miles to the southwest, that the bodies of eight student nurses had been found, raped and stabbed and strangled in the dorm they shared. This is why the date sticks. July 15, 1966. And while Richard Speck would soon become the first mass killer to set up camp in my consciousness, Jack and I had a body of our own to contend with that morning.

"Gonna be a sticky one," Mr. Blackhurst said, observing the sear of the sunrise. He would know, I thought. The red filled his face, rose from beneath his knotted tie and buttoned collar. Blackhurst was his old self, and less. The energy of the day before was absent, as was his daily pearl of wisdom.

His spirits lifted at the sight of the hotdog. The toasted bun. The zigzag of mustard.

"We've got something to show you, sir, if you don't mind." Jack steered him by the elbow to the picnic table. I dealt the cards onto the surface. Mr. Blackhurst stood, observed, chewed.

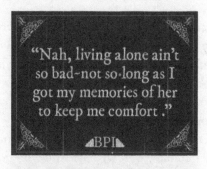

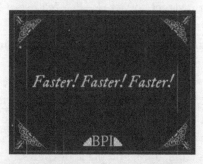

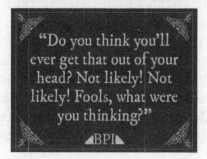

Jack said, "We're hoping you'll tell us more about your movie days."

"Hollywood North," I said.

Blackhurst's jaw worked to the rhythm of a throaty purr. He hacked, and I figured hairball. He hacked again, and Jack leaned in. "You feeling okay, sir?"

The old man went Wolf Man on us, his face obliterated by mouth and snout. A chainsaw cough and a popgun pop. And a bloodied wad of bun and wiener shot onto his palm. He teetered, knees bent to bench, grim realization dawning, as if done in by sabotage—slivered bamboo or powdered Kryptonite. He reached across the table, his fingers worming up my arms, his flesh as grey and clammy as the concrete underfoot.

He clutched his armpit and his life dropped out from under him. He reversed like a Slinky from tabletop to bench to ground, flopped flat onto his back. His eyes rotated shut and, with the disconcerting hiss of a cross-country fart, the whole of him contracted.

We stood over him. Watching. Waiting. Hoping.

His eyes rotated open, a jackpot white.

It's the one thing they never teach you in school, what to do with a dead body. Do you leave it? Touch it? Sit with it? And who do you call? And why weren't there boxes on street corners?—*Pull in Case of Death.*

Jack ran to the Marquee to tell his dad.

I packed up the cards, hid them in the canteen behind packages of napkins, and returned to shoo away the flies.

It struck me then, Mr. Blackhurst had eaten his last hotdog. I wondered if I'd know when it came down to the final hotdog of my life. Wondered if anyone knows when they're eating their last hotdog, outside of death row inmates who'd made it their last meal. Or vegetarians, of course, who could probably tell you the time, date, and place of theirs.

Two ants inspected Mr. Blackhurst's last bite. I kicked the slimy wad of pink and white onto the crabgrass. A black Lab swooped in from somewhere, but a seagull beat him to it.

The Lab sniffed Mr. Blackhurst's ear, licked an eye, the saliva bubbles on his lips. I grabbed the broom. "Get outta here," I shouted. The dog yelped off and Mrs. Dahl-Packer came yelping up from dockside.

"What have you done to the poor man? You monstrous boy, what have you done?" She dropped to her knees, pounded Blackhurst's chest, and stuck her mouth on top of his.

She kept going till we heard the sirens. "You've done it this time, haven't you? Don't think I won't tell the authorities everything I know."

"But what about you?" I said defiantly. "You French-kissed a dead man."

TEN

The best thing that could have happened

The cops and ambulance guys got right to it, measuring, photographing, straight out of *Rescue 8*, despite the absence of anyone to rescue. Boaters crowded around, too, murmurs reserved, as they kept Jack and me hopping at the canteen with requests for coffee and grilled cinnamon buns. Our busiest morning to date.

"It's our fault," I said to Jack during a lull. "We killed him with the cards."

"Don't be stupid," he said. "You saw him. He was sick before he got here. You don't eat hotdogs for breakfast and expect to live forever."

"The cards, Jack, I'm telling you, no different than King Tut's tomb. You lay your eyes on 'em, you touch 'em, and you're cursed."

"You know what you're saying, don't you? Because that'd make us cursed, too."

We told the police what they wanted to hear, omitting the details best kept to ourselves.

Mrs. Dahl-Packer spoke to them, too, pointing at me all the while.

They were wheeling Mr. Blackhurst into the ambulance when Bryan McGrath turned up. He peeled back the sheet for an I.D., snapped photos, and prodded the cops and ambulance attendants for quotes. He saved Jack and me for last.

He kept a professional distance, not what we'd come to expect from him. "Your eyewitness accounts are all I'm looking for, gentleman."

Jack grabbed the broom as if he might whack the reporter, then brushed past him and started sweeping.

Mr. Blackhurst was the first person to die before my eyes. My first freshly dead body. Till now, I'd lived with and accepted accidental death. Slip in a public washroom, you die. Go fishing from a dam, you die. Play on a construction site, you die. But now Death had a new wrinkle: He could jump you at any time, no negligence required. I'd always frustrated Mom, how I kept stuff inside, reluctant to talk it through. While I wasn't yet ready to bare my soul, I felt I had nothing to lose, and finally get my name in the paper to boot. "Well, he came by early, same as alw—"

"Cut to the chase, son," McGrath said. "Dead is dead. All I need are his last words. You got one shot, make them good."

I was eager to please, stuttered as I scrabbled for a clever parting line. Something up there with "Keep watching the skies" from *The Thing* or "To God, there is no zero—I still exist" from *Shrinking Man*. A quote to incorporate Blackhurst's fatal hot dog perhaps. Then Jack cracked the broomstick on the picnic table and stole my limelight, yet again.

"'I made movies.' That's what he said. 'I made movies in Hollywood North.' Mr. Blackhurst's last words exactly."

McGrath met the assertion with an exasperated sigh. He pocketed his notepad, his tone uncharacteristically conciliatory. "Let me tell you, Jack Levin, as sad as this day is, Norman Blackhurst's passing is the best thing that could've happened to him. Best that could've happened to all of us. May he rest in peace. And may you boys—you and you—have the respect and common decency to let him."

Jack wilted, his bravado dissipating. Guilt tugged at the corners of his eyes and mouth. Was he buying what McGrath was selling? Had he so easily forgotten what the man had put us through? For the second time this morning, I witnessed sudden death.

McGrath rested a grandfatherly hand on Jack's shoulder and would have done the same to me had I allowed him. "Whatever you boys think, whatever you have been up to—and I know you have been—let the end be the end. A man is dead here. You understand the finality—the gravity. A human being same as you and me is dead here." McGrath bowed his head.

"'Short days ago he lived, felt dawn, saw sunset glow, loved and was loved, and now he is no more.' Common decency, boys. Common decency."

He'd taken a verse from *In Flanders Fields* and twisted it. "That's not how it goes," I said.

"That is exactly how it goes," he snapped.

"It is," Jack said. "It's over, Gus."

ELEVEN

Paint by Numbers

Mr. Blackhurst's obituary was the first I'd read without self-interest or burglary in mind. (I'd never seen my dad's.) I clipped it from the *Record* and would transfer it to every wallet I would own for the rest of my sentient life. I did not do the same when Jack's and Annie's turns came. Or my mother's. I feel bad about this, though I would have been reading only what I knew or, perhaps, preferred not to know.

BLACKHURST, Norman Kingsley
Suddenly, in Trenton, on Friday, July 15, 1966 in his 72nd year. Born in the United Kingdom and a decorated veteran of the Great War, the proprietor of Sure Press Dry Cleaners on King Street, Trenton, will be sadly missed by his friends and customers. He leaves behind his cherished companion of many years, Miss August. In keeping with Norman's wishes, cremation has taken place. For those wishing, donations may be made to the March of Dimes or charity of choice.

"It's all lies," I said to Jack.

"We need to let it go. For real, this time. Like McGrath said, Gus, it's about respect. Decency."

"You kidding me? Two days ago you were ready to punch him out."

"Death changes things."

"What are you talking about?"

"I'm no grave robber."

"Who said you were?"

"What if it's just that you and me wanted something so bad, we started seeing and thinking things that weren't there? Did McGrath ever do anything to us? Did he? Really? Did he ever say anything that was so wrong? Or was it in our heads?"

"Holy cow. Death scares you that much? You're like the rest of them now, Jack? That it? You've shut your eyes, blocked your ears? You believe what you're told more than what you know and see? You gone Eloi on me?"

"You got me wrong, man."

"Then tell me."

"It's sort of like Paint by Numbers."

"Ah, Jesus. Not again."

"You start out all excited, ready to paint this masterpiece, but five, six numbers in, you realize it's going to be worthless shit, no matter how careful you are to paint within the lines. You stop. You throw it in a drawer. You have the good sense to know that even should you get it done, who's going to give a crap? You're not making art, you're jerking off. That's us, Gus. We solve the mystery—so what? What do we prove? And who do we prove it to, if no one cares to begin with?"

"I care."

"And what if it turns out the only mystery was us, kidding ourselves into believing there was a mystery?"

"The cards. McGrath. Blackhurst. Hollywood North. The accidents nobody talks about . . . None of it's Paint by Numbers."

"Don't be so sure."

"You don't read Sherlock Holmes for the solution, you read it for the steps he takes to get there."

"Annie's right—you need to have more fun, Gus."

"She tell you that?"

"You need to grow up."

"Who the hell are you?" I said. "What's happened to you?"

"C'mon, Gus, the man is dead. And we're still playing at make-believe? Not only you. Me, too, man. It's time we grew up."

Grow up. No two words did I detest more. "Fuck you."

"Gus, c'mon. Listen to me—"

"You do what you need to do."

"Let's just go back to the way it was, okay? You and me, working the dock, goofing with the girls, playing our games . . . Beach Boys or Beatles? Ann-Margret or Elke Sommer?"

"Yeah. Sure," I said. "Benedict Arnold or Judas Iscariot?"

# TWELVE

Evie III

The deep freeze carried into August. Jack and I worked together as before. We didn't argue. We talked and such, laughed at stupid stuff. But nothing amounted to anything. Life went on, with a huge chunk missing. Jack was moving on without me, again. He didn't vanish this time around. Not completely. More like The Invisible Man on a half-dose of monocaine—here, gone, partly here, gone, here, gone, partly here . . . He was the one who'd let me down, yet he was making *me* pay. *Grow up,* my ass!

We no longer walked together from the Gilbert Hotel.

We stopped hanging out during free time.

Without serving notice, I joined my mother's boycott of the Marquee.

Annie would have had to be blind not to notice the chill. "I don't know what's happened between you two, but it's got to stop. You're best friends. Please, Gus. Tell him you're sorry."

"Me?"

"One of you has to make the first move."

"Tell that to your boyfriend."

"Pardon me? Is that what this is about? You're fighting over me?"

"You wish," I said, scoffing at the suggestion, amazed she'd uttered it. Annie knew boys liked her. *How could she not?* But she'd always kept her vanity in check, self-deprecating to a T, advocating the fraud there was nothing special whatsoever about her—which drew boys to her all the more.

Yet now she had revealed an unintended truth: *He was her boyfriend*. I'd blurted it and she had pretty much copped to it. I could stop conning myself, pretending Jack, Annie, and I were a trio. And he wanted to punish *me*?

I would've launched my counteroffensive, laid into them, given them an earful, all right, had it not been for Clyde Neil, the wayward wharfinger.

It wasn't payday, yet here he was. Important, too, because the door of his pickup was full open and he was sitting sideways, heels on the running board to face us. "You boys recollect the old guy croaked, few weeks back? *Blackhearse*, was it?"

"Do we *recollect*?" Jack said, and for a disbelieving instant the two of us were gratefully in sync.

"Message come in, his lady friend or some-such wants her boat back. You boys know anything 'bout it?"

"*Evie III*," I said. She bobbed patiently at dockside where Mr. Blackhurst had left her, as if her dear master might yet return.

"Well, once you finish up here tonight . . ." Clyde fumbled with his glove compartment, found what he was looking for behind a window visor. He passed me the sheet of directions. "You're to take the boat 'cross the bay."

"Me?" I said.

"The twos of yous. The dame requested the twos of yous. Never met the lady myself, mind you. Who has, eh? Reclusive by nature, I hear. And quite the looker, some say. Funny that, eh, some people? Not quite right upstairs, if you catch my drift. Women, you know, them and their times of month—"

"How do we get back?" Jack said.

"Yeah," I said. "If we're leaving her the boat . . ."

Clyde sanded his fingertips on the stubble of his neck. "That's a stumper, can't deny," he said, hauled up his legs, shut the door, and drove off.

THIRTEEN

Evie August in August

Admiral Friggin' Jack manned the wheel, First Mate Annie all too cozy at his side, and me, lowly Deckhand Gus, on the bench behind. I'd been assigned towline duty, minding our return transportation, Annie's old dinghy bouncing and bucking in the bitchy wake of *Evie III*.

We ignored Clyde's orders and cut out early, putting a good hour of daylight in our favour. Enough time to make it across the Quinte and home before dark.

Sunset bled across the waters, an open wound poisoning the bay. Not that Annie saw it my way, of course. She shivered, reached for Jack's hand. "I ask you, how could anyone tire of anything so magnificent? How can there not be a Higher Power?"

Jack held her closer. "'Red sky at night, sailor's delight . . .'"

Annie's cheek touched his. "You look at all this beauty and you know the Devil doesn't stand a chance."

"Oh, Jesus." I was itching for a showdown. "What a load."

The grins Jack and Annie traded were benign, and infuriating. They saw me as a work-in-progress, nothing love and friendship could not heal. I knew better. By then, I was every inch, every ounce, every breath of my being a lost cause.

"You know who likes you?" Annie said.

"Nobody," I replied, and they laughed at my presumed quick wit.

"Di does. Diana Klieg. Don't ever tell her I told you, but she's had a crush on you for the longest time."

"We missed the landing," I said. The notes and drawings Clyde had provided were neat and orderly, and unlikely from his hand. "Back that way."

"Jack and I were thinking the four of us could go to a movie one night. How about it, Gus?"

I pointed. "There. See. By the rocks."

Jack got the message and doubled back with few seconds lost. "Slowly," Annie said, her hand at his back, noting how the waters here ran faster and shallower than was typical of the bay, how the rocky outcrop discouraged boaters from straying too close.

Trees and bushes competed for dominance along the shoreline, presenting an impassive front for whatever secrets awaited us inland. The domain of the late Norman Kingsley Blackhurst was the last place on the Quinte anyone would have thought inhabited.

"I can't believe I never noticed any of this before," Annie said. "I go by here almost every day."

Jack eased up on the throttle, piloted the boat between the rocks and shore, and we drifted up against the floating dock.

"Cheer up, Gus," Jack said, initiating a momentary thaw in our cold war. "I have a feeling we're going to get some answers."

"Like that matters to you," I said.

"C'mon, man."

"You guys are out of your minds," Annie said.

Thirty feet up the trail the forest receded, then conceded to a one-horse bridle path canopied by inconsolable willows. It wasn't much farther when a cast-iron fence stopped us cold. We looked to either side and up. Fleur-de-lis finials capped the pickets, sharpened spears with sharper barbs that'd gut you through the ass should you be fool enough to climb over.

"Welcome to Transylvania," Jack said, his Lugosi impression not half-bad, though not that I'd tell him.

"Shut up," Annie said. "It's spooky enough."

"Less spooky than Creighton Farms," I said.

"There are houses on those graves now," Annie said solemnly.

Jack gripped the bars, peered into the thickening gloom. "Hello? Anybody out there? Miss August?"

My mouth went dry. The Angel of Death was bearing down upon us. "It's her," I said.

"I got eyes," Jack said.

"You know her?" Annie asked. "How do you know her?"

Evangeline August was a lot more slinky than I recalled (from either memory or messy dreams), in mourning black of flowing lace and silk, a charcoal etching of ethereal grace upon a canvas of dusk. The solitary colour, her lips, a succulent slash of red. (What can I tell you? When it comes to me and Evie August, I will always be the horny teen with a downmarket thesaurus. She was fifty-three then, looked thirty-three, and would die in January 1988 at the age of seventy-four. And while older women were never my thing, until I was old myself and out of options, Evie in this moment became the standard by which I judged all other women, the enduring stimulus for my every arousal, desire, and kink.)

Evie held the gate ajar as we filed through. God, she was tiny. Then again, she'd been in heels last time we'd met, while I'd been four years and a good foot younger.

Annie promptly cued us to the appropriate etiquette. "I am sorry for your loss, Mrs. Blackhurst."

Jack chimed in, "He was a nice guy."

"He sure liked hot dogs," I said.

Evie replied with dispassion. "It was his time. Later than I expected, if you must know. The difference in our ages, you understand—a Lita Grey in thrall of Chaplin sort of escapade. May-December, should the allusion fail you."

We followed her in silence. Well, Jack and I, anyhow. Annie wasn't pleased, hushed annoyance at Jack's ear: "You promised we were only dropping the boat off. It's almost dark. My parents are going to kill me. You promised . . ." I loved the sound of that, you bet.

Knowing Mr. Blackhurst, I figured for sure we'd be arriving at the *House on Haunted Hill*. What we got was *Moby Dick*—an old Cape Cod with a wraparound porch, shuttered windows, and a widow's walk among the treetops. Evie saw our faces and elaborated, clarifying only slightly: "Norman salvaged the façade from *The Women of Butternut Bay* and built from there."

The seafaring theme carried on to the feebly lit interior as she hurried us from one room to the next. A blur of patterned sofas, barrel chairs, and driftwood lamps. Brass instruments with fancy dials and scale models of tall ships, some in bottles. Oils of craggy mariners in peacoats and mackintoshes.

Down through a passageway we went, a slalom of umbrella stands, canes, shoes, and boots. She halted by a wall of coats and scarves, took a hooded black fur from a hook, advised us to do the same, and resumed her pace. The request was nutty. Humidity hung heavy within the old house and our trek had left us sweaty. Still, we didn't question.

Kids are stupid. We were stupid. How many movies had I sat through with this plot? Good-looking women did evil things, particularly lipsticked beauties slight in stature. More than that, Evie up close was a black-haired blonde as contradictory as this sounds, venal or vulnerable, as she manipulated light and circumstance and us. I'd go only so far with her, I told myself. Should she offer us a drink, I'd know the jig was up.

9:00 5 HERCULES UNCHAINED—Adventure
A thirsty Hercules (Steve Reeves) guzzles from seductive Queen Omphale's enchanted spring, loses his memory, and becomes her captive slave and lover.

At the bottom of a short flight of stairs we came to a heavy steel door. She retrieved a key from her coat pocket, inserted it into the lock, and turned the handle. I looked to Jack, Jack to me, and Annie to Jack. A door this thick and big did not augur well for our futures. "I really have to be getting back," Annie said. "My parents will—"

"Button up, children," Evie said, and a blast of frigid air blew us back. "Welcome to Norman's Icebox."

FOURTEEN

Norman's Icebox

Little lambs, shoulders hunched, hands in pockets, anxiety rife, hearts beating a dirge.

"Wow," Jack said. "Wow. Wow. Wow." And I added several wows of my own.

The screening room was the size of a two-bay garage, with high ceilings and sloped floor. Like Brainiac had shrunken the Odeon for shipment to the bottled city of Kandor. (*Action Comics 242*.)

"It's beautiful," Annie said. "Who built it for you?"

Two terraced rows, four seats abreast. Plush velvet cushions and armrests. A wall-to-wall screen. Burgundy curtains, trimmed and cinched with gold braid. Conch-shell sconces, the light fanning upward along the walls. An ornate plaster ceiling, naked cherubs frolicking amid pastel garlands and bows. Sculpted cornices, masks of Tragedy and Comedy. And behind the top row of seats, propped on four legs of its own, the projector—a boxy contraption of black and grey metal, a reel above, a reel below.

"The chill is to preserve the film," Evie said, "what little remains."

"The movies you made? Hollywood North?" Jack said, a concessionary shrug aimed my way.

She ushered us to the front row.

We sat. Me. Jack. Annie.

Evie deposited a space heater at our feet. "If needed," she said. Heartless, she was not.

Jack gave it another shot. "Mr. Blackhurst told us you were a movie star."

"She is?" The news excited Annie. "Honest? You are? Have I seen you in anything?"

"You are here to honour Norman's last wishes. Let us leave it at that." In fact, Annie had not been invited. Only Jack and me. We'd thought Evie might question it, but this was the closest she would come.

"All set, then?" she said, and disappeared behind us.

The theatre darkened. The projector whirred to life, revved to a metallic snore. And the film wended its way down and through the sprockets, clippity-clop, clippity-clop, like a Jack of Hearts pegged to the spokes of a bike.

Silent movies, we learned, were only as silent as the projector allowed, delivering an unauthorized soundtrack to the images on screen.

Five movies would unspool, though only I kept track.

Anticipation ran high at the outset. Jack and I on the precipice of discovery. Yeah, he was back in the hunt, all right. We were on the lookout for clues—or whatever it might be Mr. Blackhurst had wanted us to be on the lookout for. And right off the bat, a card we remembered from our collection.

"Beware her accursed charms,
for behind those pearly whites
lies the bite of a shrew."
BPI

But aside from a half-decent bridge collapse toward the middle and a train piling into the canyon below, the movie stunk. Stiff-necked men and women yakking in parlours. No Keystone Cops chasing bank robbers. No Laurel & Hardy pitching pies. Music would have helped, I suppose. In a weird way, the din of the projector had shifted from grating to sedating. Maintaining focus was a challenge, even without my other problem in the two seats adjacent.

Jack and Annie were necking full-out before the first picture was ten minutes in. Two tongues sloshing together is nothing anybody wants to hear, unless one of the tongues is their own. I was yet unaware to the extent hormones trumped friendship. Or how jealousy trumped both. As unexplained mysteries go, hormones were up there with Area 51.

Despite my objections—"Cut it out! C'mon!"—and frequent elbows to Jack's ribs, they kept at it till Annie dozed off during the third feature, slumbering serenely within the crook of the traitor's arm.

And wouldn't you know, there was my best bud, fair-weather Jack, back on the job as if his tongue hadn't been swabbing my oldest friend's throat ten seconds before. Oh, I was seething. Still, I set aside our differences for the greater good, vague though it was.

We watched. Fought sleep. Drowsed. Nudged one another awake. Pointed out familiar intertitles. And yeah, sure enough, the pieces came together. For me, anyhow.

Dry Gulch,
Arizona Territory
Pop. 640 (for now)
Undertakers 64

BPI

"Hey! Did you see—the cowboy in the white hat? At the end of the bar."

Jack straightened. "What about him?"

"It's him. Mr. Malbasic."

"No way." He peered at the screen.

"I'm telling you, it's him. Same outfit he's wearing in the picture on his office wall."

"It's hard to tell," he said, as hell broke loose in the Dry Gulch Saloon.

"I'm telling you, it's him."

"You say so . . ."

Jack and Annie were back to making out when *The Black Ace* came on. Too bad, too, because the film was the best of the lot, Mr. Blackhurst's self-described masterpiece.

The hero was a one-time WWI flying ace who becomes a barnstormer. He's got it made. Swell hair. Manly moustache. Winning smile. Super-sweet girlfriend. Adoring public. But when the clock strikes midnight, he dons his canvas flying helmet, adjusts the chin strap, lowers his goggles, and makes like Jack the Ripper.

I didn't have patience for all the credits, as brief as they were. Still, seeing N.K. Blackhurst as director on three gave me that pang of excitement you get when you know someone famous.

His wasn't the only credit to jump out, either.

The Black Ace had Bryan D. McGrath down as Assistant to the Producer.

And for *The Black Ace*, *High Noon in Dry Gulch*, and *Night Fog*, an Iris Nearing was credited for Costumes. I couldn't say for certain she was Iris Lebel, too, but I couldn't say she wasn't.

As for our infamous intertitles, I counted eleven sure hits and half as many good bets scattered among the five flicks. I knew the cards pretty much by rote by then, but the lack of a notepad to keep count and my occasional nodding off put my accuracy in doubt. You sit through a silent film marathon without a note of music and you tell me how long you stay awake.

"Were you in any of them?" Annie asked Evie, after the lights had come up.

"Not if you blinked, dear," she said.

"So, then, Hollywood North is for real," Jack said. "Mr. Blackhurst did make movies in Trenton."

"Jesus, Jack, you think that's all there was to this?" I said. "If you think that's all Mr. Blackhurst wanted us to see, you weren't watching."

"I was watching," Jack lashed out. "I saw what I had to see." Who was this guy, *Jack the Blinder*? Had his horniness for Annie zapped his brain? Had love smacked him stupid? Had McGrath's guiltshit lament for Blackhurst dimmed his lights? How could he not put two and two together? The worst of it, he wasn't done. "So why is Hollywood North a secret? I mean, all your movies . . . And Mr. McGrath, why'd he go nuts when we first brought him the title cards? And then you, that day?"

I cut in before Evie could reply. "The disasters. Didn't you see the disasters? The train derailment. The buildings blowing up. The plane crash. The tanker truck—"

"So what? Find me a movie that doesn't have a train going off the rails or a bridge falling down. The old ones especially, if it wasn't a sword fight, that's all they had going for them. Any idiot knows that. I'm right, aren't I, Mrs. Blackhurst?"

Evie came around to the front, gave Jack a hard stare. "You're the boy who finds things."

Jack's extra large smile wasn't all that different from the Black Ace's. "Jack, ma'am. Jack Levin."

"Well, Jack Levin, I have a question for you: Who do you think I am? The all-knowing windbag at the end of the story who ties the loose ends into a pretty little bundle and tells the good children to run along? Is that who I look like to you?"

"No, Miss, it's just—"

"I showed you the films as Norman requested. Make of them what you will."

Annie was up and at the door of the Icebox. "Please, Jack. I need to get home."

"Only thing I don't understand is why Mr. Blackhurst told us it was fear that killed Hollywood North. Fear of what? Horror movies?" Jack was scrambling, brain cells shooting out his ears. Man, it felt good to hold the upper hand for once.

"It is late. Listen to your girlfriend, Jack Levin."

"I'd like to come back another time, if it'd be all right, Miss August."

Evie lowered her eyes as if to contain her thoughts, and abruptly ushered us through the heavy door, up the steps, and into the passageway.

". . . Like, you know, come back when we're not so tired."

I dawdled by the coat rack as Jack played the fool. All he had to do was look in Evie's face; he'd had his chance and he'd blown it.

"It was very interesting, Miss. Thank you," Annie said, and then, marching off, issued us her ultimatum. "I'm leaving without you."

"It was great," Jack said, and chased after his girlfriend. "Thank you. See you."

Calamity and tragedy had underscored the films Mr. Blackhurst had lined up for us. Watching out for our intertitles during the screenings had taken concentration and, as I said, I missed a bunch. The no-brainer was the message Jack had failed to grasp.

Not every accident or disaster in the movies struck home. A tornado. A mine cave-in. A dam busting. An earthquake. But, fact was, most struck too close to home.

A train derailment.

A bomb factory explosion (courtesy of a German saboteur).

A yacht fire and sinking.

A tanker truck blowing up.

A big-top fire.

A midair plane collision (a highlight of *The Black Ace*).

A graveyard on the grounds of a mansion (*The Black Ace* again).

A landslide above a sleepy village.

A train annihilating a stalled bus.

And thousands of drownings (most in *The Deadly Waters of Nantes*, a costume drama set in France).

I waited till the door slammed shut behind Jack.

"He had it backwards," I said. "Maybe not the train wreck, because it was earlier, but the rest . . . The accidents happened in your movies first, before they happened for real. *Before*. That's it, isn't it? Your movies made the bad stuff happen."

"Your friends are waiting for you."

"People got scared. That's why you stopped making them. That's what killed Hollywood North."

She busied herself with the tassels of her scarf. "After you've passed through the gate, please lock it." She handed me a key. "Leave it in place. I'll retrieve it later."

My heart was beating, my breath short, felt like I was running for my life. "And it hasn't stopped, has it? The bad stuff you filmed, some is still happening for real. And if it hasn't, it's coming. I'm right, aren't I? Aren't I, Miss August?"

Her eyes met mine so unexpectedly, I turned my cheek, checked my neck for whiplash. "Which would you say comes first, the chicken or the egg?"

"Pardon?"

"Does film mirror life or does life mirror film?"

"I don't—"

"Neither do I."

"But—"

"You're the one they call Gus."

"It's not my real name."

"That's okay. Evangeline August isn't my real name."

"It isn't?"

"Two complete strangers in a room, each known by their respective alias . . . Some might attach great significance to such coincidence."

"Robert Ripley would," I said, and it was the closest I would ever come to seeing her smile.

"To me, there is only one real coincidence: That each and every person's life is riddled with coincidence."

My brain was backfiring. "You're saying the bad stuff in your movies and the bad stuff in Trenton are coincidences?"

"Tell me, Gus, would you like to be famous?"

"Huh? Like a movie star? Like when you told Mr. Blackhurst we were stars, Jack and me? Stars of what?"

"Do you have a plan?"

"What?"

"You know what you need to do, of course?"

"I don't—"

"Something very good."

"What?"

"Or something very bad."

"I don't understand."

"How odd. You profess to have a perfect grasp of everything else."

FIFTEEN

The Brain Eaters

I caught up with Jack and Annie at the gate.

"Jack says you'll show me the cards, now that your wild goose chase is finally over."

I threw up my hands. "You told her about them, Jack? You told her?"

"What's the big deal?" he said. "We know the truth now."

"You don't know anything," I said.

"If you ask me," Annie said, "you've been making mountains out of molehills."

"Oh, yeah? Did Jack also tell you Bryan McGrath threatened to kill you? Did he tell you that?"

"What?" Annie said.

"It wasn't like that, Annie."

"Yeah, then what was it like, Jack? Why did we start walking her home from school, eh? Tell her that, Jack. We were watching out for you, Annie."

"You're exaggerating, Gus."

"And you're lying."

"I'm keeping things in perspective, man."

"I don't think so. You don't have any perspective. Not anymore you don't."

"Just stop it, you two. Please. Just stop it."

"The Brain Eaters, man. They finally got to you."

"Grow up, Gus. Just grow up."

"And become more like you? No thanks."

"My dad is going to kill me," Annie said. "Do you have any idea how late it is?"

SIXTEEN

How Jack and Annie drowned

We were on the bay, minutes from the Barkers' cottage. Annie was going to let us take the boat after dropping her ashore. Her anxiety was running high, speculating as to how her dad would punish her, so Jack and I were surprised when she cut the Evinrude, let the current have its way with us. She knew better than to stand, but you know how it was with Annie—when her spirit would thumb its nose at caution. "There!" she said, arms spread wide like she might hug the sky. "The stars. The stars. If you look—really, really look—you'll see God in every one."

The rest happened fast. We hit a rock. Or something. My first thought was that Jesus had snatched Annie up to Heaven. Abracadabra, I swear. She was there and then she wasn't. And Jack and me, we were jumping in after her. That's when the boat capsized.

I remembered nothing more.

Annie's father, Mr. Barker, and a friend of his found me in the morning, clinging to the hull. They wrapped me in a blanket, gave me coffee from a Thermos, asked me where Annie was.

I didn't know what to tell them. And when I did, I didn't know *how* to tell them. I wept. "I tried to save them. God knows I tried."

"It's okay, son. It's okay. Easy, boy. Easy."

"Where were her angels?"

"What?"

"Her angels. Annie's nine brother and sister angels. They were supposed to be watching out for her."

SEVENTEEN

My picture in the paper

Bryan McGrath interviewed me in the hospital.

"I know the truth," I told him.

He patted my shoulder. "The truth is exactly what I am going to give them, son." He pretended we were talking about the same thing.

Got my picture in the paper.

Was famous.

My newest fear was people pointing fingers. I had not forgotten Helmut Swartz, the rumours that dogged him after Dottie's death. Or the dogfood baby's mother, the whispers of her complicity, the pram filled with Gravy Train. I saw myself railroaded like that Steven Truscott kid.

Steven lived in Clinton, Ontario, 225 miles west of Trenton, 60 miles northwest of Woodstock, where the fifteen-year-old girl was found buried alive in 1886.

In June of 1959, when Steven was fourteen, he was arrested for the rape and murder of a school friend, twelve-year-old Lynne Harper. The evidence was weak and plenty of people believed him innocent. It didn't help. Steven was sentenced to die by hanging, the youngest person in Canadian history to receive the death penalty.

I confessed my fears to my mother. Water on my brain, I guess.

A book about the case had been in the news since January. *The Trial of Steven Truscott* by Isabel LeBourdais. My mother had read it. Her boycott of Bert Levin and the Marquee had freed up reading time.

"My poor, brave boy." She broke down, cradled me in her arms. I didn't fight it. "The lovely things Mr. McGrath wrote about you, how can you even think it? Everyone knows you did your best to save them." Could've been Annie talking.

For my homecoming, Mom bought me *The Collected Poems of Robert Service*. I didn't tell her we had an older edition in Dad's library. The book fell open to *The Three Voices*:

> The waves have a story to tell me,
> As I lie on the lonely beach;
> Chanting aloft in the pine-tops,
> The wind has a lesson to teach;
> But the stars sing an anthem of glory
> I cannot put into speech.

I would have cried had I let myself.

Got my picture in the paper.
Was famous.

I asked to see Mr. McGrath again. He'd redeemed himself in Mom's eyes with the feature on me, though she wouldn't let him inside. She left us on the back porch with lemonade and cookies.

"I might have gone about it wrong with you kids," McGrath said. "Sure, I can be rough around the edges, but I hope you see I was never out to hurt you or anyone. Only to save you from yourselves."

"But you did hurt people, the movies you and Mr. Blackhurst made . . ."

"You got it wrong, son. Our movies were no different than movies anywhere. It's the town. Something about this place . . . I can't explain it. No one ever could. The only thing we were guilty of was providing the catalysts. Like the intertitles. You should've burned them when I asked."

"We did."

He snorted dismissively.

"I swear," I said.

"A props master I used to work with, he'd joke how Trenton was built on a sacred burial ground for assistant directors."

"Others knew, then? Not just you and Mr. Blackhurst?"

"What do you expect? Anybody who'd ever worked in Hollywood North knew. But it wasn't anything you'd go and blab to the world. Some worried they'd be arrested for, I dunno—cinemacide or something. Others feared a padded cell. It was lose-lose. Nobody wanted to work here. Evie, Iris, Norm and me, but the others . . . New York. New Jersey. Hollywood. Some got out of the business. Most kept the story to themselves. And the few who did blab, well, you think anyone took them seriously? In time, Hollywood North was part of the movemaking lore, another apocryphal tale everybody wants to believe, but nobody does. Like Fatty Arbuckle's Coke bottle or George Reeves jumping out a window to see if he could fly like Superman. The critics. The intellectuals. I laugh when I hear them pontificating, how movies mirror reality. Let them come to Trenton. Let them see how movies determine reality."

Who'd have thought? It wasn't Evie August. It was Bryan McGrath. *He* was the character at the end of the story who filled in the holes. *Or so I thought.* And I pumped him for all he was worth. "But the forgetting . . . How is it nobody talks about the accidents—nobody remembers?"

"Well, they're talking about you now, I tell you."

"I don't mean me. You know what I'm saying."

"Tell me, son, you ever leave a movie, loving or hating what you saw, chatting it up with friends?"

"Sure?"

"In the moment, good or bad, that picture is important to you, right?"

"I guess."

"But what about a month later? How many other movies have you seen in the interim? And that first picture, are you and your pals still chatting it up?"

"Guess not. Well, maybe, sometimes."

"Sure. Of course. An occasional scene, a funny line, but the whole? Not likely. It's the exit effect. There's the fade-in. There's the fade-out. Life works the same."

"Okay . . ." I leaned back, took a sip of lemonade. "I think."

"Tell me a tragedy that doesn't diminish with time. Sure, it may rear its head in moments, wrestle itself into the foreground, but never for long. Loss is only forever in the beginning."

"The exit effect."

"Exactly. And today, son, you are quite the hero."

"All I did was—I didn't drown."

"That's all it takes, most often."

The mysteries weren't so complicated, after all. I should have known. The Unexplained explained, never fails to be a letdown.

Had my picture in the paper.
Was famous.

Mom's Avon sales went through the roof. A hero in the family was good for business.

Bert Levin joined his wife and daughters in Montreal for Jack's funeral. He never returned.

"Some losses are too great to bear alone," Mom explained.

"Will you miss him?" I said.

"Not as much as you miss your poor, dear friends."

"What will you do now?" I said.

She turned misty-eyed. "Perhaps I'll find an old stray somewhere and let him follow me home. They tend to be more loyal."

"Old dogs, they take one look at you, Mom, and can't believe their good luck," I said.

She hugged me, kissed me, declared it was the nicest thing I'd ever said to her.

Had my picture in the paper.
Was famous.

Annie's parents insisted I sit with them at the funeral. Mrs. Barker said, "Of all the boys she knew, she always said Gus was the nearest and dearest to her."

Susan Burgess, Diana Klieg, and Bonnie Priddy sat with us, too. "How are you doing?" they asked me each in turn and I made sure they saw I wasn't doing well. And I wasn't, not at all.

The Barkers struggled through the service. They fell to pieces when the priest quoted Annie's last words and my part in his being able to share them. "'There!' our dear Anne said, her arms spread wide like she might hug the sky. 'The stars. The stars. If you look—really, really look—you'll see God in every one.'"

The pastor singled me out. "Thank you, Leo, for extracting the sweet from the bitter." I could have been their son the way the Barkers held onto me. I cried then. Let it all out.

Mr. Barker said, "You've got ten angels watching over you now, Gus."

Had my picture in the paper.

Was famous.

For four weeks. Five, tops.

That photo of me. I looked at it once. Once was enough.

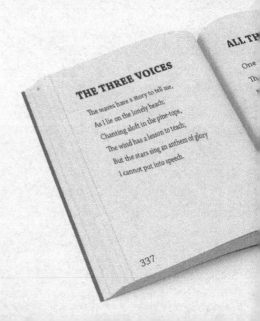

THE THREE VOICES

The waves have a story to tell me,
As I lie on the lonely beach;
Chanting aloft in the pine-tops,
The wind has a lesson to teach;
But the stars sing an anthem of glory
I cannot put into speech.

337

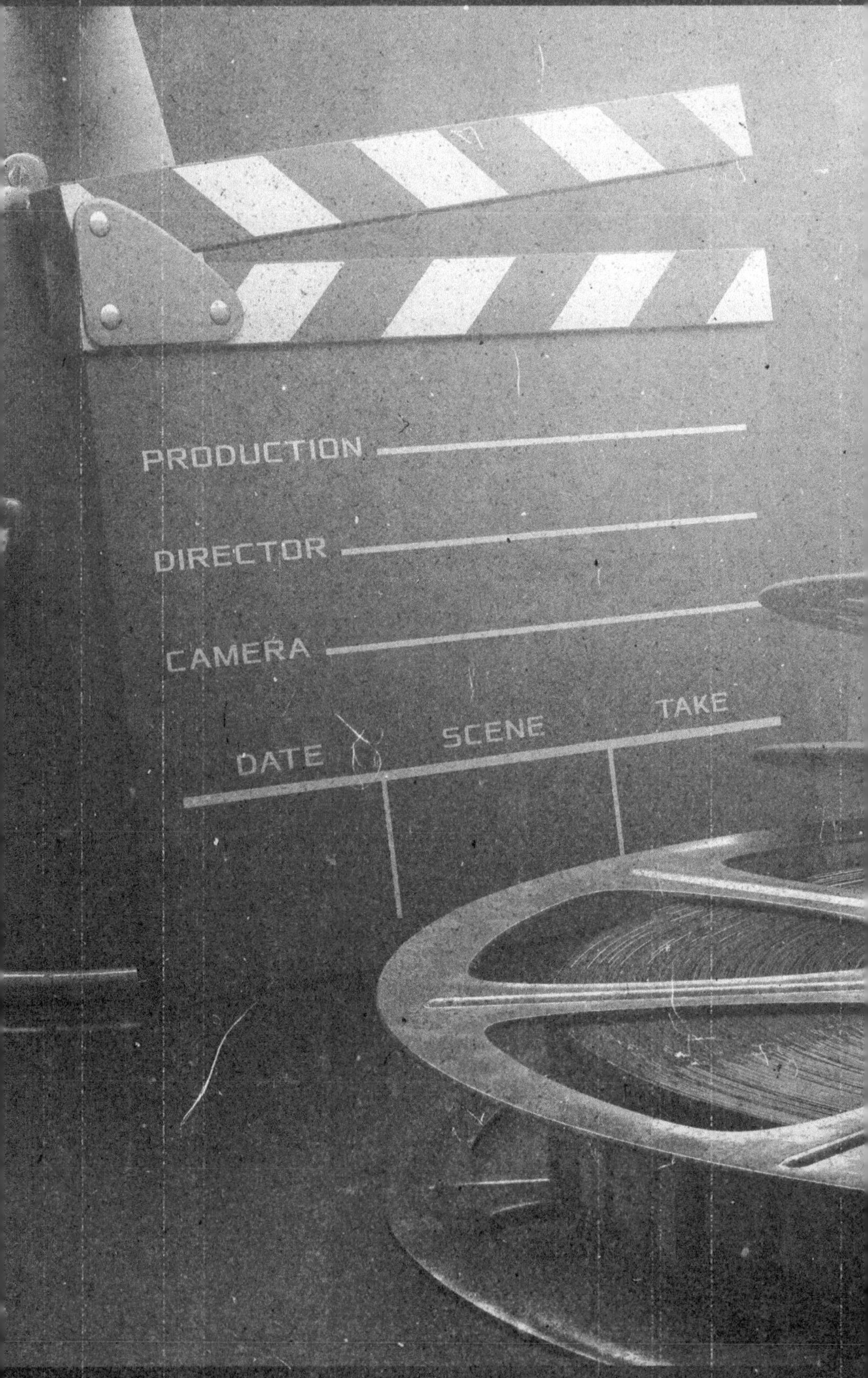
PRODUCTION
DIRECTOR
CAMERA
DATE
SCENE
TAKE

Sixth Reel

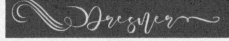

When Autumn had cast its
golden glow and the
flowers had faded and
died, he still wanted to tell
her he loved her.

–Seven Chances (1925)

ONE

The exit effect

Helmut Swartz parlayed his Dance Studio earnings into the Marquee, taking over from Bert Levin. He rejigged the sign to Dottie's Marquee Café. Few knew who Dottie was, by then, and the rest took no note.

Mom attended the grand opening and reported, "He doesn't know anything about running a restaurant."

Helmut remarried not long after. An Arthur Murray dance student half his age. His bride was said to be unhappy about the name choice and the *Dottie's* came down. Mom never went back.

I got through high school. Did well enough. Teachers cut me some slack.

Wasn't sure what I'd do next, until Mr. and Mrs. Barker handed me $3,000 for college. The money had been set aside for Annie. "It's what she would have wanted," they assured me.

I got into Queen's in Kingston. Sympathy and my survivor status compensated for mediocre marks. Maybe, too, Mr. Malbasic had pulled some strings.

In October of my sophomore year, I made my way to the school's Miller Museum and saw firsthand the meteorite Jack had found when he was eight. Should anyone yet wonder, and with the statute of limitations expired, let it be known I am the prick who stole the bronze plaque that bore Jack's name.

I graduated university without flying colours. A BA in Balls All.

Spent time in Toronto, North Bay, Thunder Bay, Saskatoon, Kelowna. Worked as a stringer for the papers. Had a piece picked up by *Time Magazine* once. Canadian edition. With a byline, yet. Thought it would be my springboard to the Big Time. The States. I ended up writing ad copy for radio stations.

Two failed marriages. No need to repeat.

Settled in Winnipeg, mosquitoes and shitty winters my sackcloth and ashes of choice.

Iris Lebel disappeared in the spring of 1967. It was said Mr. Blackhurst had willed her a tidy sum of money and she had signed an offer to purchase a property on Creighton Farms. "A sunny room for sewing," she had told the realtor. It was in the model home the last of Iris was seen.

In 1971, when Tompkins Street was being dug up for the installation of new sewers, an eight-year-old boy found the sweetheart bracelet Iris had given Simon. The *Record* did a story on the kid and another on the history of the RCAF and sweetheart bracelets.

Harvey L. Malbasic, Dufferin's longest-serving principal, died in 1990 at the age of ninety-one. His daughter found him on the floor of his bedroom. He appeared to have choked to death. A great horned owl lay on the floor at his side, a gaping hole in its feathery face, where a big yellow glass eye should have been.

It was said, as well, that Mr. Malbasic's daughter buried him with his strap.

Excluding the great horned owl with the missing eye, I do not know what became of the entirety of Dufferin's taxidermy. Remnants used to be found in the small museum housed in the old police station at King and Division. But they so creeped out the staff, the surviving pieces were exiled to the Nature Centre at Presqu'ile Provincial Park near Brighton.

When Bert Levin sold the house on Queen Street and moved into the Gilbert Hotel, he took down the newspaper clippings and packed up the finds Jack had rated *X* and *N*, and put them into storage. The Lone Ranger and Tonto bookends, too. I do not know what happened to any of it after that.

Bert tossed out everything else, including the books. Most would have duplicated what I already had, anyhow. But there are a few I would have liked.

Steven Truscott, that kid who I feared I'd become, had his sentence commuted to life in 1960. He was paroled in 1969. In 2007 he was acquitted of the murder of Lynne Harper, though there are many in Clinton, Ontario, who would tell you to this day Steven was guilty as charged.

There is a sequence in *The Black Ace* where a newspaperman believes he is close to solving the string of gruesome murders. He tracks his prime suspect to an airfield and confronts him with the evidence. Fists fly. A chase ensues. The newspaperman runs into a spinning propeller. And *The Black Ace* lives to rip another day.

In 1972, Bryan McGrath ran into a spinning propeller, too. The *Record* milked it for a week. He was one of their own, you understand.

JAMES CAGNEY TAKES LIFE OF OUTDOORS COLUMNIST

Yeah, the Cagney line threw me, too—another bit of Trenton's secret history.

In the early days of WWII, Warner Brothers' *Captains of the Clouds* was shot at the town's RCAF base. The star was Jimmy Cagney. The thirtieth anniversary of the movie's release was coming up and McGrath was aiming to make a story of it. That's what brought him to the base and his face into the tail rotor of a helicopter.

He should have known better. He'd worked on *The Black Ace*, don't forget.

The *Record* printed McGrath's title for the story he never got to write:

TRENTON'S BRUSH WITH HOLLYWOOD GREATNESS

McGrath's obituary made no mention of his screenwriting days.

 # TWO

Like a castle in Scotland or something

Evie August (Evangeline August on IMDb) died on New Year's Day 1988 and left me Captain Ahab's dream house. The lawyer tracked me down in Winnipeg and, well, you know the rest. (And no, I never saw the Pfizer rep from the train again.)

He shook my hand and ushered me into his office. "I remember your mother with great fondness. She was quite the saleslady in her day. Certainly brought out the best in my wife, God bless her."

"She brought out the best in everybody," I said.

"And you, why Winnipeg? Quite a change from Trenton, I imagine."

"I'm kind of in a rush," I said.

He opened the folder on his desk and read aloud what was required to be read. "The only proviso, you watch the movie, answer three questions to verify you did and, following that, done deal. The property and all its movables are transferred to you. There's a vintage Chris Craft you have got to see to believe."

"And if I want to get rid of any of it? Sell or whatever?"

"Abide by the terms and it's yours free and clear, Mr. Berry."

"This movie I need to watch, what's it called, again?"

"Ah, let me see now . . . one sec here . . ." He shuffled the papers. "Ah, yes, *Boy Girl Boy*. Never heard of it myself."

"Me, neither," I said.

* * *

I could have taken the highway and back roads. Would've been simpler, safer, saner. For old time's sake I took the Quinte.

I maneuvered the Tempo down the boat ramp and onto the frozen bay, past the oval cleared for skating, and out toward the fishing shanties, the cars and pickups parked alongside. Fishermen waved, extending the suicidal stranger their blessings as he glided between the markers to the point of no return. The chains on the rental's tires mocked my progress, the ghost of Jacob Marley hitched to my fortunes, Jack and Annie accompanying on celestial tambourines.

Snow drifted in spots, streaking and swirling across the surface of the ice, white snakes chasing their own tails.

As arranged, the caretaker waited on shore. He warmed himself by an old steel trash can filled with flames. A Ski-Doo was parked nearby.

I coasted around the rocky outcrop that poked defiantly through the ice, remembering how we'd overshot it all those years before. I anchored the Tempo where the floating dock would be in warmer weather.

The caretaker offered me a roasted marshmallow. "You must have one huge horseshoe up your ass," he said. "Out in the middle there, it's been looking mighty thin of late, in spite of the cold. Figgered it was fifty-fifty you'd make it."

Shit. The guy was Alan Allen. Double Fucking Al. He didn't recognize me and I wanted to keep it that way.

The marshmallow was delicious and he obliged me with a second.

"Fit as a fiddle, she was. One day to the next." He snapped his gloved fingers. "Never a peep 'bout any kin. All these years at her beck 'n' call, to come up empty . . . Just my luck, I says to the wife. Just my luck."

"I'm sorry," I said.

"But not all that sorry, eh, chief?"

I opened my wallet and offered him the forty dollars the lawyer said he'd agreed on.

"Eighty," he said. "Promised me eighty."

He'd be leaving me with five. I didn't argue, dug out the extra forty. "The keys?"

"You work all them years . . . Miss August this and Miss August that . . . and yes, Miss August and thank you, Miss August . . . and you're looking lovely today, Miss August . . . and what do you get? Could've had my way with her. Should've had my way with her. Right to the end, she had something."

"The keys. Please."

He dropped the keys into the snow at my feet. "Damn, I wish the bay had taken you under. Me and the missus, we prayed for it."

"Me, too," I said.

He saddled up his Ski-Doo and buzzed off helter-skelter down the shore.

I turned up the path. He'd cleared only so far. The gate was open, small mercy, and I trudged the final fifty feet, ankle-high boots and knee-deep snow.

THREE

Boy Girl Boy

I did not take a coat from the rack. I had my own.

"Welcome to Norman's Icebox," she said.

The 35mm reel of *Boy Girl Boy* was waiting for me in the projector.

I searched for notes, an explanation, found only detailed instructions on the operation of the projectors—there were three—and the care and storage of nitrate film.

I got right to it, dimmed the lights, flicked the switch, and took a seat, front row. What did I have to lose?

A year after Evie's death, a local writer, Peggy Dymond Leavey, published a book about Trenton, *The Movie Years*. For the record, they went from 1917 to 1934. Among the productions was *Carry On Sergeant!*, the costliest silent film ever made in Canada.

In 1992, the town erected a historical marker where the studios once stood. Should you be in the area, look for the stone obelisk on Film Street, a couple of blocks up from Hanna Park, where I found the metal box and intertitles, just sitting there. *Anybody could have seen it.*

Hollywood North, the existence of the studios, was not so secret anymore. But this was as far as it went. In a spiritual sense, perhaps the passing of Evie August had set the memories free. Selected memories, of course. There were so many bigger secrets by then.

* * *

Boy Girl Boy was no *Battleship Potemkin*, no *Ben-Hur*. The plot had to have been stale even by 1920s standards.

7:30 ⑦ BOY GIRL BOY—Silent
A classic love triangle, in
which two childhood friends
find themselves at odds over
the pretty girl they both covet.

I wasn't entirely clear on why Evie had wanted me to watch it. Until the closing minutes.

A moonlit night. A rickety rowboat in the middle of a quiet lake.

The boy, Tom, sits with the girl, Sally, at the bow. His lips are at her ear. Her fingers are in his hair.

Facing them, looking on from the stern, is the younger boy, Henry. His hands are wound tight around the oars as he propels the small boat through the waters.

There is no missing Henry's rage. In his face. In his posture. In the intertitle.

Henry can contain himself no longer. He wrenches an oar from its row-lock, lurches to his feet, and swings at Tom. Sally sees, eyes wide with terror, lunges to intercept the blow, and takes the brunt. She crumples onto the bottom boards of the rowboat. And as Tom leaps to help her, Henry swings the oar once more, connects with Tom's head, pulls back, pauses. He flips the oar end to end, shifts his grip, and rams it into the chest of his staggered opponent. Again and again and again. Until Tom lies as stock-still as Sally.

Henry blinks sudden awareness, comprehends the magnitude of his crime. Buries his face in his hands. Trembles. Cries. Panics. Thinks. Thinks. Thinks.

He rows closer to shore, amid the rocky shoals.

He cradles Sally, kisses her limp hair, drags her to the side, lifts her up, over, and into the water. Just then, Tom regains consciousness. He and Henry struggle. The boat capsizes and into the drink they go.

At dawn, two fishermen happen upon Henry. He clings to a rock, the oar yet within his grasp. He sobs.

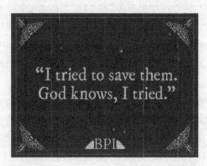

"I tried to save them.
God knows, I tried."

BPI

They wrap him in a blanket, pour him hot coffee from a Thermos, and do their best to console the grief-stricken survivor.

The oar drifts away. Slowly.

It was dark when I emerged from Norman's Icebox. I had to feel my way along the passageway before I found a light switch.

I dialled the lawyer. He asked me the three questions.

What were the names of the two boys and the girl?

Who goes into the water first?

What floats within reach of the boy's hand when the fishermen find him?

I hesitated with the last. *Why am I doing this?*

"Congratulations, Mr. Berry. Enjoy your inheritance."

FOUR

A satisfying ending

Nitrate film is disastrously unstable. It can decompose and combust if handled or stored without extreme caution. Mr. Blackhurst had salvaged thirty-two films, stowed each in ventilated containers and fireproof vaults, and maintained the ideal temperature and humidity. Evie had respected his legacy. So have I.

Since 1988, I have come and gone. Three times a year. One- or two-day visits, never more. Hunkered down in the icebox.

My favourite remains *The Black Ace*. Did I tell you how the commander of the Trenton air force base was convicted of rape and murder in 2010? Go ahead. Look it up. I was beginning to wonder if it might never happen.

Bryan McGrath, incidentally, had writing credits on eight of the films. My mother taught me never to speak ill of the dead, but I have to agree with Mr. Blackhurst: "Bryan was a mediocre and malodorous screen scribe."

I watched *Boy Girl Boy* only the one time. Forwards, that is. Backwards, I lost count. It made no difference. None that I have found. But then I never was much good at knowing where to look. As for the other films, you wouldn't believe how often. Even the rotten ones, including those penned by McGrath.

Trenton may thank me some day, but don't hold your breath. The town remains mired in the here and now. The history they don't tell you will always be greater than the history they do.

Last night, I hauled the films from their vaults, stacked the forty-seven intertitles beside them.

This morning, I shut down the cooling system and turned the heat way up. You'll find what's left of me, if anything, in my seat in the front row, Jack to my right, Annie one over.

I leave these pages in my car in the hopes they will be found. I saw somebody do this in a movie once.

NOTES

Portions of this book were previously published in the November/December 2014 issue of *The Magazine of Fantasy & Science Fiction*.

The lines of poetry on pages 28 and 315 are from "In Flanders Fields" by Canadian poet Lieutenant Colonel John McCrae, first published in *Punch Magazine* on December 8, 1915.

The DOs AND DON'Ts quoted on page 34 are from *The Hardy Boys' Detective Handbook* by Franklin W. Dixon in consultation with Captain D.A. Spina. (1959). Grosset & Dunlap, New York, NY.

The verse quoted on page 37 and 194 is from the movie *The Wolf Man* (1941), written by the legendary Curt Siodmak and produced by Universal Pictures. The words were originally spoken by Maria Ouspenskaya in the role of "Maleva, the Gyspsy Fortune Teller."

"You can trust your car to the man who wears the star . . ." on page 161 is from the classic Texaco commercial that first aired circa 1962. It came from the New York City advertising agency of Benton & Bowles and was written by musician Roy Eaton.

The poetry recited by Mr. McGrath on page 165 is excerpted from "The Cremation of Sam McGee" by Robert W. Service, first published in 1907 in his collection, *Songs of a Sourdough*.

The poetry Gus describes as "reeling ominously through my skittish brain" on page 188 is excerpted from "The Shooting of Dan McGrew" by Robert W. Service, first published in 1907 in his collection, *Songs of a Sourdough*.

The verse Annie recites on page 225 is from "The Highwayman" by Alfred Noyes, first published in 1906 in *Blackwoods Magazine*, Edinburgh, Scotland.

The lines quoted on the bookmark Gus finds in a motel room Bible on page 246 are from *This Is That: Personal Experiences, Sermons and Writings of Aimee Semple McPherson, Evangelist*. (1919). Bridal Call Publishing House, Los Angeles, CA.

The poetry quoted on page 334 is excerpted from "The Three Voices" by Robert W. Service, as published in *Collected Poems of Robert Service*. (1954). Dodd, Mead & Company, New York, NY.

ACKNOWLEDGEMENTS

Fifth grade, Dufferin School, Mrs. Franks sends us home to write a composition about a fire. I'm scribbling away at the kitchen table when my older sister, Marabelle, glances at my beginning and groans. "Everyone is going to write about a burning building," she says. "Burn something different." Days later, Mrs. Franks reads my forest-fire story to the class, and I am hooked. I have tried to "burn something different" ever since. Mara died without her own stories making it to print, but she remains with me in every word I write. I wish she were here to read this and, knowing her, to critique it. I am indebted to her and so many others.

My wife, Pat. Sure, she got the dedication, but she also deserves recognition as my first reader, despite the inherent risks and pitfalls the role poses to a relationship. Let it be said, her courage, love, enthusiasm, and intuition have no equal. Likewise my radiant and wondrous daughters Carrie, Lindsay, and Margie, who wade gingerly through every word their father writes, knowing full well the latest story is likely to disturb, same as so many stories that came before. (Sorry, girls. And thank you.)

My sister, Shandyl (or Shangle, as some in Trenton called her), who follows in our mother's footsteps as captain of my literary cheerleading squad. If she and her equally supportive husband, Jerry Wiseberg, haven't yet told you about this novel, rest assured they soon will. My brother-in-law, Andrew Davis, and sister-in-law, Maude Barlow, who have made everything I've ever published a cornerstone of their library, not to mention the libraries of their helpless friends, as well. I thank them all, though thank-you barely begins to cover it.

5

My extended family of first readers for their commitment and feedback:

Stan Reich, the longest-serving member of these intrepid volunteers and as close to a brother as a friend can be. He just might be the world's most well-read dentist.

The acerbic and insightful Matthew Cope, the one reader every writer needs *and fears*. The thoughtful and thorough Sean Campanie, Bill Shunn, Ramon Kubicek, James Thomas, and Kurt Olsson.

And the backup players who aided and abetted: Joel Ramsey, Jean-Philippe Lebel, Shelley Reich, Murray and Baila Kane, Ariella and Stephen Drooker, Dave Fisher, Ralph Lucas, and the late, deeply missed Joe Heckenast (aka Jim McGraw), Sol Shade (aka Steve Michaels), and Bernie Seidman. Also, Norman Lipkowitz because, well, he's my accountant.

The mentors who eased the doubt: Clark Blaise, who shielded me from the hellfire of literary pretension, while freeing me to be the writer I needed to be. Barry Malzberg, whose refusal to sugarcoat damn well anything keeps me on the straight and narrow. And the late Mordecai Richler who liked that I didn't have "an academic approach to anything." (A compliment, I think. I hope.)

Publisher, editor, and ultimately friend, Gordon Van Gelder, and *The Magazine of Fantasy & Science Fiction*. Gordon gave my stories the chance to be seen and read, not the least of which was the 2014 novella from which this novel grew. Indeed, I am grateful to every editor who has given me a shot, most notably Peter Crowther, Kris Rusch, Ellen Datlow, and Sheila Williams.

The Kidd Literary Agency, from the late, legendary Virginia Kidd who welcomed me into the Arrowhead fold and introduced me to her rambling old house and its ghostly residents, to Vaughne Hansen for crossing the *T*s and dotting the *I*s, to my longstanding agent and friend, Christine Cohen, who passionately carries on the Kidd tradition.

The CZP team for bringing this book to life: Publisher, Sandra Kasturi, for insisting on reading the manuscript after I told her it probably wasn't what ChiZine was looking for. (Yup, I really said that.) Erik Mohr for designing and then igniting the book cover. Jared Shapiro for his brilliant interior design and clever flourishes throughout, not only complementing the story, but lending it exciting and unexpected added dimension. Kari Embree for her shout-outs on social media. And editor, Brett Savory, for steadfastly righting my wrongs in his foolhardy crusade to make me look good. They are why CZP *is* the writers' publisher.

The invaluable sources that provided the historical perspective:

Peggy Dymond Leavey and her remarkable *The Movie Years* (www.kirby-books.ca), essential reading for anyone eager to learn more about Trenton's moviemaking past.

Deborah Chouinard and Connie Beal of the Trent Port Historical Society, The Trent Museum at 55 King Street, and the nostalgia-laden *"Trenton Town Hall – 1861"* Facebook page.

Nick and Helma Mika and their 1979 book, *Trenton: Town of Promise*.

John David Lewis, Vince Graham, Mark Goldberg, and Marg Gillies for filling the gaps in my memory. And former Trentonians, Karla Kuklis and William Crandell, for generously reaching out and spreading the word on my behalf.

And then there are those from my Trenton of long ago who inspired one way or another:

The boyhood pals with whom I shared movies, comic books, adventures, and sometimes falling-outs: Michael Foster, Geoffrey Uttley, Richard Beecroft, John Copeland, Normie Davies, Michael Lambrose, Dean Loucks, Jr., and Alan Price.

The kids who inhabit the classrooms and playgrounds of my memory: Wayne Armstrong, Diane Bowman, Susan Brown, David Calnan, Malcolm and Marie Clark, John and Bonnie Clegg, Mary Craddock, Lynda Dawson, Linda Delong, David Dobbin, Paul Eden, Ann Filion, Ricky Fitchett, Adele Fritshaw, Duncan Goldie, Peter Griffiths, Robert Halvorsen, Richard Knack, Karen Larkin, Pat Larry, Brian Macgillvray, Gordon McIllwaine, Charlotte Mountenay, Jaye Parker, Ricky Price,

Ken Proctor, David Ramsey, Valerie Rideout, Robert Robertson, Ian Scarborough, Bruce Scott, Barbara Shorey, Jane Simmons, Glenn Slaunwhite, Don Smith, Paula Smith, Diana Thompson, Billy Weese, and Peter Wilkins.

The cherished *regulars* of Bert and Mollie Libling's Theatre Bar at 122 Dundas Street West. With wistful and enduring gratitude, I thank each for bending the ear of the nosy little pest I surely was: Vic Auger, Pete Aziz, Charlie Barker, the Berry brothers, Bill Blight, Jack Carney, Jim and Frances and all the Crawfords, Laurie Dunbar, the Embleton brothers, Doc Farley, Hazel Farley, George "Frenchie" French, Foxy the Housepainter, George and Vera Friedman, Walter Gillies, Fred Goldberg, Jack and Elsie Goldberg, Peter Held, Tom Holmes, Lottie Jones, "Pepsi Cola" Jack, Orville Kelly, Ken "Mutt" Kenny, Ted Kinsella, Harry Lafferty, Augie Larry, Fred and David Lewis, Dean and Winnie Loucks, Jim MacDonald, "Scotty" MacGregor, Clyde Mason, Ray McGale, Norm and Marian McCue, Bessie McKibbon, Isabelle McCrodan, Ben Minard, Frank Miron, Dave Murdoch, Ted Parker, Pop (just Pop), Joe Scaletta, Bert Scarborough, Lloyd Seeley, Wayne Simmons, Ted Snider (CJBQ radio), Len Soifert, Sergeant Steenburg, Harry Stroll, Bud Swanson, Dick Talsma, Chief of Police Taylor, Tiny the Trucker, Paul and John Tripp, Peggy Westlake, Doug Whitley, Jack and Dorothy "Dot" Wilson, Walter Wrightman, Jack Zigman, and the priests from St. Pete's.

Lastly, I thank Trenton. I left when I was fourteen, but the town never quite left me. No matter where I go, Trenton will always be where I am from.

Hollywood North is not a textbook. It is a novel. Fiction. And while aspects might raise eyebrows in certain quarters, this book is nonetheless my tribute and fan letter to my hometown—a tourist guide, if you will, to the fact and the fantasy. May the people, places, history, and secrets of Hollywood North prevail—the actual, the imagined, and the half-truths between.

Michael Libling
mike@michaellibling.com
July 2, 2019

ABOUT THE AUTHOR

Michael Libling is a World Fantasy Award-nominated author whose writing has appeared in *The Magazine of Fantasy & Science Fiction, Asimov's Science Fiction, The Year's Best Fantasy & Horror, Welcome to Dystopia: 45 Visions of What Lies Ahead*, and many others. Set in his hometown of Trenton, Ontario, *Hollywood North: A Novel in Six Reels* is his debut novel. Creator and former host of CJAD Montreal's long-running *Trivia Show*, Michael is the father of three daughters and lives on Montreal's West Island with his wife, Pat, and a big black dog named Piper. You can find out more about him at www.michaellibling.com, where he has been known to blog on occasion.

5